THE RISE OF DEVILS

THE RISE OF DEVILS

A NOVEL BY
J.M. TOPP

MILL CITY PRESS

Mill City Press
555 Winderley Pl, Suite 225
Maitland, FL 32751
407.339.4217
www.millcitypress.net

Paperback ISBN-13: 978-1-66289-444-2
Hard Cover ISBN-13; 979-8-86850-121-0
Ebook ISBN-13: 978-1-66289-445-9

Table of Contents

I heard the voice of God during a vast and sudden
silence among the noisy heavens.
I listened to one side of that conversation
I should not have overheard.
I do not watch the skies anymore.
I do not look up.
—*Unknown*

The Bear of Devil's Peak

Two weeks before the Bullet-Catcher, somewhere in the Zappalachian Mountain Range.

If any eyes stared down at us from the twinkling stars, would they see us like bugs? Would they know the distinction? Would they know to care? Rogen lay down there in the tar-like mud beneath the shadow of a dead tree. He stared past his riflescope at countless black ants milling about on a mound, asking himself that very question. Then he looked back at the sky as the last rays of burnt sunlight revealed a black canopy riddled with stars. He stared at the ants until his vision began to blur, and his eyelids fell heavy and closed shut for a moment before he jolted up. If he were to fall asleep on that ravine, he would die. Simple as that.

He brushed his fingers through his wiry white mustache. If Lydia were to overhear his absent thoughts, she would laugh like she was known to. She didn't believe in silly stories like people living in the stars. Rogen gritted his jaw, keeping his thoughts from wandering. He didn't know how long he had been lying there holding his Lebel

1

Model 1886 rifle to his chest. His body had finally found some warmth behind the small outcrop shielded from the perpetual winds of the treacherous mountain range. He decided to inspect his rifle for the hundredth time. He hadn't moved it in nearly a day as it rested on a dried tree root. He affixed a long rectangular suppressor of his own making with steel wire at the end of his barrel. The once sharp lettering of the brand had now faded by years of heavy use. Rogen shook his head, knowing he and this rifle had been through a war together and somehow managed to tell the tale. He no longer killed soldiers or murderers. Now, he hunted the unwary, the aloof, and the innocent. Well, perhaps not so innocent. Anyone deserving his lead had sealed their life one way or another through poor decisions and folly advice.

The rifle itself had merged with the surrounding greenery in the days he had been sitting on that lonesome ravine. He lifted the rifle slightly off the ground as moss and tall grass clung to the barrel. He had to be careful and not allow mud into the well. Eight extra rounds of loose bullets weighed down his breast pocket. He was certain he didn't need them, but it was always better to have a bullet and not need it than need a bullet and not have it.

A lone howl of a wolf echoed throughout the ravine from a series of jagged peaks below, mysteriously growing louder and tricking Rogen's senses to the whereabouts of the pack. He knew it wasn't alone. He just hoped they didn't catch his scent before he caught his own prey.

Though the snows hadn't yet begun to fall, he knew winter was well on its way. A breath of frigid air beat against his face to confirm it. If his target didn't pass through in the next day or two and Rogen remained on that mountain range, it would be over for him. The snow-fall would trap him, and he would likely freeze to death. Even so, he dared not move. Not yet. His stomach gurgled with ravenous hunger. It had been nearly a day and a half since his last meager meal. It was only with momentous effort that Rogen was able to distract his mind from food. Even the peeled bark of the surrounding trees was beginning to look appetizing. It wouldn't be the first time he had eaten bark.

Something moved out of the corner of his eye, far in the distance. It was a strange initial feeling, realizing this wasn't just the wind in the pine trees or the cold dead grass swaying in its breath. It wasn't his imagination either.

This was prey.

As slowly as possible, he took the spyglass hanging from his neck and brought it up to his eyes. Six hundred meters, give or take, he judged. He let the spyglass fall to his chest and leaned forward to look into his rifle scope. The target was a young male who had stolen something of great value. Dusty Rose wanted this item back. Rogen knew better than to question the Devil of Glen Rio, so he took the job without hesitation. The target walked with his own rifle shouldered with a strap over his chest and a small green bag on his back. He had a gray kepi hat, and

Rogen smiled when he saw he had leaves and dried grass stuck into it. It was clear judging through the scope that the target had been waiting on this ravine for a while just as he was. *Great minds think alike*, he supposed.

Rogen centered the crosshair of his scope directly over his head as the target slowed to a crouch. The young man had no clue Rogen was there. For two days, they had been waiting each other out, not knowing exactly where the other was, playing a dangerous game of cat and mouse. Rogen was relieved the tip paid off. It was such a long shot his prey would show here and now in this remote mountain range. He supposed he was the lucky one this time. Even so, Rogen knew that trying to rush the shot would only turn the tides against him. If he were to miss, he would lose his prey forever. He only had one shot. Rogen looked away from the sight and took a deep breath and let it all out slowly, his breath forming a faint mist puff.

He had to remain calm.

Rogen returned to the scope and peered through it. His target hadn't moved very far. In fact, at that moment. the man was nearly staying motionless, revealing the white of his ass. He was taking a crap.

Rogen looked away and swore beneath his breath at the target's terrible luck. He didn't want to shoot him mid-crap. The man was dead to rights anyway, so the very least Rogen could do was let him relieve himself in peace one last time. Of course, this is why Rogen had a few waste bags and a wad of rubber bands with him. This meant his target probably hadn't been doing this tracking and hunting thing for very long. He took his eye off the scope and peered at his target with his naked eye.

There's a lot you could learn from a man just by the way he craps. *Where* he craps. *When* he craps. Control over your basic urges is control over your mind. If you can control your mind, you can improve the possibility of your desired outcome. This man wasn't patient enough; therefore, this man was dead. He just didn't know it yet. Rogen took in another deep breath and let it out slowly. He looked through the scope and saw his target pull his pants up and reach for his rifle.

Rogen squinted, aimed up a few breadths above the target, and squeezed the trigger. With a small flash, his rifle *popped* softly. Mud and rock burst up as the round pierced the man's torso, causing him to drop like a sack of potatoes before lying motionless in the grass.

"Damn," he whispered. The thought of potatoes made his mouth water. He yanked the bolt back as the spent brass casing twirled to the grass beside him, leaving a twirling trail of smoke. Then Rogen picked up the still hot long casing and stuffed it in his coat pocket, and he slammed the bolt forward as another round cycled through and peered through the scope again.

He meant for a headshot. No need for the dude to know he was dead. The man lay still, his rifle on the ground just a few feet away as blood pooled beneath him.

Rogen pushed himself up from his hiding place, tearing away the greenery and roots stuck to his rifle. A searing pain of atrophy shot up his legs as clumps of dirt, mud, and dried grass fell from his brown pants. He couldn't stretch them out totally, so he took a premature step forward but stumbled as blood poured fresh through his veins. He then waited for the pain to fade entirely before he slung the rifle over his shoulder and cautiously made his way up a narrow path to the site of the kill.

When Rogen came up to the edge of the ravine, he heard a soft cough. He dropped his bag and slung his rifle into his hands. How the hell was he still alive?

"You ratty bastard," came the raspy voice. "How long were you sitting there waiting for me?"

Rogen rounded a large boulder and kept the body in his sights. The man was trying to reach for the gun beside his feet, some kind of retrofitted carbine with a make-shift scope attached by what used to be barbed wire, by the looks of things. Rogen's bullet must have pierced his spine and gone clean through as he only seemed to be able to move his arms and nothing beneath the torso. The man saw Rogen and made a desperate effort to reach his rifle.

"Don't think about it," Rogen said. The man coughed blood and glared at him, laying his head back and holding the gaping hole in his stomach.

"I didn't think you hunters were allowed outside Mawbury Hills," said the man.

"They aren't."

"Liar. You're one of Dusty Rose's hunters. You're a Devil."

"I'm not, though she is my boss."

The wounded man squinted to take a better look at him. "Aw, Jesus. I know you. You're the Bear, Rogen Fletcher. Goddamn it, why did they have to send *you*? Had they sent anyone else, I might have gotten away with it."

Rogen looked the man over to realize he was barely a man at all. Only fuzz adorned his cheeks, and his face sported no wrinkles. Rogen knelt beside the young, wounded buck and shoved his hands into the boy's pockets. He had a stick of dynamite in his belt, so Rogen took that and hooked it to his own belt along with an old lantern that sported a crack in the glass. He searched the man's back pocket and pulled out what this dude was dying for: a small pocketbook with handwritten scribbles on it.

"I knew when I left Glen Rio, I would have a bounty placed on my head. If I was fast enough, they wouldn't catch me. But here I am caught, and all for the Rifler's Pamphlet."

"What does this mean?" asked Rogen, holding the pocketbook and flipping through the small pages, which revealed a series of symbols etched within. It was a foreign language unlike any he had seen before. Then, the strangest thing happened. The symbols seemed to crawl and move on the crumpled yellow pages the longer he stared at them. A dull pain in the front of his head began to squeeze like a vice. He looked away and felt strange relief in doing so.

The boy shook his head and coughed up spurts of blood that dribbled down the sides of his mouth. "Why do they call you the Bear, anyway?"

Rogen snorted and shook his head as he slammed the small book shut and held it before the man.

"Why would Dusty put a bounty on your head to deserve my lead?" Rogen stuffed the pocketbook into his coat and crouched over the boy's knapsack, holding his rifle on his lap. With the other hand, he pulled the string and opened it. He had loose ammo and a rope.

"No one knows who wrote it." The boy coughed. "Some say it was a witch from Tickfaw Bog. Others say it was the Devil himself. I just know the Salem Twins would pay a pretty penny for it."

"Where's your food?" Rogen asked, rummaging through the bag but finding nothing more. Pain squeezed his stomach.

"I ran out yesterday."

"Damn," Rogen snarled and let the bag go. Nothing but cold wind accompanied the two of them. The boy had both hands on the bullet hole and was trying in vain to apply pressure. Rogen had to admire him; he was fighting death hard with every breath.

"I'm getting too old, I'm sorry. I was aiming at your head."

"Yeah, I'm sorry too," said the boy, spitting a bloody wad at his boots.

Rogen let the bag down beside him and the rifle on top of it, outside of arm's reach.

"What's your name?"

The boy swore and tried to spit, but his mouth had run dry.

Rogen pulled out a knife from his boot and began to cut a square into the boy's right pant leg by his thigh. His mouth began to water.

"What are you doing?" asked the boy, panicked now. "You're not going to *eat* me, are you?"

"Not all of you. *Damn.* I apologize. If I were a better shot, you would be dead now." Rogen spotted a clump of dried branches that would suffice as kindling. "You weren't supposed to be here for this part, but I can't spare the ammo to kill you. Besides, your bounty was open, and I don't know how many others took the task. I can't risk a second rifle shot."

"Please. Don't eat me," he whispered, tears falling from his eyes.

"Don't worry. I'll wait till after you leave," Rogen said, sitting against the rock. He stuck the knife into the dirt beside his boot. "Unless you would rather die alone."

The boy's breaths were becoming more rapid, and he could hear the crackle of blood flooding his lungs.

"No. Don't go," the boy finally whispered.

Rogen nodded and looked down at him. "You're brave, I'll give you that. Most men die crying and pleading, but not you. I am sorry it had to happen this way." Rogen looked him over, feeling a strange twinge of sadness as his lifeblood leaked out.

"Tell me something," stuttered the boy. "Wh-what is waiting for me on the other side?"

Rogen glanced up at the gathered celestial forms of stars, who watched in reverence for a life about to snuff the wick. He cleared his throat. "My mother used to sing to me when I was a child. My father was a German fur trader, and she was a poor Unangan woman. During the cold nights in the mountain ranges of Alaska, she would cuddle up to me and sing a song. I can't recall the words. I never learned her language. I do remember the tune, though."

He curled his lips and let out a long whistle. Rogen was impressed he still remembered how the tune went. His whistle was clear and effortless, ebbing into the night sky, forming crystalline echoes that reverberated through the mountain range eerily like the call of a banshee.

"That's beautiful," whispered the boy, his breathing slowing down, his eyes turning glossy.

"Before she died, she said—" Then Rogen mimicked her accent. "'Little Cub, look into the sky. See that cloud? There begins the path to the pearly gates. I will wait for you there.' She then walked out into the snowstorm, and I never saw her again. Father said she was sick and didn't want us to see her die. Shortly after, we left these lands. Only I returned. Sometimes I look at the sky, and I see the same cloud there. I can almost see her shadow now, waiting for me." Rogen looked down at the boy.

The boy hadn't moved or spoken for a few moments, and his eyes were bolted to the sky, unblinking. Rogen let his head down and uttered a short prayer but had to get moving. He had already stayed too long.

He pulled the knife from the ground and knelt beside the body.

Chills ran up his spine, he sensed eyes on him, and in one fluid motion, Rogen snatched his rifle and slid into the shadow of the stone he'd been leaning on. He then poked his rifle over the side, close to the base of the rock.

A howl echoed over the basin. There were a dozen yellow eyes in the distance. Six night-smothered silhou-ettes observed him cautiously, their hunger evident. Rogen relaxed the grip on his rifle and set it beside him. Without turning his back on the wolves, he grabbed the knife and walked backward until his shadow swallowed the dead boy. Then, he plunged the knife deep into the thigh and began sawing against muscle, then bone and sinew.

Another howl, this one much closer.

"Don't worry, boys. I'll leave more than enough for you."

A week and a half later, Rogen rode atop his brown pack horse, Grunt, up the narrow dirt path as snow fell lightly all around him. He refused to shiver, hardening his lower lip against the frigid wind. His bear pelt coat was sufficient, but he could feel the bite of the cold as the frigid wind carried mites of snowflakes through the air.

Eventually, he spotted a wood cottage at the end of the trail, which looked down over a small valley adorned in a guise of marbled snow. When he got closer, he caught the scent of what may have been porridge. His boots crunched frozen leaves as he dismounted and walked to the rickety wooden door and pushed it open just enough to hear the sound of a bow lightly running against the strings of a violin. He hesitated as the song had just begun, unwilling to interrupt the harmonious tune that tugged at his heart.

The musician in the cabin played with adept precision. He saw Lydia's beautiful red hair braided onto her right shoulder, back turned to him, and arm arched expertly as the song crescendoed into the pre-chorus. She tilted her torso back and forth as if mindlessly dancing its sweet melody.

"Set your rifle down and sit, my love. Do not break this moment," she said, still not turning to him as the song flew into a sad, melancholic tune. Rogen did as he was instructed and sat at the dining room table, setting his bag and rifle beside him. He leaned back on his chair; tears welled in his eyes.

"Was it a hard hunt?" Her back still turned to him.

Rogen nodded. "Went longer than expected. There was this boy. I shot him."

"A boy?"

"No older than Vincent, when he . . ."

"Ah-ah. No bitter memories, Rogen. You know better than that."

He hung his head on his chest. "The look in the boy's eyes. I felt for him. What a waste, to end a life for . . . for what? A small book with symbols no one can understand?" Rogen opened his eyes, took the small pamphlet from his coat, and set it on the table. "Dusty owes me for that one."

"Perks of the trade."

"He called it the Rifler's Pamphlet. I don't know what that means."

"Means you have to go back to Glen Rio?"

Rogen nodded. "On the morrow."

"I wish you wouldn't go to that hell of a place; there's no heaven above Glen Rio."

"I know," said Rogen. The lights and sounds faded like a groggy waking dream. He sat alone in a dark room, a chill following in from the open door. He saw her beloved violin leaning on a corner, veiled in dust and cobwebs. Some of the bowstrings had snapped in the time he had been gone, curled on the floor. The house was dark. A bitter presence of sorrow lingered near the piano.

The scent of porridge vanished like forgotten memories as he stood up and grabbed a candle from the larder. "No bitter memories. I know better than that," he said, relishing whispers of the past.

Then he heard the crunch of leaves and snow just outside his window, then nothing more. Rogen froze in his steps, sharpening his ears to the outside. Nothing but the soft howl of wind came from the open door. For a split second, he wondered if he was still hearing things. He reached into his belt and rested his hand on the hilt of a Bornheim pistol.

Then he heard a body collapse outside in the wake of a hushed whimper. Rogen bolted to the door, pistol at his hip. He saw someone lying face down on the ground. Seeing the long black hair, he realized he knew who she was.

"Nilah," gasped Rogen. He holstered his pistol and ran to her side. She was badly beaten and bruised, her face a swollen, nasty purple mess. Her breaths were shallow, and when Rogen tried to pick her up, he heard a crunching sound in her chest. Her ribs were broken.

"Dear God, above. Nilah, what happened?"

She could barely breathe, so Rogen instead brought her into the cabin, closed the door shut, and set her on his small cot. He quickly lit an oil lamp and set it by the end table. She would need warmth. Rogen threw a few logs into the furnace and tossed a match onto the kindling. Within moments, tongues of fire lapped against the wood, quickly spreading light and heat to the room. He ran outside, grabbed a steel pail, and drew some water from the well behind the cabin. Then, he paused. He realized he was holding the pail with all his strength, his knuckles going white along the handle. He struggled to catch his breath while sweat beaded down his face. Rogen then shook his head, freed himself from the moment, and pushed the well spring lever up and down. After swallowing hard, he turned back into the cabin with a pail full of water.

He set the pail just above the fire on a metal grate and turned to her.

"I have some deer meat left over from the trip—" began Rogen, but then he stopped suddenly. "Nilah, where is my son, Jacob? Where are my grandchildren? Why are you alone?"

Her left eye was swollen shut, but she stared at him with her raven-black right eye. Tears streamed over her bruised cheeks, but she didn't sob. Her voice, though broken, was firm and came as barely more than a whisper.

"Fur traders. French. They killed Jacob. They used a garrote to cut his head off."

Her words hit Rogen like an axe to the gut. He clenched his fists and held back tears.

"Reva and Jonah?" he asked, fighting the break in his voice.

Nilah choked on her words. Rogen stood up and grabbed a small towel from his cupboard. He then grabbed the pail of warm water and dipped the cloth into it. Then, he began to clean the wounds on her face and neck.

"Reva and Jonah. Are they . . .?"

"Father, I had to leave them. I broke my ties, but they almost caught me. I ran as fast as my legs could carry me. I didn't know what else to do."

"You *left* them?" The question was poignant, and Rogen's pity turned to rage. "You left my grandchildren to *die*?"

"What was I to do, Father? Your son, they quartered him. Tied him to four horses, they did. I can still hear him scream. I can—" She began to sob, wheezing with every breath. "They set fire to the farm and took my two children. The Frenchmen took them from me. They raped me and then—poor Reva, and I don't know what they did to Jonah. They took him away."

"You shouldn't have left them. A mother must remain with their children until death," growled Rogen through his teeth.

Then, Nilah stopped sobbing. "I know where they are camped. Please, help me."

Rogen stood up and grabbed his rifle and a handful of bullets from a brown box beneath the table. He heard Nilah grunt and saw her sit up, holding her side.

"What are you doing?" asked Rogen.

"I know where they are camped. I'll take you there."

"You should stay here. You abandoned your children for safety. Well, this is as safe as you can get. Enjoy your sanctuary."

"Father, please," begged Nilah.

"My son is dead. My grandchildren might be as well. You might want to stop calling me Father."

"Rogen!" she shouted. "Please. Help me get my children back."

He turned to the side and spat on the ground. "Grunt can only carry one. If you slow me down, I'll leave you behind just like you did my own blood." Nilah grabbed his arm. At that moment, Rogen looked deep into her eyes. There was a pain that he had only just begun to understand through the waves of anger crashing against his soul. There would be time to mourn later, but not now. Whoever it was that did this made the mistake of pissing him off. There would be nowhere they could run or hide that Rogen couldn't find them.

He saw an elegant bow and a quiver full of arrows in a corner of the cabin. They once belonged to Lydia.

"The quiet sheathe their arrows in darkness," came her long-lost voice. *"Evil men must taste evil then die."*

Grunt trudged through the snow, creating a trail that Rogen followed close behind. Nilah rode atop his mule in silence, not even risking looking back at him, and for that, he was grateful. Fortunately, the snow had ceased, leaving behind a quiet and still morning along a narrow, winding path. They came across a small brook, and Nilah winced as she fell from the saddle and landed unevenly on her feet. Rogen knew she must have been in extreme pain riding on Grunt, yet that was the price she must pay for running and leaving her children behind. She knelt at the edge of the brook and cupped her hands, bringing it up to her lips and drinking silently.

"The rifle is loaded, and there is spare ammo in the saddle bag. If we *do* come across them, I want you to make yourself useful," said Rogen, pulling the bow and a quiver full of arrows that were tied above the saddle bag. He threw the quiver over his shoulder and tested the bow string. The string was still stiff, and the weapon itself was strong. It was a well-crafted wooden bow that still retained its rigid quality. Rogen looked up and down the brook.

"Where are you going?" asked Nilah, wiping moisture from her lips.

"There are good fish in these waters and farther down to the lake. Stay here with Grunt. I'll be back shortly."

Rogen left her behind without another word as he wandered into the white frosted undergrowth. He walked up to the creek and began to follow it, keeping an eye on the horizon. Suddenly, he felt his legs give way, and he reluctantly sat behind the base of a tree and set the bow at his side.

He felt a wave of emotions crash over him.

"Jacob," he whispered, choking back tears. He clutched at his chest as memories began to spill over him. He saw the first time he and Nilah had come to visit his homestead when little Jonah had been born. The newborn could barely open his eyes then, but they were as blue as the sky. He remembered when Rogen heard his first words echo in his ears. Why did he let them live so far away? He should have been there. What kind of a grandfather was he to allow himself to live while his offspring were snuffed away into darkness? Why the hell was he still alive and not them?

Not yet, my love. There'll be time to mourn later. Evil men yet draw breath.

As if snapping up from a horrid nightmare, he sat up straight. Rogen quickly gathered himself, looked around just in case Nilah had followed him, and cleared his throat. He had to get back on the trail. He had to find those French bastards.

Then, he heard the splashing in the water. It wasn't in the direction behind him where he left Nilah but ahead, farther along the river. Someone else was at the lake. Judging by the sound, it was more than just *one* someone. Rogen's heart fluttered. Was there a chance God brought these devils to him?

Rogen quickly kicked his boots off and reached into his knapsack. He pulled a series of bandages and began to wrap them around his feet, his mouth pooling with saliva with stark anticipation, like a bear who sniffed out a wounded animal. Only blood could satiate his ravenous anger. When he had finished wrapping his feet, he made a mental note of where he left his boots and proceeded to go after the sound, his footfalls now completely silent. He drew an arrow and notched it. Rogen realized the trappers were headed through Devil's Peak into Mawbury Hills to the south. This being the only way through, it was lucky the traders hadn't been in a hurry. Tracking them would have been significantly harder if they had crossed over the pass. They didn't expect allowing a grieving widow to live would have serious repercussions for them. Rogen would make sure they were paid in kind. He crouched low as he moved silently, like a ghost in the snowfall.

As he crept to a line of bushes, he came upon an opening in the undergrowth from which he could see the entire crystalline lake and the camp of a group of men scattered along the banks. They were heavily cloaked in many layers of jackets and furs. A few congregated by a waning fire, and a few more were on the sandy banks with fishing nets. They cast the nets off into the crystalline waters and pulled them in. There were no fish in their nets, however. The Frenchmen swore at their poor luck and laughed at each other. Rogen studied them for a moment, counted them one by one, and realized their rifles were in a pile beside the fire. They had an ox and a cart with all their wares, and it seemed like they would move off at any moment.

Then, he heard footsteps crunching the snow just a few feet away. Rogen remained still, crouched, hand on the quiver at his thigh. A thick man with bright red hair emerged from the camp, but he didn't see Rogen. He reeked of old ale and burped loudly to confirm Rogen's suspicion of a drunken night. The man stopped at a tree, turned to it, and pulled his member from the folds of his pants. After a few seconds, Rogen heard the stream of urine hit the tree and a satisfied *ahh* from the burly redhead.

Rogen gritted his teeth, notched an arrow from his leg quiver ever so silently, and pulled the string back. The man continued pissing against the tree. Rogen released the barb, and it flew so fast that the arrow pierced the man's neck, went clean through, feathers and all, and hit the tree in front of him with a *thud*. The man stumbled back, put his hands on his neck, and tried to scream. Gore burst from his mouth and sprayed through his fingers like a geyser. He fell into the thick snow cushioning his fall and flopped there like a fish until he finally fell still. Blood dripped from the arrow's feathers, tainting the snow bright red.

Rogen was already searching for his next target with a new arrow notched. There, just beyond a row of bushes, crouched a man by his horse. His thick coat would make it complicated for a clean shot. Rogen snorted softly and carefully flanked the distracted man.

"Oy! Who's out there?" came the call of a man.

Rogen stood still and realized there was a man on the other side of the horse staring right at him. He hadn't fully seen Rogen by the looks of him hesitating and standing up with a squinting look on his face. This was his mistake. Rogen pulled back, aimed for a breadth of a second, and released his arrow. It buzzed at the man and thudded into his skull between the eyes. He fell limp by the horse, dead in the snow. The crouched man stood up and tried to pull a revolver from his belt.

His cold fingers fumbled at the grip, giving Rogen enough time to notch another arrow and release it at the man. This one landed in his cheek. The man stumbled, said something unintelligible, and fell face forward into the snow. The horse whinnied softly, but overall, the camp still seemed undisturbed. He heard the splashing again and saw the two men in the river with their net. They were wrapping it up, apparently giving up on their search for fish in the water.

Rogen snorted and drew his bow when, suddenly, he heard the rippling of gunfire on the other side of the camp. The sound caught him off guard that he nearly lost his barb. He released the stress on his bow as the two men on the sand bank dropped their net into the water and drew their revolvers, backs turned to him.

He heard a terrified scream as a hulking mass of fur burst through the tree line, clawing at a Frenchman, tearing the flesh off his face. It was a boar, the largest and ugliest Rogen had ever seen. It was missing both ears and half its nose. Its fur was pocked like it had been shot dozens of times before and survived, its wounds hardening like iron scales. This was no ordinary boar; it was a man-killer. Its tusks jutted out four feet from its face, glistening in the sunlight like bloodied swords. Its eyes were white with fury.

The Frenchman turned away, revealing a face without skin, only bare white bone. His screams made Rogen's mouth flood with saliva as the boar charged him and impaled him with razor-sharp tusks. Then, it trampled him, making the tusks slice the man clean to the shoulder.

"Good," grunted Rogen as he shot a wad of spit from his mouth. He rotated closer to the camp that erupted in complete and utter turmoil. The eight-foot beast became a frenzy of fur in the camp. It seemed like the boar didn't very much like these fleshy humans coming to his watering hole. A few more rifles cracked in the camp, but their bullets seemed to have only pissed the thing off as it charged another trader and gored into his back. Rogen crouched by a tree and began to laugh.

He had to quickly stifle his laughter, though, because by now, the fur traders had completely surrounded the boar and unloaded round after round into the angry and confused beast. It hadn't quite calculated the number of men in the camp. It stood on its hind legs and gave a thundering roar, kicking and squealing.

He saw a man with a shotgun approach from behind the boar. Rogen stood up with an arrow notched, pulled back, and in one fluid motion, loosed the barb. It sailed in an arc at the man and landed in his chest with a thud. He fell down to the mud, dropped the shotgun, and clutched at the arrow in his chest just as the boar turned and trampled him into the ground, crushing his head like a melon with a sickening crunch. Rogen then saw a man point and

23

spot him in the tree line and scream at him, but Rogen already had another arrow ready. He let the arrow fly. The man ducked, however, and the arrow buzzed overhead, landing on the snowy ground. Rogen drew again and loosed, but the man leaped behind a tree. The man, not at all phased by the sight of a killer boar just a few feet away, pointed his revolver at Rogen and fired his gun at him.

The boar seemed to have been so content with the bodies piled at his feet that it seemed to have forgotten the immediate danger the other fur traders posed to him. It grunted as it tore the fresh flesh at its hooves, ignoring all else, swallowing chunks and drinking blood.

Ah, well—It was on Rogen to finish the job.

Suddenly, a muffled shot rang out on the eastern side of the camp. The trader's head burst like a pumpkin, and he fell into the snow. The men returned fire into the forest, but there was no telling where the shot came from. A can affixed to the end of the barrel can have that effect.

Even so, Rogen saw the slender outline of his daughter-by-law Nilah in the shadow of a tree. She racked the bolt forward, cycling a new round into the chamber, and caught Rogen's eye. There was a ferocity in her battered face that Rogen was relieved to see. He nodded at her and then turned to the remaining trappers.

Arrow after arrow, he fired the barbs with abandon as Nilah fired bullet after bullet. A squat man saw Rogen, shouted at him, and fired his rifle. The round whizzed above Rogen's head, and he ducked behind a tree. A trapper with pale skin and a patchy beard charged at him, which was probably his saving grace, because just behind him, Nilah switched targets. A man brought his rifle to aim at Rogen, but she shot him in the back. The man grunted as blood exploded from his chest, and he fell against the tree.

Rogen moved to grab another arrow, but his quiver was empty. He grabbed a revolver off the gun-belt of a dead body and pulled the hammer back, spotting the man charging through the thick snow at him. Rogen fired one shot, but the man was much quicker than he looked. The bullet grazed the trapper's shoulder, but he shrugged the pain off. He dropped his rifle, and Rogen heard him draw a long knife from his boot. Rogen stepped behind a tree, but the trapper rounded it and launched at him. Rogen wasn't caught off guard.

The moment the man with the patchy beard rounded the base of the tree, Rogen shot through the trapper's boot. He yelped but continued his charge. Rogen dropped the revolver, grabbed the squat man's knife hand, and used the momentum of his charge to throw him over his shoulder. The man fell into the mud, and Rogen dug the point of the man's own blade into his neck, drawing blood. He realized there was an arrow stuck in his other shoulder. Rogen *had* hit him once. He pulled the arrow from the man's shoulder and set it back in his quiver.

A few more shots from Nilah's rifle went off, but then, everything went silent. Rogen looked around. Everything ceased to move except for the gruesome sounds of a boar consuming man-flesh. Rogen knew Nilah had dispatched the other stragglers.

"Lucky bastard. If that boar hadn't attacked us, it would be *you* at *our* mercy," grunted the man in a heavy French accent.

"Mercy. That's a strange word from your mouth," said Rogen, further digging the knife's edge into his neck. The trader gritted his discolored teeth in a pained smile and held his hands up. A drop of blood trailed down into his coat. Nilah walked just behind Rogen, keeping her finger on the trigger of her rifle, nervously regarding the monstrous boar.

"What do you want?" coughed the squat man. "We're goddamn fur traders. We've got no gold and no food."

"She look familiar?" asked Rogen, grabbing the squat man's cheeks and forcing him to look at her. She brushed a strand of bloodied hair behind her ear, her knuckles going white as she gripped her rifle.

"I asked you if you recognize her?" asked Rogen grabbing a clutch of his hair and pulling it. He yelled and opened his eyes. His face turned from pain to sour as he saw her battered face.

"I was wondering where you got off to," spat the man. "Nice killa you hired."

"She didn't hire me," said Rogen, leaning in close licking his mustache. "Reva and Jonah. Where are they?"

"Who?"

Rogen placed his knee in between the squat man's legs and began to set his weight on the man's genitals. The squat man winced, but there was little he could do with his neck pinned by Rogen's blade.

"Please, I-I—."

"Are they alive?"

"The boy, the young one," coughed the man.

"Yeah? What about him?"

"A Rose Hunter. He came through here just a day ago. We sold the boy to him. He said he was headed to Glen Rio," said the man.

"How do I know you're not lying?" asked Rogen through his teeth, putting more weight in between the man's legs.

Tears began to fall from his eyes, and spittle collected at the edges of his mouth. "I'm not lying, you old bastard! The hunter found us a few miles back. We thought about killing him and taking his stuff, but he had a strange companion who wore a hooded gator-skin coat. They seemed like bad banditos. They took the boy, paid us in spit, and left."

"What about the girl?"

At this, the man hesitated.

"Well?" said Rogen, leaning forward.

The man squealed as tears burst from his eyes. "I had nothing to do with that. I told them it was foul."

Rogen steeled his jaw and pressed on the man's balls until he felt a pop. The man howled, frothing at the mouth in delectable pain. Then, Nilah rushed to the man and knelt beside him. She pushed Rogen off and cradled his twisted face.

"That was my daughter. Tell me what you did with her?" she pleaded, rubbing her fingers against his cheek.

"The men were restless and bored. I told them not to. I told them," sobbed the man, tears running down his to his chin.

"Where is she?"

The man turned to look past Rogen. Nilah followed his look and began to run in that direction. Rogen grabbed the squat man by his coat and pulled him to his feet.

"Go," said Rogen. The man stumbled, holding a bleeding spot between his legs. He was about to pass out. Rogen jabbed the point of the dagger into his back, and the man screeched and began to walk faster.

They reached a clearing in the underbrush, and Rogen saw a small bundle of fur and a small, pink, bloodied body resting face down on top of it. The small arms were already covered in swathes of ants as well as the rest of her naked torso. The long black hair was a tangle atop a sapphire unblinking eye. It stared down at the ground with no light within. Nilah fell to her knees and began to sob over the remains of her daughter.

"I told them to stop. I told them it was foul," said the squat man, tears running down his cheeks.

"If anyone were to harm any of my children, it would be better for him to have a large millstone hung around his neck and to be drowned in the depths of the sea," growled Rogen.

"What?"

"It's too bad we are thousands of miles from any coast, and I'm fresh out of millstones. But maybe I can do something to remedy this situation." Rogen grabbed the man by the collar and pulled him up. He dragged the man to the edge of the lake.

"If I could have stopped them, I would have. You have to believe me," pleaded the man. He grabbed Rogen's arm in a failed attempt to pull his bear-like grip away. It was an entirely hopeless effort. His fate was sealed. "That girl and her mother there are my kin. That boy you sold is my grandson."

"Please, I am innocent. I didn't do anything!" screamed the trapper. Rogen dunked him into the frigid waters, but then he heard footsteps running up beside him. Nilah grabbed the trapper from Rogen's grip and pulled him back to the bank.

In complete utter shock, the man sat up, wet and blinking. Nilah grabbed the bloodied arrow from Rogen's quiver and jabbed it into the man's eye. He screamed and fell on his back with Nilah on top of him, slamming the arrow into the man's face. Rogen stood back as she slammed the point over and over into his eyes. The man stopped moving, and his arms went limp, and even then, Nilah didn't slow her blows down. After a few minutes, his face was a bloodied flesh clump of mush.

She began to grunt with each jab. Finally, Rogen walked over to little Reva and began to brush the ants off her cold body. He wrapped her in her own coat and picked her up in his arms. Tears flowed down his cheeks.

"Granddaughter. My beautiful granddaughter," he sobbed. He walked away from the camp back to where Grunt was tied to a post. He set the body on the ground and pulled a fur from the pack. Carefully, he wrapped her small body and then heaved it up onto Grunt, tying it with a leather strap. He turned to see Nilah just behind him with a bloodied arrow in her hand, strands of hair falling over her face. She panted, tears streaming down her cheeks.

"We cannot stay here, Nilah," said Rogen, unable to wipe the tears from his face. "These bodies will attract other animals. We have to leave. You still have a son we need to find."

Nilah nodded, but then they heard the crash of the snow-fallen underbrush. Rogen reached for his pistol but knew it would be no use. They stood just a few feet away from a battered hulk of a boar. It snorted and pawed the ground. Nilah closed her eyes and fell to her knees, not making a sound, keeping her back to the cursed beast.

The boar snorted and walked to her. It sniffed her, and Rogen could smell death on its breath. Blood and chunks of flesh fell from his tusks, but it didn't charge Nilah. It sniffed her a second time. Then, it looked at Rogen.

Its eyes were devoid of light, like staring at a dark abyss. Rogen felt a tightness in his chest as the seconds spanned decades as he looked into the behemoth's eyes. Then, just as suddenly as the thing had appeared, it vanished like a ghost in the snowfall, like it had never been there to begin with.

Black smoke clouds hung over Glen Rio like a cursed canopy of soot and ash. Rogen walked through the dirt street as the stench of burnt flesh wafted in the air. Burnt-out beams pierced the sky like exposed ribs, the remains of what must have been the brothel.

He turned to Nilah as she rode atop Grunt, carefully studying her surroundings. Small tongues of fire still lapped at the sides of collapsed buildings, ushering pillars of smoke into the sky. Rogen walked with a hand on his hip as a group of men carried a body each and tossed them onto a smoking pile of flesh and ash. He could see the bronze stars pinned to their chests.

"What the hell happened here?" asked Rogen.

"The Bullet-Catcher. Something must have gone horribly wrong," said Nilah.

There was an aura of strange, somber solitude in the air as they made their way through the burnt town. Sweeney General Goods store had mostly burned to the ground, only the northernmost part of the building being the only portion still standing, with the *Sw* of the sign untouched. Everything else was burnt to a char.

Rogen pulled the reigns left onto the main street into a collection of small wooden shacks. Most of them were in the same sad, burnt-down state of the town. A few people milled around the wreckage, looking for valuables or bodies. A few women milled together, sniffling and weeping over a few bodies on the ground with coats over them. Two of the bodies were small.

Rogen looked away and gritted his teeth. "I hate Glen Rio."

He turned on a gravel road leading up to a large conglomeration of lavish buildings untouched by the fires. It was an architecture so far out of the ordinary Glen Rio housing it seemed so out of place. The arches were jagged like that of a castle, and the peaks were black and pointed to the skies. This was the Rose Manor.

They passed the main gates that were open, and Nilah dismounted Grunt just outside. Rogen tied the reigns to a hitching post and then walked into the manor. He pushed into the main hall, followed closely by Nilah, who shrunk into his shadow. The hall was mostly empty as they walked the carpeted floor up to a man who sat behind a small counter, rifling through a newspaper. His skin was black, and he had a completely shaved head. He wore spectacles on his nose and regarded Rogen and Nilah with a cold stare above his glasses. Rogen stopped just before the counter as the man set his newspaper on his lap. Rogen had seen the man in previous visits to Glen Rio and knew him as Mr. Donaldson.

"I need to speak to Dusty," grunted Rogen.

"She's preoccupied at the moment," said the man.

"I don't think you understand. I am going to speak with her now."

"I don't want to hurt you," said Mr. Donaldson as he stood and rolled his sleeves up. He pulled two brass knuckles with three gold-plated spikes on each. "Do you know what they call me?"

"The Gilded Ursa."

"Do you know what that is?"

"No," grunted Rogen. "It's them golden knuckles that give you that name."

"Ursa means bear. I suppose you also know that the adult bear has no natural predators in the wild, except maybe another bear. You sure you want to die for this, Bear to bear?" asked Mr. Donaldson.

"I've killed many men for this. What's one more?" asked Rogen, slipping his jacket off his shoulders.

"The only way you're getting through here is if you give me your Bornheim pistol."

"You've wanted it for a long while," said Rogen. "Come and take it."

"Stop!" came the calm command behind Mr. Donaldson. He turned slowly to the voice.

"Let him in," said a woman garbed in a tight-fitted navy blue suit with hands behind her back. Her hair was pulled tightly into a simple bun, and not a single facet of her visage was unpolished or ruffled. She emanated power held back by great discipline and restraint. Her face was torn by a dozen scars. She was missing her lower lip, exposing yellowed teeth, and her eyes were like sharp needles.

"Maddie," said Rogen with a nod. "I'm here for my grandson."

"I know. Dusty is waiting for you."

"Follow me," said Rogen to Nilah. She nodded in silence.

"Next time, you better be willing to part with that pistol," said Mr. Donaldson with an evil grin as they passed. "It's a beauty."

Rogen walked past Gilded Ursa, casting a sideways glance at him as he entered the small study. The metallic scent of blood struck Rogen like a slap, making his mouth water. A maid held a bloodied mop in her hands and scrubbed the crimson floor vigorously. Blood was not coming out easily. The room had a fog-like haze of what could only be gun smoke. The scent of gunpowder singed his nostrils, making his mouth water. Many men had died here less than a day ago.

Rogen saw a severed hand and a few loose fingers in a corner. The mud tiles sported streaks of blood, and the nurse gave a nasty look to Rogen as he walked through.

He then turned to a woman with shoulder-length white hair and a black eye patch standing behind a counter. She wore a black skirt and a white shirt with silver buttons in the middle. Then Rogen realized they were not buttons at all but bullet-holes. She wore a brown wide-brimmed hat from which she did not look up.

"What the hell happened here?" he asked.

"Just business. I didn't expect you so soon, Rogen."

"My grandson. I know one of your men bought him from French fur traders and brought him to Glen Rio. Where is he?"

Then, a door opened on the opposite end of the study. Maddie walked in, followed by a small boy in a brown coat.

"Jonah!" sobbed Nilah, who then ran to his side. He had scratch marks on his cheeks and nose, but overall, he seemed unharmed. Tears flooded Rogen's vision as he watched his daughter-by-law embrace the boy. Jonah started to cry, kissed his mother's cheek, and clutched her coat with no sign of letting go. Nilah kissed Jonah on the neck, holding him hard. A reluctant tear dropped from Rogen's eye, but he didn't wipe it away. Even Dusty set her hat on her desk. She stood side by side with Maddie. Rogen made his way to them.

"You saved the life of my grandson. I am forever grateful to you, Dusty Rose."

"I cannot abide the harm of little ones," said Dusty. "If by my life I could save them all, I would heartily do so. Now, I do believe you have something that belongs to me."

Rogen nodded, pulled a small pamphlet from his coat, and held it out to her.

"The symbols scribbled on those papers. What do they mean?" asked Rogen.

"What do they mean, indeed," said Dusty as she shoved the pamphlet into her coat. "Stay here a few nights before you return to Devil's Peak. I have lodging for you and yours. The danger has passed. You will be safe here."

"I just might take you up on that offer," said Rogen, glancing at Nilah and Jonah. "I believe we could use a rest."

His eyes went dark as the sudden pain struck him. "I must dig a grave first."

"There is a familial graveyard out back. You would honor me by laying little Reva to rest there," said Dusty. "Jose Amador was the one who found Jonah. He informed me of the entire event."

"I'll have to remember to give *El Cabrón* respect next time I'm unlucky enough to see him," he said. Jonah looked up from his mother and ran to Rogen. He knelt down, and this time he could not contain himself. Tears flowed as he held his grandson.

"I love you, Pappy," squeaked the boy amidst his sobbing.

"Thank you, Dusty. Thank you."

She cast a sideways glance at him. "If I may speak to you in private. I have a task for you."

"A task?"

"Nothing comes for free, and no good deed goes unpunished," said Dusty with a tired smile.

"Whatever you may need, Dusty. I'm your man," said Rogen. He gave a tight squeeze to his grandson, and he ran back into his mother's arms.

"We'll be all right," said Nilah.

Rogen followed Dusty into an adjacent room. There was a faint humidity that clung to his shoulders, and he realized he stood in some sort of study, yet above him was fitted with a large glass spanning the entire ceiling. Rogen paused as he looked through it. Though it was the middle of the day, the sky was dark, only illuminated by countless stars like flecks of salt on a black cloak. Several telescopes were fitted, staring up at different parts of the glass.

Books lay in uneven stacks like pillars strewn throughout the study. Papers were scattered on the floor, some crumpled with strange writing similar to what was on the Rifler's Pamphlet. The longer he stared at them, his mind began to wander, and the pain returned to his head.

"Close the door, please," whispered Dusty, snapping him from staring at the papers. Her voice carried hesitation and unease. She turned to him with a look he didn't understand. Long gone was the tired smile now replaced with a look of regret. Rogen closed the door shut.

"What is this about, Dusty?"

"You have proven yourself time and time again. I'm afraid I have found my hero."

"Hero?"

"A man admired for courage in the face of evil. Long ago, before I came to these lands, I was tasked with finding a human, one to bear a mark for a task no other human could possibly endure. I've been searching year after year with not very much promise. The Bullet-Catcher was supposed to be an answer to my search. Turns out, I didn't even need that blood-fest. Turns out, it wasn't even a Hunter of the Rose that was to be my hero."

"Dusty, what the hell are you talking about?"

"I was considering making you a hunter, but I now see you are meant for much more," said Dusty. "There will be no token for you. I hope it's not too late."

"Dusty!" Rogen grabbed her shoulders, and she looked into his eyes. "What are you on about?"

"You put your life on the line for your kin. How much further would you go to protect them?"

"I would give my life for them. I will never let anyone else harm my grandson and daughter-by-law," he said.

"It is good to hear, Rogen. Then, I indeed have my hero," said Dusty. She pushed him off and then drew a strange device from her belt. It took a few moments for Rogen to realize it was a gun.

The weapon spewed sparks from the sides with a mechanism Rogen had never seen before. He instinctively reached for his pistol but didn't draw.

"No, no," said Dusty, making Rogen hesitate. "This won't kill you."

"What is it?"

"It's a brand."

"For what?"

"I can't tell you now, but one day, much sooner than later, you will have a chance to protect your kin. You said you would do anything."

"If you shoot me, how can I protect my kin?"

"Again, this won't kill you. This will mark you and erase your memory of this moment. You will wake up with a sharp but bearable pain in your chest."

"So, I won't even remember this choice?"

"I'm not giving you a choice, Rogen. Our existence relies on you to make this sacrifice. Even then, you won't remember this moment, but I will. I love you, Rogen. You are indeed my favorite." A bright flash blinded him, and he felt his body fall to the ground.

The sun had begun its crimson descent, casting a canopy of burnt orange rays across the sky. Rogen leaned on his shovel and wiped the sweat from his forehead. He felt an uneasy pain in his chest, and he rubbed his sternum, feeling relief as the pain faded away. He found himself in a row of marble tombstones and crosses. Reva's body would rest well among the Rose family. It was up to them to care for her now. He looked up to a cloud and, for a moment, he thought he saw a shadow there. He smiled.

"Reva will keep you company for now, Lydia. Until I join you and Mother," said Rogen. He heard footsteps behind him and turned to see Nilah draped in a beautifully stitched orange and blue blanket. Her head was bandaged, and the swelling in her eye seemed to have gone down just a little, though she still could not open it.

"Jonah is fast asleep, and Maddie has chosen to stay and watch over us. Father, Doc Jennings needs to tend to your wounds," she whispered.

Rogen looked down at his arms and torso to see flecks of dried blood caked on his clothes and skin. Some of it was his. "If you hadn't run, I would never have looked into the face of my only remaining grandchild. I would never again feel the heat of his cheek nor ruffle my hands through his hair. You coming to find me is what saved his life. If you hadn't, I would never again see your face or the face of Jonah. I will never let you out of my sight again."

Then, Nilah jumped with a short gasp and touched her belly in a way Rogen understood. She raised her eyebrows slowly as her gaze met Rogen's.

"Could it be?" whispered Rogen, his voice breaking. She walked into his arms. He embraced her as the sun gave way to the moon, and its entourage of twinkling stars above watched silently.

I have a rendezvous with Death
At some disputed barricade,
It may be he shall take my hand
And lead me into his dark land
And close my eyes and quench my breath
And I to my pledged word am true,
I shall not fail that rendezvous
— *Alan Seeger*

Gator Tears

Four years before the Bullet-Catcher, on a horse farm far away.

"Helena! Where is she?"

Earnest Conley burst into the anteroom, where a dozen of his men stood in riding gear thumbing their revolvers and shifting the rifles at their sides. Grim looks were etched on each of their faces. They regarded Earnest nervously and avoided his gaze as he stood there eyeing them. He could taste the disgust reek from the presence of every man in the room. Their trigger fingers ached like hounds salivating for their prey. Good.

"Mr. Conley," said a middle-sized man with a kepi-cap atop his head beneath a mop of salty-gray hair. He brushed past to stand at attention in front of the other men. His wiry black mustache blew back as he breathed uncertainly.

"Rogen, tell me you found them," growled Earnest. He caught a glimpse of himself in a mirror just by the door. He was covered in dirt, and his clothes were browned because of it. His brown hair was matted back from wearing a hat for hours of being under the sun atop horseback. His mutton chops were caked with mud, as was most of his face, and even his once finely curved mustache was a tangled mess over his stiff upper lip. His silver eyes were thin slits, and he looked back at his right-hand man staring deep into their faces. They were scared, as they very well should be.

Rogen hesitated, his gruff backwoods accent thickening like molasses as he tried to find the words to speak. "We found little Helena a stone's throw from Serpent Creek. She did not have the strength to even pick herself up. She's bleeding badly."

"Is she in there?" asked Earnest.

Rogen nodded and put a hand on Earnest's shoulder. "I advise patience, Earn. She has been through a lot. Have pity—"

"Do not tell me what to do," growled Earnest, tossing Rogen's hand away, his face growing red as he clenched his fist. "Who was the man?"

"It wasn't a man," said Rogen. He hesitated as he looked at his riders and then back to his boss.

"Spill it. Who was the son of a rat that abducted my daughter?"

"His name is James Doyle, and he's just a kid. He's one of my stable hands."

"You hired him?" asked Earnest through gritted teeth. "I thought I could trust your judgment. Looks like I may have been wrong about you."

Rogen frowned and looked at his boots. "I hired him seven months ago. He comes from a neighboring farm."

"Did you know about this?" asked Earnest with a snort.

"No, sir," said Rogen. "He was always diligent and hard-working. He was a good boy. None of us saw this coming."

Earnest glanced at the men standing about in the anteroom. He gave a hard look to one of them, and they snapped to. Without saying a word, they straightened their backs and began to mill out the room. The last one closed the door behind him with a squeak. Earnest turned back to Rogen.

"Wake Doc Jennings up."

"Already done, boss. The moment I knew what James had done, I sent for her," said Rogen, clearing his throat as he ruffled his fingers through his mustache.

"Well, did you catch him?"

He stiffened his back and looked at Earnest from the corner of his eye. "Not yet. It seems he left Helena by the river and continued to ride on. We think he wants to cross over the McCadden farm into Mawberry Hills swamp. My men are on it."

"I want him alive. Do not return without him. Now, get the hell out of my sight," said Earnest as he brushed past Rogen and entered his daughter's room.

His wife, Sallie, and three house slaves stood around a large bed. Each one wore a combination of worried and frightened looks on their faces. Sallie sobbed in a corner, holding herself in a rocking chair, going back and forth, mumbling unintelligibly. Helena sat on the corner of the bed with the head house slave, Flora. Blood pooled between Helena's legs. Her swollen belly bulged awkwardly, issuing a heavy grunt from her. Flora looked up, blood splattered on her once white apron, and saw Earnest. She swallowed hard and stood up from the bed, handing a towel to another slave. The other girl sat beside Helena, placing the towel between her legs.

Flora approached Earnest. "She's bleeding so much. I can't imagine how rough that ride on horseback must have been. Master Earnest, please."

Earnest pushed her out of the way and towered over Helena. His daughter looked up at him, sweat pouring from her brow. She could barely keep her head up.

"Look who you're about to meet, *Father*." She spit the last word out. "It's your grandson. His name is James Jr."

"Why would you do this to me?" His hard gaze cracked momentarily, revealing a sorrow in his voice. Helena glared at him.

"It's always about you, isn't it? It's about your pride. It's about your status and honor as a glorified horse farmer. I'm nothing but a token to you."

The door creaked open, and Rogen stepped through with a hooded woman holding a black bag following closely behind.

"Ah, Doc Jennings. Thank you for answering the call at this late hour," said Earnest. The woman doctor took her hood down to reveal brown hair in a bun and rounded spectacles resting low on her nose. "Least I could do, Earn."

The moment Helena saw the doc, tears flowed from her eyes, and she began to whimper. She looked back up at Earnest as all defiance had turned to fear.

"How far apart are her contractions?" asked the doc.

"It doesn't matter," said Earnest, his lips thin lines. His words evoked a gasp from Flora, and even Sallie stopped crying, still staring at the wooden floor, straining her ear to what was about to be said next. Doc Jennings cleared her throat and pushed her spectacles up on her face. She approached Earnest and grabbed his arm.

"Are you sure?"

He nodded. "She was raped."

"No, I was not!" screamed Helena, forgetting her fatigue. "I love him. He and I were running away to get as far as possible from *you*! You're a monster!"

"Do *not* say you love him!" Earnest screamed in return. "Doc, do your goddamn thing."

"No! Get away from me, you *whore*!" Helena kicked and screamed, but there was very little she could do in her condition. Flora held her arms tight and rested her head on her shoulders, tears streaming down her face.

Doc clenched her jaw and walked over to her, drawing a syringe with transparent liquid from her bag.

Helena lashed out and tried to bite, but Doc slapped her cheek hard, sending her back on the bed. With a sudden quick movement like a viper, Doc jammed the needle into her neck. Helena screamed, and kicked, but her movements grew slow, and before too long, her upper body fell limp.

"Stand here, Flora, if you please," said Doc Jennings as she kicked the pail of bloody water just between Helena's legs.

"Her exhaustion is carrying most of the effect. I didn't give her much sedation, but we don't have much time. I don't want her to be too far gone, having lost so much blood," she said. She pulled a pair of steel forceps from her bag and began to work.

A hand rested on Earnest's shoulder, drawing his attention away. A saddened look adorned Rogen's face as he looked at Helena's drugged body. "Poor girl. Does she really need to go through this, sir? She's only fourteen."

"I'm *not* the monster here," said Earnest through his teeth. "That rat-faced son of a bitch *is*. Now, why the hell are you here? Aren't you supposed to be hunting him down?"

"We found him. I had him brought to the stables," said Rogen with a heavy sigh. Then, he grabbed Earnest by the shoulders and looked him in the eye. "This is foul, Earn. The men aren't gonna like this."

"Who gives a damn? They work for me. *You* work for me. That's *my* daughter."

"You may not like James, but he's a good boy. He worked really hard and showed promise. The men really liked him, too. There has to be another option. He can work this off—I know he can," said Rogen.

"He raped my daughter," Earnest said slowly.

"That's not the story they paint, Earn. He's a kid. They both are. Kids do stupid things. You deserve to be mad. That's a father's right, but they are young and dumb, and they just don't deserve this."

"Get out of my face, Rogen. If you don't like the way I do things, see yourself off my land."

"Earn, we've known each other since we was in the war. You can always trust me to tell you the truth," said Rogen, letting go of his shoulders. "This is wrong. You have to listen to me."

"I don't have to do a damn thing," said Earnest as he shoulder-checked Rogen and passed by him.

Earnest left the house and made his way to the stables. Dogs barked into the light of the waking sun that painted the skies red like a pool of blood above him. He spat on the ground and marched through the gates to see twenty of his men standing in a semi-circle, rifles at their hips. Their hats tilted as they made way for him. Three big hounds barked rabidly, braying for flesh on a single leash held by a mountain of a man, Paul. Two were black, and one was brown, but they had nasty-looking snouts that dripped thick saliva as they barked. Their muscles strained against the leash, cloying for flesh. Earnest gave one look at the man, and he grunted at the dogs in return.

They instantly held their barking and lay on the ground with a few whimpers.

A boy sat with his back to a bale of hay. His face was badly bruised and beaten, and his left eye was swollen shut. Blood was caked on his sandy yellow hair. His hands were tied together with rope behind his back, and Earnest realized the kid had no shoes on. His feet were bloody, meaning he must have lost his horse along the chase and ran barefoot. Big mistake on his part. His shirt was shredded, and bite marks scarred his arms, chest, and back that were crusted with mud and blood. The hounds had done a number on him. Even so, the kid's eye stared up at Earnest with a hard glare.

He walked up over to the boy and leaned down to look him in the face.

"James? Is that your name, kid?"

The boy didn't answer. His face betrayed the hard attempt at being courageous. He couldn't have been older than fifteen or sixteen. Earnest did indeed remember seeing him from time to time. It's the stuff closest to home that bites you the hardest.

"Look away from me, boy," growled Earnest.

The boy's gaze didn't waver. Earnest reared back and kicked James hard in the ribs. The boy grunted and fell over into the dirt. The men stared, but Earnest could tell in their faces there was a look he hadn't seen there before. There was respect, yes, that much was true. There was fear, as it should be, but there was something else in the gleam of their eyes. It was sadness or maybe resentment. Since when had his men grown soft?

Earnest spit at the boy as he gasped, attempting to catch his breath. He leaned down and grabbed the boy by his hair, pulling his head up. "You are scum beneath my boot. I should have you shot." He shoved the boy's face back into the dirt.

"That would be too good for you. That would be too easy," growled Earnest, taking a few steps back. He heard a faint scream from within the house. His blood boiled, and he gritted his teeth. "You bastard. Every breath you take is an affront to me and my home. Paul, do it."

Paul hesitated and glanced at Earnest and then back to the boy.

"Do it now!" he screamed, spittle collecting on the edge of his mouth. "Let the hounds loose!"

Paul shouted something, let go of the leash, and the dogs charged at the boy.

James screamed as the hounds attacked him, biting into his flesh and tearing him piece by piece. Earnest stared as the boy helplessly tried to shield himself, but his efforts with hands behind his back were in vain. The dogs were just too strong and starved. He heard a window open behind him, and he turned to see Helena standing in the window. She cried out, but the terror she saw choked the air from her very lungs. Her eyes were full of tears, and she tried to fight Doc Jennings behind her. It looked like she wanted to say something but was unable to fight the knot in her throat. Flora pulled her back, cradling her head, whispering in her ear, and the window slammed shut.

The boy's screams had stopped, and all that could be heard was the growling and barking of the hounds as they tore the boy's body apart. Earnest stared into the carnage as saliva pooled in the back of his mouth. His eyes watered, and he heard Paul call his hounds back. The men were looking at him, shocked with scared looks on their faces.

Earnest realized he had been screaming. He took a breath and stood himself straight. Wiping tears from his eyes, he looked at his men.

"That rat raped my daughter! He deserved what came to him," he said, stumbling away drunkenly. "He deserved it. That son of a bitch."

He glanced back at what remained of James. His head lay crooked beside the mulch of what remained of his body. His mouth was open, but his eye stared fire into Earnest.

A surge of anger and hate burst into Earnest's chest, and he ran at the head and kicked it away. "I said look away from me!"

He looked at his men to see unusual looks on their faces. It was disdain. How? Did they not see the injustice done upon him? Did they not see that his daughter had been defiled? Their hats were all off, and they turned their backs, milling away from the stables.

"Don't walk away from me! I am *not* the monster here!" he screamed, but they did not listen. Then, he saw a shadow on horseback emerge from the barns. He recognized Rogen's outline and saw his satchel and roll of blankets on the saddle behind him. His favorite rifle, a Lebel 1886, was tucked into his saddle scabbard by his leg.

Rogen held the reins of his horse loosely in his gloved hands. He stopped the horse just before Earnest.

"What are you doing? Get down from there," said Earnest.

Rogen glanced at what remained of James. The hounds had done such quick work of the small boy; it was a wonder it hadn't all been consumed already. He stiffened his upper lip and then looked back at Earnest. Without a word, Rogen turned his horse away and kicked his steed, galloping off into the rising sun.

The look of disdain in the eyes of his men never faded. Months after that fateful morning, Earnest couldn't spit out the taste of blood in the air every time he neared the stables. Despite his daughter healing nearly to her complete capacity, she refused to even look at him, let alone interchange words. Try as he might, he wondered if perhaps more time would need to pass for her to realize what he had done for her. He had saved her.

"Sir?"

Flora's voice shook Earnest from his thoughts, and he looked up from the mass of papers on his desk.

"What is it?"

"Oscar from Sweeney General arrived with his goods. I know how dearly we are in need of salt."

"I'll see him right away," said Earnest.

"You also have another visitor, sir."

"Oh?"

"He comes with a proposal."

"What kind of proposal?"

"He seeks to sell you his land."

"I don't need any land, Flora. Send him away."

"It's Mr. McCadden from the McCadden Farmstead."

Earnest's eyebrows flew up on his forehead. "That old bastard is finally selling? If he gives me his land, I'll finally own the river. Of course, let him know that I intend to run my business with Oscar, and I will be with him after that. Tell him to wait in the gardens. Oh, and offer him chilled sweet tea if you please."

Business with Oscar concluded quickly, and before long, Earnest found himself walking through his sprawling garden. It was a delight of his, a garden kept in what some considered to be a wasteland. It wasn't only vegetables that grew there but also a beautiful assortment of wild-flowers. A man, short and kyphotic, sat at a table sipping a cup of tea.

"Mr. McCadden, what a pleasant surprise," greeted Earnest with a charming smile.

The old man grinned jovially and raised his teacup. "It's a meeting long overdue, Earn. You and I have known each other for years. Call me George."

"Right, George. Well, can I get you more tea? Perhaps a sweet bread? Flora is an accomplished cook and has been perfecting the family recipe."

"Oh no," said George, waving his hand. "I don't wish to take too much of your time."

He let out a belch, and Earnest winced. The man smelled of days of un-wash. He looked terribly ragged as even his clothes were in tatters, torn and patched, and torn and patched again. Earnest didn't think there was a shred of original clothing on him. His skin and white hair were in equally disheveled condition. Old age had caught up to George since the last time Earnest had seen him.

George flashed a toothy grin with as few teeth as he still had and gestured to a pedestal with a revolver and several medals pinned beneath it. It was quite the polished display of silver and steel in the gardens. "You fought in the war, didn't you? My, my, that is a beautiful piece," he said, leaning over the revolver with hands behind his back.

Earnest couldn't help but smile back. The medals and the revolver were displayed on a marble pillar just beside a collection of scarlet corn poppies. "I was a First Sergeant during the first war, then Major in the second."

"Ah, that would make you my superior officer twice over. I was a private in both, unfortunately for me."

George didn't look much like a man to rise above his station. He flashed a second smile, revealing even more missing teeth and blackened gums. He took his hat off, and Earnest nearly wished he hadn't, seeing a flaky scalp with flecks of hair missing.

"I hope you will accept my respect as a fellow soldier. We really let the Greys have it, didn't we?"

"That we did," Earnest nodded.

The old man stood up from his chair and tipped over the glass of tea, spilling some on the grass at his feet. "Oh, clumsy me. Terribly sorry."

"Never mind that. Flora will take care of it. Shall we get to our business?"

"I would like to make you an offer. I am leaving these lands for a while, but I will return in three years' time to check up on things. I want to make sure it falls into the right hands. Seeing as how you keep a tight ship on your land, I don't think I'll have any issue leaving it to you."

"I'm afraid I don't understand. You want to sell me your lands for three years? After that, what? You want them back?"

"Oh no, the lands you can keep them for as long as you can. I just want to make sure my homestead doesn't fall into disrepair while I'm gone. It is my family home, you see, but it was recently broken."

"I'm sorry to hear that. My family home is breaking apart at the seams as well," said Earnest. He looked at the door leading into Helena's room. She hadn't left there since the event. He wondered if she would ever leave. "I think I know the land you own. It's by the river bend that leads to Mesa Frio a few dozen miles back?"

"That's the one."

Earnest couldn't conceal the smile that spread across his face. It was too easy. "How much are you asking for it? Name your price."

"My price? I only ask you hear my story and accept a gift for your troubles," said the old man as he fished a small wooden token from his pocket. He rolled it in between his knobby fingers as he spoke. "Five years ago, I hurt my leg plowing my very own fields. For a long time, I have lived alone as a hermit, selling my scant wares only to return to a lonely land. I've never been blessed with a wife and thus never had the chance to have children. So, I hired on a young buck back to help me with the day-to-day duties. I saw in him not only a good heart but also a spirit that was unbreakable. He knew the role of a man, and he took the farm over. However, I learned that he could do more by working for you and earning increased wages at your farmstead. I would look after the farm, but it would be up to him to put food on the table. I saw him as something of a son, you might say. I know my time on this earth is nearly over, so I willed it all to him."

"I fail to see how this is related to me, Mr. McCadden. Is there a point to your story?" he asked—his patience running thin.

"Do you? Interesting that, isn't it? The boy's name was James. James Doyle."

"I'm sorry. The name doesn't ring a bell."

"Honestly? I am shocked. A man of honor and prestige like yourself." The old hermit chuckled, gesturing to his medals. "I would have thought you the type to remember the name of a man you murdered."

Earnest's smile faded, and the air went hot in the garden. He could feel chills run up and down his spine. He looked at the revolver on the mantlepiece.

The old man chuckled. "Oh, I can't shoot like I used to. I'm not here for revenge. Well, I am, but—not exactly by mine own hand."

"I think it's time you leave," said Earnest.

"His name was James Doyle, and *you* murdered him. He was like a son to me. I loved him. He was young and made a stupid mistake, but his mistakes didn't warrant death. Your mistake does. Fortunately for me, I traveled to Glen Rio, and I was able to get *this*," said George holding the wooden coin up in the sunlight. It was a token with crude cuts and the initials *DR* engraved on the face. "I only ask that you accept *this*, and I recommend you keep it safe. It's worth more than gold in these parts."

Earnest stood up and snatched the revolver from the marble pedestal, feeding two bullets from his belt expertly and pulled the hammer back. He held the gun aimed from his hip at the old man.

George held his hands up just slightly. "I don't have an iron on me, and besides, I intend to leave right away. Before I do, you must first accept my gift."

The old man flicked a wooden coin, and Earnest snatched it out of the air. Suddenly, a stinging pain surged through Earnest's arm, and he dropped the coin onto the floor. A symbol like a fiery brand appeared in the shape of an upside-down triangle with the point missing at the bottom and a horned skull with mouth agape in the center. The pain was so unbearable that he dropped the revolver with a clank onto the wooden floor and went off. The gunshot blast made Earnest jump as smoke traced a line into the air. He gasped and clutched just above the brand. Then, just as suddenly as the brand appeared, it vanished, leaving behind a thin trail of blood behind. Even the pain faded, begging the question as if Earnest had imagined the whole thing. He stared at the coin on the floor beside his boots.

He reached down to the floor and grabbed his smoking revolver up. "I don't know what the hell that was all about, but you're coming with me. You have some questions that need answering."

The door burst open, and four of his handymen entered the room. Each of them with revolvers in hand.

"We heard a gunshot," said one of them. They aimed their guns at the old man.

George reached into his belt and drew a small paring knife with a curved edge that glistened in the sunlight. He laughed at Earnest. "For months, I have rehearsed what I would say in this moment. I wish I had tears to spill, but I'm afraid a life of many sorrows has drunk them all. Just take care of my land. I have become very attached to it. In a way, I will never leave, and now, neither will you."

"I don't know what you think you're gonna do with that," said Earnest. "It would be best to drop it for your own good."

"You're a monster, Earnest. I'll see you again, that I promise."

Then, he did something that, even while watching it happen, Earnest couldn't believe his eyes. George brought the paring knife to his neck and dragged the sharp edge across his neck, painting a crimson line on his flesh. The knife was so sharp it took several seconds for the blood to begin to drip. When it did, it rushed out the gash and his mouth. He choked and fell to his knees, his eyes casting an unwavering gaze at Earnest.

The handymen froze in shock, unable to even speak or move. Earnest watched in utter confusion as the old man collapsed on the hardwood floor, and his lifeblood seeped from his self-inflicted wound. He began to twitch and squirm in his death throes.

"What the hell?" was all Earnest could utter. Then, the old man went still. Just like that, the tension in the room was released, and Earnest looked at his men. The look of confusion was shared by all. They hesitated, unsure of what to do.

"Get him cleaned up and buried on his land," said Earnest after a few moments. "And tell Flora to get this blood cleaned up."

"What the hell did we walk into?" he heard one of his men whisper. Earnest glanced back on the body and saw a symbol, the same one he had seen on his forearm just moments before, appearing on George's forehead. It flashed bright yellow and then vanished in the same manner he had seen his own.

Earnest felt sweat bead on his brow as he approached his daughter's bedroom and felt his footsteps slow. He had put on his Sunday best, consisting of a powder blue suit, a starched collared white shirt, and a thin black tie. His shoes had been polished and had very little wear as he preferred to wear his boots. Even so, he would make an above-than-normal effort in light of the upcoming event. The tie felt like a noose as he knocked twice on her finely carved door. There was no answer, but there usually never was.

He opened the door as it creaked and let himself in. The room was poorly lit, with only a sliver of light coming from a partly drawn curtain. Helena cut a harsh silhouette on the windowsill as she sat at a desk with a book closed before her. Her hair was tied back in a ribbon, and her blue dress was beautifully ironed, only showing shined shoes with white ribbons on her feet. The scent of lavender soap still permeated the room, as she must have recently had her bath.

Earnest cleared his throat, walked over to the desk, and set a tight bouquet of flowers on the top beside the book. He saw a golden cross on the book and realized it was a Bible.

"That was your mother's favorite book," he said, running his fingers over the hardened leather spine. "She would be happy to see you read it were she still alive."

Helena stared out the window. She never spoke, never even looked at him. Perhaps today would be different. It was a hope he carried every day.

"I prepared the carriage for this afternoon, just in time for the party. You should see it. The ribbons I bought from Oscar are breathtaking, and I bought a few other goodies as well. Seeing as it's your seventeenth birthday, I thought you would enjoy your first cup of wine. Only one glass, though, seeing as I've also prepared a dance and invited anyone in a five-mile radius. I hear Lores and his girls will attend the party. They're your friends, right?"

Helena gave no indication that she heard what he said. Earnest touched his oiled mustache and followed the fine curves to the end. It was a nervous tick he had when unsure what to say. Normally, this awkward pause would be enough to make him leave, but this time he had one thing more to say.

Earnest put his hands behind his back. "I have given thought to what your future might be. I have spoken to your Uncle Levi in York. It seems he is willing to give you room and board for your education. The university there would accept you with open arms. I have it on good authority that the climate there would do you wonders. I fear this place has worn your welcome out. What do you think?"

Nothing.

"Your carriage leaves in the morning. I hope you enjoy yourself tonight, my dear," he said, turning on one heel and walking to the door.

"I have caused you enough frustration. You're finally sending me away?"

Her voice nearly made him jump out of his skin. It was the first time he had heard her voice in three years, and he looked back at her. "What? I—"

"You should be relieved. You no longer have to walk on eggshells around me. You will no longer have to make an excuse as to why I am not present at autumn balls or midnight dances. You have finally gotten rid of me, along with anything else that spites your pride."

Earnest was dumbstruck. "I have done nothing but work for the best for you. I—" but she had turned her face away from him and resumed her stare of contempt through the windowsill. His ears began to burn red hot, and he knew it was pointless to argue with her. So he was sending her away and wouldn't have to feel the searing hatred from his own daughter. What of it? If she so desperately wanted nothing to do with him, what better way to give her what she wanted than sending her north? Let Uncle Levi sort her out. Ungrateful child. He should have tanned her hide more often to instill the fear of the Lord in her.

Seething thoughts ran rampant through his mind as he stormed outside. The banners of the party were being tied to posts as his slaves worked to prepare the grounds.

"Rogen, you bastard. You always had sense when it came to things like this. Where the hell did you go?" he whispered to himself.

A scream pierced the peaceful afternoon. It came from the stables.

"Goddamn it. What now?" snapped Earnest as he marched his way around the house. He was the first to arrive and see Flora with tears in her eyes, clutching at her dress. She seemed to be yanking against a root in the ground, but Earnest couldn't see what. The moment she saw him, she held her arms out to him.

"Help me!" was all she could manage before she seemed to sink into the dirt. What bewildered Earnest the most was that it was impossible. There was nothing but hard compacted earth beneath his feet. The ground became soft only on the other side of Mawberry Hills. Then, Flora lifted her dress to show what had made her stuck.

A hand held a grip on her ankle. It was the strangest sight. It wasn't just any hand, however. It was black and blue, like rot had set in, and he noticed the flesh of the fingertips was missing, revealing the pointy white bone beneath.

A feeling like being touched by a searing iron made Earnest wince, and he saw the strange brand appear on his forearm. Its eyes and open mouth were glowing hot white on his flesh, and blood spilled from the uneven triangle around it. He clutched at it and squeezed, unable to understand what was going on.

Flora screamed again as two other arms shot up from the ground and grabbed her shoulders.

Earnest's handymen arrived behind him at Flora's horrific beckoning. She fought against the grasp of the three arms sticking up from the ground when the sky, despite it being mid-afternoon, went pitch black like the darkest of nights.

He looked up to see the moon, as he was watching, grow into a colossal size shining brightly over him, casting jagged shadows across the stables. It was almost as if the moon had grown sentient and was now watching his every move.

"Jesus Christ!" shouted one of his men. Earnest looked back down at Flora to see her completely pinned to the ground. More hands had sprung up from the ground. A blast of wind blew against them from all directions, as if to keep them away from running away.

"Please. Someone do something," she gasped. No longer was she screaming and then blood spurted from her mouth onto the dirt ground. Her eyes went to the back of her head as a dead hand cracked through her back with bits of guts and flesh caught in between the digits.

A cursed cacophony of deep, grating voices erupted all around them in an unceasing chorus. This sound was accompanied by what could only be described as a thousand drums pounding to the beat of a damned rhythm that reverberated in his ears. They crescendoed into a deafening roar all around them as if the very hills had come alive and were beckoning their doom. Chills ran up and down Earnest's spine as he saw what was left of Flora pulled into a gash in the earth, and a burnt, red fire began to flicker from within. Then, a man emerged from the crevice, but a man was too loose a term to describe what Earnest and his men were looking at.

Torn flesh hung to his exposed bones, and he looked like he had been decomposing for a long time. Small clumps of raven-black hair stuck out from scant pieces of skin, still somehow stuck to his skull. Then Earnest saw a symbol he could never forget branded on the creature's forehead. It was the horned skull brand, and it was glowing like burning coal. Earnest's eyes opened wide as he heard a low rumble of laughter emanate from within the skeleton as it stood up straight, clutching a paring knife in its hand.

"It can't be," was all Earnest could utter. He felt scalding pain in his forearm, and when he looked, he saw the same mark etched in his flesh, and it was bleeding. It almost looked like the horned skull was crying as it opened its mouth.

"Look out! There's more," shouted another field hand, yanking his attention away from Earnest's arm. By now, all his field hands, cowboys, and working men had gathered in front of the main house, around thirty all. A man, Earnest couldn't remember his name, emerged from within carrying a bundle of repeater rifles. He began to hand them to the men around him. Another dude carried a bucket of bullets and distributed them by the handful to each man. They stuffed the ammo into their pocket.

The looks on their faces betrayed their fear. The hellish sound of singing continued in the distance like braying hounds on a tireless hunt. Earnest took a rifle and a handful of ammo. He had to rally the men. He was about to speak when he heard a cold *click* beside his ear, bringing his breath to a grinding halt.

He glanced at his side to see a man in a black hat pointing a revolver directly at him.

"This is all your fault!" said a man with black hair and fierce black eyes. "No one has ever had the guts to tell you to your face. God's gonna cut you down for what you did, you son of a bitch."

"John, stop that," said another man, grabbing his sleeve, but John instead pulled the hammer back with his thumb, keeping his arm steady.

"No! The others weren't there three years ago. I was. I saw this *monster* break a mewling babe from his own daughter and tear it to pieces before it even had the chance to breathe. He fed the father, a boy no older than sixteen, to his hounds and watched without even a moment of hesitation. You are an animal, Mr. Conley. You're a filthy monster."

Earnest's ears went red. "Now listen here—"

But the man wasn't done. "The Devil has come to the Conley plantation."

No sooner had the words left the man's mouth when they heard a series of animalistic coughs and screams erupt all around them through the thin trees. Glowing red eyes blinked in the darkness surrounding them and coming closer. Their skin was as tattered as what remained of their pants, shirts, and skirts. They stumbled like drunks at them, mouths agape, and a combination of a moan and growl emanated from their swollen throats.

The man named John nervously turned to the crowd of monsters surrounding them, the metal in his revolver clinking in his hand. "The devil has cursed us too. Run! All of you, run for your lives!"

The ground beneath John broke, and three hands sprung from the hole, grabbing his ankle. Flames licked the edges of the hole. He yelped, turned his revolver to the ground, and fired all six shots to no effect. The hands began to pull him under, as if there was a little hell just beneath their feet.

The men scattered.

"No! Stand your ground, men!" shouted Earnest, but there was no ear to hear. John grabbed the earth with his arms and pushed, attempting to stop the cursed hands from pulling him. More hands shot up and held his torso and neck. Then, he was gone.

Earnest screamed as the ground closed up, and the cracks disappeared as if they had never been there. He looked up to see the line of glowing eyes come closer. Now he could see the dark outlines of their bodies as they came closer, strings of flesh clinging from their arms and torso, revealing bone beneath.

He heard footsteps just behind him and turned just in time to see the corpse of Mr. McCadden lunge at him. Earnest fell to the ground with the *thing* on top of him, clawing at his clothes. Its jaws snapped at him, attempting to bite into his neck, but Earnest held him at bay. He shouted and tried to kick him, but the *thing* was too strong.

He heard a guttural laugh emanate from what used to be Mr. McCadden's throat. Tears flooded Earnest's eyes.

"Please. Please, don't," gasped Earnest. "I want to live."

This made the thing hesitate for a split second, almost like it was taken aback. That was all Earnest needed. Summoning all his strength, he threw the living corpse off him and tumbled to the side. He grabbed a repeater rifle, racked a round, and put the thing's head in his crosshairs.

He pulled the trigger and burst his skull like a melon. The undead's body stopped moving. Earnest stared in awe as he realized one very important detail: *these things can be killed.*

A sudden flash and a heat wave at his back made him turn his head to see the main house alight with fire. Pillars of smoke erupted from the windows as a handful of men, some had taken shelter within the house, ran back outside engulfed in flames. They fell at Earnest's feet, their skin melting to the ground like hot wax.

"No," was all Earnest could whisper as he stared at his livelihood being consumed by fire. Then, he saw her.

Helena stood on the windowsill. Her dress flapped in the torrential winds, fanning the flames. Smoke blew behind her, but the look on her face wasn't that of fear. She was laughing. Her eyes were wide as she stared at the burning chasm two stories below. Then, her eyes made contact with Earnest.

For a split second, the hellish landscape seemed to go still. The very deadened moans and guttural screams seemed to fade to silence as she smiled wide at him. Earnest looked down as a dozen hands emerged from a chasm below on the ground and seemed to clutch for her, beckoning for Helena to join them.

She stepped onto the windowsill. Earnest shouted for her as she fell into the chasm that swallowed her up. He ran to the chasm, but the earth sealed up before he could get there. He spotted a shovel by the house and grabbed it. He began to dig.

"Helena!" he screamed, but the earth was hard and compacted. He saw shadows grow taller and saw that a line of four undead had surrounded him.

"Get the hell away from me!" He swung the shovel and smashed the face of one, but another was just behind. It lunged at him and struck him in the chest, knocking his air out and tearing his shirt. Another one just behind him charged and sunk its teeth into Earnest's shoulder. He screamed and yanked the biter off him, but another grabbed his other arm and tore his flesh with sharp fingernails.

Earnest swung his arms and knocked them down. He ran as fast as he could away from them.

He looked for his other men, but no one else was standing save for the undead surrounding him. The chorus of angry voices seemed to get louder, and more glowing red eyes bobbed at him in the distance. There was no end to them.

The house collapsed in on itself, spewing flames and ash clouds into the dark skies. Earnest's heart pounded in his chest at the very same rhythm of the cursed drums beating somewhere deep in the swampland. The moon seemed to scream and grow larger in the sky. Looking up, he thought he saw a mouth on its pale face howling in agony.

Earnest dropped the shovel into the ground and ran into the trees. His mind was numb, and he knew he was bleeding. There was no time to tend to his wounds. These devil creatures would catch up to him. He needed help.

"Dusty Rose. Only *she* can help me."

All he had to do was make it to Glen Rio. Then, a thought crossed his mind. There was a swamp in between Earnest's horse farm and Glen Rio. Those things wouldn't be able to make it through very easily at all. The dark waters would make it nearly impossible for them to rise from it. Hope filled his thoughts, and he charged into the darkness.

Earnest didn't know how long he had been trudging through the muddy swamp waters, but the moon that had been staring down at him for the last few hours suddenly disappeared. He stopped in his tracks and blinked, staring at the sky. Disappeared wasn't the correct word, though it did seem like it. The moon had returned to its place in the clouds far above him.

Then, he realized the demonic chorus and beating drums had also ceased. The brand on his mangled arm had also vanished. He heard a lone scream in the distance behind him and looked back.

A line of glowing red eyes atop crooked shadows stared at him longingly. Then, as Earnest watched, they melted back into the ground out of sight until there was nothing there.

"Yes!" shouted Earnest, a wave of relief washing over him. He splashed and kicked in the mud puddles. "Yes, you goddamn bastards! The Devil take you all. Hah! You couldn't get me. How's that taste, George McCadden? Who's the rat now?"

Earnest spit on the ground and then winced as he looked himself over. The wounds on his arms and legs were bleeding profusely and would need medical attention. He knew Doc Jennings now lived in Glen Rio. *Lucky that*, he thought. It was a welcome relief to hear silence. Not even the insects and other creatures of the swamp were making their music. It was so peaceful to him that he couldn't help but feel the weight lift off his shoulders. He began to make his way farther into the swamp when he heard a sound that made chills run up and down his spine. It was the sound of something big moving in the waters beside him. He looked down on the swamp floor.

Dozens of beady eyes reflected in the moonlight stared at him from the waters. He gasped as his heart fell to the pit of his stomach. Maybe if he was slow and careful, he could make it out.

Suddenly, a loud splash doused him in mud to his left, and he felt the snap of powerful jaws on his hand. Earnest screamed as the gator did a deathroll and fell to the ground. Then, it scurried away.

Earnest wanted to run, but the mud had taken hold of his footfalls as if he had fallen into a trench of tar. He wiped mud from his face but noticed two things. It wasn't mud on his face; it was blood. Second, his hand was missing. He was staring at the stump of his arm. The gator had taken his appendage, and Earnest hadn't even noticed.

The bite of powerful jaws crushed his right leg and dragged him down into the mud. He turned and slammed his other fist into the eyes of the gator. Somehow, for some reason, the thing let go and scurried away. It was a different gator, much smaller than the first. It had broken his leg, having punctured his calf muscle.

Earnest knew the gravity of his situation. Wounded and bleeding would usher a feeding frenzy, and judging by the growls and heavy movement in the swamp around him, he had scant seconds to do something. He had to get high up in a tree. He only needed to look a few feet away to see a cypress that would be his salvation. It wasn't tall and had no greenery on it, but it would do to get him off the swamp floor. He pulled himself there, hearing more sloshing of mud behind him. He dared not look back.

He reached the base and pulled himself up, leaving a trail of heavy bleeding behind. A growl shook his very core as he felt another set of jaws clamp down on his other leg and pull. Then, he went free. He shouted as he no longer felt his left foot. Earnest fell back into the mud below.

"God. Please. I don't want to die," cried Earnest, tears, blood, and mud covering his face. He felt more jagged teeth bite into his side and tear flesh away, but it didn't hurt anymore. One bit into his cheek and punctured his left eye, but he couldn't move. The moon stood witness far above him, the face of agony gone, now replaced with an apathetic blue gaze.

Suddenly, they stopped. Bleeding and torn to pieces, Earnest lay at the base of the large tree. Blood poured from the chunks missing in his flesh. Then, to his stark and utter surprise, he heard footsteps not far away. Light from a small lantern revealed a woman dressed in a black and red shawl. She held it up to her face, and he saw a black eye patch over her left eye and a right eye glowing bright red. In her other hand she held a longrifel with a long scope, as if it could do anything against the gators.

Then again, Earnest could no longer hear their growls or movement through the swamp. It was as if the ravenous beasts were scared of this lone woman. She knelt beside him and looked him over, licked her teeth, and pulled a thin cigarette from her breast pocket. She lit a match and puffed the end, then tossed the spent matchstick into the mud. She breathed in deep and let out a puff of white smoke into the cool air.

"Honestly, I hoped you'd be dead before I got here," she said, blowing smoke from her nostrils. He couldn't speak or move his neck. He felt hot dripping from a wound just below his chin and realized his vision was beginning to blur. The woman sighed, slung the rifle over her shoulder, and drew a syringe with green liquid inside.

"Why is it that good people suffer and die while cockroaches such as yourself get a second chance? Doesn't seem fair, does it?" She knelt beside him and pierced his neck with the needle. She pushed the liquid in and pulled the syringe out, then tossed it into the mud. She looked up at the moon, taking puffs of her cigarette.

"Your daughter Helena was a beautiful rose. I wish I could have saved her."

She flicked the cigarette away and turned her back on what remained of Earnest. "In three years' time, you will wake up again. Maybe this time you'll make something of yourself to amount more than just hot mess."

Earnest raised a mangled hand, reaching for her, and tried to speak, but nothing came out except for the bubbling of blood in his throat.

"I wouldn't worry about the gators. They won't mess with you now, you lucky prick."

Her footsteps faded in the swamps, and he was alone again. Earnest felt his lifeblood seep from his body, and he felt nothing more.

Sunlight struck his eyes, and he felt the moisture of sticky mud as he lay in a swamp bed. Earnest realized he was laying beneath a large cypress tree just outside of the shade above. He sat up and realized his lower body was submerged in mud. How he was still alive was a wonder. Whatever that woman had injected into his neck sure did the trick. He looked around and indeed saw no sign of the gators that had attacked him the night before. Even the blood trail was gone. He would have to go to Glen Rio and find out what she had given him.

He pushed himself off the swamp ground, but then, it hit him. He had his hand back. He brought the once amputated limb up and jumped back, startled. Where his arm had once been pale, it was now green. Only, not just the color was different, but also his skin itself. He looked at his other arm to see it covered in thick scales leading up to sharp claws that glistened in the sunlight. His arms were bound in pure muscle, and his torso was absolutely carved. He felt something strange close to his mid-back and saw a thick and long tail behind him.

What the hell? he tried to say, but only a series of snarls and clicks emerged from his throat. Shocked, he found a puddle with just enough water to create a reflection. He couldn't believe his eyes.

The face Earnest had become accustomed to seeing in a mirror was long gone. In its place was a scaly gator-face staring up at him. Yellow eyes looked back at him beneath pointed growths at the top of his head like a crown. He turned his head left and right, then opened his long jaws to see countless teeth. Disgusted and completely bewildered, he fell from the puddle and screamed. He screamed and screamed until the sun went down and the moon woke from its slumber.

Only a few remember that night. It is said that his screams were heard all the way to Glen Rio. The only reason they do remember is because of the unnatural braying that ushered in the most horrific visage of a demon beast lurking in the swamps. Only Dusty Rose had been expecting this day, and she leaned on a wooden post, staring up at the night sky, relishing the echoing howls. She held a thin cigarette in between her fingers.

"That's not a polite way to show your gratitude." She snorted smoke from her nostrils, holding her black and red shawl close to her neck. She puffed a cigarette and watched the smoke rise into the blood-red moon.

Whoever appeals to the law against his fellow man is either a fool or a coward. Whoever cannot take care of himself without that law is both. For a wounded man shall say to his assailant; "If I live, I will kill you. If I die, you are forgiven."
Such is the rule of Honor.
—*Omertà*

If I Had a Bullet

Two years before the Bullet-Catcher on a forgotten field.

Mack

If I had a bullet for every time some bug-eyed inbred freak told me to get the hell off his land, they might indeed have reason to leave me to my business. Perhaps the tendency of rancid smells when brewing my potions caused the strong distaste. In that case, I suppose I could understand it. The patchy blonde mustache on the hillbilly blew back and forth as he growled, holding a sawed-off shotgun over his shoulder, tapping it every now and again threateningly.

"I saw the smoke from my ma's house. You-ain't-supposed-ta be-here." He patted the gun on his shoulder with each word, as if to make his threat more pronounced. I kept my hands held high and glanced at the shadow of a man with a wide-brim hat on the other side of the smoke huddled beside a few crates at the foot of my donkey.

"Care to pitch in just a little?" I grunted, unable to hide my frustration.

"You hired me to protect you against any threat," grunted the shadow, not even looking up at me. "This man's not a threat."

"Anton. He's holding a shotgun!"

"It's empty."

"No, it's not!" protested the hillbilly with a curled lip, bringing the shotgun down and aiming it at my chest. I had no clue how Anton could possibly know that it wasn't loaded. He shrugged, and I heard the faint snoring rumble from beneath his stupid wide-brimmed hat.

"Useless," I whispered. If I had that many bullets, maybe then I wouldn't have to waste money on a trash bodyguard. Why did this place not work like it should?

"I want you and yer friend off my land, or I will get my three brothers and Little Millie, and we will make you leave. Trust me, it won't be pretty."

I had no clue who Little Millie was, whether a rabid hound or a milk cow; I didn't want to find out. Yet, exhaustion clung to my shoulders like a wet blanket. "We have been traveling for eight days, and we're finally in Mawberry Hills headed to Glen Rio. This land is without end. We just want to find a safe place to stay for the night."

"Well, this ain't it. Yer trespassin'. This is yer last warning."

I heard the shuffling of feet and looked back to see Anton already had the crates loaded onto my donkey. He grabbed his bag and slung it over his back, not even looking up from beneath his hat. He grabbed the donkey's reigns and began to walk away.

"Anton? Where are you going?" I asked, glancing nervously at the hillbilly. I took a few steps back. Then, I grabbed the brewing pot and dumped it into a large phial. The glass quickly heated up in my hands, and I jammed a cork in the top and threw it in my satchel before it got too hot to burn my hand. I tossed the pot away and kicked dirt over the fire. With an awkward wave and smile, I charged after my worthless ward.

"Anton!" I ran after him and stopped beside him, matching his pace. "What the hell? A little resistance, and we pack up with tail between our legs? I thought you were supposed to protect me? Why the hell am I paying you?"

I glanced back and saw the hillbilly just stare at us as we walked away.

"You haven't paid me yet," he said and stopped in his tracks, staring dead ahead. "Speaking of pay. If I find out you lied to me, I will take your life as payment. A hillbilly with an empty shotgun will be the last of your worries."

His voice was calm and calculated, and he didn't even turn to speak to me, yet I felt the cold threat run shivers up and down my spine. He resumed his walk allowing the threat to massage deep into my shoulders.

We walked for a while on the dusty road.

"How did you know his shotgun was empty?" I asked after a while, breaking the stiff silence.

He grunted and didn't answer for a moment. Finally, he sighed and looked at me from his side.

"Every time he patted the shotgun on his shoulder, it clicked. One, a loaded shotgun doesn't click like that when loaded. Two, if it really was loaded, those shotguns have a tendency to misfire when treated too roughly. Though that man *did* seem like the type to not understand something as basic as self-preservation, I opted to believe the former."

I chewed on his words for a moment. "So, you didn't know?"

"It was an educated guess based on possibilities."

"I could have been killed."

"Maybe. You've paid me with a promise, so why should I deal in lead?" grunted Anton, and he said no more. I gritted my teeth.

"You will get what I promised once we kill that beast and turn in the bounty, not a moment before," I said, trying to convince him just as much as myself. He grunted again and continued his walk. I gathered my cloak over my shoulders and pulled a small parchment from my belt. Adjusting the spectacles over my nose, I squinted at the writing.

There wasn't much to go on except for a short description and the name of the region. The beast was said to have been spotted just outside a large town called Glen Rio.

"Mack, I've been throwing this question around in my head for a while. Why would a chemist go after this beast anyway? It seems the sort of creature a man like you would want to avoid," said Anton. "How much *is* this bounty exactly?"

A man like me. I knew I couldn't tell him the real reason. If he knew why I needed this bounty, he would be the sort to turn to greed and try to steal it from me, or worse, kill me for it. However, there may not be much harm in lying to him.

"My grandfather hunted this beast in his youth. My father did, too. The thing killed them both. I aim to finish the job," I said. It was a simple yet convincing lie I had rehearsed in a mirror for months. Apparently, Anton bought it, and we walked in relative silence for a few miles.

It wasn't until we found ourselves walking on a wide dirt road leading through Glen Rio that the sun began to rise high in the east, and Anton turned his head sideways to me holding the reigns of my pack animal. Sweat beaded his coffee-colored skin and blew through his well-trimmed mustache.

"Does this creature have a name?" asked Anton.

"My father called it a Scrapper."

He nodded as we stopped before a seedy saloon with the name Silver Bullet on a sign above the entry. "I'm going to see if anyone has heard of such a beast."

"Wait!" I grabbed his shirt by the sleeve. He clenched his jaw and looked down at my hand. Quickly, I let go of him and patted the wrinkle away with a nervous chuckle. "If others know we hunt this beast, it could impulse them to try and find it too."

"Why the hell would anyone else care?" asked Anton. He then bowled his shoulders forward, and his stature seemed to rise above me, his shadow enveloping me. "Is the bounty worth that much?"

He had me.

"It is, isn't it?"

I nodded.

"So, this garbage about your grandfather and father is a lie?"

I cocked my head. "Not exactly, you see—"

He grabbed my shirt by the collar and shoved me into the wooden side of a shop.

"You are a coward, Mack. Don't you think I know when I'm being lied to? I know about this beast, and I knew about the bounty well before you begged me to be your bodyguard. Don't you think it curious I took a contract *before* being paid?" he snarled, letting my collar go. I fell to his feet and coughed as dust rose into my nostrils.

"I lied, maybe, but this bounty is important to me. It can set me up for life. I want to be a hunter just like you, of course with my unique chemist skills."

"You can never be a hunter like me," said Anton, baring his teeth. "Now get up and stay with the donkey. Don't get lost here. Newcomers don't last long in this place alone."

"Where are you going?"

"I'm going to ask some questions." He walked away and disappeared into the Silver Bullet. I picked myself up and patted the dust off my coat. If I had a bullet for every time someone pushed me against a wall, I might have had enough to actually *be* a hunter. I spat on the ground and walked to the donkey.

"He's a bastard, isn't he?" I patted her back, and she snorted. Well, even though Anton knew the truth, he would still help me kill the beast. I would have to start thinking of a way to deal with him afterward, though. I'll be damned if I have to split a bounty with that son of a bitch.

I heard the whinny of a horse and looked up. Two men sat atop their steeds in black coats with shiny revolvers at their hips and rifles in their saddle-sheaths. One had orange-red hair and a nasty scowl on his face. The other had a finely curved mustache and clean-shaven chin and wore circular sunglasses that reflected sunlight back at me. They both stared from the other end of the street in silence. I smiled at them and gave a quick half-wave, but they remained still like statues. Finally, the one with glasses spat on the ground and kicked his mount, pulling the reigns away. They guided their horses down the empty street and were soon out of sight.

I realized I was sweating, and I pulled a gray kerchief from my vest. "Surely, they are just passing through," I whispered to myself. "Nothing to do with us."

"Wishful thinking," boomed a voice behind me. I jumped and nearly shat myself. Anton stared at me with jaw clenched.

"You scared me, Anton."

"You *should* be scared, but not of me," he said. "Those men are legendary hunters, E. Gray and Jose *"El Cabrón"* Amador. Very few have traded lead them and are left living. That Mexican is a particular kind of nasty. Very few men have a devil's heart, and that one beats no longer. They are after *this*."

He handed a yellow paper to me, and I took it. On it was a vague picture of what looked like a farm and had $4000 written in bold black ink at the bottom.

"It seems Dusty Rose caught wind of this beast and put a bounty on it herself, so the cat's out of the bag. Apparently, it has been ambushing caravans going west and eating them alive. I have a good idea of where it is. We have to hurry if we want that cash," said Anton, grabbing the donkey's reigns and began pulling it away. Thunder rumbled in the distance as dark clouds gathered overhead.

I was pissed. Not only did everyone know about the Scrapper, but there would likely be other hunters looking to poach that bounty. "Who the hell is Dusty Rose?" I asked.

"Damn, you really *are* new to these parts. Maybe you shouldn't have come here," said Anton, lifting his hat up and giving a smile, the waning sunlight glinting off a golden incisor. "People lose their heads in this place. You wanna know who Dusty Rose is? She's the one who calls the shots. With one breath, you could end up with a face on a paper just like this one. Though you probably wouldn't amount to more than a few dollars, she's the Rose of Roses, and every man with a token like this one is her hunter." A wooden coin appeared from in between his fingers with an engraved *DR* on the face. "Her name has weight, Mack. I would be careful how you use it."

Before long, dark had already begun to haul the moon in from its roost, but it shone no light on this cloudy night. The wilderness was alive with the chirping of crickets and the howl of cicadas. The only weapon I had was a tiny derringer that once belonged to a lover of mine. I pulled the quad barrel out and realized I only had two bullets left. I smiled to myself. If only I had a bullet for every time she slapped me across the face. A man can handle only so much abuse, it seems. Good on me for letting her leave into the darkness.

A thick fog came as a precursor to the night, and the crisp air blew softly through the trees rustling branches and making me nervous. I had to take my mind off the darkness of the night.

"Why did you take this job, Anton? Now that the air is clear between us."

Anton remained silent.

"I mean, say what you will about me not telling you the whole truth when we met in that seedy booze-hole I found you in, but you didn't seem to hesitate, and in fact, you *didn't* ask for details about money. Why is that?"

Anton grunted, and we walked in relative silence.

"Oh, so you're gonna play it like that, huh?" I asked. "You know, if we're gonna go up against this thing, it might be a good idea to build a little trust between us."

"Trust?" asked Anton. At first, I thought he was gonna make a joke, but he remained quiet as if he was thinking. He eyed me curiously. "Nah, we ain't about that. Once our business is concluded here, we'll go our separate ways. I don't trust dead weight."

I was about to say something smart when Anton halted abruptly before a fallen log, and only as I got closer, I realized it was no log but a body lying face down.

"Who's that?" I grunted.

"I don't know. Why don't you ask him?" he snapped.

I kept my mouth shut as he knelt over the body.

"Just one?" I asked, daring to break the silence and peer out into the darkness. Suddenly, a sharp howl echoed into the night sky, filling the air with a sticky sense of dread. It was difficult for me to see clearly. I pulled a small lamp from my belt.

"Don't," he grunted.

I hesitated, but he didn't elaborate. I put the lamp back onto my belt.

"Did the creature kill him?" I asked.

Anton shook his head and tilted the body into the scant moonlight. I could see a small hole in the back.

"It's a .44 bullet hole from what I can tell. Looks like he was running away when he was shot. Safe to say we are not alone. Keep your eyes peeled," said Anton. He let the body back down and pulled a rusty-looking revolver from the dead man's holster. He aimed down the sights and then held the gun out to me.

"You'll need this," he said. "It's better than what you have anyway."

I took the weapon. I had no clue what kind of gun it was, but it was heavy in my hands. I tried to open the well, but it wouldn't give way. Mud was caked on the barrel, and I did my best to try to wipe it off.

"I need more bullets."

"Don't worry about that, Mack," said Anton. "That thing has seven rounds. If you miss your shots, you won't have time to reload. Not against Hunter of the Rose."

He pulled a sawed-off shotgun from behind him and slammed the well open, loading a single shell into it. I saw he had a small hatchet attached to the end. He strung it back behind him, and then he pulled a Winchester lever-action rifle with the barrel sewn in half from a strap around his chest. It had a scope on it and a beautifully carved bear on the wooden guard. I stared at the rifle as Anton cocked the lever back.

"If there are others, let's hope they find each other before they find us," whispered Anton.

"Aren't they Hunters of the Rose just like you?"

Anton smiled. "That only makes it more dangerous for us. If they take this token from me, bad things happen."

A howl broke the sudden chorus of night creatures plunging the night into dread. We were getting closer.

"What kind of things?" I asked.

"You wouldn't believe me if I told you. Tie the donkey up here."

I followed Anton into a dry creek bed, and we followed the howls of the creature. Suddenly, he stopped and crouched, putting his hand up. I knelt beside him.

"Why are we—?"

He turned around with a look that could murder. Then, I heard the crunch on dry leaves not more than a few feet away on the southern bank of the river, and then, it stopped suddenly. I couldn't see in the thick underbrush, but I knew someone was out there. I heard another set of footsteps just a little further away on the eastern side. There were more Hunters, and we were surrounded.

Anton silently pulled his shotgun from its sling. Then, I saw the flash of a gunshot in the distance and the zip of a bullet passing overhead. I ducked, but Anton grabbed my cloak to prevent me from running. The two hunters crouched at our sides both stood up and began running toward the gunfire. They had no clue we were even there.

We waited a few minutes until we could hear no more footsteps.

"I count three," whispered Anton. "That sniper must be the dead guy's partner."

"How do you know that?"

"You do something like this long enough; you get to understand hunters and their bonds simply by how many gunshots you hear in the distance."

"Did E. Gray and *El Cabrón* do this?" I asked, afraid to move.

Anton shook his head. "We would be dead by now if it was them two. Best pray to God they haven't found the beast's lair."

We heard more gunfire rattle off and then a dying shout.

"Guess that's the sniper. Now, it's just two," said Anton. He walked in a crouch in the direction of the wailing beast. For a moment, no sound other than the rumbling creature could be heard. I pulled a phial from my belt, and the liquid glowed green.

"What is that?" asked Anton.

"The creature is a chimaera from the north. Some experiment gone wrong. This serum will attract it."

"We don't want to *attract* that thing," muttered Anton.

"Not to *us*," I said. Then, I drew a modified flare gun and fit the end of the phial into the barrel. "I have an idea. Let's get closer."

I saw the outline of a barn and heard the hulking sounds of a monster rampaging within. Whatever the other hunters were doing to it caused the thing to go berserk. Two hunters ran circles outside, shooting into the barn.

Then, I saw the thing. It towered over the hunters and roared at them; a blast-wave of wind blew against me as it screamed. It stood at eight feet tall and had a cloak of feathers interspersed with barbed wire that stripped against its flesh. The monster had some sort of bag on its back with shovels, pickaxes, tin cans, medic bags, bullets on its arms, and spent casings strapped to its legs like ornaments on a macabre, bloody Christmas tree. It seemed like a cross between a starved bear and a de-feathered crow. Its eyes glowed red, and it charged the two hunters but then stopped and disappeared back inside the barn. For some reason, the creature wouldn't chase the hunters out, only get to the doors.

The hunters shot at the beast, but the rounds didn't seem to do much damage to it. Then, the hunters charged into the barn.

"What the hell?" I grunted.

"They're using eclipsinthe bullets," Anton said. It was clear they were not your average killers. "The beast in the barn doesn't belong to this world in the traditional sense. Therefore, untraditional hunting methods must be taken."

"What's eclipsinthe?" I asked.

"They are what you call slow bullets. They aren't designed to kill. If you hit a target with two rounds, it creates an electrical field between the two, stunning the target. One is ineffective, so you have to hit your shots. They say, to shoot an eclipsinthe bullet, you must trust the bulletsmith who smithed it. It's just as likely to kill you as to shoot."

I could tell by Anton's body language that he was clearly nervous. "If these cats have eclipsinthe, that means they have serious firepower."

I wouldn't believe things like that normally, being a man of science, but here roams a creature that defies all logic. I had no reason to distrust Anton, not yet.

"We have to get to them *before* they kill the beast."

"What happens if they kill it before we do?" I asked.

"They will hunt us down and kill us," Anton said. "It would be easy for them, especially since this is your first fight against Hunters of the Rose."

I couldn't see his expression in the darkness, but I knew the darkness in his eyes. We found ourselves at the edge of the small compound surrounding the barn. The creature screamed again, and the loud echo of a shotgun thundered within. The beast roared, shaking the very fibers of the wooden walls and the ground beneath my feet.

Anton walked to the barn door, pulled it open, and found himself face-to-face with a hunter. He was barely a man with any hair on his face and was drenched in sweat. The hunter raised his shotgun up.

Click!

He'd forgotten to reload.

Anton snorted and fired his shotgun, blasting the young man in half and bursting him into a mist of blood and gore. He fell to the mud in pieces. The beast screamed, and I saw the other hunter realize his partner was dead and charged Anton with dual pistols raised.

He fired his weapons, peppering mud into the air as Anton ducked behind a wooden panel. It wouldn't be much cover for long as the hunter's bullets chewed away at it.

He screamed as he pulled the hammers back with his thumb and fired over and over again. Anton was pinned, so I rounded the other side of the panel. Just before the hunter could turn and shoot me, I aimed my modified flare gun at him.

The phial flew at the hunter and exploded all over him. He hesitated and looked down at his soaked shirt.

"This smells like piss!" he sniffed, completely befuddled. Suddenly, we all stopped as we heard a loud snort rumble through the compound. The hunter turned and realized he stood in the shadow of a hulking beast towering over him. The beast backhanded the hunter in the face, tearing flesh from bone and cleaving barbed wire through his eyes. Then, it bit the hunter's arm. Anton said something, but I did not hear over the sounds of the beast tearing the screaming hunter limb from limb.

The creature dropped what was left of the hunter's torso in a heap at its feet. Then, it stopped for a moment as if its eyes were adjusting to the darkness and then spotted Anton and me.

"Run!" I shouted at Anton, but it was too late. The monster was on top of him.

I heard the tell-tale sound of an explosive being cooked, and I saw him lob a stick of dynamite at the beast.

Then, with all the calm sense in the world, he pulled his shotgun up and fired into the dynamite stick. The blast shook the ground, blinding me and sending Anton off his feet into a bale of hay. I heard a ringing in my ears and was frozen to the ground, afraid to move.

After a few moments, I heard no movement around me and no other sound save for the undergrowth filled with the howling chorus of insects. My eyes adjusted to the darkness, and I saw where the monster once stood now lay a pile of barbed wire, fur, and feathers.

I ran to Anton's side and patted out the tongues of flame dancing on his body. He was bleeding heavily from his chest and his face, and his shotgun was broken in two. I grabbed a bandage from my satchel and began to apply pressure to the wounds, bandaging as I went along. Then, I pulled a syringe and stuck the needle into his arm. His eyes opened ever so slightly.

"Thank God, you're alive," I gasped, washed in relief.

"What the hell did you inject into me?" he asked amid a series of coughs. The bleeding had stopped, and I let out a sigh of relief. I heard the *clop, clop, clop* of approaching horses and felt the hairs at the top of my head stand on end. I tried to grab Anton's rifle, but I was too late. The riders were upon us. Unable to move, I looked up at two gunmen helplessly.

"E. Gray and '*El Cabrón*'," was all I could manage to whisper. I raised my rusty revolver and aimed at them, but my fingers were shaking too weakly to pull the trigger back.

The men chuckled to each other.

"At least you get your nickname. It seems mine don't stick," said the rider with red hair. "I am Edward 'The Rookie' Gray. Wait no, I am 'The Rebel' Gray."

The revolver clicked violently in my shaking hands.

The other one, I assumed to be Amador, didn't answer but instead lifted himself off his horse and landed heavily into the dirt beside me, his spurs spinning as he walked. The barn had caught fire, and the flames were beginning to lick the sides of the wood paneling. This cast an eerie shadow over him as he approached. Surprisingly, he still wore his sunglasses, and I could see myself in their reflection, yet he walked right past me.

He stopped at the heap of fur and broken metal and pulled out a knife. He jammed it into the beast and began a sawing motion. Finally, he yanked the head of the creature from its body and walked back to the horses holding the bleeding head.

"Thanks for dealing with the creature for us," said the redheaded hunter E. Gray. "We would have had some trouble, it looks like. Well, I guess it's just the way the butterscotch cookie crumbles."

Amador strapped the head of the creature to his saddle and pulled himself onto his horse, grabbing his leather reigns. He then tossed a coin from his purse that landed on my lap. It was a wooden coin with a simple skeleton etched onto the face, unlike currency I had seen before.

It looked like a worthless piece of garbage. The letters *DR* were carved onto the back of the coin.

Suddenly, I felt a hot flash of pain sear up and down my arm. A small symbol appeared in the middle of my forearm that looked like a devilish skull in the center of a triangle. Just as soon as the symbol appeared, it vanished like it was never there to begin with. "What the hell is this?" I asked, picking up the strange coin.

"Hurry back to Glen Rio and present that coin to Doc Jennings. Do *not* let that man die," said Amador. Then, he pulled the reigns of his horse, and the two hunters disappeared into the darkness of the burning underbrush. I stared in disbelief. I don't know whether I was surprised to be breathing or learn that the man with a devil's heart had a soft spot for Anton.

I pulled the donkey into town by her bit, making sure Anton didn't fall off her back. The sun had risen once more and was beginning to shine hard down over us. I led us to the front of a small house with a red cross on a white circular field painted above the doorway. I threw the reigns over the hitching post.

"Help! Help!" I said, pulling Anton down from the donkey, but he was too heavy. He fell out of my grip and landed with a thud on the dirt street. He let out a pained moan and opened his eyes slightly. They were erratic and unable to focus. I knew he didn't have much time before it was too late for anyone to do anything for him.

A man with arms strewn with muscles nearly twice the size of Anton's emerged from within the house, a tangled mop of brown hair resting on the top of his head. He looked at me and then at Anton.

"What the hell?" he blurted.

"Hurry, please. He's been hurt!"

"How did you manage to get him onto the donkey in the first place?" asked the man as he picked Anton up in his arms as if he weighed only as much as a sack of potatoes.

"Get him in here, now."

I turned to see a woman standing in the doorway. Her hair was cut ear-length and sandy brown-colored. Her brown eyes pierced into us. She wiped her hands on her bloody gown.

The beefy aide gave one look at her and silently obeyed, bringing Anton into the doc's house.

"Doc Jennings, I was told to hand you this," I said, flicking the coin at her. She caught it in her palm and then flicked it back at me, landing it square onto my forehead.

"I *know* who he is. Keep that coin. You might find yourself in great need of it in the future," she said. She then closed the door behind her without further words. I looked down at the wooden piece in my hand. It didn't seem precious in the least. I'm sure I wouldn't be able to get any money from trading it. Perhaps there was more to this coin than met the eye. I clutched it in my hand and stared at the door with a bright red cross.

There was something more to Anton than just a simple brute.

I felt something hot and wet drip down my face, and suddenly, the doors burst open, shaking me awake. The moon was high in the sky, and Anton stood there, bandages on his arms and legs. He stared at me, fresh cuts on his face. His left eye drooped down in fresh stitches.

I realized our donkey had fallen asleep over my head, and I pushed her off me, wiping her saliva off my face.

"Anton, you're alive!" I said.

He grunted and took in a deep breath. "I-I'm not good at this."

"Not good at what?"

"Thank you."

I was speechless. "I-uh, You're welcome?"

He nodded, and I realized he had his rifle and bag with him.

"Wait, you're leaving?"

"I need that bounty, Mack. I can't let Gray and Amador get away with it." He began walking down the dirt road.

I snapped myself out of confusion. "You just got back from death! Are you so eager to leap back into the fire?"

He didn't respond and continued to walk. I felt a heavy hand rest on my shoulder and turned to see Doc Jennings and her muscle-strewn aide.

"You can't go where he is going," said the doc softly. "That's Anton Hudson, one of the best hunters this side of the Castor River. If he needs this bounty so badly, that must mean he's in deep trouble. Heaven help whoever gets in his way."

"Don't think he's going alone," I said, wrestling myself from her aide's strong grip. "I hired him for a bounty, and I intend to see it through and pay him."

I paused for a second. "Oh, I need that money, too, if I'm going to eat sometime in the next week."

The aide crossed his arms over his burly chest. "You won't last a minute."

If only I had a bullet for every time I heard someone tell me that. Though, I had to admit, it was the first time I had heard it from a man. Maybe that changes things?

I grabbed my donkey's reigns and pulled her to her feet, slinging the satchel over my head. I guided her out to the road after Anton. I can't tell why I was feeling what I was feeling. Was it that we had come so close to death and somehow made it out alive? Was it the heat of gunfire purged away menial trifles? I didn't care. Whatever happened next, I would be there by his side. Whatever happened next, I wouldn't let him down. I saw his shadow at the edge of town, leaning against a fence post.

He grunted and looked at the ground, the brim of the hat covering his eyes. Regardless, I saw a smile shine beneath.

"I didn't know if I would go alone, friend."

This place is evil.

The Preacher's Whore

Eight months before the Bullet-Catcher, in a brothel.

"The Black Manor, the Black Manor, the Black—"

A murder of crows sprung up to the skies on the road outside, making Emil jerk up from a chorus of whispers tormenting his restless sleep. His heart pounded in his chest, and sweat beaded his brow. The sun was beginning to rise, casting orange-yellow rays through the bedroom window. Thin white sheets were wrapped around his ankles, and he kicked himself free. Sitting up, it took him a moment to gather himself. "I was so close to finding it. How did they catch up to me so fast?"

"What's the matter?" purred the sleepy voice behind him. He almost forgot his most recent sin.

"Though we are overwhelmed by our transgressions, you forgive them all," prayed Emil, wrapping a rosary around his fingers. "Forgive me, Lord."

"You really *are* a preacher, ain't 'cha? It was hard to tell if you were telling me the truth. Most men who enter our establishment claiming to be men of the cloth don't end up enjoying me so much."

"I used to be a long time ago." Emil turned to see the slender outline of a woman staring at him draped in thin sheets, her hand on her hip. He could still see the shape of her hips and the curvature of her breasts in the rays of rising sunlight. Her raven-black hair was a tangled mess on her head. It was enough to make him want to take her once more, but he had to fight the urge. He had already lost once, and hell was bearing down fast.

"Blessed are the merciful, for they will receive mercy," he turned away with a whisper, clutching a black cross with silver inlays and pointed ends to his breast. Then, he heard the crash of glass outside.

"Laura, you need to leave," he whispered. "Now."

"Why? It's Saturday. It's a day to sleep in and do nothing," said Laura, throwing herself back onto her pillow. "Come, spend the day with me. Besides, most of my suitors are from the mines and so, so dirty. You are the most handsome suitor I've had in a long while and—"

"You are paid to say that."

Laura shook her head and reached over to ruffle her fingers through his brown hair. She touched the carved muscles on his abdomen, her reach going down between his legs, and began massaging his member. "You've already paid me. My shift ends at sunrise, and look, the sun is almost up, and I'm still here. With any luck, it won't be the only thing that rises this morning."

Emil shook her off and stood up, bare as the day he was born, and turned to her. Dozens of small black marks dotted his shoulders, neck, and chest, and they all had the same symbol of a star with five jagged points and a skull embedded in the middle. Laura's jaw dropped as she gazed upon him.

"I didn't see those marks last night," she said as she reached up to touch them. "Strange tattoos. What do they mean?"

"They aren't tattoos, and you didn't see them last night because they weren't there," grunted Emil, looking out the window. He sighed deeply. It probably wouldn't hurt to tell her now that she was going to die. "I am being hunted by hellions. If I stay in one place too long, they will find me and consume my flesh. I usually have a day or two. I should have gone to Glen Rio," said Emil as he reached down and pulled his pants up. He strapped a revolver to his hip and threw on a white shirt, then brought suspenders over his shoulders.

Laura stared at the revolver.

"I've seen that gun before," she whispered. The gun was a six-shooter Colt open-top revolver with a sleek silver barrel. The hammer was unlike any other hammer she had seen before. On the tip of the hammer was a winged skull with black eyes. "It's the Devil's Ruin, from the 'Bullet-Catcher' championship top prize in Glen Rio six years ago. It's said to never miss."

Then, she paused. "Wait, did you say you're being hunted by hellions?" Laura shrunk away and hugged the sheets to her chest. "What do those symbols mean?"

Emil slid three bullets into the cylinder of his revolver. He pulled the hammer back and walked to the window, holding the gun to his hip. "Demons."

"Wait, you aren't kidding?" asked Laura as the sheets fell from her chest and her breasts bounced lightly. "Usually, when men talk like that, they only mean to impress and sound mysterious for another quickie. You mean you are *actually* being hunted by demons?"

Suddenly, a scream pierced the peaceful morning air. Laura shot up and glanced out the window with a worried look on her face.

"They're here," he whispered. "It's too late."

"You're lying," said Laura with a smile, but Emil could tell there was a hesitation.

Muffled gunshots erupted in the distance like the spray of fireworks, and they heard the sound of more breaking glass. Then, Emil saw a man stumble into the street. He was covered in blood, and his arm was missing as if it had been torn clean off. The man glanced erratically to his sides, but there was nothing there. He screamed for help and fell to his knees, sobbing.

Suddenly, he rose into the air off his feet as if something had picked him up, but they couldn't see what. Then, his body contorted and twisted, and his torso burst into a mist of blood and guts. His body, torn in two pieces, fell into clumps in the middle of the street. It was then Emil saw bloodied footprints leading away from the mulch of gore. Then, all went silent.

"Holy hell," gasped Laura.

"And David spoke to the Lord the words of this song on the day when the Lord delivered him from the hand of all his enemies," whispered Emil, closing his eyes. He tucked the cross into his pants, then grabbed a Bible from the nightstand.

"Why can't I see them?"

"They appear visible to the naked eye only in the moonlight or at a very near distance. Thank the stars you can't see them now, but that changes when you get too close. You wouldn't be able to even run if you could see what they really look like. Fear would grip your feet like a vice."

Laura swung her legs off the bed and pulled a blue skirt up her body. Emil snuck a glance at her ass and gave a sigh as she tied the skirt to her waist and then slipped her arms into a white shirt, fastening the two buttons. She pulled a knife from behind a dresser and strapped it to her leg.

Suddenly, a shotgun blast rang out in a hallway, followed by a series of screams. A few seconds later, another shotgun blast rocked the wooden floor beneath them. The door flew open, and Rebecca and Lily burst into the room with disheveled hairdos. It seemed like Mr. Daily had them working last night too. Rebecca was a Mexican woman from Laredo, and Lily was a pale girl with burnt-red hair from up north somewhere. Emil had almost chosen Lily for the night until she started crying. It seemed like any little thing made that girl's spine turn to jelly.

"Laura! Mr. Daily is dead," said Lily, who immediately melted into tears and ran into her arms. Laura held her by the shoulders. Rebecca slammed the door shut, holding a smoking shotgun in her arms. Her eyes betrayed a chilling terror.

"All right you two, what happened?" asked Laura.

"He was doing his morning rounds when a man came up behind him and bit his neck," said Rebecca. "I-I shot him then."

Lily stopped sobbing for only a moment to look into Laura's eyes. "Then Mr. Daily got back up, but he wasn't himself. His skin was falling off, and I could see bone—" Tears flowed from her eyes, and her words choked in her throat.

"He tried to bite Lily. I had to shoot him twice," said Rebecca. "I was lucky enough to be in the rifle room when it happened."

"How many rifles do you have?" asked Emil.

"Five and one shotgun."

It wasn't much, but it didn't matter. Emil stood up and walked to the window. He saw footsteps in the sand close to the window, but he still couldn't see the hellion. If he started firing at them, they would know where he was and swarm his position. Then again, he could do that and let them tear the women down, allowing him the time to escape.

They were only whores.

Emil grunted and was about to take aim when a hand pressed on his shoulder firmly. He turned to see Laura staring at him with a grim look. "We found a way out of here. Come with us."

Emil shrugged. It wouldn't hurt to follow them. They had no clue what they were up against.

Rebecca and Lily left the room with rifles at the ready. Laura held the shotgun and grabbed Emil's hand, leading him out onto the hallway of the second floor. The other two girls had already gone downstairs.

Suddenly, a man burst from the door across from them and launched himself at Laura. She grunted and tried to shoot him, but the barrel of her shotgun was too long. The man had tattered strands of skin peeling off his cheeks as if he had raked his face on the street outside. His one eye was popped from his eye socket, but he barely seemed to notice. His breath reeked of rotting flesh, and his jaws snapped at Laura as she pushed the man off.

"What is wrong with you?" she screamed in vain to push him off. Emil kicked the man's shoulder, tossing him off her, and then shot the man in the head, exploding it like a melon. The man's body fell to the floor, headless, and twitched there for a moment.

Laura gathered herself and then aimed her shotgun at the body. "What the hell was that?"

"I don't know," said Emil. He wasn't entirely lying. "As I said, the dead are after me."

"Why? What did you do?"

"It's more what I *didn't* do," said Emil. "C'mon, we have to get out of here."

"You've got some explainin' to do," growled Laura. "Once we get out of Mesa Frio, I expect answers."

Emil shook his head. She had no idea whom she was talking to. One thing was certain; he knew she was a firecracker the moment he laid eyes on her. She was apparently more than just a good lay.

Once on the ground floor, not a soul stirred within the saloon, a strange sight even at this hour of the morning. The floor below was barren. Not even the bartender, a man known to be meticulous in the cleaning of his establishment, moved about cleaning glasses and scooting chairs closer to their tables.

Emil saw a chair move on its own out of the corner of his eye. He knew those unseen dead were in the room, too.

"Where did the other two girls go?" asked Emil.

"Out the back, probably."

She nodded in the same direction, and they both crept to the window and looked out. It opened up to a balcony.

Slowly, Laura unlatched the window, and she lifted herself over the windowsill onto the dirt street. Emil followed after, and he saw the door to the general store swing open by itself. The dead were in there waiting. Laura must have seen the same thing and caught her breath.

"Now we know where they are," he whispered. "We can leave the other way. I saw a barn on the—"

"Mr. Varbinsky is a friend of mine. He's in the general store. We must help him."

"Help him? Did you not get that we are being hunted by demons? He's very likely already dead."

"Shut your mouth and follow me," said Laura. Emil heard movement on the other side of the saloon and saw Rebecca and Lily poking their heads over. Emil tilted his head as they approached him.

"What are you doing?" he asked.

"I dunno. I saw footprints in the dirt on both ends of the street. I think we're trapped. The only way out is through the alley from the general store," said Rebecca as the girls huddled up to Laura. They all stared at the store with black GENERAL STORE letters above the entryway.

"The undead are in there," said Laura.

"Oh no, Mr. Varbinsky," gasped Lily. "You think he's okay?"

"I don't know. We have to check before we leave. Then we take the alley to the hills behind the store. It's our only way out of Mesa Frio. Now, come along."

Emil half-smiled but didn't protest. Even though her chances of survival were slim at best, he would, at the very least, enjoy her presence until their end. They crossed the dirt road and kept away from the pile of gore in the middle of the street that was already amassing a cloud of flies over it. Laura pushed her way into the grocery store, all four keeping their footfalls as silent as they could.

Laura held her shotgun to her side and swept the aisles as Emil followed close behind, Devil's Ruin in hand. The store was empty, just like the saloon. Or at least, it appeared that way. It was strange. Even though the town of Mesa Frio was small, it still had the typical regular day-to-day bustling of townspeople, miners from the northern camp, and travelers milling south to reach Glen Rio before winter. Emil had visited the town when he was a miner himself for a few years. Though he rarely frequented Mesa Frio, he knew it was typically busier than this. Had the demons been on his tail *before* the sun came up?

He noticed the backroom door ajar and pushed it open. A swathe of flies blew up at him, accompanied by a fetid stench of rot, and stepping back, he forced an involuntary gag silent.

"I found your Mr. Varbinsky," said Emil, covering his mouth with a red cloth. Lily began to sob, and tears streamed down her cheeks.

"Keep quiet," snapped Rebecca, shaking her head.

Laura approached and looked through the door. A man hung by his neck with a small stepping stool knocked over at his feet.

"Mr. Varbinsky," gasped Laura. His face was bloated and blue.

"He's been dead for a while," said Emil. "Can we go now?"

"These creatures with rotting flesh that we can't see, you said they are hunting you down. Why?"

"We don't have time," said Emil.

Laura poked the end of the shotgun into his face. "We got a minute."

Emil's eyes went thin as he glared at her. "Fine. I'll need to show you something. It's in my pocket."

"I know that trick. You best be careful. Any sudden movement, and I'll blow your brains out."

"Fair enough," he said as he reached into his pocket and pulled out a wooden coin. He held it up to her and flicked it at her. Laura snatched it from the air and looked at it. The coin appeared to be nothing special save for the initial *DR* engraved in the center.

Emil smiled at her. "The reason I'm being chased is because I am a Hunter of the Rose."

"From Glen Rio?" asked Lily, tears still somehow falling from her eyes.

"The Hunters of the Rose are blessed with uncanny abilities that hone their fighting chance, but they trade their souls for a simple wooden token. You've heard of my gun, the Devil's Ruin, from the Bullet-Catcher, yeah? Well, every three years, a championship between Hunters of the Rose takes place, and any Token Holder who is not present gets marked, like this." Emil took his shirt down from the collar, and now there were many more black marks on his chest.

"If a Hunter of the Rose misses a Bullet-Catcher Championship or is absent from Glen Rio at that time, they are marked. When a hunter gets marked, demons are spit up from hell to run down the prey until the token is claimed again. I missed the last one, and I've been running ever since."

"So, you're just going to keep on running?" asked Laura. "The dead will chase you where you go?"

Emil shook his head. "The Black Manor is the only way out for me. If I can only find the damn thing. I'm so close. The way of the innocent is paved with mercy. The Lord forgives them all."

Laura rolled her eyes. "Enough with the verses, Preacher. How the hell do we get out of here?"

Before he could answer, the glass windows of Mr. Varbinsky's store burst in as a dozen grunting undead poured in. They were close enough to no longer be invisible to their eyes. The stench of putrid decaying flesh hit them like a wall, filling the air with terror. Emil saw a crowd of them gathered outside, fighting to get in. Laura, Rebecca, and Lily turned their guns and opened fire. Laura's shotgun poked a hole through two undead, and they fell onto the ground, gurgling blood, and shaking uncontrollably. Rebecca aimed down the sights of her repeater and expertly fired headshots, dropping one after another. Lily fired her gun, but she closed her eyes shut with every shot, her rounds hitting the walls and ceiling. Emil smiled and looked to the back of the store. The door was wide open, and he saw no footsteps on the other side.

The exit was free.

Suddenly, Rebecca let out a scream as an undead man grabbed her from behind and bit her in the neck. She tried to elbow him off, but he locked his arms around her waist and squeezed tightly, forcing the air from her lungs. Rebecca grunted and fell hard to the floor with a thud. Lily turned to shoot but missed horribly, her shot landing on the floor of the store.

"Rebecca!" Lily screamed.

Laura racked a shotgun shell and turned to help, but two more undead jumped her. She swung her shotgun and poked it into an undead's mouth. "Bite this." She pulled the trigger and blew his brains out. The second one grabbed her blouse and tore it open, exposing her breasts. Laura didn't miss a beat. She pulled her knife from her leg strap and plunged the blade into its brain.

Emil realized that now was his chance. The horde would be busy with the girls for just enough time before they overrun them.

He ran out the back of the store.

"Lord, forgive us sinners now and at the time of death," he prayed, closing his eyes. He walked up a small hill overlooking Mesa Frio. Most of the town was on fire now.

Then, something caught his eye. At first, he thought it was a mountain range, but it was to the south, and there was nothing but plains to the south. It poked up into the waning sunlight like a black dagger against the sky. Its jagged arches turned into peaks at the top like a dozen majestic, pointed hats. Blue and yellow lights shone from beneath the shadow like rays on piles of gold and precious gems. Emil gasped as he realized his search was at an end.

"The Black Manor."

He could hardly believe his eyes. After all those years of running and searching, he had finally found it.

"Thank God!" he shouted to the heavens.

Before he could move, he felt a sharp pain in his leg and a ringing in his ears. He looked down to see blood pooling at his feet. His leg buckled, and he fell into the dirt. He heard the racking of a shotgun slug behind him, and he turned to see two women standing over him.

"Laura?"

She was draped in blood, and her hair was a mess on top of her head. The folds of her torn blouse flapped lazily in the wind.

"Why?" he wheezed, every breath an increasing struggle.

"You dare ask me that after leaving us to die? You're the reason our home is on fire."

"I found it. I found the Black Manor," said Emil, but when he looked back to see the cursed manor, it was beginning to fade.

"No! No, I am so close! Please, help me get there," said Emil, attempting in vain to stand up. He fell into the dirt.

"You are something else, Preacher."

"I am chosen of the Lord's to find the Black Manor. Look, there it is!" said Emil, a smile beginning to decorate his face. He turned to look again, but this time, there was nothing on the horizon. The Black Manor had all but vanished.

"No! Lord, why have you forsaken me?"

The rustling sound of footsteps alerted Emil to a ring of demons rising up to the hill, closing in like a cursed noose. They were completely surrounded. Lily shrieked as a crowd of undead surrounded them with terrifying grunts and gurgles. Laura looked on nervously. She held her shotgun at her hip as the cannibal crowds came closer. They moaned with horrid snarls, yearning for their flesh. Emil knew they had to act fast if they were to survive.

"Help me up," he said.

Laura slipped her arm under his and helped him to his feet.

"Nasty wound you gave me," he said drawing his revolver. "I'll deal with you after."

The crowd of undead lurched, but just as they reached out with furled fingers for their flesh, another shotgun blast rang in Emil's ears. The surrounding demons stopped suddenly in their tracks, staring at them with mouths agape. They simply stared, no longer snapping their jaws or shrieking for their blood. Emil looked down and saw a hole in the center of his chest. He looked at Laura with a smoking shotgun.

"When I was a young girl, my mother took me to church from time to time. I remember the preacher saying one thing that I'll never forget. 'And the dust returns to the earth as it was, and the spirit returns to God who gave it.' That same preacher ended up raping me before I did to him what I just did to you. I'm sending you to meet him. You lot deserve each other."

Emil fell into the dirt, eyes wide open. Laura racked another slug and turned to the undead bystanders. Their eyes glowed red, but they did not advance. In fact, they began to retreat from them. Laura aimed her gun at them, but before long, they disappeared from view into the burning town.

"We cannot stay here," said Laura. She turned to Lily, but she was no longer at her side. The young girl knelt over Emil's body and picked up a small coin from his jacket pocket. "Lily, no! Wait, it's cursed!"

She gasped and jumped up, letting it fall onto his dead body, but it was too late. A mark appeared on her wrist, the same shape and symbol as the ones on Emil's body.

"Oh no," she squeaked. Then, the symbol vanished as if it had never been there at all. "I didn't mean to." Tears welled in her eyes, and she began to sob. Laura let out a sigh.

"We must go to Glen Rio if we want some answers," she muttered. "Stop crying."

Lily shrunk into Laura's shadow. She knelt over Emil and took the Devil's Ruin from his hands. She stared at the sleek silver barrel and the winged skull on the hammer. She felt the weight of it in her hand and was surprised to find it not as heavy as it looked. She shoved the revolver into the folds of her dress.

"See you in hell," muttered Laura.

"I have a friend in Glen Rio who can take us in. She's a bulletsmith. I hope she's still alive," said Lily, tears streaming down her face.

"It wouldn't hurt to look."

"What about poor Rebecca?" sobbed Lily. "We should at least bury her?"

"I should have put a bullet through his head the moment those things attacked us. Had I known it was that easy, I would have."

"Laura, look!" Lily pointed at her arm.

A stinging pain in Laura's wrist made her wince, and she dropped to her knees into the dirt road. She gritted her teeth as a small black mark appeared on her arm. It looked like a small diamond with a skull in the center. It flashed bright red, and then it disappeared. She touched her forearm and stared hard. It was almost as if she had imagined the brand appearing at all.

"But you didn't touch the token. Why did you get marked?" asked Lily, wiping tears from her eyes. Then, Laura remembered she had held that very same token just a few hours before Mr. Varbinsky's shop. He had simply tossed it to her, and she took it without hesitation. It seemed Emil had sealed Laura's fate.

"Aw, hell."

The Union-American government fell silent shortly after the Second Civil War. Most predicted a third war after the armistice at Houston, Texas. Yet, the Yanks, suddenly and without warning, fled to their lands and never returned. It was as if they were running from something. All communication was lost after a thick perpetual fog descended upon their lands. Many said their souls were collected for a reckoning. Many scoffed at those superstitions and decided to find out for themselves. Those who went to investigate never returned. Now, it is an unspoken rule not to even mention the north. To do so might incur the fog to bring the south to that same fate.

The Rifle's Spiral

A year after the first Bullet-Catcher (eight years ago), in Glen Rio.

A gunshot rang out in the early morning sky, and Oscar's heart jumped into his throat. He ran to the window of his store with his Colt army revolver in hand and stopped at the windowsill. He waited a few seconds, and when he looked through the glass, he let out a sigh and relaxed his shoulders.

It wasn't a gunshot. Mrs. Ann Blankenship snapped her whip with a crack over her four horses again, and they began to pull her empty carriage away. She had a bright look on her face. She must have made a killing with the moonshine she sold to Sarah in the Silver Bullet Saloon. Oscar swallowed hard and forced his shaking hand to holster his weapon. He noticed a costumer staring at him. Oscar turned and forced a smile, trying to control his breathing as sweat beaded on his brow.

"Sorry, ma'am. I'm a veteran of the Last War. I gets the shakes from time to time," he said as if that was enough of an explanation. He wrung his hands, made a beeline to the backroom, and shakily sat on a sardine barrel to gather his thoughts. He could feel chills run up and down his spine. His bushy white mustache blew back and forth in the wake of his rapid breathing, poking his lower lip. After a few moments, he wiped the sweat off his brow and cleared his throat. The door opened, and a young man stood in the doorway.

"It happened again, Mr. Sweeney?" asked Percy, the store aide, as he set a box of bullets on a shelf above him.

Oscar grunted sheepishly and stood up. Percy put a hand on his shoulder.

"It's all right, sir. I'll watch the shop. Take all the time you need in here," he said. Oscar closed his eyes at him and sat back down on the barrel reluctantly. He knew the fear was coming, and it would grip his soul and squeeze like a vice. Someone so young as Percy wouldn't understand that. Even so, Percy left the door ajar, leaving just enough room for a thread of silver light to poke through. He was a good boy, Percy. Always willing to help. Always willing to lend a hand.

Oscar's calloused hands were still shaking. Thunder of cannon fire roared overhead, making him bolt upright. It startled him, and he began to unclip his gun belt. He heard the shout of a man and the firing of a row of rifles. Sweat began to collect on his forehead, or was it blood? It sure smelled like blood. He squinted in the face of muzzle fire and the sound of a hundred blaring trumpets. He set the gun on the shelf beside a jar of pickles. The cannons roared again. The smell of sulfur rose to his nostrils. He heard the click of a dozen rifles readying and the bark of a captain.

Fire!

After a while, Oscar closed the door to the backroom and took in a deep breath of the crisp and quiet Glen Rio morning air. He could tell Percy was studying him as he walked back to the flour bags and lifted one up, setting it high on a shelf.

For a man in his late seventies, he was cursed with good health. He emerged from the wars with little physical trauma. Some called it luck, but Oscar never would dare say he was lucky. Quite the opposite, really.

"Sir?" asked Percy from behind the counter.

"All better." Oscar smiled at him, flashing his green eyes in an attempt to dissuade his aide from prodding further. The old man's attempt to reassure him seemed unsuccessful as Percy merely stared on in silence with a skeptical look.

Movement on the street caught Oscar's eye, and he heard a terrified squeal. A man stumbled from the Silver Bullet, dragging a small boy by the collar of his shirt. The man had a mutton chop beard on his cheeks and a hard double chin. He tossed the boy into the street and then reared back and kicked the boy hard in the ribs. Once, then twice.

The man spit over the boy's curled-up body.

Oscar's eyes widened, and he walked to the doorway as the man melted back into the saloon. He heard the howl of laughter from within.

The boy lay on the dirt street, unmoving, blood dripping from his lips and chin. He couldn't have been older than twelve. Oscar stiffened his upper lip and growled as he pushed the store door open. Two men in fine-fitted suits and golden-hilt canes walked past the boy without so much as a cursory glance.

Oscar growled at them as they passed, and they turned to him as if *he* were the odd one out. Oscar saw a cart pulled by two horses round the corner. The driver showed no signs that he saw the boy lying in the dirt directly in front of him. Oscar hurriedly ran into the street and scooped up the boy in his arms as the horse cart thundered by just in the nick of time.

He sat down on the wooden platform of his grocery store and set the boy on his lap. Now, staring at him up close, Oscar realized the boy was no older than seven or eight. His eyes were rolled into the back of his head, and blood and vomit had accrued on the corner of his lips. Oscar rubbed the child's chest.

"C'mon, boy. Don't die on me."

He sat there for a few minutes, unsure of what to do. Then, the boy's eyes fluttered open, and he coughed and sat up, his head twirling on his shoulders. Oscar let out a sigh of relief. "Dear God, boy. What the hell did you do to earn that man's wrath?"

"Let him go!"

Suddenly, the air was split by a shout, and Oscar looked up to see a woman in a ragged dress that had once been white but was now browned with dirt from everyday living. She rushed Oscar and tore the boy from his arms.

"What the hell do you think you're doing?"

Oscar stood up with hands clenched. "You're the mother?"

"Of course, I am," spat the woman. "Who else do you think watches over him?"

Oscar stood up as a dark shadow overtook his features, and his eyes shone deadly. "He could have died."

"He talked back to his father. Spare the rod, spoil the child, and I'll be damned if I raise a spoiled brat."

"He probably needs to see a doctor."

"Why do you care? He's not your blood. I am his *mother*. If I see you even look at him again in that creepy way, I'm placing a bounty on your head. You will learn what it means to mess with Hunters of the Rose Manor. Pervert!"

She spat at Oscar's boots and cradled the startled boy in her arms. She kissed him on the forehead. Oscar stared with fists clenched as she rushed out of sight back into the saloon.

The following day, a mule from Glen Rio arrived on schedule at the Sweeney General Store with silk, nails, wooden boards, horse bits, horseshoes, and booze. When Oscar and Percy had finished unloading the cart, the only crate remaining was the box of dark beer for the saloon.

"I'll take it, Mr. Sweeney," offered Percy. Oscar shook his head and brushed his aide off. This was a shipment he was delivering himself.

He slammed his boot on the wooden door of the saloon open, and he walked through into the pantry.

"Good morning, Mr. Sweeney. That box looks awfully heavy. Why is Percy not helping you?" said Sarah as she approached him, wiping her hands with a towel.

"Hullo, Sarah," said Oscar. "He is busy at the moment. Where can I set this?"

Sarah pointed to a corner in the pantry.

"Thank you," he said, bending over and setting it where she had indicated. Then, Oscar heard the clanging of a glass on the bar counter.

"Coming," said Sarah, turning to the sound of a customer who called for a refill, giving a quick wave. "Have a nice day, Oscar."

He smiled back, but his eyes were scanning the saloon floor. Cigar smoke created a fog in the saloon, and though the sun was poking through the windows, a few men were still at their seats on tables. The working men of the small town allowed Sunday and Saturday to become one, as was typical, for drinking, whoring, and gambling.

Sarah let out a laugh as she poured a mug of beer for her customer. Then, Oscar saw a man in a corner, along with two others who had cards strewn on the table. They had cigars in their mouths, and their hats were low on their brows.

125

Oscar brushed his hands on his apron and rounded the counter.

"You all right, Mr. Sweeney?" came the sweet voice of Sarah, who had eyes like a hawk. She knew something was up as he rarely ever entered the establishment. She approached him, setting a pitcher on the counter and eyeing him quizzically. Oscar didn't look, however. His eyes were bolted to the men in the corner.

"Whiskey. One shot, Sarah dear."

"That has to be the first drink you've ever asked for since I've known you the last fifteen years. Everything all right?"

Oscar fished a nickel from his apron and set it on the polished wood. He turned to her. "If you please, dear."

Sarah gave a worried look but grabbed a bottle from beneath the counter and poured a yellowish liquid into a small glass. Oscar took it and slammed it home. He set the empty glass upside down on the counter and gritted his teeth as the warm liquor burned down his throat.

He slipped his apron off his shoulders and set it on the counter.

"Oscar?"

"One more thing. That man with the mutton chops in the corner. That dude have a name?"

"That's Roy Briggs. I have to ask, what are you doing?" said Sarah with a hint of worry in her voice.

He ignored her and made his way to the corner table and sat down beside the three men.

"Huh, Mr. Sweeney?" asked one of the men. "I never thought to see you in *this* establishment."

Oscar realized he was an old Hunter of the Rose who would always frequent the saloon, Mr. Edward Gray. His red hair spilled from beneath the brim of his hat. The other man only grunted with a smile, but Oscar didn't recognize him. The third man, Roy, stared back at him with raven black eyes. He flashed a drunken smile.

"Well, if it ain't the general storekeeper. Perhaps business has been good, yeah? Perhaps he has a little extra money to spend?" He laughed. Then, he rounded the cards all into his hand and began shuffling them expertly. "I should thank you for saving my son yesterday. From what I understand, you were touching him inappropriately, in the middle of the street, no less. However, that came from my stupid wife. She has a tendency for hysteria." He spread the cards across the table until each man had seven cards.

"I assume you know how to play the game, old man?"

Oscar nodded.

Roy set four cards on the table. "Whaddya got there, old geezer?"

"The boy."

He raised an eyebrow. "You got a boy?"

"No, you do."

Roy sighed and looked at the other men. They simply shrugged. Sarah walked to the table with fresh mugs of beer, and E. Gray began nursing his drink. The second man simply stared at his cards and would not look up again. Roy then tilted his head at Oscar. "Aye, what of it?"

"Do you claim ownership?"

"Hardly," he laughed. "Why? Are you interested in buying him?"

"Is he for sale?"

Roy rubbed his chin. "As much as I wish, his mother would never hear of it."

"His mother?"

"That rat is not my son. He was born here while I was off to war. When I returned, that runt was crying, causing a ruckus in my house. If not for the lust I have for that brainless wench, I would have shot the boy then and there and been done with it. The law is on my side on that matter, haven't I said so, boys?"

E. Gray nodded with a mouthful of beer.

"You see, the doc in Glen Rio said I can't have children. My wife, in her infinite stupidity, thought she was doing me a favor by getting pregnant with the town fool while I was away, putting my life on the line for my country. What a joke," said the man.

"Sometimes, that's just the way the butterscotch cookie crumbles," grumbled E. Gray, setting his cards face down with a scowl.

"Hah! That's exactly what I told the town fool when I put the barrel of my iron in his mouth and blew his brains out the back of his head. The war had just come to an end, and no one said a damn thing to me, not even the old sheriff. Apparently, he had impregnated a few too many wives, so no one gave protest."

"I was in the war too," whispered Oscar.

"Which one?" E. Gray laughed. "You look like you could have fought in the First Civil War."

"That too," snapped Oscar. This made E. Gray cut his laugh. He returned to his beer.

"Well, judging by the looks of things, you were on the winning side," said Roy with a grin.

Oscar shook his head. "We lost."

Roy turned to his compadres and then back at Oscar.

"You're a filthy Reb?" he asked, his hand wandering to the gun tucked inside his pants. Oscar saw the motion and smiled.

"Draw that gun and see how long it takes you to pull the trigger before I tear your throat out. I've done it before. It's a lot easier than you might think," said Oscar, baring his teeth. "All I ask is to lay off the boy. Be a father to a son even if he does not belong to you. You claim ownership; in that matter, the law is on your side, yet a son scorned by his father is a son damned to hell on earth."

"It isn't Sunday, and I didn't ask for a sermon. Why do you care?" asked the man as a telling quiver danced on his lower lip.

"I'll be watching you," Oscar said as he stood up and spat on the floor. "And today *is* the day of the Lord."

Then he left the Silver Bullet Saloon without another word.

By the time the sun had gone down that day, the saloon had begun to empty as the working men returned to their homes to sober up to return to the mines early the next morning. Oscar stared through the glass of the general store as Roy stumbled down the dirt road. He grabbed his brown coat and slipped into it, then grabbed his kepi hat and fitted it on his head. He reached beneath the counter to pull a slim steel revolver. He slid six long bullets into the cylinder, then spun it and expertly shoved it into the holster at his hip.

Then he paused as he felt someone watching him from the dark corner of the store.

"Mr. Sweeney?" asked Percy, coming into view. "I know where you're going."

"I can't let it happen. How long before it's too much? How long before it becomes a supposed accident that can't be forgiven."

"Why, Oscar? Why? What the hell does this boy mean to you? The boy's living conditions are terribly unfortunate, but that is the way of the world. Why are you so fixated on meddling in someone else's business?" pleaded Percy softly. The veins of Oscar's neck popped, and he stiffened his upper lip. He lit a cigar and puffed it in his mouth.

"You wouldn't understand."

"Then help me understand. I can't let you go after him. You'll get yourself killed. Forget the boy. He's not worth your life. Simply alert Constable Skinner and be done with it."

"He's worth everything!" shouted Oscar as his smoking cigar dropped to the ground. Tears flooded his vision, and his hands began to shake violently.

"Oscar," whispered Percy, grabbing his shoulders and squeezing them.

Oscar gave a heavy sigh. "I *was* that man. The drink possessed every moment of my young life. Even after I, by sheer luck, found a beautiful wife and had a son, I still let the Devil dominate me. I beat them both hard at any flash of anger. I caned her, and I kicked him. I was worse than that man. Then, the war broke out, and I signed up without saying goodbye. Good riddance, I said. Months turned to years, and finally, we had been beaten, and I returned home. I was met with ash and destruction. As it so happened, a faction of the enemy didn't know the war was over, and they wiped out Richardson Villa. I found my house burned to the ground and the burned bones of my wife scattered on the consumed foundation. Then, I saw what was left of him. His skull stared at me through the ash, condemning me to hell, to a life of tortured thoughts and a bed of thorns. The second war happened, and I signed up to die, but somehow, I lived no matter how many charges I led, no matter how many times I stared bullets in the eye. That is my curse. I wish someone had stopped me. I wish someone had shot me before I did that to them. I can't let the boy live like that. I won't let it happen again."

Percy knelt down and picked up the cigar in his hands. "I-I didn't know."

"That boy has maybe a few days before he is just another grave without a cross. I'm not about to sit by and let it happen," said Oscar, taking the cigar from Percy's hands. "I'll be back in the morning. Don't wait up."

He brought the neck of his coat together in his hand and vanished into the night, headed after Roy, a stream of cigar smoke rising from his mouth. The wind's icy chill bit against him, but Oscar clenched his jaw. He saw a stumbling shadow ahead and followed him down the dirt road.

Roy stopped and knelt beside a tree. He belched and threw up loudly on all fours. Oscar stopped a few feet away and puffed his cigar. The wind beat at him, carrying the icy slap of cold inclement weather. This winter would be a fierce one.

Roy shouted something, wiping sweat from his face and walking into the brush. Oscar's hands began to shake, so he grabbed his wrists and squeezed them hard.

"Just go home and go to sleep. Just go home and go to sleep," whispered Oscar as the man stumbled off the tree and back into the road. Oscar followed not too far behind, keeping the sound of his own footsteps out of earshot. Finally, they rounded a bend in the road that led down into a small farmstead.

As Oscar came closer, he heard the burst of voices from within and the crash of glass. He could see a man in the window holding a bottle, and as soon as Roy entered, stood up and spit.

"Well, took you long enough. I suppose you return with nothing to your name, don't ya?" thundered the man's voice. He was twice the size of Roy, with a black beard reaching nearly down to his waist over his beer belly. His face was redder than a beet, and he scowled at Roy. This must have been his brother.

"You guess right, you dumb bastard. Jesus Christ, how you came from the same womb as me, I'll never know. Suppose Mother wasn't the pious type to keep her legs together, was she?" snarled Roy.

A scowl crawled onto the man's face as Roy howled with laughter. He sat down at the table and took a swig of his brother's drink. Suddenly, the door behind them swung open, and his wife stepped through, pulling the boy by a rope tied to his neck.

"Roy, he has to be punished. Everyone saw what happened in the street. Now the townsfolk have begun speaking ill of us, and it is all his fault."

"Do what you will. Don't you see I'm trying to relax?" grunted Roy, taking another swig from the bottle.

"How long should the punishment be?" asked the mother.

Roy chewed his lip. "Ten hours got to do the trick. Remember, boy, you earned this punishment for yourself. Accept it like a man."

The mother nodded and pulled the boy into the room by the rope. His face was already red, and Oscar could see red marks on his neck. The boy began coughing.

"Shut your mouth. If you cough while in your punishment, you get caned, got it?" barked his mother, who then pulled him close to a peg high on the wall and strung the rope to it, leaving just barely enough room for the boy to stand on his toes to breathe. They were strangling him as a punishment.

"Not seen and not heard," said Roy with a laugh. The brother snatched the bottle away and slammed the tip into his face.

Oscar's heart beat wildly in his chest like a war drum. He stood up, but then he saw the boy struggle with the rope. He slipped his neck from the rope and made a run for the door. With uncanny speed, Roy jumped up and grabbed him, nearly yanking the boy's arm clean off.

"You little pissant," growled Roy. His mother handed Roy a cane, and he grabbed it and began to whip the boy. Oscar's lip twitched as he watched the boy get beaten viciously. Roy reared back with every blow, mercilessly striking the boy with all his strength. The boy cried and pleaded, but there was no end in sight to the onslaught of lashings. Oscar's lip stiffened, and he stood up from the undergrowth and drew his revolver. He walked to the window just beside the doorway.

The boy's pleas turned to silence, and a look of numbness spread over the boy's face. Then, in a motion Oscar couldn't have predicted, the boy grabbed the revolver from Roy's belt and pulled the hammer back, aiming it at Roy's chest.

Out of breath and clearly dizzy, Roy let out a smile. "You have earned yourself a week in the hotbox. You sure you want to make it two?"

The boy whimpered, his legs shaking and his back clearly in pain as red stripes began to bleed through his shirt.

Roy looked at his brother and laughed. He wasn't so jovial and eyed the boy nervously.

"Drop the gun now, and I stop beating you. If you don't, I will make sure you're never able to use your hands again," said Roy, balling his fists. "Do you realize you have signed your fate by this stunt? Your mother and I have taken you in, fed you, made sure you were clothed, and this is how you repay us? You will feel this one, I promise you."

The boy didn't say a word. He pulled the trigger, and the bullet zipped through Roy's chest and pinged off a cast-iron grill on the wall, casting sparks over his brother. Roy fell to the ground in a puff of smoke. His brother stood up, but at that close range, the boy didn't have to aim.

Spittle dribbled from his brother's lips as he held his hands up, shattering the bottle as he let it from his hands to the ground.

The boy pulled the trigger again. The bullet hit the brother in the head. His body went limp, and his arms fell to his sides. His eyes rolled to the back of his head, and he remained still, blood dripping from the hole in between his eyes. In mere seconds, both men lay dead at the boy's feet. He dropped the gun just as his mother screamed from the other room. She had watched the entire display in utter shock. She emerged, loading a shotgun.

At the sight of her with a gun, the boy ran through the door into the dirt road with tears streaming down his face, but he tripped on a tangle of brush just a few feet away from the house. Light from within shone on him but was quickly blotted out as his mother emerged with a cruel look on her face.

The boy spotted Oscar and ran behind him, clutching at his pant leg. He could feel the little boy shaking uncontrollably beside him, permeating fear and the sharp smell of urine. Oscar held his gun as steady as he could, but he knew the clicking sound gave away the shakes in his hands.

The mother panted as she saw Oscar and then wiped strands of hair from her face. "I know you! You're the shopkeeper. What the hell are you doing out here?"

"I'm taking the boy away."

"No, you're not," said the mother, shouldering the shotgun and aiming it straight at him. Oscar chewed on the stub of a cigar that had gone cold a few hours now.

"He's not yours to torture anymore."

"He's my son!"

"No, he's not! He's lucky to be alive. If I ever see you again, I will shoot you. Stay away from Glen Rio and stay away from him," said Oscar. He turned his back to her and put his hand over the boy's shoulder.

"Everything's going to be okay, boy."

Oscar heard the clap of gunfire and a sharp bite in his side. He whipped around with his thumb on the hammer of his revolver. He fanned the hammer and shot the woman three times in the chest. She fell with a whimper into the dust and lay still.

He looked down at a bloody hole on his left flank. It looked like someone had taken a bite right out of him.

He heard small footsteps, and Oscar glanced back and saw him kneeling beside his dead mother.

"It's all right, boy. It's over now. You are safe."

The boy stood up and took a step back.

"What's your name, boy?"

"Jonesy."

"Come, Jonesy, I'm going to take to you to a better place."

"I killed them," he said, tears falling from his eyes. "I killed them all."

"It's okay. I saw the whole thing happen. I will help you."

"They will hang me."

Oscar hesitated and looked back at the dead inside the house. It would be a grim explanation. Then, Oscar took a step toward the boy, but before he could get too close, he darted into the darkness.

"Jonesy!" He could hear rustling in the darkness, but then nothing. He had vanished like a ghost.

Oscar then saw a rider on horseback holding a torch approach from the far road.

Oscar thought about calling again for the boy, but in fear of the rider hearing him, he darted into the farmstead. He cut across a field and ran as fast as he could in the direction of DeGuello Canyon. He turned to see the shadow on horseback had disappeared.

Thunder rumbled in the distance by the time Oscar found a cave with his own distinct OSY mark above the entryway. It was not the first time he had to sleep beneath this rook roof in one of the easternmost caverns of the canyon stretch. He reached beneath a rock and picked up a leather satchel with dried crackers, flintstone, kindling, and a paring knife. There was a handful of bullets, so Oscar took the bag and watched as rain began to fall down into the crevice and create a small creek in the old rock. The moon stood vigilant in the lone night sky above him. He began to think about what to do. He would have to leave Glen Rio now.

He didn't know how long he had been sitting there when he heard the telltale *clop, clop, clop* of a group of horses. He didn't run. He didn't speak.

He remained still.

"I'll talk to him. Just stay back, please," came the voice at the opening of the cave. It was Percy. Oscar heard footsteps come closer. "Mr. Sweeney?"

Oscar looked up to see Percy standing before him. The usual worried look was chiseled into his face. It didn't melt into a smile, however. Oscar saw pistols at his hip.

"You are here to take me in?"

"I have E. Gray and a few Rose Hunters with me. Dusty Rose put a bounty on your head. The neighboring farm rang the alarm at the sound of gunshots. There are twelve men to bring you in. You must surrender to us."

"Only twelve?" whispered Oscar with a hint of a smile. This made Percy's face sour.

"I told you to leave it alone, Oscar. I told you it wasn't worth it."

He shrugged. "Maybe not, but at the very least, I gave him a new chance."

Percy shook his head and glanced to the side as if to see he was out of the posse's earshot. "If only your aim had been true, Mr. Sweeney. You shot her up good, but you didn't kill her. She was rushed to Glen Rio two hours ago. Doc Jennings will patch her up. She said the mother will live."

"Shame. So, the boy—?"

"He was found with her. If she recovers, they will both be fine."

Oscar let his head down. "I looked into his eyes, and what I saw was fear. He saw a monster in me, and I allowed myself to be overtaken. What was I to do? Stand by while he suffered?"

Percy shifted onto his hip.

"I was prepared for a shootout, but I won't fight you, Percy," said Oscar, tossing the revolver at his feet. "Take care of that weapon. You have no idea how many I had to kill to acquire it."

"I will," said Percy as he reached down and shoved it into the back of his pants.

"The gallows then?" asked Oscar.

"No. Secretly, E. Gray is relieved that Roy and his brother are dead. He said, 'That old bat Oscar saved me of a large debt. The least I owe him is to look him in the eye when I shoot him. No hard feelings. That's just how the butterscotch cookie crumbles.' You're to be killed by firing line and buried in these caves."

"I accept that," said Oscar.

"They are waiting for you."

The term *mosquito* is often used in a derogatory way when referring to a gun fixed with a suppressor. These types of weapons are considered cowardly, and whoever uses them is considered a lower class of bounty hunter or an "unskilled" gunman. Most users of these types of weapons don't advertise their use, yet nearly 20 percent of all bounties turned in to Rose Manor belong to kills with *mosquitos*. Someone is clearly lying . . .

The Mosquito

One year before the Bullet-Catcher, in Glen Rio.

Joel pushed the Silver Bullet Saloon doors open and stood in the doorway, his torn coat flapping in the dusty wind behind him as he caught the barkeep's gaze. The establishment was packed with patrons despite it being still early on a Tuesday afternoon. All tables were taken, so he made his way through to the bar. Patrons melted away from him, most likely due to the putrid stench of mud, crap, and old blood. Honestly, he was surprised to still be breathing. His hands still carried the shakes as he approached the bar.

He let out a sigh and sat on a stool, taking his wide-brimmed straw hat, which sported a nasty tear at the top, and set it on the counter. He would need a new hat now.

"Well, well, well, if it ain't Joel Whitney. Goddamn, you're alive," sneered the barkeep, shaking his head. "When you took that bounty, I was sure I'd seen the last of you."

Joel flashed a smile, fished a crumpled piece of paper from his breast pocket, and slammed it onto the counter. The grim face of Lester McBride stared back with one eye missing and scars scissoring his face. The $500 sign was in bold black for all to see. "I got lucky."

"You have proof?"

He pulled a patch of leather from his pocket. It was a gator-skin patch belonging to the jacket Lester McBride was known to wear.

"You're telling me you single-handedly killed not only Lester McBride but also his fifteen gunmen in Castellan Crow Cave? All by yourself. With that modified revolver that looks about to break apart at the next pull of a trigger?" asked the barkeep, leaning onto the counter, staring needles into his eyes. "Nahhhh."

Joel gave a nervous laugh. "Of course, how do you think I got this? Maybe a guardian angel watches over me?"

There was blood on the picture, and Joel was sure some of it was his own. At least, it *looked* like it could be.

"Hardly broke a sweat. Two shots of your top-shelf whiskey," Joel said, holding two bruised fingers up. To tell the truth, he *really* was surprised to be alive.

"Not so fast," said the barkeep. "You have to see Dusty Rose and claim your bounty before you drink here. I won't take none of your credit anymore."

"I wanted to have a quick drink right before I claimed the money," Joel pouted. "You wouldn't believe how thirsty shooting *banditos* makes a man. I'll be back to pay you pronto, I promise."

"Not off your promise of a bounty, you don't. You've maxed your tab, and I'm tired of your grand stories. You want a drink? I gotta see some coin," muttered the barkeep.

Joel frowned. "Fine, hold my seat. I'll be right back."

The barkeep chuckled, giving him pause.

"What's so funny?" asked Joel.

"Dusty is not in Glen Rio at the moment. She left on business nearly three days ago. She was supposed to return yesterday, but I imagine she got held back. You have no option but to wait, it seems. Well, if you are thirsty—"

"Yeah?" asked Joel.

"Well, I just got a new shipment of—" began the barkeep, leaning forward on the counter and gesturing Joel to come closer, lowering his voice to a whisper, "—fresh horse water."

He let out a roar of laughter. "Been distillin' all day in the sun just for you!"

Joel growled but knew better than to fight with the man. He fished a bronze coin from his pocket and tossed it at the barkeep. The coin fell against his stomach and then into his hands.

"A single then," said Joel.

The barkeep wiped the edges of his mouth and grunted, patting the coin into his pocket, and poured the transparent liquid into the shot glass. He slid it in front of Joel, still chuckling from his own joke.

Joel tossed the shot of whiskey into his throat and winced at the burn. The voices of the table behind him began to grow louder with enthusiasm. He craned his head to hear better.

"They say only eclipsinthe bullets can actually kill that thing for good. The swamp is its perfect hiding spot. Honestly, it's too bad our bulletsmith works exclusively for Dusty Rose now."

"It's too bad our bulletsmith is a *woman*!" The men roared at the joke, slamming their fists on the table.

"Wait, wait—no. It's a whole lot worse—it's too bad that forge is run by *two* women!"

They howled and hooted. Joel stared at the bottom of his shot glass and saw a tiny drop left. He slammed it back and felt the burn on the tip of his tongue. He stared pitifully at the barkeep, who only grunted in response.

The men behind him resumed their gaff. "The world's gone to hell in a handbasket. Now, some towns are straight up disappearing. They call her the Trapper. She operates a devil train with legs, not wheels, mind you, like a centipede, and it doesn't run on tracks either, oh no. It is said this thing runs underground like a damn mole digging through the ground," said the man, shuffling through his cards and setting one in the center of the table. This must have been the end of the game, for the other two scowled and tossed their cards before them. "They say she experiments on the men she captures. They say she uses their bodies for science and then discards the bones in the desert."

"How could we defend ourselves from something like that?"

"Again, eclipsinthe bullets would be where I would start. Too bad our bulletsmith is a woman with a stupid name like Elsie!"

The table shook with laughter as if it was the funniest joke ever uttered. Sometimes, Joel wished he was deaf.

"There is a $10,000 bounty on the Trapper. If only there was a way to penetrate the armored exterior of the train."

Joel's eyes nearly popped out of his head at the mention of the bounty amount.

"Good luck to anyone who catches *that* train. No way anyone would have a chance to penetrate that armor if you can't even find the damn thing. Perhaps the best way to defend ourselves would be to dig holes and fill them with explosives."

"They would sooner blow up beneath us, you idiot. No, there has to be another way," mused a bystander Joel didn't recognize, who sat at their table and began shuffling the cards.

That would do for him. Joel knew words only complicated things. You could gain all you needed to know by simply listening. He fit his torn hat on his head and left the saloon. He had to find himself a bulletsmith, one who happened to be a woman named Elsie.

Joel walked along the dirt road thinking of the $10,000 bounty and all he could do with that money when he heard the loud clanging of hammer onto anvil. He followed the sound to a barren section of Glen Rio. He found himself close to the outskirts of the town. The sun hid behind a swathe of gray clouds, and rain was on the way; the smell confirmed it. Before long, rain pattered on the rim of his busted hat, and he walked through the mud up to the bulletsmith shop. He found a woman beneath a red tarp in front of a shop with a sign reading *Bulletsmith*. This must be the woman those men spoke of.

Elsie had coal-colored skin, and her hair was made into thick dreads and tied together behind her head. Her arms were strewn with muscle, and she wielded a small hammer in her hands with extreme precision. Then, she nodded and slammed her hammer onto a thin metal slab, and it cracked. For a moment, Joel thought she had ruined the piece, but then, the bulletsmith grabbed a pair of tongs and plucked a hidden gem from within the cracked metal. Or at least it looked like a gem. It glowed dark green, and she pulled a brush with fine bristles from her belt and brushed the metallic contents away. She hammered once, ever so precisely, and this blow crushed the gem to fine dust. It was clear she was no amateur. Joel watched her work in awe of her masterful display. She pulled a thin bullet case from a pouch on her belt and, with a tiny spoon, scooped up some of the fine dust into the brass casing of the bullet.

"There has to be a perfect balance. Too little eclipsinthe, and you miss the effect of the bullet. Too much, and you melt through the brass casing the moment the hammer strikes, blowing your fingers to bits. To use a bullet like this, you must trust the smith who made it."

Joel glanced around, but there was no one else in the dusty street. Was she talking to him?

The bulletsmith brought her round to a press, placed the round in the loader, and leaned into the lever. The loader dropped the bullet, but she caught it with her hand and held it out in her palm for Joel to see.

"Perfection," she gasped.

"How did you get a hold of eclipsinthe? I thought it was extremely rare," said Joel, reaching out to touch the bullet. Elsie frowned as if just then realizing he was there and snapped her fingers over the bullet like a clam.

"Only comes from meteors. Even more reason to handle with care," said the bulletsmith. How she had gotten a hold of eclipsinthe was beyond Joel, seeing as it was so impossibly hard to find. The bulletsmith finally sighed as if annoyed that he was there. Perhaps it was the stench. He couldn't remember the last time he had had a bath.

"What do you want?" she asked. Joel pointed at the bullet in her hands.

She laughed. "You cannot afford this."

He shrugged and pulled the bloody bounty from his breast pocket. "I just killed Lester McBride and his gang."

"No, you didn't," she smiled. "It would take a lot more than you to kill *that* lot."

"Well, *I* did. I got myself $500."

"Not yet, you don't. You have to turn the bounty into Dusty Rose for dollars. I don't take credit. Go away. I don't need beggars, and I don't need tricks. I need cold, hard cash."

"But she's not in Glen Rio," protested Joel.

"Sounds like that's your problem."

A door creaked open behind her, and a girl in a blue dress and burnt-red hair emerged, sniffling with tears in her eyes. Her skin was as pale as the bulletsmith's was black. She held her knuckles to her chin and sobbed quietly.

"What now, Lily?" growled Elsie.

"I-I-I forgot to keep the fire going. I fell asleep," she sobbed. She was younger than the bulletsmith but that much more frail-looking. There was no meat on her bones, but she didn't look starved, only very frail in comparison.

Elsie let out a sigh and closed her eyes as if trying very hard not to snap at Lily. "Did you think to light it again? I need that fire for the forge, Lily. We have six orders of horseshoes to complete before the end of the week."

The sobbing stopped for a second as if the idea hadn't even crossed her mind.

"Go and start it again," said the bulletsmith, calmly but clearly losing her patience. "And *stop* crying."

The girl nodded and left, sniffling away and wiping tears from her eyes.

149

Elsie turned to Joel once more. "You're still here?"

He nodded.

"Look, unless you are willing to cross through the swamp for me, I don't need you hanging around warding customers off with your stench. Piss off before I shoot you myself."

Joel cocked his head and looked in the direction of the swamp.

"You're not from around here, are you?" she asked, eyeing him up and down.

"Not really. I've visited Glen Rio a few times in the past, but I've since become a hunter."

"A bounty hunter? You don't look like much."

Joel looked down at his muddied clothes. "That's the trick. It's easier for someone to underestimate me so I can get the upper hand. They call me the Mosquito." He held his hand out to her.

Elsie looked up at him and then his hand and sighed. "You play the part well."

She leaned back, brought up another slab of metal, and set it on the anvil.

"You want something from my shop? I have an idea," said Elsie. "An employee of mine, Russell Hart, went into the swamp, and I haven't seen him in two days. I need to know where he is—if he is still alive."

"Your employee, huh?"

"One who crossed me."

"What did he do?"

Elsie hesitated, like she was thinking how to phrase what happened. "He stole something," she said, chewing her lip. "A crate of gunpowder and other valuables. I need that crate back, but I can't leave the shop or Lily by herself. If I *do* go, we won't complete the contract we so desperately need. I've asked so many others, but none have returned. I wonder if the box was stolen a second time."

"Done. Throw in a meal, and I'll find your dude and the crate."

"Do this, and I'll even throw in a warm bath. You smell like ass," said Elsie. She pointed down the road. "He went east down Lorenzo Path into the swamp. I can't tell you how far you have to go but that he's there somewhere. If you go past Devil Rock, you've gone too far. That's all I can tell you."

"Got it," said Joel, who then turned in the direction instructed. He noticed silence as he walked away and stole a glance behind him. Elsie simply stared at him as if in disbelief at where he was going. Perhaps this was a mistake.

"Bring him back alive. I need to have some words with that son of a bitch," she called after him.

Joel nodded. There was not much he could do without Dusty Rose being out of town. He threw his mud-caked cloak over his shoulder and left Glen Rio.

The road turned to slush the farther Joel went into Glen Rio's swamps. The tall, crooked trees created a thick canopy of dried branches and brown leaves that nearly blotted out the sun. He clutched his silenced revolver to his breast. It was an old Russian-made revolver to which he had attached a bottle to the end with wire. A small piece of broken mirror was wrapped to the left side of the revolver just above the thumb rest. It was the laughingstock of any who laid eyes on the weapon, but Joel just ignored them. The additions made him silent and very aware of his surroundings. Its benefits were worth the mocking.

Before long, he found his footsteps slowed by a muddy path. The swamp itself seemed to grasp at his shoes as he walked by. He could no longer see Glen Rio behind him, and he rounded a curve in the path that then gave way to a muddy lakebed. He saw the peak of a hill and a jagged rock jutting from it into the sky.

"That must be Devil's Rock," he whispered to himself.

He heard a crunch of leaves not so far behind, and he froze in his steps. Someone was trailing him. He didn't dare turn around for fear that the very sound of the rotating bones in his neck would give him away.

He was still for a few moments, but Joel heard nothing else behind him. Whoever was stalking him was a smart man and was staying just as still as he was, matching his motions. Did Elsie send someone else after Mr. Hart? Whoever it was made the mistake of alerting Joel to his presence. Then, he saw a spot of dry ground. He leaped from the mud and pushed himself off the ground to the base of a tree into its shadows. Here, he would wait.

There was no need to see him. All the stalker needed to do was make a move, and Joel would know precisely where he was. He didn't have to wait much longer as he heard a soft sigh and the soft pattering of movement. He could tell three things. One, whoever was after him didn't have boots but instead slippers or even barefoot. Two, the footsteps were light, meaning whoever it was had on a thin sweater at best, which indicated someone not geared for a hunt. Three, judging by the pitch of the sigh, it was either a thin-boned man or a woman.

Finally, the stalker came into view, and Joel's suspicions were confirmed when he saw a frail woman with long burnt-red hair kneel where he had previously been standing. Suddenly, a gust of wind kicked up, and the woman scrunched her nose. She then jumped and stood still as she saw Joel with a revolver trained directly on her. She raised her arms up slowly as tears began to flow from her eyes.

"Lily?"

"Please," she whimpered, "don't kill me."

"Why are you following me? Did Elsie send you?" asked Joel.

Lily shook her head and spoke mid-sobs. "I don't think-*sob*-she would want-*sob*-me to go into the swamp by myself-*more sobbing*."

"Then, why?"

"Because I—that's none of your business!" she said, her tears momentarily stopping in the strange outburst. Joel holstered his revolver and flashed a smile. "The dude I'm looking for, Russel Hart—" He paused to see a light red tint on Lily's cheeks.

"You fancy him," whispered Joel. "Does Elsie even care about what he stole?"

Lily nodded. "She does, and if she knew Russel like I knew him, she would know he would never steal from us. He took a stack of eclipsinthe to trade for a new forge. It would set us up for a long time."

Joel's eyes widened. "She didn't tell me there was eclipsinthe in the crate."

"Oh," gasped Lily covering her mouth with her hands.

"How much was stolen?"

"Oh, I'm not sure, but I know he didn't steal it."

"Yeah, you said that."

Joel pointed his revolver at her head. He had no intention of shooting her, but he needed to know the amount. He also knew it wouldn't take long to get an answer out of her. She indeed folded like a wet napkin.

"Five pounds. He took five pounds of eclipsinthe. Dusty gave it to Elsie for safekeeping. Elsie is mad about that too. Once Dusty finds out, there will be trouble for us."

"Jesus Christ, five pounds," Joel gasped. How the hell had Dusty come across so much eclipsinthe? He let his pistol into his holster again and threw his cloak over it.

"So you have a crush on someone who stole from you. Poetic, huh?"

"He-he was always nice to me. I still can't believe he would steal from us."

What a sob, Joel thought. *Russel probably tricked her, and she very likely gave him the eclipsinthe willingly. Even now, she still has feelings for him.* Joel didn't have the heart to tell her she had been completely and utterly conned.

"Well, I suppose you can tag along then. You will have to keep up," said Joel. He turned and continued down the muddy path, with Lily following close behind.

"Did you actually kill Lester McBride and his gang?" she asked.

Joel hesitated and gritted his teeth. He remained silent, but Lily showed no signs of dropping the topic.

"They say his gang was made up of savage men with no souls and itchy trigger fingers. It must have been quite a fight, you shooting all twelve of them. Then you killed their leader, the worst one of all. Even if they lined up for you, it would be a difficult task."

"I—damn it," began Joel.

"You didn't kill them, did you?" asked Lily.

Joel's hand wandered to his holster, but she didn't even seem to notice the gesture.

"What *really* happened at Castellan Crow Cave?"

Joel bit his lip. Her curiosity had sealed her fate. Now, she would never leave the swamp. He supposed it wasn't too bad. People disappeared in the swamp all the time.

155

Dangerous creatures roam about. It wouldn't be too hard to convince everyone she simply fell into quick sand and never came out. It would only take one small bullet. Not even she would see it coming. He craned his neck, but they were completely alone.

"I took the bounty from the bounty board just outside the Rose Estate. I had wanted to be a hunter for as long as I can remember," said Joel. "No one seems to want to hire me. I'm not like the other hunters. I'm not quick at the draw like E. Gray. I can't intimidate and make men run away with a single look like Anton Smoll. A man still needs to eat, right?"

Cicadas chirped deafeningly in the thick swamp as the two walked deeper and deeper. Only their footsteps broke the monotony.

"I reached Castellan Crow Cave at night. I can't tell you how nervous I was. My hands wouldn't stop shaking. The Lester McBride gang had been on a killing spree and were in a feeding frenzy. I mean, cannibals, right?" Joel smirked but then quickly cleared his throat.

"I don't know what kept me there. I should have just run, but something kept me from turning tail."

"What happened?" asked Lily. She was polite in asking, and Joel remembered what he would do to her after he told her the truth. Maybe he shouldn't. She was sweet, young, and innocent. He glanced at her. It was the first time he was looking at her with dried cheeks. It was strange because she was pretty in a unique sort of way.

It almost was enough to make him change his mind, but he wasn't there for her. If there really was a lost box of eclipsinthe in the swamp, he would never have to fight for bounties again. The hunters wouldn't shun him anymore. It was too bad for her, really.

Unlucky.

"I crept to the cave and heard gunshots within. I remained in hiding for a while. After a few moments of silence, I realized it was safe to peek my head out. I saw a dead body on the ground. Then, I saw another just a few feet into the cave. I realized someone else, probably another hunter, had come this way for the bounty, and I was overtaken with curiosity. Whoever it was had torn through the gang like they were simple straw targets. Each one was shot in the head dead center. This hunter with extreme skill had killed each and every one of them seemingly with very little effort. I nearly turned tail and ran. I mean, who would have the ability to take on such devils like McBride and his gang, let alone someone like me? Then, just as I was turning to creep away, I saw an old hunter with long white hair stand over Lester McBride's body with his back to me as he cut a piece of leather from the legendary cannibal's coat."

Joel drew his revolver and aimed at nothing, squinting his eye through the iron sights. He flicked his wrist up emulating a gunshot. "I saw the old hunter emerge from the cave, so I shot him in the chest, and he fell over dead. I took the piece of leather from his dying hands and realized it was my lucky day. The bastard had killed the entire gang by himself, but I had the token. Then, I ran out of those caves as fast as I could manage without a second look back."

"So, you lied about the whole thing?" asked Lily, shaking her head. "That's just rat behavior."

Joel turned and aimed the gun at her head. She caught her breath, and he was about to say her sorrys when he saw movement out of the corner of his eye behind her. Tears began to fall from Lily's eyes, and Joel quickly holstered his revolver. If someone were to see him kill her, it could mean more trouble along the way. Joel had to make sure they were completely alone.

"You weren't—you weren't really going to shoot me, were you?" sobbed Lily after realizing he had put his weapon away.

"Shh, shh," said Joel, holding Lily's shoulders. He leaned into her ear with a whisper. "Someone's been following us. Pretend nothing at all is the matter, and please, stop *crying*."

She wiped the tears away, but it was pointless. There was no dam made by man that could hold back her tears. Joel stared past her head to where he saw the movement, but now nothing stirred in the underbrush. Had he imagined it?

Joel realized they were well beyond the length of Lorenzo Path and didn't know how far they had walked. He turned and stepped on a branch that made a loud crunch. Only when he looked down, he realized it was no branch. He had to stifle a gasp from his throat. His foot was firmly planted inside the ribcage of a skeleton. Joel pulled his foot from the dead body. The bones were covered in moss, and there was very little meat and muscle on them. Whatever was left was burrowed with maggots and other insects that now claimed his body home. His head was the most intact area of his body, and he still had one cloudy eyeball in the eye socket. A worm wriggled endlessly within his pupil. Joel didn't have to ask about the identity of the body as Lily gasped, instantly confirming that this was indeed what remained of Russell Hart. She began to sob, but this time, Joel didn't have the heart to stop her. However, he knew they couldn't stay.

"Let's go. Whoever is following us may be who killed Mr. Hart."

Joel was about to turn when he saw a small ornate box tucked into the torn folds of the not-so-recently departed Mr. Hart's armpit. He reached down into it and pulled the small box to his face. He could hear his heartbeat pump in his head and feel tingling in his fingertips. The eclipsinthe in this box would set him up for life. "Let's go."

Joel heard the sounds of sloshing footsteps through mud not too far behind. He pulled Lily by the hand into a thick collection of bushes, and they crouched for a moment. They waited for any movement, but there was little sound in the marsh. Joel could hold his curiosity no longer. He pried the top off the box, and his heart sank.

"Oh my God. It's empty," whispered Lily. The small, nondescript box had small traces of eclipsinthe that glittered like excess flakes of silver. Tears began streaming down her cheeks. Joel frowned.

Damn. He had come so close.

He tossed the box into the marsh just as a figure came into view from the other side of the brush. Joel wished he could say he was a man, but what he saw defied anything he ever had seen. He nearly pinched himself that he might be in a nightmare.

He was not dreaming.

The man, if it could even be called that, walked on two feet, but that was the only similarity Joel and *it* had. Its skin was scaled and shone in a green gloss. Its arms were strewn with muscle, and its chest was thick and full of scars, yet the magnitude of strength was clearly displayed. It had a tail that came to rest just a few inches from the ground, with tiny ridges on the top leading to the tip of the tail. The most startling feature of this creature would undoubtedly be the head, which, instead of a face, sported the snout of a gator.

Its cruel yellow eyes positioned at the sides of the head scanned the marshland, and it hissed, mouth open, displaying rows of jagged teeth. Joel realized he was frozen in place, unable to move. Even by miraculous intent, Lily behind him had stopped sobbing and remained absolutely still.

The gator-creature knelt to the body of the deceased Mr. Hart and seemed to be rummaging through his body for something. Joel looked at the discarded box in the reeds and then back to the creature.

"It can't be," he said.

Then, the creature stood up once more and hissed loudly, turning to the bush the two were hiding in. Its mouth glittered with silver specks in the dim light poking through the canopy of dead trees above them.

"It *ate* the eclipsinthe?" gasped Lily, echoing Joel's realization. She gasped too loudly, and the creature dropped on all fours and darted out of sight into the greenery.

Silence.

Not even the characteristic humming of insects could be heard. A sudden feeling of panic began to overtake Joel. It was like knowing a poisonous snake was in your room but not knowing where it was exactly. Perhaps the analogy was a little too similar.

Joel wondered if he could even take on a creature like that. He turned his head to Lily and put a finger to his lips. She nodded.

He brought up two fingers to his face and made a walking gesture with them. Then, he pointed behind her. She nodded again, wiping tears from her face, careful to keep her sobbing quiet. Joel then began to creep away from where he last saw the creature. Whatever it was, it was fast, strong, and deadly. He wasn't about to test his luck. They crept farther and farther away until he was certain, if they were being followed, he could hear its movement in the swamp.

He turned to Lily to make sure she was following him when he realized she was no longer there.

If he returned with no eclipsinthe box, it would be a major disappointment, but if he returned and Lily let out his secret, he could be in danger—danger in the swamp or danger in Glen Rio. He should have just shot her and never returned to Glen Rio like he originally planned. Then again, he needed Dusty Rose's bounty money. It probably wasn't worth his own life, though, right? He sat there in a crouching position, sharpening his hearing. He heard the snapping of a twig and turned to his left. Joel saw nothing and raised an eyebrow. He was sure he heard something—.

Saliva dripped onto his shoulder, and he looked up, slowly.

Two yellow eyes stared at him from above, hidden in the shadow of a tree. The creature leaped at him, and Joel darted back, but the creature still sliced through his clothing with dagger-like claws. Joel fell back and instantly felt the warm drip of blood on his chest. He raised his revolver but realized that he was only holding onto the grip of his gun. The drum and barrel of the gun were gone as if cut in half, and Joel's mouth dropped in shock. A stench of sewage hit him like a cast-iron pan, making his eyes water and his nostrils burn. The gator-thing hissed at him and reared back for a killing blow.

"Stop!"

The creature hesitated at the shout and turned his head to Lily, who stood just a few feet away with hands to her mouth.

"Don't kill him."

The gator man tilted his head at her, as if he understood what she was saying. Joel was unable to move, and he could feel blood pooling on his chest.

The creature could understand, at the very least, what Lily had screamed. Or maybe it was just startled that someone was scolding it as if it were a child. Lily looked shocked that it stopped too, the look on her face only growing more and more pale. Then, the gator man did the strangest thing. It stood up, chest outward, and simply walked away. It disappeared into the darkness of the marshes like a damn ghost.

Before long, they couldn't even hear the footsteps of the thing, and even the marsh life seemed to let go of a deep breath that had been held for far too long. The insects resumed their chorus, and frogs chimed in with their song.

"What was that?" sobbed Lily.

"I wish I knew. Whatever it is, I'm sure it had something to do with that box of eclipsinthe—agh!" Joel fell into the mud. The wound on his chest was deep, and he felt pressure in his lungs squeeze the air out of him like a vice.

"We have to get you to a doctor!" shouted Lily. She shot her arm beneath his and lifted him up with surprising strength for a woman a quarter his size.

As they approached the town, the bleeding had stopped surprisingly, and Joel realized he wasn't hurt so seriously. He even regained enough strength to walk on his own. Joel wondered what to do about Lily. She *did* save him, after all. He shouldn't have said anything about the bounty. Why did he think it would be all right to tell her what really happened in the caves? Then, he smiled at himself. How could he have predicted a gator-like man emerging from the marshes and attacking them?

Unlucky.

Suddenly, Joel saw a figure on the road running at them. He squinted his eyes and then gasped as a person with long black dreads rushed at them at full speed. Elsie crashed into Lily, knocking Joel to the ground.

"Lily, you dumb wench!" She hugged Lily's neck and squeezed her tight. "Why the hell did you leave without telling me?"

"I-I left you a note," whimpered Lily, the tell-tale signs of crying fast approaching.

"No-no," said Elsie, standing back, revealing her own cheeks already wet from tears. "We haven't been separated since you got here from Mesa Frio. Oh, please stop crying. You'll make *me* cry." She squeezed her arms around Lily's neck.

"Russel. He's dead. I saw him, and then this croc monster appeared. I think it killed Mr. Hart."

"Well, I figured," said Elsie. "I can't say he didn't deserve it."

Joel tried to leave silently, but Elsie turned to him.

"You have my thanks. I didn't know I would ever see Lily again. Thank you."

"Uh—you're welcome." Joel nodded, not turning around. He could hardly look into her eyes after what he was planning on doing to Lily. He still had to solve the issue of her knowledge of what really happened in Castellan Crow cave.

"Oh!" shouted Elsie after him. "Dusty Rose arrived in town. I figured you would like to know."

Now, that was *good* news. He would claim his prize and get the hell out of dodge before that story got out. Maybe his luck had made a turn for the better?

Joel approached Dusty Rose's mansion, the only place in Glen Rio with actual grass growing on the land. The sprawling lawn of lush greenery was guarded by men in navy blue uniforms with masks that had no eye-slits. Joel wondered how the hell they could see to aim the strange rifles on their backs that seemed heavily modified. He set foot on the stone road that led to the doors of the mansion. A rose carved from wood had been set above the doorway. He had to be quick if he was to claim his prize unharmed. If Dusty Rose were to hear about the truth behind Crow cave, she would surely shoot him as an example or, worse, place a bounty on his head.

The doors of the mansion were opened, so Joel simply entered and found himself in a grand hall with a sprawling polished marble floor. He kicked sandy dust that licked at his boots in the wake of a soft, warm wind that drifted through the hallway. It blew eerily against his coat as he walked by, staring at the trophy bounties on display on the sides of the hall. Behind each glass case, separated by an even space of ten feet, were pieces of cloth, necklaces, and even guns. Each piece depicted a bounty note below it, meaning whatever was in the glass case was proof that said bounty was claimed. Joel soon realized it wasn't just paraphernalia belonging to the bounty targets but also fingers, clumps of hair, and cuts of skin. Then, he reached the end of the hall, where there lay a single glass case that was empty.

"Maybe Dusty is keeping this empty for something special," muttered Joel to himself. Dusty Rose was a particular breed of human. She used criminals to her own ends and had a unique brand of biased justice. Even within her mansion, there was no killing allowed. Every three years, there was a championship between bounty hunters to see who was the best of them all, called the

Bullet-Catcher Championship. The prizes were always unbelievably legendary, but they always cost something great, something personal. Joel knew he could never participate in such a tournament. He could barely complete a middling contract, and it would have cost him his life had he not gotten lucky.

He turned into the final hallway of the manor and saw a dim yellow light come from Dusty Rose's office. He could feel the warmth of a fire, and he could hear voices from within as he approached. He pulled the bounty note from his coat and, with the other hand, clutched the piece of leather from Lester McBride's gator-skin jacket. He only had to lie one more time, and there was no one left alive who could contradict his story. The only person who knew the truth was Lily, and she was currently being berated by Elsie. He had to turn this bounty in and get the hell out of Glen Rio.

Joel pushed the wooden door open and peered inside. Two persons were by the fire, one standing and the other with back to him. An aide, the one standing, was dressed in a slim navy-blue suit, and she stood staring at the fire with her hands behind her back. Her hair was pulled back tightly into a simple bun, and not a single facet of her visage was unpolished or ruffled. She seemed like the epitome of discipline and restraint. She turned to the sound of the door squeak to reveal a face torn by a scar. She was missing her lower lip, exposing yellowed teeth, and her eyes were like sharp needles.

"Hullo," muttered Joel weakly, clearing his throat and stepping into the warmth of the room. He walked to a table beside the fire and set the bounty note as well as the token on a stack of books. "I have a bounty token to turn in—"

His voice died in his throat as the person in the chair stood up. Dusty Rose turned to reveal her left arm in a sling and her brown coat covered in blood.

Joel shot his arms up. "Um, on second thought, I don't think I have a bounty to turn in. I must have got heat stroke and clearly don't know what I'm talking about. You gotta remember to hydrate 'cause heatstroke is serious business."

"Joel Whitney, how kind of you to show up," growled Dusty, "—again."

"Oh hell," he gasped, taking a step back but feeling nothing but the closed door behind him.

"Oh, hell indeed. Now, sit down before I fill you with holes."

Joel sat down at the table. He could hear his heart pumping in his ears, and he could hardly do anything to close his mouth.

Dusty kicked the chair to face him and flashed a cruel smile. He could see her features better when she sat down. She had a full head of white hair that went down to her shoulders, and she had an eye patch over her left eye. Her right eye glowed dull green as she sat back and set her hand cannon on her lap.

"Draw your weapon," said Dusty.

"What?"

"You heard her," said the aide. "And if you try anything, just know that her pull is the fastest in the region. Try and find out for yourself."

Joel shook his head and knew this wasn't a bluff. He hesitantly reached to his hip and pulled what was left of his revolver.

"Ah, I remember you. You are the rat with a modified revolver and a silencer. See, Maddie, that's why I didn't hear it," said Dusty, with a chortle. "That mosquito nearly killed me. Can you believe that?"

"Barely," said the aide with a glare.

"Must have run into some trouble, though. Who carries their guns in pieces?"

"I-I didn't think someone else had the bounty. I was the note holder," said Joel, shyly.

The aide glanced at Dusty and then back at him. "What are you implying? That you are justified in shooting the legendary Dusty Rose in the back?"

"I had the note. I had a claim to that bounty."

The aide began to laugh and break the stillness of the room with her cackles. She was even uglier as she laughed. "You think you, of all hunters in Mawbury Hills, would be able to take on Lester McBride and his gang alone? With a trash gun like that one? What a joke."

Dusty held her hand up, and the aide bit her tongue.

"Now, Maddie, he's right."

Now, it was the aide's turn for shock to grip her face. She remained silent.

"The bounty holder has a right to the token. When I sanctioned the bounty, I waited for months for it to be picked up. After a while, I didn't think anyone would take it up. When I went north, I figured I would clear that bounty and give myself a raise when I returned. So, I did. I killed each of the McBride gang and cut a piece of leather off Lester's still-warm body, only to get shot in the back. You knocked me out for a few hours, but you missed my heart, unlucky you."

Joel bit his lip as Dusty leaned back in her chair.

"I can't kill you here and now because, despite your cowardly approach, you *did* hold the bounty note. I respect that. Also, if I were to kill you, I would have to take you off the property. Therefore, with the turning in of this bounty, I recognize you as a bounty hunter of Rose Manor. Welcome to the family."

He straightened his back as Dusty said this. "Really?"

"Of course! You now have the respect given to bounty hunters in Mawbury Hills. However, though you are safe from harm at my mansion, the same cannot be said for other hunters outside this property, let alone Glen Rio and anyone else who hears how you *really* got the reward. You see, we are a select few, proud and arrogant. We consider ourselves greater than our fellow man and regard our ranks with prestige. I would suggest laying low for a while."

"Okay—"

"I will make sure the bounty is cataloged, and you may approach the treasurer in the basement. He will give you the payment if you present *this* to him," said Dusty, pulling a wooden chip from her coat. She flicked it at him, and it landed on his lap. An elaborate *DR* was carved into the face of the chip. "That is worth more than gold in these hills. I would not treat it carelessly. If you lose it, you lose your bounty reward and your life, so be careful."

"Okay," said Joel, standing up. Suddenly, he felt a burning pain in his wrist like someone had cut him with a piece of serrated glass. He gritted his teeth as a small black mark appeared on his forearm. It looked like a small diamond with a skull in the center. It flashed bright red, and then, it disappeared as if it had never been there at all.

Joel came back to his senses and held his tongue in fear that they might change their mind and kill him despite Dusty's promise. He brushed wrinkles off his coat.

"Not so fast," said Dusty before he could get to the door. Joel stopped, feeling sweat drip down his neck.

"The bulletsmith, Elsie Crosswell, is a close friend of mine. Seeing as she's the only bulletsmith in the region, well, except for the spineless whimpering jelly of a companion she has, I have to keep them close. From what I hear, you saved Lily from that crocodilian in the swamp, and for that reason, you don't have a bounty placed on your head right now."

Joel froze. How had she heard about that so fast?

"I need to know more about that *thing* you and Lily encountered."

How had she heard so soon? He was sure Lily didn't beat him to the manor and tell her. She must have eyes and ears everywhere. Dusty leaned forward in her chair.

"Two questions I want answered. Is Russell Hart alive? He was a conman, but I'm sure you can relate. If he is dead, I need to know where his body is right now. Second, where did you see that crocodilian? It has a debt to pay, and I think it has been more than enough time. You are going to tell me everything that happened and be sure to leave no detail out." She scrunched her nose. "But first, you're going to get washed. You smell like ass."

"That's Jonah McDaniels. He cries every time a heavy carriage mills through the town or he hears a horse racing to the stables. The tremors remind him of a demon wurm with a hide made of iron who would spit up countless minions and swallow entire villages into his gaping maw, never to be seen again. He blames his blindness on what he witnessed, but many doubt his word, for he and he alone was left behind to tell the tale. He sits there to this day, crumbling under a broken roof, succumbing to shakes and shivers, whispering to ghosts tormenting him in his sleep. He wakes in soiled breeches at every sunrise." —*Mother Moranna, when asked by a sister who the decrepit old man was staring at them.*

Cupid Carries a Gun

Three months before the Bullet-Catcher, on board a cursed train.

August poked his head out of the engine car, feeling the rushing wind beat at his sandy brown ear-length hair. He glanced at his train master, Shamus, an old curmudgeon with a severe spinal condition that bent his back forward nearly in half. George, an old Swiss engineer, sat in a corner of the cab rummaging through a newspaper. His spectacles reflected the sun's rays as he read, holding the paper low on his lap to stop the wind from stealing his tabloid. He was teaching August how to read, and despite his age, August was a quick learner, but he had to wait for George to finish the papers first.

Shamus pulled the horn string twice, announcing their entry into Mawbury Hills with a piercing whistle.

"Coal," grunted Shamus, but August wasn't paying attention. George glanced over his spectacles at the boy with a sly grin. The Antoinette Express chugged onto the sprawling plains at a slow march. Before they reached Glen Rio, August knew the view would give way to swampland.

Dried grass spanned the flatland in clumps as far as the eye could see behind them. August wondered what so many passengers were doing going to these lands. There wasn't much, as far as he could tell, *to* these lands. No oil, no commerce, very little trade. He supposed everyone had their reasons, though. Why else would anyone come here?

"You little rat, you—get me *COAL!*" shouted Shamus as he grabbed a small wrench and threw it at the boy. The metal clanked directly above August, and he jumped from his thoughts, slipped gloves on his hands, and grabbed a shovel. He swung the furnace door open and scooped coal into the furnace as fast as he could. George snorted and resumed his reading.

"Goddamn it, young bull, if you mind your job more than your daydreams, you might actually amount to something more than hot mess. Focus," grumbled Shamus. He had a glob of snot at the back of his throat that made his voice sound like he was constantly about to cough but never was able to. August knew that giving a response would be the equivalent of arguing, so he simply bit his tongue and continued shoveling coal.

"One-hundred and twenty passengers headed to Glen Rio," said George. "Is that the most we've ever had on this train, Shamus?"

The old man glanced at his engineer and sat back into his beaten leather seat, pulling a black kerchief that once must have been red and wiping his forehead of sweat. "One time, long before you were born, I had one-hundred and eighty-six tickets. Of course, it was an entirely different scenario. That time, we were running from war."

August shoveled a clump into the engine and glanced out the back window. People sat in rows huddled beside each other, keeping their heads down to avoid the whipping winds. They seemed like refugees to August despite the fact that most of them had paid a hefty price for passage into these hills. They didn't care there was no roof on the passenger cars. Were they running from something?

"I feel bad for them. I suppose the plague really *is* coming to the south. I didn't believe it at first, but now, it seems to be all the papers are talking about. First, evidence of a failed Mexican invasion years ago comes to light just a few hundred miles away, and now there's talk of a new epidemic plaguing the land," said George.

"They'll figure it out," said Shamus. "The place has gone to hell in a handbasket. That's what happens when you piss God off. Enough drunken debauchery, and that big guy upstairs gon come down and tan your hide." He pulled a small bottle of liquor from his coat as he said this and gave August a large wink. "Bottoms up, young bull."

George snorted, turned the page, and ruffled the papers, apparently ending the conversation. August tossed a clump of coal into the furnace and slammed the iron door shut. His face was drenched in sweat, and he took his gloves off, wiping his forehead.

Suddenly, the train lurched, knocking August onto his back. A spray of black droplets fell onto the train conductors. George spat on the floor and stared at the black sticky liquid on his fingers. He slowly looked up at Shamus.

"Tar!"

August spat out bits of black mulch from his mouth. "What the hell?"

A chorus of gunshots erupted beside them, and August peeked out the window, his heart dropping to the soles of his feet. Eight men atop horses raced beside the train, keeping pace. They had bandannas tied over their faces, leaving just enough room for their glistening eyes to gaze over from beneath their hats. One, in the lead with a brown and white poncho and red bandanna, aimed his revolver and fired. August ducked back into the cab just as sparks burst beside his face. He looked at the speed dial. Tar was clogging up the wheels, stealing their momentum.

"We're being robbed!" shouted George, huddled in a corner, trying his best to make himself small.

"Ya don't say!" Shamus pulled a sawed-off shotgun from beneath his chair and chambered two slugs. "This ain't my first rodeo. Come and get it!"

Bullets whizzed overhead, zipping through the cockpit, bursting pipes, and breaking levers with every shot.

"Goddamn, why the hell are they after us? This is just a passenger train. We have nothing of value!" shouted George, to no avail. August heard the sound of a body slamming onto the side of the train. A head peeked up with a black bandanna, and the bandito aimed his revolver directly at him.

The bandit's head burst into a puff of red mist, and the body tumbled off the side. Shamus let out a whoop and broke the barrel forward as two empty shells ejected onto his chest. He loaded two more and slammed the action back.

"Didn't expect that, did ye, bugger? That'll give you sorry sonsabitches something to think about, ye?" shouted Shamus. August wiped bloody slime off his face and dared his heart to hope. Perhaps they *could* defend the train. On some weird level, he felt the old codger was enjoying it. August thought all the stories Shamus had told around a fire about him being a bounty hunter once upon a time were full of lies. Perhaps not everything was embellished. Then, the old train conductor aimed his shotgun out of the cab at the gunslingers. A small bullet pierced his throat with a sudden *crack*, creating a clean hole and a thin trail of blood out the back of his neck. The old man fell into the cab beside August, dropping the shotgun, gurgling, and clawing at his throat. Blood spurted from his open mouth with each struggling cough.

A man, the one in the red bandanna and brown poncho, poked his head over the cab. George rushed to grab the shotgun, but the bandito was too fast. He pointed his silver revolver and shot him in the arm.

George screamed and fell back. The bullet seemed to have grazed his shoulder.

"Stop the train!" shouted the bandito. "Do it, or I kill the boy." He pointed the revolver at August, pulling the hammer back. The silver inlays of the barrel caught the rays of the sun and nearly blinded him. August held his hands up, eyes open wide.

"Okay, okay," gasped George. "Please don't shoot."

"Do it! Now!"

He picked himself up, squeezing the bloodied wound on his shoulder, and pulled the brake lever. The wheels squealed and spewed sparks as the train came to a screeching halt. August glanced at the passengers through a crack in the back plate. They were staring wide-eyed at the robbery, very likely trying to stay as still and silent as possible. They knew what was about to happen.

August looked at Shamus and realized he had stopped moving. The old codger had a glazed look in his eyes, and the blood in his mouth was no longer pumping. He looked back to the hijacker.

"Thanks," said the bandito. He then shot George in the back of the head, exploding brain matter and chips of bone onto the furnace door. He fell over in a heap and remained motionless beside Shamus.

"Why? We are just a passenger train," stuttered August, his hands began to shake uncontrollably. "We have no money."

"Sorry kid, no witnesses," said the bandito in a thick Mexican accent as he pulled the hammer of his revolver back and held it pointed at him. "Empty their pockets."

"Really? You're robbing us for our pocket change?" August hesitated, but the bandito kicked his leg.

"Get to it, now."

Relieved that death had been warded off, but in a few moments, August moved and reached into Shamus's and George's pockets. He didn't find much other than a golden pocket watch on a chain on Shamus's body. Then, he pulled a wad of banknotes from George's inner chest pocket. A small picture fell out onto the bloodied floor, and the bandito reached down to pick it up.

"That was his daughter in Plainview. He was saving for her to have a wooden horse for Christmas," said August through his teeth.

"Guess she ain't getting nothing this holiday, huh?" grunted the bandito. He stuffed the wad of money into his coat pocket. August didn't know what got into him, but in that moment, all he wanted to do was look into the face of the man who was about to kill him. He pushed himself up from the floor against the gun and stood up.

"What are you doing?" asked the bandito, clearly surprised by the reaction. "You aren't going to cry or beg for your life?"

August lunged at him, but the man caught him by the neck. Then, August pulled the bandanna off the bandito's face. The gun was still held firmly at his forehead. He had bright brown eyes and bony cheeks. His thin lips were firmly pressed, and there was scarring all over his face like he had been a victim of frostbite. He had a deep gash on his forehead where an animal had clawed him, or perhaps a long knife had cut him.

"Happy? What did you expect to see?" asked the bandito, tossing him to the ground beside his two dead crewmates.

"You don't know who you're transporting, do you? Unlucky for you. Someone worth hundreds in a bounty is hiding among the passengers, someone very valuable to us. We just have to pretend we're after your pocket change for a short minute before our sniper on the ridge sees our target."

August glanced over his head and saw the glint of a scope on a ridge far, far away, as if on cue.

"We just have to make enough of a spectacle. If you play along, you'll live. When we hear the killing shot, we take our bounty and leave," smiled the bandito as his poncho flapped in the soft wind. His eyes caught the glint of sunlight.

Suddenly, a tremor shook the ground beneath them with a muffled crack. The bandito raised his eyebrows, and he caught his breath for a moment. A look of fear gripped him, and his voice cracked. "It can't be." He put his fingers in his mouth and whistled hard. "Boys! We have to go now!"

It was too late.

The compacted earth just a few yards away began to swell up like it was made of sand. Higher and higher, the mound of dirt rose until it exploded into the air, and a hellish machine burst up onto the plains. It was a train of sorts, for it had an engine car at the front, but it clearly was not fueled by coal or anything August had ever seen before. A maw of circular saws with razor-like teeth whirred on the engine car's face, but instead of wheels at the base of the machine, there were a thousand small metallic legs like that of a centipede. The engine car pulled forward from the ground, dragging strange armored cars up behind it.

The mechanical earthworm surrounded the downed Antoinette Express and bellowed a devilish roar. For a moment, August's heart stopped beating. Such was the quality of the force and tone of the roar that stunned August and, judging by the looks of it, the bandito as well. It was the echo of the abominable sound reverberating in his mind that gripped him to the very core. It was like he was in a vivid nightmare, and his worst fears were about to become reality. What made it all the more extraordinary was that the moment the sound faded, it was as if the banditos woke up from a trance. They, in unison, opened fire on the bizarre train. Bullets buzzed and pinged off the machine's thick armor, but it remained still as if whoever was inside was still unsure of what to do or biding their time.

The bandito's smoking guns halted their fire, and a thick silence descended on the plains. All that could be heard was the whistling wind in their ears as a few panicked men began their failed attempts at reloading. The bandito standing above August gasped as the side of the engine car door flew open, and a hail of bullets from within the train rained on them. August ducked and put his hands over his head at the roar of gunfire. The bandito fell over, and August realized they were not bullets at all.

Five darts had embedded into the bandito's chest just beneath his red bandanna. His eyes were glued to the floor and glossed over. August dared to look up and saw the other banditos run, attempting to climb up to their horses or even legging them away from the hellish machine, only to be met with darts in their chest or back. Another spray of darts rained from within the darkness of the machine. Finally, the gunfire stopped. A loud whistle burst from the machine like the call of a dozen foghorns.

August didn't dare move a muscle until he heard a hissing sound and the faint clicking like that of a large clock. No, a dozen large clocks. He peeked his head over the edge and caught his breath in his throat. It wasn't just one machine; it was a whole host of mechanical men that emerged from within the maw of the engine car. They had bulbous bellies that, where the belt should be, gun barrels poked from. Their heads were faceless, and they sported tin top hats. Their metallic black boots clicked when they walked even on the dry grass of the plains. August glanced over to the passengers and saw strange darts in their necks as well. The mechanical men moved from the train and began picking bodies up and bringing them into the darkness of the centipede train.

Suddenly, it struck August. Why wasn't everyone dead? Even the banditos were still breathing, just paralyzed. One mechanical man slung a sleeping woman over his shoulders, and she, too, disappeared into the train. It made no difference to these things; everyone was going into the throat of the cursed machine. Another sound like the call of a foghorn burst into the sky, and then the mechanical men turned to him.

Though August didn't see any eyes on their blank faces, he felt a terrible stare burn into his mind that made him turn away slowly. Then, he felt a stinging in his neck, and when he turned to look, he saw a long barb stuck in his throat. He fell to the floor of the engine just beside Shamus. The last thing August saw was four mechanical men in their silly top hats staring down at him as his world went dark. He felt his body being lifted, then nothing at all.

August felt a strange sensation around his neck, like a vice slowly releasing pressure as his vision began to clear up. When his eyes adjusted to the low light, he strained his eyes to focus. He stood in a vat of thick, viscous liquid that drained out onto a grated floor. He flew into a fit of coughs as his lungs emptied the strange liquid and took back in air. It was such an asphyxiating feeling as if he were drowning standing up. As he began to retake his breath, he realized there were dozens of other vats on both sides of him, and each one contained a person sealed beneath thick water. They looked like pickled vegetables standing side by side in those pods. August realized the vat directly across from him contained the bandito who had shot George and Shamus. Suddenly, a strange but marked ticking like a clock brought his attention back to the figures standing over him.

Four mechanical men stared down at him. These were different from the ones he had seen before. These had painted mustaches and hollow red eyes staring dully at him. They put their arms beneath August's armpits and pulled him from the vat. He tried to stand, but his legs buckled under his weight.

"Where are you taking me?" he coughed out. The mechanical men didn't respond. Instead, they pulled him away in silence, dragging his boots against the grates. It was such an awestriking sight to be in the belly of an earth-train machine-worm *thing*. August still struggled to come to terms with what had happened. It was almost as if his brain was unwilling to come to terms with his kidnapping. The machine's insides were reinforced iron plate, but it had spaces that were connected by a fleshy red substance like a thick fold of skin. August supposed this aided in turning omnidirectionally as needed beneath the ground. Liquid sloshed and dripped from his pants as he attempted to walk. The mechanical men dragged him through the winding, rumbling corridor. Then, it hit

August. All hope of escape was gone so long as the devilish machine was underground.

Finally, the mechanical men stopped him just before a rounded ornate bronze door with a great locking wheel. One of the men in a top hat reached over and twisted the wheel over three times. He heard the grinding of gears and spewing of steam echo through the hall. The clicking men pulled the large door open. By then, August had found his footing, and though his head still spun, he could, at the very least, stand.

The men pushed him into the room, and he stumbled inside only to be faced with what he would recall for the rest of his life as the most daunting visage of dread he would ever see. It would also be the most beautiful.

A woman sat upon a throne made of scrap metal with two mechanical men by her side. She wore a dress made of black leather with steel pauldrons over her shoulders. Her hair was snow-white, and its length nearly reached the floor. Her face was just as pale, and even the irises of her eyes were white as if she were blind. However, the most distinguishing feature of her body was the fact that she had no legs. Well, that wasn't entirely true. She *did* have hundreds of them. They were thin metallic tendrils that looked very similar to the legs of the train itself. They poked from beneath her dress like that of a centipede. She didn't seem much older than August, but her grotesque appearance brought him to his knees.

"What is your name?" asked the woman. Her voice was crystal clear like a running brook in a still forest.

"August," he gasped, still trying to make sense of what he was looking at.

"Do you know who I am?" she asked, with a smile. Then, he *did* know.

"You're the Trapper."

The woman's smile faded away, and she leaned on her elbow. She bent forward, staring at him. Her white eyes seemed to drill holes in his mind as silence poured over the room. She certainly wasn't blind. Finally, she leaned back.

"Tell me about Mawbury Hills. Tell me about this mysterious land of strange occurrences. I hear so many odd things."

August hesitated for a moment. The question took him by surprise. The woman stood up and approached him with the sound of countless metallic legs clicking on the metal grates of the floor. Standing, she was nearly eight feet tall, and August was sure if it weren't for the ceiling of the engine room, she would be taller. Then, the Trapper knelt to eye level before him.

"This young man is thirsty. Bring water, now," said the woman to her henchmen. August tried unsuccessfully to swallow. A mechanical man turned and left the engine room. A rumble shook the grates beneath, making him snap his arms out for something to steady himself. He grabbed a pipe alongside the wall, his face reddening at his clumsiness before her. He realized those countless legs would make easy work of keeping balance within a constantly moving train, especially underground.

The woman smiled again. "Do not be afraid; I wish you no harm. Do you like my train? It is a wonder to be sure."

August stole a glance at her. There was something innocent about the way she spoke, almost like a child.

"Why?" he asked.

The Trapper's smile faded. "What?"

"I've heard your stories. Why are you doing this? Do you intend to harvest our body parts? Are you going to kill me?"

She recoiled up as the mechanical man returned with a small glass of water. She took the glass, and then, in a gesture that shocked August, she cupped his chin against the cup and tilted the edge up to his lips. The water was cool and tasted better than any water that had flooded the inside of his mouth. He drank greedily until the cup was empty. Finally, she took the empty glass away from his lips, and he coughed twice.

"Thank you," he wheezed.

"You called me the Trapper," she said, handing the empty glass back to the mechanical man. "I wish I could explain to you why I do what I do. I am bound by oath to secrecy, but one thing I can divulge to you is my name isn't the nickname that your people have given me. My name is Emma, and I come from afar. Well, not too far away, as a matter of fact. I was born just beyond the Ridge of White Wolves."

"I have no idea where that is."

"The land called that is called that no longer. Believe it or not, I was born there and taken away."

"You mean you were born in Glen Rio?" asked August.

She turned her head away. "No. I mean, I was born on this planet before—"

The train lurched, and Emma's eyes opened wide as each of her metallic legs shot out from beneath her and grabbed onto a grate like the legs of a spider. It happened so fast that she hardly seemed to notice. "We've arrived. Get the others ready. Take Mr. August back to his pod. I must prepare myself."

"Why did you take me from the pod? Just to ask me about the land?"

"I like seeing the world from your perspective. It allows me to experience it once more as if I were free to do so," said Emma. "Now, if you'll excuse me. I must prepare."

"*Free* to do so?" whispered August as the mechanical men moved in on him and put their arms under his. They began to drag him away, but not before he stole one last glance at her pale face. Their eyes locked together for an instant as she turned her head away, her hair flapping like a white banner. The bronze doors slammed shut.

There was a strange sorrow in her clouded eyes August couldn't understand. If she wasn't going to kill or harvest their organs, why the hell did she kidnap everyone on the Antoinette, *and* the banditos?

The mechanical men marched him down a narrow corridor. Having found just a bit of courage, August spat at one just to see what would happen, but it didn't seem to notice the gob of spit trickle down its face. They shoved him into his pod and were going to close the door when the floor beneath them shook, nearly knocking them off their feet. The mechanical men turned to each other and stared at one another for a moment.

August realized they were communicating, but he could not hear any sound at all. After a few moments, they clasped a steel collar around his neck and slammed the pod shut, but it only partly closed. One pressed a red button. They didn't seem to notice the ajar door and rushed away.

A thick liquid pooled around August's ankles and began to rise around him. He began to panic, but then, just as the liquid reached the crack in the pod door, it began to spill out onto the grates.

"Pssst! Hey, pendejo!"

The voice startled him, and he looked up to see the bandito in his own pod that had a small crack in the glass near the bottom. The trembling must have caused a crack in the glass for a few pods. The trickling of viscous liquid onto steel grates confirmed the theory.

"Hey! Listen up. You see that needle?"

Just as the bandito said that, August heard a whir beside his head and turned to see a thin metal arm approach. On the end, he saw the glistening sharp point of a needle.

"Now relax and open your mouth. The needle will pierce your cheek and inject that liquid out the side of your mouth. Make sure you don't swallow it, or you'll go to sleep. Just spit it out. Do *not* swallow it."

"What?"

"It pierces your neck, and you fall asleep. Listen to me or die!" shouted the bandito.

The needle pierced August's cheek, and he had the urge to close his mouth, but to do so would be to seal him to his fate. A liquid squirted out his mouth just as the bandito said, and then, the needle retracted back into the wall. August spit it out on the grate and pushed the pod door open, rubbing his cheek. A droplet of blood was all that remained from the injection. His boots were drenched, but at the very least, he was awake. He stepped out of the vat and couldn't resist the urge to stretch. It was almost as if he had been curled in the fetal position for hours and was finally able to stand.

"Good boy," said the bandito. He had already partially broken through the tough glass, and his upper half was mostly free from the vat. "I can't get myself out," he grunted. Then, he stopped for a moment. "You see that lever over there?"

August turned where he was pointing.

"Pull it quick and free us all. I promise you I will get to the bottom of this."

August caught a glance at the silver revolver in his belt. In an instant, he reached in and pulled the hand cannon free from the leather holster. He held it aimed squarely at the bandito's chest.

"*Ah, cabrón?*" he said as he stopped fighting the vat door and raised his hands slightly in the air. "What do you think you're doing?"

"You shot my friends, Shamus and George. You were going to kill me next."

"Oh," snorted the bandito. "No, you're looking at it all wrong."

"Don't tell me how to look at it!" shouted August through gritted teeth.

"Okay. Okay. Damn, boy. When did the fire grow in you?"

August licked his lips. "Next time I see you, I'll kill you. Count on it."

The bandito looked like he was about to say something when the train rumbled side to side. August turned and ran down the hall, but he wasn't sure exactly where he was going. He stopped and found himself standing in a break in the machine. He realized the machine was much bigger than he had originally thought. He looked up to see hallways above and below him like a series of elongated tubes stacked and wrapped in the machine's exoskeleton. The walls were a bizarre hybrid of mechanical and flesh interwoven, and August hesitated to even touch it. Everything looked the same in each congested hall. Countless tubes and pipes lined the walls, intertwining like a bed of seaweed all around him. The squealing of belts screamed in his ears, and steam blew in his face as he emerged into the next car, and each was full of sleeping people in their pods. When August took a closer look, he could see their faces through the glass as if they were unconscious. He saw each pod had a needle in its cradle beside them.

Then, a strange sound caught his ears and snapped him to a halt. It was the sound of a woman singing. It was such an odd thing to hear in the belly of a mechanical earthworm. The crystal-clear song captivated his body, and he was helpless to fight the trance as he began to move to the sound.

Folks say that I look like Death
Lived in the hotel of my eyes.
Blinds wide open like a whore,
Paid in spit from that hearse between her thighs.
Keep your halos tight;
I'm your God or your guardian.
Keep your halo tight;
One hand on the trigger, the other hand in mine.

August peeked around the corner into a sprawling oval room nearly thirty feet high that was thick with gray steam. He squinted through the warm mist and caught a glance of a naked woman in a pool with her back turned to him. She filtered through her wet hair with a brush, the length going down past her firm buttocks. It was Emma, the Trapper. He crept into the room, mesmerized by her visage. She had metallic implants in her spine that blinked soft blue. Her shoulders had strange symmetrical gold scars inlaid to her wrists that ran all the way up to her neck. She held soap in her hand and began to rub it onto her skin. She lifted her voice into the second chorus of her song. August felt a stiffness in his pants and realized he had stayed too long. He clutched the silver revolver and crouched to leave when suddenly, he heard the rhythmic march of mechanical men behind him.

Because now
Cupid, cupid carries a—

His boot kicked over a loose bronze tube. He froze and turned back to Emma slowly.

She was up from the pool facing him. Her breasts were exposed, and droplets of water and soap suds dripped from her nipples into the crystal pool around her. She covered her womanhood with her hand. Beneath that, where her legs should have been, was an amalgamation of tiny metallic tendrils. August realized each tendril was nearly twenty feet long. He braced himself for death as Emma rose up from the pool. But nothing happened. She leaned down and stared at him in just as much shock as he must have displayed on his face.

"How did you escape your pod?" she asked above him. Her hair fell down in front of her face as droplets fell on his body and all around him.

"I—I," began August. The sounds of mechanical footsteps began to grow louder as Emma's henchmen drew closer. They must have found the empty pod.

"Hurry! Hide behind that crate there," said Emma, pointing to a dark corner. "Do not move until I tell you to."

She descended back into the pool until the water was at her neck. August, unable to believe what she had just said, moved his feet to where she directed and crouched there in the darkness. Two mechanical men entered the bathroom, their top hats clinking on the top of the door as they entered.

"Still no fix on my door, huh?" Emma pouted, lazily pointing at a broken lever.

They clicked and clinked, but August didn't understand what was being said.

"Very well. Go and make sure I am not disturbed further. He wants us to hit the town within the hour."

Who was she talking about?

They nodded and left her room, their footsteps a rhythmic motion. Finally, when August was sure they were out of earshot, he emerged from behind the crate.

"You didn't tell them I was here," he said, astounded that he was still breathing. "Why?"

"You are full of questions. Turn around," said Emma. He obeyed and watched her shadow rise from the pool. Emma, keeping a close eye on him, grabbed a towel from the edge of her pool and began to dry herself off. He heard a gurgling sound as the water from the pool drained almost instantly.

"How did you escape?" she repeated.

"I don't know," lied August. "Maybe your henchmen are defective."

After a few moments of the sound of rummaging behind him, she spoke. "We are exhausted. We've been doing this for a long time. You can turn."

August obeyed. She was in a burgundy armored leather dress. Her shoulders had thin steel pauldrons that mimicked crows on each face. She wore a thin chest plate with a foreign insignia on it. She sat on the edge of the pool and began to dry her hair with a strange cone-like device.

"What does that symbol on your chest mean?" asked August.

"It is a family crest. I belong to the Bludwuld family. I fear I am the last surviving member," said Emma, a hint of sadness flavored her words. "For thousands of years."

August snapped out of his trance. He raised his revolver and aimed it at her. It felt wrong to do that, but he had to get out. He had to escape this hell machine. His hands shook as he held the gun up to her.

"I just saved your life. You would threaten mine the very next moment?" asked Emma, a dark frown adorning her face.

"Sorry," said August, quickly bringing his sights down but still keeping the revolver at his hip. "Help me."

"What?"

"Help me get off this death train."

"Please. He hates it when you call him that."

Now, it was August's turn to be confused. "*Him*—you mean the train?"

Emma nodded. "He knows. He always knows. Well, at least he makes me think that. What's this plan you have?"

"Plan?"

"Of course. You don't have a plan? I thought all heroes had plans."

"I'm not a hero; I'm just a coal boy—"

The train lurched forward, nearly knocking August off his feet. He looked at Emma and saw the countless legs strapped to the grate floors and welded tubes on the wall. He realized how useful her differences were despite the initial gruesome appearance.

"If I help you get off the train, would you take me with you?" asked Emma.

The question caught August off guard. He realized that the Trapper was just as trapped as he was. She was running from something. Was it the train?

"We are set to take on a small village on the edge of Mawbury Hills. It is said that the Confluence will pass through there. If we are to leave, we have to leave now," said Emma. "We have to hurry."

"I don't—I don't know what to do, but I do know someone who might help," said August. "He also just as easily could shoot me. See—I took his gun. He killed my friends. Do not trust him, but I don't know how to use this."

"You don't need to worry about that," said Emma. Suddenly, two long daggers jutted out from the palms of her hands. The edge glistened in the low light. Then, the blades simply retracted back into her arm, and she held her palms out. August shrugged and led her back down into the pod cart. They were fortunate not to run into any mechanical men, and he wondered where they had all gone.

They stopped at a pod that had belonged to August just a couple hours before. He turned to the bandito across from him. The liquid was obviously missing, and a crack had grown just a little larger since August's departure. The bandito had his face squished against the glass, and his eyes were closed as if he were asleep.

"Him?" asked Emma.

August nodded. As soon as Emma pressed a lever on the side panel, the bandito charged them with a grunt. He stopped like a statue when he saw himself staring down the barrel of his own gun.

"Take it easy, cowboy," said Emma.

"You little rat. You take my gun and leave me for dead, only to rat me out?" His eyes became narrow slits, but then, he looked past August, as if for the first time noticing Emma was there.

"Holy hell. *La Ladrona*," he said, taking a step back in his pod.

"Wait," said Emma. She approached them and pushed August's gun down from the bandito's face. He stared at her like he had just seen a ghost, or an angel.

August held the gun at his hip. "You're going to help us escape this place."

The train shook beneath them, but this time, it was different. They heard a few muffled pops.

"Are we underground again?" asked the bandito, quickly standing up.

"No, we resurfaced nearly an hour ago. That's something else," said Emma, glancing down the hallway. "That was an explosion."

"Someone is attacking the train?" asked August. "Who would dare do something like that?"

"I know a few bounty hunters who would," the bandito shrugged. "Dusty Rose and her gang have a bounty on this hell machine. That crazy wench."

"Now is our chance. We have to make a break for it!" said Emma.

"What?" asked the bandito. "I thought you were the Trapper. Isn't this whole operation your idea?"

"She is just as trapped in here as we are. It's the train," explained August. "The train has a mind of its own. It's keeping her caged in here."

"*Hijo de puta*," gasped the bandito, shaking his head.

"Follow me," said Emma, leading them down the hall.

"What about your other mates?" asked August.

The bandito scowled and then slammed his fist against a lever. The liquid began to pour out. Before long, they would begin to come to. They would, however, be trapped in their pods.

"The hell with 'em. I never liked 'em cutthroats. I was planning on leaving and starting my own gang anyway," he grinned. "Let's get out of here."

August looked on in disgust as he ran after the Trapper.

Suddenly, the left wall bubbled up and burst inward, spewing flames and smoke in their faces.

"Watch out!" shouted Emma. She flapped her dress wide and blocked the flames from touching the two men. In that moment, August caught a glimpse of her face. There was a grim determination etched in her eyes, like a woman who had to carry an unbearable weight for far too long. Yet, in that same look, there was a spark of light. Those moments made August feel something he had never felt before, something deep within. It was the mixture of a choking warmth and the icy touch of a heartthrob.

The fire quickly dissipated out of the gaping hole in the side of the train car, leaving them beneath a canvas of stars amid the dense trees of a swamp. When August looked out, he realized he, indeed, was in the middle of a swamp. Insects had caught fire in the wake of the explosion, their wings alight as their burnt bodies fluttered to the damp floor at their feet. Emma was the first to step out, her countless legs clicking as she walked—if it could be called walking.

She took in a deep breath as if it was the first time she was breathing air that wasn't recycled.

"It's been so long," she gasped, confirming his suspicions. The train shook furiously as if it were a giant serpent that had just been wounded and was writhing in pain.

"We cannot stay here," said the bandito.

He took the lead, and they left the hellish machine behind. Gunshots rippled not too far away, and August could hear the robot-like ticking of the mechanical men. They stopped at the edge of a bush line and crouched in the shadows, watching the trail with peeled eyes. Another explosion lit the sky, outlining shadows of men on horseback.

"Now what?" asked Emma.

Suddenly, a rustling of the undergrowth alerted them to the fact they were surrounded by a row of mechanical men. Their midriffs opened up to expose three machine gun barrels each. The bandito grabbed Emma and August and dragged them down to the ground. The barrels spewed gunfire at them as mud and dirt splashed up into their faces. August glanced up and realized a rock was taking most of the beating from the hail of bullets. This time, they intended to kill. They must not have realized that their very own Trapper was with them.

The mechanical men began to flank the rock, but the bandito grabbed the silver revolver from August. Suddenly, thunder roared overhead, and a streak of lightning cut the sky in half with blinding light as he leaped from behind cover. August stared in disbelief as the bandito's revolver seemed alight with sparks and roared like a cannon with each pull of the trigger. It all happened so slowly, like he could feel the strain of every muscle in the bandito's arm, like he could feel the revolver's hammer strike each bullet like a mallet slamming on an anvil at the beat of his heart. He felt a wave of heat, like an intense fire, slap against him with each pull of the trigger. August saw two mechanical men explode in a cascade of sparks.

The third instantly closed its midriff and spun to walk away.

"No, you don't," the bandito said as he laughed. His revolver sang, and the bullet smashed the mechanical man to pieces onto the ground. Suddenly, the giant shadow of a train moved and rose up into the sky. The head of the train turned like a metallic viper, and a red light shone over the bandito.

A loud scream emanated from deep within the machine that sounded like the growl of a ravenous bear. Then, the ground saws on the face of the hellish train turned and bit into the ground, pulling the rest of the train down into a hole with it. August's jaw dropped as the train disappeared beneath the earth in an explosion of mud and swamp trees.

"What the hell?" gasped Emma, standing up from the bushes. She stood a full three feet above the bandito, and it was somewhat daunting that a thing such as her, with her height and awestriking visage, could be shocked at a mere cowboy with a gun. Well, it clearly wasn't just any gun. The drum glowed white hot, and steam spewed out from the barrel.

"That train thing has heard about the Kayoro-moon. He didn't want any more of that smoke," the bandito chuckled. The earth rumbled beneath them. "Guess that's where those strange earthquakes were coming from." He pushed the hammer home and shoved the revolver into its holster. "You're welcome."

"It's gone?" asked August.

"Yeah," said Emma. "They won't notice I'm not there for a while. It's enough time for me to disappear."

The bandito led them farther and farther away from the battle site out of the swamp to the east. After a while, he stopped at a formation of boulders that would make it incredibly difficult for anything to come up from the hard-packed ground. If anything did, they would be able to feel it coming. After a while, the singing of insects rose again from swamps around them, and they were surrounded by darkness. The bandito was the first to give a laugh of relief. Emma turned to him and joined him, laughing softly. August couldn't believe his eyes and clenched his fists, glaring at the bandito.

"Why are you laughing?" he said, gritting his teeth. "We almost died back there."

The bandito turned with a mess-eating grin on his face. "Isn't that reason enough?"

He began milling through the swamp floor.

"What are you doing?" asked Emma.

"I'm going to build a fire. It's cold now, but this is nothing. In a few hours, it might snow, the first snowfall of this bitter-looking winter. I would like to get a little ahead of the frost if possible. Boy, search over there. Grab as many small sticks as you can."

August was going to do no such thing, but then he caught Emma's gaze. Despite her white eyes, he could see the look of worry on her face. Something inside him pushed his body to move to where the bandito had indicated, and he began to pick up firewood.

Emma also helped gather kindling not too far away. Before long, they had a rather large collection of wood, and the bandito set upon building the fire. Finally, the flames caught as a light snow began to fall over them.

"Just in time. The heat should melt any snowflakes that touch it," said the bandito. "We can't let it go out, though. Then we're proper done for. Soon, this whole valley will be covered in heavy snow."

August held his hands to the flames for warmth. Even Emma sat beside him and put her hands close to the fire.

Despite her alien-like visage, August figured she was still very much in need of basic human necessities.

"If only I had a nice cast-iron grill and a slab of steak. Boy, I would make us a feast." The bandito grinned, showing off yellowed teeth and chapped lips.

"That weapon you have. It is no ordinary gun, now is it?" asked Emma.

"Nope," said the bandito, drawing his revolver and holding it out so that she could see. A strange white glow emanated from within the drum that made it seem like it carried the heat of a thousand stars.

"I killed a Rose Hunter a long time ago who had this at his hip. This was the grand prize of the Bullet-Catcher Championship."

"You wield it with great confidence," said Emma, but her tone was not that of a compliment. In fact, there seemed to be sorrow in her words.

The bandito shrugged. "I don't know much about this thing except any bullet I slide into the drum turns into something like a bolt of lightning that causes things to explode. It only works at night, too, from what I can tell. In daylight, it's as useless as any other gun. I have a feeling it has to do with the moon, hence the name. Kayoro-moon." Emma nodded but turned her gaze into the fire. The bandito holstered his weapon and let out a sigh.

"You killed my friends. They were like family to me. Don't think you're getting away scot-free," warned August, finally breaking the silence.

"Hmm. Took you long enough to pipe up. So you'll kill me in revenge?" asked the bandito, tilting his head to him. The musky smell of unwash assaulted August's senses. If only he still had that revolver. He should have shot him when he had the chance.

"You didn't have to kill them," whispered August. His grit melted away. "We were just doing our jobs. We didn't mean anyone harm."

"If you think you can form attachments in this world and not expect a sacrifice, you're naive. The strong prey on the weak. Either get strong or die," said the bandito. He caught Emma's glance, and his shoulders seemed to soften. He spat on the ground. "Remember my name. Felix Quintana. When the time comes you've grown scruff on your chin, and your voice drops a few octaves, I want you to come find me and give me your best shot. I'll even let you pull first, but you better make it count. Fair enough?" Felix glanced at him and chuckled. "You wish you had shot me when you had the chance. Well, you should have. You were an idiot not to."

The words made August's face redden. "You're sick."

Silence fell on the strained company. Emma stood up and turned to walk into the swamps, wrapping her armored coat around her chest.

"Where are you going?" asked August.

She turned her head slightly. "More firewood. We're almost out, and it is indeed getting colder."

Without waiting for a response, she vanished into the greenery, but August could still see her shadow. He glanced at her from time to time.

"If it means anything to you, I'm sorry."

The words took August's breath away. It was the last thing he'd ever expected the bandito to say. He stared at Felix.

"Why?" asked August.

"No hard feelings," grunted Felix. He rested his head on a smooth stone and closed his eyes. They were silent for a few moments.

"No hard feelings if I kill you," growled August, leaning his head onto his knees.

"That's cute—"

August straightened his back and peered out into the darkness of the swamp. He no longer saw Emma's shadow.

Snow continued to fall steadily, and the moon shone brightly through the swamp trees far above Emma. She stared at the twinkling empyrean in awe. The sky didn't look so bright the last time she had seen it with her own eyes. She gasped when she heard the snapping of a twig and turned to see a rabbit with antlers leap into the clearing, study her for a moment, and then scurry away into the undergrowth. Emma picked up the snapped twig.

"Looks like you're enjoying yourself, dear thing."

The screeching whisper in her mind made her freeze. It was a voice she knew too well, a voice that had spoken into her mind for thousands of years on a dozen planets.

"You found me rather quietly," said Emma, dropping the branches underneath her arm to twiddle the last twig in her fingers. "I expected to feel you."

"Why would I do that? So you could avoid me and run? Why are you running?"

Suddenly, the serrated voice in her mind turned into the soothing feeling of a cool spring on a warm day. She knew it was one of the luring mechanisms of the Great Machine. That and it being able to read her mind like a book.

"Have you forgotten why you were given permission to return here in the first place? Did you forget the plea you made before the Council of a Thousand Planets?"

Emma shook her head. "I just wanted to see what it was like to walk on the surface once more. This place was much different the last time I was here."

Silence for a moment. She took a deep breath and sat down at the foot of a tree. The ground was cold as flecks of snow stuck to her fingertips and face.

"Winter was my favorite season. The beautiful snow and the glistening light on the cold just made everything so wonderful."

"They took your legs for a reason, dear thing. You wish to lose more of your body to augmentics? It can be done rather easily."

Emma found herself staring into a fleshy smile full of teeth. The Great Machine had been spliced together with a train engine car long ago. He was almost twelve feet tall from chin to smokestack and rounded like the face of a giant clock without the arms of time. He smiled again, revealing a row of nasty flat teeth within. His eyes were crystal blue and piercing. It was always unsettling to look at, yet at the same time, she had lived inside his belly for the better part of a thousand years, working as his steward. What made it so unsettling was the grin. She knew he could slice her up into a hundred tiny pieces in the blink of an eye and put her back together again.

"That look of disdain, is that for me? What have I been except for a friend in dire need? You lack nothing, and still, you fear me. I have never hurt you."

That was true. He had never been cruel despite his appearance. Until now.

"You wish to take more of my body? You have taken so much. What difference does it make? I want to be free. I want to live here for the days of my life I have left. I don't care about saving them any longer. Haven't we saved enough to avoid the invaders from causing extinction?"

The Great Machine's smile faded to one of a sad frown.

"It is disheartening to hear you say that. I still see you there standing upon the towering pearl podium, addressing the lords with such passion and conviction. It moved the hearts of the council that only you would make a plea for anyone other than her own people. Then, I was spliced into this machine against my will. They didn't ask me, yet I knew I would be their salvation. I hoped what we are doing together is making all the difference in the world."

The Great Machine sighed and looked past her into the shadows of the swamp. "If you don't return willingly, I will not take any more parts of your body. Instead, I will have to kill the men who broke you out."

Emma gasped and looked over to where August and Felix were still talking. She could see their shadows whispering in hushed tones.

"Ah, you are fond of them? What is it? Their daring escape? Their willingness to get what they want despite the overwhelming odds? Or is it something else?"

Emma's cheeks flushed unwillingly, and she felt a strange tug at her heart. "Ah, it *is* something else. That young boy, the one thrice victim, once to the thieves and twice to us. Such a weak creature compels you so? It would be a shame to kill them just to make a point. It almost contradicts why we are here in the first place."

Emma spotted the shadows of at least four mechanical men's top hats just a few feet away in the darkness. She knew their tranq-guns were trained on August and Felix, and they had no clue what was about to happen. The Great Machine wouldn't just tranquilize them this time. He would torture them and turn them into mechanical men, too.

"Don't do it," Emma whispered softly. "I don't want you to hurt them."

"Please understand I hate to do this to you. I would love nothing more to return here when our work is done and watch you frolic in the wintry fields. We have a mission to complete, however, and we must do it for the good of humanity, including those two men you have found a soft spot for. If we are not efficient, as is our primary directive, all will fade for the last time. A Bad 'Un will show no mercy," said the Great Machine with hundreds of echoing whispers in her mind.

"I will obey," said Emma. "Just don't harm them."

"Good, I—"

"They are moving closer, Oh Great One," came the voice of a mechanical man in her mind.

The Great Machine looked at where the mechanical men were hiding. Suddenly, a flash of lightning streaked over them and struck the tree, bursting into sparks and little tongues of fire. Emma shrieked and fell to the ground.

Felix leaped from the bushes with August close in tow. However, at the sight of the Great Machine, Felix froze. Before, when he had shot at the machine, he had not seen it in full view. Now, standing merely a few feet away, he didn't miss a single detail.

The Great Machine smiled, revealing his flat yellowed teeth. Suddenly, a dozen mechanical tendrils shot from within the machine's throat. The tendrils caught August and pulled him to the ground with a wail. Felix leaped out of the way just as a mechanical man moved to grab him.

Felix whipped around and shot the man, blowing his head clean off. A sputter of sparks and blood bubbled up as the bulbous frame clanked to the frozen ground. He then stood up and fired into the bushes, the crack of his weapon like the blasts of bellowing thunder. His poncho flapped in the wind behind him as each electrified bullet burst a mechanical man into a puff of red mist and sparks.

"Stop!"

The scream halted everyone in their tracks. The only sound came from the labored breaths of the Great Machine.

"Please, no more," said Emma. At that moment, the tree that Felix had shot fell over and crashed onto the ground. She stood up and knelt before August.

"Are you hurt, cowboy?"

August swallowed hard and patted his body. He shook his head. "No, I-I don't think so."

"Good," said Emma. She threw herself at him, wrapping her arms around his neck. "I am so glad I met you."

Panting, Felix sat on a mound of frozen mud, reloading his gun. He regarded the mechanical men with a cold stare, ready at any moment to begin firing. They seemed to think the same if a metallic faceless man could feel disdain. The Great Machine's eyes were bolted onto Emma and August. The arms from his mouth were poised as if to strike like reinforced metal scorpion tails.

Emma caressed August's face and saw a hint of sadness in his deep brown eyes. She didn't know why she felt the way she did, but she couldn't help it. "You are the first person

I had spoken to in years who wasn't intent on killing me. Given the chance, you stayed your hand. I pray this is not the last time I see you. Don't you forget about me, cowboy."

She kissed his cheek and stood up.

"Spare them. If you abide by this request, I will go willingly," said Emma, turning to the Great Machine and wiping tears from her eyes.

"I abide, dear thing."

Emma nodded, and the mechanical men peeled back from their positions. The Great Machine opened his mouth three times the size of his face for them to enter the hellish train. She stood at the lip of the giant face and turned. The mechanical tendrils wrapped themselves around her torso gently and lifted her up. Then, the machine pulled her into his throat. Emma caught August's gaze in the last instant before the titanic maw closed over her. Suddenly, the face of the Great Machine was closed over by a series of spike grates, which was, in turn, covered by a carapace of rotating buzz drills. The hellish train lifted itself into the air as the buzz drills began to spin and squeak. Then, it plunged into the compacted earth, spewing clumps of mud into the air.

Felix stood up and holstered his weapon as the train disappeared into the earth.

"Jesus Christ," he snorted, pulling a wad of tobacco from his breast pocket. He poured it onto a white piece of paper and licked it, wrapping it into a fine cigarette. The final train car vanished, leaving behind a gaping hole in the ground. The earth rumbled beneath them, shaking the stones and trees around them. Felix struck a match and lit the end, taking a deep breath. He glanced at August and shrugged.

"Never thought I would see a sight like that before. You would be crazy to believe something like that, right?" He tossed the spent match into the hole and let out a chuckle. "Well, see ya, *cabrón*."

"What? Where the hell are you going?" asked August, quickly standing up.

Felix paused. "The closest town to here is Plainview. I suggest you head there now. The cold is only going to get worse."

"We have to go after them."

"What?" asked Felix. "You've got to be kidding."

"You owe me," growled August.

"I'm not sure you've been paying attention. That train isn't killing people. It's an ark of some sort. They are kidnapping everyone and bringing them onto that *thing's* belly to save them from something. I'm not about to get caught. I'm going to run as fast as my legs can carry me."

"Coward."

"No. You're just thinking with your dick. I saw how you looked at her. What do you think is under that dress, huh? She ain't even have legs. She probably doesn't have anything between her legs, and if she did, it would probably be all teeth or tentacles or whatever the fu—"

He wasn't paying attention. August closed the gap and clocked him clean in the chin. Felix nearly fell to the ground, rubbing his jaw. "*Hijo de puta!*"

"You owe me."

"I don't owe you a damn thing," said Felix as he reared back and swung hard, catching August's nose in return. The coal boy fell like a heap of bones, and Felix kicked him in the ribs three times. He then pulled him up by the collar and punched him hard, knocking him against the ground. Again, and again, he struck him. He grabbed August by the collar and dragged him to the edge of the newly made cavernous hole in the ground. The sounds of creaking machinery could still be heard digging deep below.

"Damn, it's too bad. Emma won't be seeing your pouty face again," said Felix, holding him by the collar. He raised his fist to punch him again.

"You're a murderer. You never needed a reason. You just wanted to take something that wasn't yours. You're a cockroach, and one day, you're gonna get yours," spat August.

"Truth is, I'm a worse monster than that train could ever be . . . Maybe it's best you stay dead. No hard feelings, kid."

With that, Felix slammed his boot on August's left leg, creating an audible snap against the ground. The boy could barely do more than whimper, and then, he went limp. The sudden pain knocked him unconscious.

"If I killed you, you deserve to die. Just let the cold take over. It will be a peaceful death, I promise."

Then, he let go. August's body fell into the dark hole left behind by the hellish machine. Felix didn't think he heard the body fall.

"Hmm, deep hole," he grunted. Then, he took another drag of his cigarette and turned, keeping his steps in rhythm as he began to hum.

Keep your halo tight;
One hand on the trigger, the other hand in mine
Because now
Cupid, cupid carries a—

It's better to be a gunfighter in a garden than a gardener in a gunfight.

The Bulletsmith

Elsie

Eight years before the first Bullet-Catcher Championship.

I still hear the rhythmic and constant *pang, pang, pang* of a heavy hammer on an anvil echoing in the streets of the God-forsaken town by a river. I was pretty sure I was in Glen Rio, but there was no sign or way to tell before sunrise. I followed the sounds and reached a lean-to shop with a torn black tarp tied to two wooden posts. There was no name but only a symbol of an anvil painted white over a ragged black sign. The blacksmith was a tough-as-nails man when I first saw him, hunched over a small anvil as a line of horseshoes dangled over him. I can still hear his gruff voice stir the early morning air with a grunt as he brought the hammer down over and over. It was a makeshift shop with a tattered brown tarp affixed over the working area.

The blacksmith huffed, casting a sideways glance at me as I approached, but said nothing. He was a giant of a man with fair skin and a crown of long, wavy white hair. His mustache had a little yellow on the ends and blew back and forth as he breathed on each blow of his gigantic hammer. He wielded his smithing tool with massive arms that were as wide as my midriff. Of course, I hadn't eaten very much in the last few days, so that didn't mean very much. His steel gray eyes pierced through his eyebrows, which were framed in a permanent frown. I knew I wasn't the image of cleanliness, seeing as I couldn't remember the last time I showered. My clothes were tattered and patched, and I'm sure the smell was unbearable. Even so, I had to do something. I would be dead in a week. I didn't even feel the pang of hunger in my belly anymore. Despite this, my mouth watered at the smell of boiling water in a pot over a fire just behind him. He was fixing to eat, it seemed.

The blacksmith snorted and waved me away with his hand. He then moved to a small press beside his anvil beside a pile of bullets next to a box of black powder. He pulled on a lever at the press, and a single long bullet fell out into a crate at his feet.

"I noticed you don't have anyone to help you. Everyone needs a helping hand. You know what they say, idle hands are the Devil's workshop. Please, I promise I won't be in the way."

He remained silent, not even looking at me. He thought I wasn't worth his time. I needed to prove I was.

"I don't ask for much."

He pulled the lever again, and another long bullet fell from the press into his bucket.

"I don't have a home," I said. "I was at an auction in the north, but my family ran from our masters. Only I made it here. Tell me, is it safe?"

For the first time, he turned to get a good look at me. His face was covered in white scars that scissored over his rough, hide-like skin. His pale complexion was only accentuated by the crown of white tangled hair above his head and below his nose and chin. His breath was mad hot, and his teeth all kinds of crooked. He pulled a cigar from a table and lit it with a match. He took in a few tokes and blew the smoke from his mouth. I felt his hard gaze on me, which made me avert my eyes from him.

Then, I saw the pot of hot water spill over into the flames. Almost without thinking I walked over to the pot, careful to grab a rag so my hands wouldn't burn on the iron handle, and pulled it from the flames. Then, I went to the drain by the anvil and dumped a quarter of the water into it. Then I set the pail down on the wet ground and returned to the fire, grabbing the black poker. I pulled some of the wood from the fire to let it cool.

"It's just a tad too hot," I said, afterward jamming the poker into the dirt.

The blacksmith stared at me and let out a puff of smoke.

"Barely more than a toothpick, aren't ya?" he asked, his voice sounding like the crunching of gravel. I couldn't find the words to speak. I just stood there as the cool morning breeze brushed up against my coffee-colored skin, running goosebumps up and down my arms.

"I can't run anymore. I need food," I said. "I don't know how much longer I can make it."

"I don't have money."

"I don't need money," I said, my heart skipping a beat. "I just need food."

"Don't we all?" he grunted. "It's all sideways for everyone here, but you think *you* deserve a bite to eat? What makes you so special?"

"Listen, at this point, I would eat dirt if it didn't give me the runs. Looks like you're not too long away from being dirt. Maybe I'll just wait around for you to keel over and roast you over a spit," I gasped quickly as soon as the words left my mouth, not knowing what possessed me to say that.

The old man stared for a moment and then burst out into laughter. "Over a spit, huh? I like that. Bill," said the man, taking one last pull and setting the smoking cigar back on the table. "That's my name."

"Elsie Croswell," I said. I knew giving my real name would only stir trouble. Best to keep that part a secret.

"Hmmm," he grunted. "Put that pail back on the fire. I still need to keep it hot."

He turned his back on me.

"Do you need it *that* hot?"

"I didn't ask for an inquisitor. Do as you're told."

I did. Setting the pot back on the fire, he leaned down and, with a knife, began to peel potatoes from a basket I saw at his feet. Then, he tossed them into the pot of hot water. My mouth watered even further. He turned and pulled black garlic and two yellowed onions from a bag dangling above me. His breath smelled like booze, and his body odor was nearly enough to make my eyes water, though that could have just been the gravity of my situation. He cut the onions in his massive hands, the gleaming edge doing nothing to the rock-like callouses and tossed them into the boiling water from where he was sitting. The cut vegetables sailed in an arc to the pot, barely making a splash. I couldn't help but smile. Bill smiled, too, but it was a shame. His smile was like the smile of a croc, torn and ugly. Even so, I was relieved by his smile. It meant he could enjoy my presence. There was a shine in that ugly smile.

That was the only time I ever saw him like that. He reached over to the table and picked up a rifle. It was some sort of Springfield conversion rifle with a strange modification on the side of the chamber, like some sort of automatic rifle loader. The weapon seemed odd to me, but I had very little concept to compare it to. I had never seen or even held a weapon, but the masters did. They always brandished their guns to prove their authority in my time at the plantation. Even so, this man was different. He didn't threaten or spit at me. Bill picked up one of the bullets from the bucket and slid it into the chamber, but it only went halfway in. The round poked out of the receiver, striker side out. Bill grunted, but his sausage-like fingers were too big to manipulate the round like he wanted to. He peered into the receiver and blew as hard as he could. He then slammed his fist on the round, but it did not give way.

Finally, he set the rifle beside him and huffed in frustration, pinching the bridge of his nose. Without even thinking, I reached over and grabbed the rifle. The lip of the chamber was bent inward, preventing the round from properly entering its seating. I realized the lip wasn't so much bent as much as actually chipped. I pushed the metal piece back with my thumb, and it tore off. I didn't so much as tear it off as I did bend it, and it fell off. The sidepiece was broken, but it was better than bent inward, preventing a reloading action. The weapon should still fire without any more issue. For a reason I can't explain, it was surprised at my own hands. It was like when I touched the gun, I could feel it speak to me. I knew what to do to set it right. For the first time in my short life, the gun made more sense to me than words. It made more sense than breathing. I set the rifle beside Bill, who watched the whole thing happen in silence as a feeling of satisfaction filled my stomach. He was probably just as surprised as I was.

He grunted.

"When the potatoes go soft, we eat. You watch. Until then—" Bill said, his face turning back to a stone-like frown as he grabbed the hammer that rested atop his anvil. Then he reached up and pulled a horseshoe from a string that was clearly bent at an odd angle. The head of the hammer was made of old iron, and the wooden grip left splinters in his hand. His arms were thick with bulging muscle the size of my waist, but I suppose that wasn't saying much. His back was like a small mountain, and his head seemed small in between the boulders that were his shoulders. He glanced back at me, and his face changed to that of shock.

The blood on his face seemed to drain, and he became deathly pale, if that was even possible. I realized his eyes were glued to something *behind* me. I turned and saw a line of *vaqueros* standing in a line in the middle of the street. Their shadows clawed at the shop as they approached, evil reeking before them. I smelled spent gunpowder on them, even from where I was standing. These men were killers.

I felt a hand rest on my shoulder. Bill pushed me behind him as he faced the men. They wore cowboy hats and brown dusters. Their spurs clinked in the soft breeze roaming down the street. I counted six and saw weapons at their hips and rifles slung over their backs.

Bill grunted at me as he set his hammer on the anvil with a sharp clang. He stood up, wiped his hands on his apron to no avail, and walked to the line of gunmen. I watched him walk over to them, and to my surprise, he dwarfed them all standing as tall as a mountain, looking down at them while they were on horseback. Even from where I stood, I was fairly certain he could tear them limb from limb if he wanted to. The gunmen showed no fear, however. They didn't cower. They stood defiant.

Bill spoke to them in hushed tones where I couldn't understand a word that was said except for the low bass of Bill's voice. Then, the line of gunmen rippled with laughter. One of them, probably the leader, drew a revolver and pointed it up at Bill. The blacksmith turned his head down and took a step back. This caused the gunmen to laugh even more. The leader holstered his revolver. The wind broke the silence of the street, but the tension could be tapped with a hammer. Finally, Bill nodded, said a line of hushed words, and turned his back to the gunmen as they turned their backs and went their separate ways. Bill didn't show an ounce of fear, but his hardened stare made chills run up and down the nape of my neck.

He stood before his anvil, and his eyes darted back and forth as if he were lost in thought. He mouthed something, but I couldn't tell what. It wasn't until I looked over to the pot to see it boiling over once more. I quickly grabbed the handle and spilled out some of the water, careful not to toss any vegetables out with it. I walked over to a table and filtered through the contents of the pot. There were spices in there that made my nose tingle and my tongue wring with excitement.

A large, heavy hand rested on my shoulder, and I looked up to see Bill staring down like a giant made of stone.

"Eat up, young pup. Tomorrow, your work begins in earnest."

I can't remember Bill ever leaving his anvil for very long. He would sit there, back arched, slamming his heavy hammers, forging horseshoes on most days. Sweat dripped down his arms strewn with muscle. With large tongs, he would dip the molten metal into a bucket and draw clouds of steam from it.

At first, as was usual, he would receive very few new customers. Most of his clientele at the time were farmers and the odd wanderer in need of a horseshoe repair or purchase.

He had only just purchased the state-of-the-art bullet-press, but now, even strangers, more dangerous men, would walk into the smith on business. Usually, it was the Loya's men, killers and murderers. Twenty bullets here, thirty there. One time, a man asked for one hundred rounds of 7x57mm. He was an infantryman, and he was to prepare a defensive against the northerners. It was a dying war, and everyone knew it. At first, Bill was reluctant, but after seeing his fist full of dollars, he agreed. He became known as the Bulletsmith of Glen Rio.

He bought a large loaf of bread and a chicken after such a large order had been completed. I remember that was the first time I went to sleep with a full belly. I suppose I lied; it was the second time I saw him smile.

From then on, I was Bill's right hand. I would fetch his water for him. I would clean his hammers and throw logs on the fire for his forge. He did everything for the town of Glen Rio. It was a small town owned by the Loya Family, whose primary export was horses in competition with the Conley farm a few miles away. Not many have anything good to say about the place, and Bill surely echoed that sentiment. "This is the Devil's Cesspit."

The war in the north was proving to be so lucrative for these Loya cats. Over time, I could feel strength build in my arms and legs. I could now hold his hammer, though not as easily as Bill could. Anytime he needed a heavy tool, he could count on me.

"Come here, kid," said Bill one afternoon after the day's grueling tasks had been completed. I sat beside him by the anvil as heat from the forge blew at my back. We both had sweat beaded on our brows, but I was proud of it. It was like a crown atop my head.

I had earned it.

"Four months, and you have never once complained. You never once said no. You did everything I asked of you," said Bill as he pulled up a brown package from behind the main black anvil. "You deserve this."

He handed the package to me, and I held it on my lap. It was heavy and smelled of grease and hot metal. When I opened the package, I found myself staring at the most beautiful hammer I had ever laid eyes on. The handle was sleek polished wood, and the head was a heavy metal with a stamp of Bill's sparrow flying over an anvil insignia on the face.

"I had it made special from the canyon dwellers on the east edge of Mawbury Hills. Wasn't cheap. Greedy bastards."

I couldn't contain myself. I threw my arms over his thick neck and squeezed hard. "Thank you."

"Hmmm," he grunted. He didn't hug me back, but I knew he understood the sentiment. "Don't think this makes your work easier. In fact, now you will have even greater responsibilities. Those horseshoes need to be mended, and more bullets need to be made. We have a great order to fill, so get to it."

I grabbed a horseshoe from the pile and, grabbing tongs, stuck it in the hot coals of the forge. The hammer felt like an extension of my arm in my hand. For the first time in my life, I felt my heart heat up, my chest warmer than the forge before me. I blew hair from my face.

"We have to do something about that," said Bill. "If the fire catches your hair even a little, say goodbye to the lot of it. That's if you're lucky."

"I got just the thing," I said as I grabbed a string from above and tied my hair into a thick ponytail.

Then, something in the street caught my eye. It was a shadow hobbling just outside the blacksmith shop in the street.

"Bill?" I asked, turning to get a better look at the figure. He saw what I saw and stood up, leaning down to not smack his head on the roof. He exited into the waning sunlight of Glen Rio. The shadow stood at six feet tall in a wide-brimmed hat and a brown overcoat. Even in the gathering darkness, the shadow's hair was clearly marble-white. Though I couldn't see the features of the persons' face, it was clear the shadow was a woman.

"Bill?" The shadow fell into the street, and blood spilled out onto the mud. It glowed blue. All was silent save for her raspy breaths. Bill stood over the figure, and we both looked into her face. Her eye was missing, and scorch marks adorned her white face. Then, I looked at the wound in her stomach. Wound wasn't the proper term for it. Though the flesh around her wound was scorched and torn, what lay beneath wasn't bone and sinew. Instead, transparent cables with blue liquid and strange mechanical tendrils moved within. It wasn't blood that pooled beneath her either, but instead, the same strange blue liquid from her abdomen.

"I guess it's about that time," muttered Bill. "You said we had until the end of the year. I guess it can't be helped."

"What are you talking about, Bill? Do you know her?" I asked, then took a step back as blue liquid began to spread beneath her. "She came from Loya Manor. I'd hate to be her right now."

He leaned down to pick her up from the ground.

"Wait, Bill," I said, grabbing his arm and glancing both ways down the street. "If we help her, won't the Loyas be on our ass? We don't even know who she is."

He glanced down the street and gritted his teeth. "*You* don't know who she is. Soon, her name will dance on the tongue of everyone who even thinks of coming to Glen Rio. Get the bed ready."

I shook my head but knew better than to argue with him. I did as I was told. Maybe Bill knew something I didn't. It was worth trusting his intuition. I held the door open as he brought her in and set her on the bed. Then, in the lamplight, I recognized her torn face. Even I, a new-comer to Glen Rio knew who the most dangerous person was on this side of the Mississippi. I had no idea *she* was in town. Blood drained from my face, and my stomach turned in a knot.

"Holy hell. That's Dusty Rose!"

Bill set Dusty on my cot as blue liquid spilled from her mouth. Her white hair was matted the same color cyan, but what caught my attention was the machinery in her exposed belly. Tiny metallic tendrils writhed with the sound of small levers squeaking and whirling.

"What the hell is this?" I asked, unable to close my mouth in awe of what I was witnessing. "She's not—"

"Human," said Bill, matter-of-fact.

"What do we do? I doubt Doc McCraggar would know what to do with a wound like this one," I said, looking her over. "I wonder what she said to piss the Loyas off."

Bill sat down beside the cot and stared at the steel machinery inside her. He was fascinated by whatever she actually was. I looked into Dusty's face and realized her right eye was open and staring at me. She opened her mouth, but what came out sounded like a conglomerate of voices, like she was many people in one.

"My gun," she said, reaching for her holster.

"No," said Bill, putting his hand out. "I've been waiting for this moment since I first met you. Use some of mine, please."

He pulled a small black box from beneath my cot that I had no clue was ever there, and he pulled the lid off. When he did so, my eyes widened because the contents of the box were full of stones that glowed the same color as Dusty's blood.

She tried to speak, but only blue blood spewed from her lips. She reached her hand into the box and pulled out a small rock that glowed blue. She tossed it into her mouth and swallowed hard. Then, just before our eyes, steam began to emanate from her belly, and her flesh began to close up. Just as soon as she had done that, she sat up and looked at us.

"I can't believe they shot me. I gave them every opportunity to do this peacefully, but they decide to gank me with twenty men. They asked me a question with lead. I will answer in blood. I won't be so kind the next time that bitch Annette sees me," said Dusty, her face turning red. She wiped the trail of blue liquid from her lips and then looked into Bill's eyes.

"What was that?" I asked. Bill slammed the box lid shut.

"It's called eclipsinthe. It's a delicacy in some parts, but here, it's best in a bullet unless you're me," said Dusty, sitting up. The wound in her belly began to close before her eyes as a tangle of web-like tendrils spread underneath the wound and began to seal up the blue hole in her belly. Despite this, the wound in her eye remained unchanged, a scorch mark where her eye had been. She seemed not even to notice, displaying absolutely no discomfort anymore.

"I won't let that happen again. I tried the peaceful way once. Never again. The Loyas have asked for death," said Dusty.

"What did you do?" I asked.

"It doesn't matter anymore," said Dusty. She looked up at the hulking shadow standing in the doorway. "I hear you're the new apprentice. Tough time for you. Bill, I need bullets."

"As I said, I'm ready, Dusty," said Bill. "No one in the world knows how to forge eclipsinthe into bullets. Only I do."

"The Loyas will see this as a betrayal, Bill," I said. "They will kill us and burn this all to the ground in retribution."

"It's fixing to rain soony, and You're not from 'round these parts," said Bill, then turning to Dusty. "I know why you were at the Loya Manor. You want to bring in your Hunters of the Rose to Glen Rio. It's always been your plan."

My mouth dropped. I had never heard Bill speak more than a few words at a time sprinkled with grunts and *hrmms*. Dusty studied the man with one eye. "You're sick of them, aren't you?"

"It's the disrespect. I've worked in this blacksmith shop for thirty years, and my father did as well before me. They come down on their horses drunk and cavalier, waving their pistols and spittin'. The Loyas weren't always like this, but ever since Hector Loya's death, I've endured three years of this nonsense."

"What are you saying?" asked Dusty.

"You're the Pit Viper. Time to make that name shine."

She bared her teeth. "I hate that nickname."

"Most people don't know it, but you've earned it. I will help you take control of Glen Rio just as we agreed, but I want to know that you will protect the people of this town. There are cutthroats, and there are innocents. I would rather not see innocents die in your fight," said Bill.

"I need your ammo more than I need your horseshoes. If you help me, you know it won't be just my fight. Those *vaqueros* will come for you, too," said Dusty. "Better hope I finish this tonight."

Bill took the hammer on his belt. "Elsie, you go with her back to the manor. They will follow the blood trail here. I buy you time."

Bill stood just outside his shop, surrounded by writhing shadows. Lightning streaked overhead, followed by the rumble of thunder as the sound of pattering rain rattled on his tarp. He half-smiled to himself as his mind wandered. Elsie had indeed learned a lot in the time she had been with him. He was proud of her. He could never tell her that to her face, of course, but in a way, Bill knew she knew.

A small creek flowed down the muddy street just a few feet away, and thunder rumbled overhead once more to the beat of a thousand drums. Then, he saw the shadows rise. Like banshees in the mist, they appeared atop horses. There were at the very least ten of them, and they all had revolvers in their hands. They approached like a claw, reaching for him, but Bill was ready.

He slipped a glowing blue stone through his lips and bit on it, crushing it instantly. His vision blurred for a moment, but then, he could see them clearly. The night turned to bright purple, and the outlines of the hunters became bright red. Bill clenched his teeth but held his ground. His belt pulled against his waist as a few hammers dangled against his black leather apron.

Then, the *vaqueros* rushed at him. They raised their weapons and fired, wildly cracking with bright flashes in the night, but Bill was ready. He reared back and threw his hammer with all his might. The hammer slammed into a *vaquero's* face and crushed it instantly like a melon and sent him flying off his horse. Bill pulled another hammer from his belt and threw it with just the same hulking force he threw the first one. This one hit the face of another *vaquero* but instead cleaved clean through it. The headless horseman's body fell into the mud with a faint splash, the horse neighing nervously. The *vaqueros* continued their rush, their horses kicking up mud in the wake of their charge.

Bullets zipped over Bill's head, and he ducked into his forge as sparks flew up from his anvil. He grabbed another hammer and threw it, but this one sailed too far over a shooter's head. He heard a shout from the killers, and then, the horse steps faded away. Bill looked over the surface of the anvil and saw nothing but purple skies through the rain. The two dead bodies lay in the middle of the road, one of them twitching his leg uncontrollably. Then, the figures materialized in the street like phantasms. They crept along the sides of the street, careful to hide behind crates every few feet. They knew on horseback they would stand very little chance against him. But on foot, that was a different matter altogether.

Bill gritted his teeth and reached for a double-barrel shotgun he had prepared for the fight. It lay on the table just a few feet away. He reached out to grab it, and a hot round zipped over his head. He ducked back into cover only to feel a hot liquid in his hand.

When he looked at his hand, he realized the round didn't go over his hand but through it. He could see clearly through a two-inch hole in his right hand. He also had his index finger blown clean off. This wasn't good. He could hear the footsteps from the *vaqueros* coming closer and closer. Their aim would become more careful and precise.

He grabbed a hammer from his belt and reared back, but when he stood to throw, two rounds pierced his right arm.

Bill knelt back behind the anvil as sparks showered over him. The killers were too far for him to reach with his bare hands and too close to simply throw hammers before being gunned down. Dismounting and pushing on foot was smart play. The Loyas didn't gain control of Glen Rio by being stupid. He heard one set of footsteps go right, and the other go left. They were going to flank him. He had to think about something fast.

Bill glanced at his shotgun on the table, but it was too far away. If he were to make another reach for it, he would lose much more than a finger. He only had two hammers left, and the *vaqueros* were closing in fast like a claw. He heard the shuffling of spurred boots just outside his shop.

"Bill? Which anvil are you behind?" called out a *vaquero*.

He knew the sound of that voice anywhere "Anton? The hell are you doing out here?"

"The Loyas aren't happy with you. You sheltered the wrong shooter."

Though Bill couldn't see him, he knew Anton was still on the road just behind the sound of footsteps in front of him.

"I wish it weren't you, Anton. Out of all Loya's killers, I hated you the least," he shouted.

"I'll take that as a compliment, Bill. I wish it wasn't you either. Damn, you have a hell of an arm," said Anton. That was all Bill needed to know where each shooter was without looking. He wrapped his bloodied arms around the base of his anvil and heaved up. Gunshots went off just in front of him, ricocheting off the hardened iron of the anvil. Bill looked slightly over the side to see him stare into the face of a surprised and slightly confused killer just a few feet away. With a guttural shout, Bill tossed the anvil at the *vaquero*. The anvil fell heavy against the man's chest, and he folded over like a wet napkin. When the killer fell, the anvil instantly cracked his legs, and he sank deep into the mud, screaming like a howling banshee, slamming his fists against the hardened iron as if it would magically roll off. Bill heard a man sneak up behind him, and he turned with such speed and ferocity that when he threw his hammer, the man had no time to even squeeze the trigger of his revolver. The hammer smashed into his chest, caving his ribs and crushing his lungs. The blow knocked him into the forge with a soft grunt. The hot coals instantly singed his skin to a crisp as he flailed around wildly, attempting to scream, but his lungs could carry no more air. Before long, he ceased to move. The smell of charred flesh permeated the forge.

Then, Bill heard a *click* behind him. He turned to see a *vaquero* with a silver revolver aimed directly at his chest. Bill knew he was dead to rights. No matter how strong he was, no matter how fast he was, he was no match for a bullet at point-blank range.

"Before I shoot you, do you want to know how much Hector would pay for you?" asked the *vaquero*. Then, his head burst into a puff of red mist. The killer fell in a heap, his loaded revolver falling onto the floor of the shop. His gun fired three times wildly into the air in his final death throes, and then he ceased to move.

Bill let his hands down and saw Anton emerge from the darkness with a smoking gun. A shadow overtook his facial features beneath a wide-brimmed hat. He wore a brown poncho with red zig-zagging lines and brown pants with mud caked at the ends. Anton smirked, revealing a pearly white smile. Sweat glistened over his coal-colored skin.

"Seems a shame to let you go like that after putting up such a good fight," said Anton, glancing at the bodies of his fellow killers. "These men were some good shots too. They underestimated you."

"What's the plan now? Are you going to finish the job?" growled Bill.

"A thousand dollars. That's how much Annette put on your head."

"You won't have to split it anymore. No one will know you shot that dude in the head for it," said Bill, pointing at the man whose brains were spilling out onto the shop floor.

"Very true," said Anton as he flipped the drum cover of his revolver and pushed the empty case out. The brass fell to the ground by his boot, and he slid a thin bullet in its place. He flipped the cover back with his thumb and holstered his revolver. "I pride myself on knowing what the future holds. Dusty and her hunters are going to kill every last Loya. They don't stand a chance. There's something devilish about that woman. It seems she is impossible to kill. I don't think anyone stands a chance in the way of Dusty Rose."

A ripple of gunfire went off in the distance amid the perpetual pattering of rain. Anton tilted his head. "Sounds like things are heating up at the manor right now. If I were a betting man, and I am, Dusty will own the Loya Manor for herself in the next few hours. It will be a death sentence to be on the Loya payroll."

Bill began to nurse the hole in his hand and try to stem the flow of blood from his palm. "So, what'll you do?"

"Contract work, probably. There's a foreigner who will pay big money for bodyguard work. We'll see what can come of that. I want to make myself scarce of Glen Rio for a while," said Anton. "I have a lot of respect for you, Bill. You beat us without firing a single bullet. That's a story that will never get old."

"I wouldn't say I respected you before today, but this changes things," said Bill, nodding his head. "Go on. You're dead if Dusty *or* the Loyas find you."

"Best be on my way then," said Anton. He tipped his hat and promptly turned on his heel and vanished into the darkness as if he were nothing more than a ghost.

Bill sat back and looked over his arm. It dangled by his side. He tried to move the fingers of his hand with the hole in it, but it didn't move. There wasn't even any pain. He fell from his small chair and hit the cold ground with a thud beside the other two bodies. Rain fell on his head through a hole in the tarp, in a thin line trickling over his face, but he didn't have the energy to move. He closed his eyes, and the only thing he knew was that thunder rolled overhead like the closing of a sarcophagus.

My hands shook as the sun came up. Dusty was bathed in blood, and a dozen or so of her hunters milled over the bodies of the Loya gang. I stood in the wide courtyard holding the hammer that Bill had given me. I realized I stood over a man I had killed. I smacked him in the face just as Dusty started shooting. Then, everything went red.

"Well, it was a thorough kill," said Dusty, winking at me. "Even if it was the only *one* you killed. You froze and started screaming after that."

I remembered. It was the overwhelming roar of gunfire in my ears that took me a long time away.

"You're lucky we're such good shots," said a Hunter of the Rose. "You just stood there begging for a bullet."

He laughed at me as did the other hunters, creating a chorus amid the dead.

"Enough, Gray," said Dusty. "Leave her alone. I believe you have all tasks to complete, Amador. This is just the beginning. You all owe me now."

"Oh? Why do you say that?" asked the one named Amador in a thick Mexican accent. He had a long, bushy black mustache below his hard nose. His eyes were black and sharp.

"You put holes in my manor. Look, there is not a window without busted glass. There's a fire over the barn. Each of you will fix where your guns shot. The Rose Manor will be the spectacle of the land, the paradise of the Hunters of the Rose of Glen Rio."

"Is that so? I'm good at shooting. Not so much repairing where my bullets go," said Amador, placing a hand on his revolver threateningly.

Dusty glanced down at the gesture and then peered needles into his eyes. She then relaxed her stance and placed her hands over her belt buckle. This move took Amador off guard.

"I'll make it easy for you, Amador. You're my best, but that doesn't mean I won't bust a dog that bites back."

Amador looked at the other hunters for a boost in confidence but quickly realized they were just as scared of her. His confidence deflated and growled, but then he nodded his head, taking his hand away from his weapon.

"I'm sorry, Dusty. Bloodlust. You know what it does to a man."

"And what it does to a woman, trust me," said Dusty patting her belt buckle. "Now, get to work. I want my manor christened by dawn."

The line of men broke, and Dusty turned to me.

"I'll bet Bill is waiting for you. Well, either he is or his body is. It would be a shame if he wasn't able to hold the line. If so, I will make sure to give him a proper burial. He served me well."

My heart dropped to my feet. I found my legs again and turned tail down the street from the Loya Manor.

"The Rose Manor now," I whispered to myself, knowing things wouldn't be the same in Glen Rio. I rounded the bend in the muddy road, and just as the rains began to clear up and give way to the first rays of sun, I saw the blacksmith shop. I gasped. Horses whinnied by the side of the road, tied to a post. I saw bodies face down in the mud. I walked over one and saw a hammer embedded into his crushed skull. His brain matter had spilled into the mud. I saw another body with the head torn clean off. Whatever happened here, it must have been a hell of a fight.

I grabbed a dead man's revolver from his hip and checked the rounds. Only three bullets remaining. Then, I pulled the hammer back and walked into the shop. A Loya man could be hiding in there. I walked past another dead body, but an anvil lay on his chest. His eyes were blood-shot and held an expression of shock. Then, I saw him.

"Bill," I gasped and ran to a body lying face up. He was still breathing, but his eyes were erratic, and his skin was pale white and clammy. I knew if I didn't do something, he would be dead by nightfall.

I quickly sprang into action, setting my weapon and bloody hammer to the floor. I tossed kindling and a small log on the fire, which quickly reignited the flames and then, grabbing the pail, filled it with water at the spigot behind the shop and returned to Bill's side. I glanced at the tepid waters, hoping the flames would begin to do their work.

"Bill, speak to me. Say something," I said. He only mumbled, his eyes unfocused and wavering. His breaths were erratic and rapid. I grabbed some tongs and shoved them into the fire just as the water had begun to steam. I dipped a clean rag into the water and began working on his wounds. He had taken most of the damage on his right arm, but he also was shot in his lower gut. It would all need to be cleaned and the bullet removed, or infection would set in. I knew better than most what infection did to a body. When the tongs were hot, I took them and inserted them in the bullet wound in the shoulder. The tongs seared his flesh and bubbled the skin around the wound. Bill grunted, and for the first time, I saw the spark in his eye return in anger as he turned to me and grabbed my arm.

"Hey there, Bill," I said, smiling nervously and letting out a sigh of relief. "Welcome back. I'm sorry I left you. Never again, big guy. Never again."

He gave me a twisted look of evil, but then his eyes met mine in recognition. He looked around his shop and saw the dead bodies and strewn tools on the floor. I pulled a bullet from his shoulder and set it on the table. Blood spurted from the wound, but I quickly applied a bandage to it and began cleaning it out.

"I can't move my arm," he said. "I can't even feel my hand."

Bill never could feel his grated arm after that. Though the wounds closed up without infection, and even the hole in his hand became a mass of toughened flesh, he would only ever wear it in a leather sling. I knew it hurt him to see his body unable to do the things he requested of it. At the same time, this forced me to take on the full duties of the bulletsmith shop. This was my time to shine.

One sunny afternoon, after all the day's tasks had been completed, Bill sat beside me with that same ornate box on his lap. He held it out to me.

I took it from him unceremoniously and opened it only to be met with a strange blue sand that glowed white.

"Eclipsinthe?" I asked.

Bill nodded and held a small bullet casing with a glass within. It was unlike the usual bullet casing as this one wasn't made of brass but of something else entirely. "Dusty says this alone is the future of our race. With this, we will conquer the stars."

He brought his hand up in an arc above his head. Then, he promptly frowned. "But who knows what any of that means. Dusty is a strange woman. One thing you must remember if you are to smith this bullet. There has to be a perfect balance. Too little eclipsinthe, and you miss the effect of the bullet. Too much, and you melt through the casing the moment the hammer strikes, blowing your fingers to bits. To use a bullet like this, you must trust the smith who made it."

"I understand."

"I hope so. Your legacy rests on the quality you produce. Word of mouth is everything to a person of our profession."

"I got it, Bill. Why does it sound like you're leaving?"

He nodded with a *hrmm* and stood up, and I realized he wore a leather trench coat that fell to the level of his boots. He slung a bag I hadn't noticed over his back and put a wide straw hat over his head. He grabbed a walking staff and leaned on it.

"Where are you going?" I asked, standing up beside him.

"My time in Glen Rio is done. Bulletsmiths will be of the highest of demand when A Bad 'Un arrives. Dusty will need orders filled each day. When I return, I hope to still find you alive and well."

"You're just leaving me?" I asked, as he walked into the street. He took a deep breath and smiled.

"If you have to know, I can't quite do my profession with a bum arm like this. I intend to get it fixed. The next time we meet, I will be formidable once more. I may meet you as my equal, maybe not."

I shook my head. "You're all chatty again. I don't get it, Bill. What happened to the strong silent type? What the hell are you doing?" Tears unwillingly flooded my eyes.

I will never forget the look on his face, nor how he let out a laugh when he tilted his head up to the sun. It sounded so guttural, almost as if I wasn't looking at him; I would think he was choking. I saw a tear run down his cheek, and he wiped it with a meaty finger. He composed himself, and his face returned to a look of grave gravitas. "I owed Dusty Rose my life and service. Every day, I put my head down and did as I was told without thinking about what tomorrow may bring. It wasn't until I met you that I realized I had much to show you. It was as if I were witnessing this profession through fresh eyes, eager and willing to discover what it means to sweat lead. It wasn't until you started to apprentice under me that I saw your incredible potential. I saw mine too. One day, you may be a better bulletsmith than me, maybe not."

"I still have no idea how to make an eclipsinthe bullet," I said.

"On my bed, you will find the diagram and measurements on how to make them. I trust you will know what to do when you see them," He turned and waved. "Dusty has components you will need, and she is expecting you any minute now. In fact, you're late. Better get a move on."

My vision went red. "You bastard. You just up and leave me with the shop? What the hell?" I grabbed a pail and threw it at him. The pail clanked on the dirt road after him but he only waved. Tears fell from my eyes, but then my anger dissolved as I realized that the shop belonged to me. The anvil, the hammers, the bullet press. He was right. In his state, he was no help to me. In fact, he was removing himself from my burden. I will never forget the hulk of a man disappearing into the swamp of Glen Rio, never to be seen again.

Suddenly, I heard a clashing of pots at the back of the shop and turned, chills running up my spine. Bill had just left, and of course, the rats were here to steal from me. Time to teach them a lesson. In anticipation, I grabbed my hammer from the anvil and squeezed the polished wooden handle. I couldn't throw hammers like Bill, but I could hurt.

I walked quietly to the doorway. The sounds came from my small kitchen. Another crash of pans, and this time, I heard a gasp and a faint sob. Only, it sounded like that of a child.

I held my hammer up, ready to strike, and peeked around the doorway. A sickly pale girl no older than myself sat in a pile of pots and pans, attempting to pick herself up. She was exceptionally filthy. Not a single spot on her skin was devoid of mud or dirt. Her blue dress was in poor shape, with tears and loose brown strands, as if she had recently been in a fight for her life.

"What the hell are you doing here?" I asked, growling at the girl. She jumped and looked up at me with tears in her reddened eyes.

"Please—*sob*—I just need some food—*sob*. Anything you can spare," she begged, tears streaming down her face anew.

"I don't give handouts," I said with a curt sniff wiping away a stray tear from my cheek.

"I can cook well and keep the fire going for you—*sob*."

"You want to work for me?" I asked.

She nodded.

"Well, you're in luck. A position just opened up for me, and I need more eclipsinthe. Do you know where the Rose Manor is?"

She nodded again, choking on her tears.

"Okay, well, Dusty has something that I need to complete her order. But she will turn her nose up to you if you appear like that," I said, looking her up and down. "Barely more than a toothpick, ain't ya?"

"I won't let you—*sob*—down-um, what do I call you?"

"My name is Elsie. What do I call you?"

"Lily."

"Fine, put a pep in your step. There's a washtub out back and a bar of soap. I'll have to find you new clothes in the meantime. Oh, and please, stop *crying*."

. . . For a Hunter of the Rose, the sound of gunshots in the distance is like a gator catching the taste of a wounded animal stuck on a muddy bank. It's the call for a feeding frenzy. —*Glen Rio proverb*

The Hunt

The Bullet-Catcher.

The shuffling of boots outside the office disturbed the commissioner from his nightly routine of dossier audits. The door swung open with a light squeak, and a man with a well-trimmed mustache and newly stitched brown jacket stepped in with a shining golden badge pinned to his chest. He took his hat off and held it before him. The commissioner resisted the urge to roll his eyes in his presence and instead opted for a cheap and exaggerated smile. "Sheriff Erik Matthews. What a pleasant surprise. What brings you to my office in the *middle* of the night?"

Erik didn't have a single wrinkle on his suitcoat that had recently been pressed by the looks of it. He sported a curled goatee, and it twitched when he spoke. "You are a representative of supreme authority of the region, are you not, Sam?"

"It's Commissioner Skinner to you, and yes, that is what commissioner means, Erik. Is that why you are here? To discuss my terms of office?" asked Sam, wincing at the grating sound of Erik's voice. He looked back to the dossier in his hands.

"I don't want to take up much of your time, but I have it on good authority that Felix Quintana and his newly formed gang are in Temple. Felix has a hefty bounty on his head, and he has just doubled it by killing Sheriff Hardy. I want him hung for his crimes."

"Right. Nasty fellow, that one. And you wish to take him on by yourself?"

Erik stiffened his lower lip. "It would be suicide to go alone. I want your permission to deputize twenty of my men to hunt him and his gang down. He's headed into Glen Rio, so there is very little time to lose."

This made Sam pause. He closed the dossier and set it down on the table before him. He reached over to his cup of coffee, but when the black water touched his lip, he recoiled. It had gone cold hours ago. He set the cup down with a heavy sigh. It was a night for disappointments.

"You realize that Dusty Rose is the authority of that town and the surrounding region, don't you?" asked Sam.

"But your authority supersedes hers. You can tell her to stand down."

Sam chuckled and leaned back in his chair. "Perhaps on paper. You haven't met Dusty Rose before, have you?"

Erik tilted his head as if to smirk, but he hesitated. It was clear to Sam even *he* had heard countless stories in bars, whorehouses, and saloons about the legendary Dusty Rose and the nasty cabal of hunters from Glen Rio.

Sam leaned forward in his chair, setting his elbows on the desk. "I have kept the peace by allowing her to run the town as she sees fit. She doesn't cause much noise for me, and I keep my affairs out of Glen Rio. I intend to keep this peace. Even so, I will give you what you ask. Mr. Quintana deserves to hang. Be warned, however. Dusty Rose is not a woman to be crossed. In many ways, she is worse than any member of the Quintana Gang, including Felix. If she deems you worth dying for, I will not retaliate. No one will mourn your shallow grave should Dusty get her hands on you. You go there with my authority but *not* with my protection. Do you understand?"

"My men will protect me."

"I sure hope so. Normally, I would say God be with you, but not even God dares to venture into Glen Rio."

Ren stared through the reeds of a river, keeping his head low and holding a mud-crusted revolver in his hand. He was crouched by the edge of a small town, and though the sun was still rising in the sky, a thick fog clouded his vision. Even so, he knew that the fog was very well the reason he was still breathing. He had lost his hat somewhere in the chaos, and his brown coat was torn to shreds, revealing a dozen cuts on his shoulder. Dried blood crusted his sleeves. Thus is the effect of getting caught in a barbed wire concertina trap. He was lucky to still be breathing. The same couldn't be said of some of his brothers. The moon shone brightly in the cloudless skies, and that was a problem. He knew the winds would pick up soon and reveal them in the sunlight. They were running out of time.

Ren heard the movement of carriages through the fog and saw several white covers being pulled by horses riding into town. It was some kind of caravan. Something moved to his right, and he turned with a revolver at the ready, sweat dripping down his face. A dirt-colored face with black hair beneath a crumpled hat emerged from the riverbank. She held her hands slightly up.

"Wait! It's Maria," she snapped, a flash of fire in her raven-black eyes.

He relaxed and gave a sigh as she emerged from the darkness.

"*Que carajos* are you waiting for? We gotta get out of the river," she whispered harshly.

"It's Glen Rio. There are so many people here. Some kind of celebration or something," said Ren, licking his lips. "They will recognize us."

Maria poked a hand through the reeds to get a better look at the town. Glen Rio was possibly one of the most dangerous places in the region. Bounty hunters had very little regard for their own lives, let alone others. It was said they all worked for Dusty Rose, the owner of the Rose Manor and taskmaster to her hunters. Maria spotted the carriages entering the town, and her eyes widened. "It's the Bullet-Catcher."

"What's that?" asked Ren.

"You never heard of it?"

He shook his head.

"The Bullet-Catcher Championship is a competition between dozens of famed gunslingers for a prize out of this world. They come from all corners of the land." Maria crouched beside him and stared just as intently as a group arrived on horseback, their rifles and shotguns glimmering in the scant moonlight. Ren pulled a bag of dynamite from his belt and handed it to Maria. "Only one left. I say we round the town and go south. Let the feds think we stayed and hid. That will give us enough time to run."

"They have dogs, remember? No way we can outrun those mutts. I think we can swing this opportunity in our favor," said Maria as she took the dynamite and strapped the bag to her belt. "It could be the perfect cover."

"What do you mean? The moment we step in, the feds will be on our ass."

"That's the fear talking, Ren," she said, pulling a crumpled map from her belt and pointing to a clump of brown squares.

"Let me show you. Unfortunately, it's the only town for a few dozen miles. But there is not a man that walks those streets without blood on his hands. How could they distinguish gunmen from gunmen at a glance? They would have to come in close. Too close, and that gives us the advantage of surprise. Besides, there are plenty of places to hide. I think this will work."

"What will work?" asked Ren.

"Think for a moment, Ren. The feds will have a harder time finding us in a group of gunmen, right? When the championship is over, we can slip out while everyone is not looking."

"I don't know; it sounds risky."

"It is. I just wish Felix hadn't killed Sheriff Hardy. We would be on our way out of Mawbury Hills with a cartload of gold by now," growled Maria.

The reeds ruffled behind them, and Ren and she jumped and turned as their hammers clicked back, revolvers at the ready.

"Some men deserve to die. It's a shame I didn't kill that son of a bitch sooner," said Felix. His brown eyes had circles beneath them, leading down to bony cheeks. His thin lips were firmly pressed, and there was scarring all over his face from when he had been a victim of frostbite. He had a nasty look on his face that only softened when he glanced at the unconscious woman in his arms. Maria glanced at her.

"Is she gonna make it?"

"Not if we don't find her a doctor," said a voice behind Felix. It was Mateo.

"How many made it out?" asked Maria.

"I saw Levers and Beau get gunned down by the feds," said Mateo. "Dimitry got caught in the concertina, and the hounds tore him apart. Denholm and Grego are lost. I'm almost certain they are dead."

"Only five of us left?" asked Felix.

Mateo moved over to the edge of the bank with Ren and surveyed the town of Glen Rio. Maria moved closer to Felix and looked into the face of the woman.

"Louisa?" asked Maria.

Felix gritted his teeth. "I tried to wrap her wounds, but the concertina tore her up bad. Those feds knew our escape plan almost too well," he whispered so that Ren and Mateo couldn't hear. "Someone sold us out."

"Could it have been one of the lost?" asked Maria.

"I don't know. It could have been, but I can't be too sure yet. Keep an eye on Mateo. He's the only one without a scratch."

"Mateo?" asked Maria. She turned to look at him. "It can't be him. He would never sell us out."

"Right now, you're the only one I can trust. What did you see across the river?" asked Felix, changing the subject. They needed to hurry. The feds would be on them at any moment.

"You know Glen Rio better than anyone. It's the Bullet-Catcher."

"It could work," said Felix.

"Do you think Dusty would speak with you?"

Felix shook his head. "She hasn't forgiven me for killing one of her favorite hunters. The last time I saw her, she asked for either the Kayoro-moon or my life. I sometimes wish I had just tried to fight her for it. No, she has no loyalty to me. She would just as likely sell us out to the feds."

"Well, we don't have a choice. If we choose to bypass the town, we get hunted down in the swamp. Those hounds will make short work of us. Our ammo is almost out, and we are exhausted. This is our only opportunity, and its fortunate timing. The feds cannot use hounds among the hunters and have to expose themselves to us in the crowds," said Maria. "Besides, I heard that Doc Jennings lives here. Lu needs to see the doc."

"Agreed, but we can't go together. If we are found as a group, it will only be a matter of time before we find ourselves hanging by the neck beneath gallows. We must split up. Mateo takes Ren. I go with Lu. You go alone."

"Alone?"

"You're the only one whose face Sheriff Hardy's posse hasn't seen. You can move freely around the town as if nothing happened and keep contact between us for when the Bullet-Catcher is over and it's time to leave. Help me get Lu to Doc Jennings, and then we wait for this thing to blow over."

"Okay," said Maria. It was their best shot.

"We leave now," said Felix, his deep voice booming to alert the others. They rushed through the knee-deep waters of the river. They were fortunate the waters weren't at high tide. Perhaps their luck was beginning to look up.

Maria knew better than to entertain those thoughts for very long.

Once the five remaining gang members crossed the river, they found themselves in the midst of a gun-toting crowd as the rising sun poked its face through the fog. Most of the men and women wore irons at their hips. Felix covered Lu in a brown cloak as Mateo and Ren melted away out of sight. When other bounty hunters saw Felix and looked at the woman in his arms, he shrugged. Either they didn't care or didn't have enough interest to ask further questions. No one interrupted them, and they moved along with the crowd.

They passed beneath the shadow of a marble statue depicting a Native American holding a bow in one hand and three arrows in the other. On the other side of the statue was the Glen Rio bank.

"Where is this doc?" whispered Felix. Maria pointed farther down the road to a sign with a red cross on it. She ran to the door and slammed her fist onto the hard wood. "We need help! Please open up!"

The doors opened up slowly, and she found herself face-to-face with a giant and a growling, stone-cold face. Maria pulled her hat off.

"What you want?" grunted the mountain of a man.

"Help. My friend, she's—"

"Concertina trap," said Felix, brushing past her and pulling the brown cloak away from Lu's body. Her chest, all the way up to her neck, was scissored with cut lines. She was breathing, but it came in short gasps. She was barely holding on. When the giant saw this, his eyebrows flew up.

"Inside, quick!" grunted the man, taking a step back, leaving enough room for them to enter.

The room smelled of singed flesh like a wound had recently been cauterized. The smell was staggering. A woman with blonde hair tied in a tight bun walked out with blood on her apron and her sleeves rolled up. Her hands were covered in blood.

"What is it then?"

"Concertina," grunted the giant.

"Jesus Christ. I've got a brand new amputee in one room, a wench with an ear torn clean off, and now another one who found herself in barbed wire, and all on the eve of the Bullet-Catcher. Dammit!" the doctor yelled. She tore her apron off and pointed to an empty room. "Set her on the table, quick."

Felix did as instructed, and they closed the door behind them. Maria stood there for a moment, wondering if she should wait for them. After a few minutes, the thought of finding a hiding place began to warm her mind against the chills of the feds catching her and interrogating her. She felt the cold iron of the revolver tucked in her pants at her back. It would be better to find a place to hide now. She realized she hadn't slept in days, and the exhaustion of the run was beginning to thaw over her.

Maria cleared her throat and put her hat back on. She walked out into the morning rays over Glen Rio and took in a deep breath. Her boot clicked on something at her feet, and she glanced down to see a piece of wood in the dirt.

Maria leaned down to pick it up and inspect it. It was a wooden coin the size of a quarter in her hands with the initials *DR* engraved in the center. Suddenly, she felt a sharp pain on her shoulder, like a bug biting deep in her flesh. She winced and pulled her sleeve up. Her eyebrows flew up as she bore a strange mark on her shoulder. It was a symbol of a star with five points and a skull embedded in the middle. She stared at it and then turned to the coin in her hands, bewildered beyond belief. Then, the mark disappeared from her flesh as if it had never been there at all.

Maria heard the sharp whinny and the clopping of twenty horses stampeding into town. She caught her breath as she saw silver stars on each of their breasts. Quickly, she shoved the coin into her pocket and averted her gaze.

Twenty men atop beautiful black and brown horses charged through the dirt road. People rushed to give way in fear of being trampled. The men looked tired and had mean looks on their faces. Their prey had just bought themselves a little more time, and it was clear they were outsmarted and pissed off at the prospect. The one in the lead, a man with no hair anywhere on his face but a fancy curled goatee, glared at her as he passed by. Maria looked at the ground, allowing the brim of her hat to shadow her eyes. The feds did not disturb her. Felix was right; they couldn't tell if she was part of the gang if they had never seen her face.

Lucky her.

All they had to do was wait until the end of the Bullet-Catcher Championship, and they would be free to sneak out and run south. The border was their salvation.

The riders passed by without a word to her and stopped just in front of the Silver Bullet Saloon. She melted into the crowd of arrivals as she eyed the feds mill into the saloon, leaving their horses by a water trough.

A gunshot rang out into the morning sky. Maria's heart leaped to her throat, and she snapped her hand to pull her revolver when a loud cheer erupted all around her. She gasped as a woman with marble-white hair stood up with an eye patch over her left eye and a sling over her left shoulder. She seemed to have had a day not too dissimilar to the one Maria was currently having. She put two fingers in her mouth and blew a piercing whistle into the morning air.

"Welcome to Glen Rio!" she shouted, and a hoot of cheers erupted in response. She waited until the laughter and whooping died down. "The sixteenth Bullet-Catcher Championship starts on the morrow, and so the festivities can begin. As always, the Rose Manor is at your disposal as a participant in the championship and as a legendary bounty hunter in the service of the Black Rose. Only those who carry bounty tokens may enter and enjoy the amenities of the Rose establishment. The pleasure has been earned, and I know each carrier has sacrificed much to attain such a valuable object. Present your token and your name to Mr. Donaldson at the manor gates. He will give you your room and your direction for the championship. Let the gunshots ring!"

Everyone around her, in unison, pulled their revolvers out and began shooting up into the sky. Even Maria pulled her revolver out and shot a few rounds before the crowds began to dissipate and meander to the manor. She holstered her piece and shoved the wooden coin back into her pocket. She didn't want whoever dropped the token to recognize it. However, she could see that inside the manor was all the ruckus. What else was she to do in the meantime anyway except try to pass for a bounty hunter of the Black Rose? It was the perfect cover. What could possibly go wrong?

Maria let out a sigh and trudged along the dirt road. Characters of all types walked beside her. Some had long black or brown coats that went down nearly to their boots. Their shined pistols glinted like silver in the morning sun. Others carried simple shotguns and rifles across their backs or in their arms. One bounty hunter of note wore the token pinned to his chest. He was a half-man with stunted legs who rode a mechanized wheelchair. The wheels were wooden, and it creaked like a wailing banshee. What was of note, however, were the miniguns strapped to both ends of the wheels. They seemed terribly rusted, but the very sight of them made Maria swallow hard. However, the man in the wheelchair had earned his bounty token. It must have been one hell of a sight.

A metal gate with sharp points like pikes surrounded the grounds, separating the manor from the rest of Glen Rio. Maria followed the path the bounty hunters milled over to a manor grounds with the most beautiful building she had ever seen. The lavish marble pillars and intricate angelic designs were almost mathematically carved into the stone. Maria entered the manor; she found herself in a rotunda with the ceiling portraying a gorgeous depiction of a dozen hunters holding rifles aimed at each other, and in the background was a sprawling canyon. *It must have represented some kind of battle long ago*, she thought. She saw a golden plaque beneath that read: The Hunt of Scarwigg Pass.

"Token, please!" came the crisp command that yanked Maria's attention from the beautifully ornate canvas.

A man with no hair and a top hat sat behind a front desk that was supposed to be a reception. That must have been Mr. Donaldson checking tokens from the line of bounty hunters that had formed. Maria hurried to place herself at the tail end. The hunters smelled raw, like sweat and lime juice. She supposed she must have smelled pretty miserable herself. She couldn't remember the last time she had had a bath.

Before long, she found herself at the front of the line, being stared down by the man in the top hat.

"Token, please," Mr. Donaldson said, raising one eyebrow. "Can't say I've seen you before. You must be a fresh hunter."

Maria pulled the coin from her pocket and hoped she had the right token. The man took the wooden coin from her hand and stared at it. He studied and sniffed it like a hound.

"Huh, not a fake, but also not a token I recognize. Every token has a distinct smell, and yours is unfamiliar. This must mean it was acquired more than ten years ago. This was before I was hired as majordomo of Rose Manor. That must mean you are one of the first bounty Hunters of the Rose Estate. You participated in the battle you were staring at just now on the ceiling. Reminiscing, perhaps?"

Maria turned red and snatched the token away. "And don't you forget it," she growled. Mr. Donaldson grinned despite the threat. "Welcome to the Rose Manor. Name?"

It was probably not a good idea to use her real name. "Darien Jacobs."

The man raised his eyebrow but wrote her name down in a book at his side. "Now, since this is your first time at the Rose Manor, a few things must be conveyed to you. There is only one rule we live and die by. This is a safe house for any Token Holder. On these grounds, no blood must be spilled on penalty of death. If you crave revenge or blood, there will be plenty of that in the championship. You are number twenty-two." He held a small paper out to her with the number in black ink.

Maria gasped. She didn't mean to participate in the championship; she only wanted a warm place to spend the night. Her participation could expose her to the feds. However, it could also help corroborate her cover story.

"Well? Everything in order? Please, miss, there is a line behind you," said the man. Maria glanced at her side to see a dozen gunslingers with sour looks glaring back at her. She took the paper.

Mr. Donaldson flashed a grin. "If you aren't familiar, since you are in the twenties, you will find your room on the far-eastern wing of the manor. I wish you to enjoy your stay, bounty hunter."

Maria moved out of the line with parchment in hand, catching a glance of a golden arrow plaque with the name far-eastern wing on it. She supposed the best thing to do was follow the direction it pointed in. After a while, she was alone and couldn't even hear the rumble of conversations from hunters. Her footsteps were her only accompaniment. She walked along a winding hall with an immaculate red carpet on the floor and kept to the direction the plaques pointed in. Finally, she entered a section of the manor that seemed largely abandoned except for a few candles on a table. Everything she saw was immaculately cleaned and dusted. The hint of lavender danced in her nostrils. It was the cleanest and most expensive place she had ever been to. Maria never imagined she would even stand in a place like this. How did she get lucky enough to stay there a night?

Maria hoped the original owner of the token had died because she would kill him just to spend the night in the hall, let alone room twenty-two. She heard footsteps behind her and turned to see a hulk of a man nearly walk through her.

"Move," said the Black man with bulging muscles and a muddied brown cloak. He shoulder-checked her, knocking her back slightly. She dared not try to challenge him, especially after seeing a mean-looking sawed-off shotgun beneath his arm. The man opened a door and slammed it behind him.

"Don't worry about Anton," said a voice behind her. "He is just tired. We have traveled a long way to be here, you see."

Maria turned and stood face-to-face with a clean-shaven man wearing thin wire glasses on his nose. He had a protruding chin and kind blue eyes. He held his hand out, but she didn't take it. After a few moments, he chuckled. "I guess it is better not to trust me," he said. "After all, I *am* your competition. My name is Mack."

"Mine is Darien Jacobs."

"Well, Miss Jacobs. I believe *that* room is yours. Seeing as this is your first time, you should enjoy it thoroughly. If you crave company, I will be out here smoking a little later if you wish to speak to someone. I have a feeling you have questions about the championship," said Mack. "Seeing you *are* new and all."

"What do you mean by that?"

Mack eyed her inquisitively, and Maria turned red and nodded, then turned into the room beside the one

Anton entered. She closed the door shut and let out a deep breath. She realized her heart was racing. She stood just behind the door for a few moments, attempting to process all that had just happened. Finally, she walked into the room where she was going to stay. The room was immaculately dressed and smelled of conifer and pine, a refreshing aroma that instantly soothed her anxious spirit. Maria took her jacket off, but before laying on the large beckoning bed with a blue bedspread, her eyes caught a large white tub just a few feet away.

What's more, the tub had a spigot over it, meaning she didn't have a need for a bucket-boy. Maria couldn't remember the last time she had had a bath. She turned the spigot, and hot water instantly poured from the pipe. Maria quickly took all her clothes off, fumbling with the buttons of her blouse and the buckle of her belt. When all lay at her feet, she drew her revolver, climbed into the rising water, and let out a soft moan as the steam enveloped her in a cocoon of watery warmth. She lay her head at the back of the tub and let out a sigh, holding her gun on the side of the tub. The cuts on her arms and legs began to bleed, but she was glad of the cleansing. She saw a bar of soap on the end and set her revolver down beside it. Maria began to scrub herself, and after a while, she drained the bloody muddy waters only to fill it back up with clear steaming water. She lay her head back and closed her eyes. She didn't know how long she lay there in the tub soaking, but she knew she would kill anyone who disturbed her just for a few more minutes in the water.

After reluctantly dragging herself from the embrace of the warm bath, Maria thought better of simply going to sleep despite the most comfortable-looking bed beckoning for her. She would need some information, and she hoped she could get it from Mack. She found him sitting down in the wing lounge, smoking a pipe, and sitting beside an obviously pregnant woman. She had raven black hair and wore a white shirt that supported her belly tucked into a black skirt. There was a single-shot long-barrel shotgun leaning against the arm of her chair. They were speaking in hushed tones until they saw Maria emerge.

"Well, all settled in, are we?" asked Mack with a smile, letting out a puff of smoke from his mouth. The other woman simply stared at her.

"Thank you," said Maria.

"She has manners, it seems. *That* I can appreciate," said the woman. "A liar, not so much."

Maria tilted her head and, in an instant, whipped her pistol out from behind her back, holding it aimed at the two, thumb on the hammer. Mack raised his eyebrows, his smile unwavering. "You sure you want to do that here? It's not the smartest play, I guarantee you."

"She knows she's been caught," said the woman.

"Does she know the consequence of spilling blood within the Rose Manor?"

"Likely not. She does have spirit, though."

Maria licked her lips. "What do you intend to do about it?"

"Do? Absolutely nothing. Maybe chuckle a little. How does that sound?" asked Mack, leaning back. It's almost as if he didn't care he was staring down the barrel of the gun; he was so casual, as if her pointing the gun at him had the same equivalence as her tipping her hat in his general direction. She supposed it only made sense to these bounty hunters. "This is Laura. She, as you can see, is about to give birth, but I haven't known this woman to buckle down from a fight, pregnant or no."

Maria still didn't know whether to run or pull the trigger.

"We mean you no harm. If anything, you might have just taken out our greatest competitor. He made us very worried. We should be thanking you," said Laura, putting a hand over her belly.

"Is that so?"

"That bounty token you found belonged to none other than E. Gray. Likely the craziest gunslinger of all of Mawbury Hills. He has won two Bullet-Catcher championships and has stolen a trophy or two from myself and Anton," said Mack. "Our run-ins have not been pleasant, but at the very least, we are alive to tell about it. So many others aren't that lucky."

"To say he's not the nicest would be an understatement," said Laura. "I saw him nearly kill the doorman, frustrated that he lost his token a few hours ago. If he finds out you took it, I promise he will kill you."

Maria shuddered at the thought. She had heard of E. Gray before, and none of it was good.

"We aren't going to hurt you," said Mack.

"Thank you. I would have hated to have to shoot you," said Maria.

Suddenly, she felt the cold steel of a rifle at the back of her neck. She held her breath.

"She's cocky," said the voice behind her. It was Anton.

"*Hijo de puta*. I didn't even hear you," snapped Maria, bringing her revolver up and shoving it into her pants. It was clear these three wouldn't be intimidated at the sight of a gun. What else did she expect? These were legendary hunters of the Black Rose Manor.

Anton let the short rifle from her neck and then held it beneath his arm.

"So, you stole E. Gray's token. Ballsy."

"I didn't mean to. I just happened to cross it," said Maria.

"As I said, you did us a favor. Now, he won't be able to enter the challenger grounds, at least for the moment. Unfortunately for you, you have to enter the championship yourself or risk leaving Glen Rio tonight. If you do leave and word gets out you stole the token, Dusty will place a bounty on your head. There is no place you can hide if that happens. Bounty hunters will fight tooth and nail to kill you and claim their prize," said Mack. "If you don't leave, E. Gray will find you and end you rather quickly. Of course, that is if the feds don't find you first."

Maria clenched her jaw.

"Ah, so it is true. You are a member of the Quintana Gang," said Mack, then he turned to Laura. "I saw the feds enter town and heard them talking about these cats, a dangerous bunch of banditos led by none other than Felix Quintana. An ugly one inside and out, or so I hear."

"You don't know a damn thing about us. Felix would lay down his life for any one of his gunfighters," growled Maria.

"Yeah, I've heard that too," Mack nodded. "So, you are stuck between a rock and a hard place. But, while you are with us, you are relatively safe."

"Only three can enter on a team at once. You'll have to come up with a plan," said Laura.

"Wait, you mean you're not . . .?" began Mack.

"I sure as hell won't be in the tournament. Are you kidding? I'm with child," snorted Laura. "You know why I'm here."

"Oh, I thought you were here to visit *me*," said Mack with a coy grin. He pulled a box at his side and opened it to reveal eight phials with orange liquid within. He caught Maria's gaze. "I am a chemist, you see."

He turned to Laura.

"Take one just before bed and one in the morning after breakfast. This should help with the nausea."

She stood up and, despite her belly, leaned over and kissed him on the cheek, taking the box of orange phials from his lap. Mack turned red instantly.

"I do wish you both the best," she said with a nod at Anton, then she looked at Maria. "Three, I suppose. I still can't tell whether you were lucky or unlucky."

"Guess I'll find out," said Maria.

"Guess you will. With that, gentlemen, I take my leave. Good night *y vaya con Dios*." Laura left the wing, closing the door behind her. Anton sat down where Laura had been sitting and stared at their addition.

"First of all, what is your name?" asked Anton.

"It's Darien Jac—"

"Your real name, please," said Mack.

She held her breath but didn't respond.

"I suppose I could just call you Twenty-two? That I think I prefer," said Mack.

"I need your help," said Maria, finally.

"We haven't agreed to take you with us just yet, Twenty-two. Why would we help you? You happened upon that coin by pure luck. I don't even know if you can use that revolver or not. You only have three bullets in there," said Anton.

"He has a knack for knowing whether a weapon is loaded or not," said Mack, who then mouthed *showoff* at her.

"I *do* know how to use this," she said, patting her revolver.

"Prove it," said Anton.

"What?"

"I said prove it. Why should we take you with us? What reason do I have to put my life in your hands as opposed to shooting you the moment the challenge begins?"

Maria licked her lips.

"You don't even know what the prize is. You've found a coin and accepted Dusty Rose's hospitality, but you don't even know why you're risking your life?" sneered Anton.

"If you want to find out what I am capable of, draw your weapon. Consequences be damned. I'll take you on *and* anyone who dares cross me, *pendejo*," said Maria, taking the stance of the gunslinger, her hand inches away from her revolver, prepared to draw. Even Anton held his silence for a moment, studying her very carefully. Then, he craned his head. "You're lucky I find you interesting. You have guts."

Finally, Mack shook his head. "Enough, Anton. We aren't rats. We sure as hell aren't talking to a damn fed."

"Maybe," said Anton. "Just so you know, Twenty-two, the prize on the line is always some mysterious object that is priceless. Some say the rewards are imbued with magic. Who knows if that's true, and things always have a price on them, no matter what people gossip."

"This year's prize is said to be a device that can block bullets even when you're not looking. Even that whoreson Jibbs swore he caught a glance."

"Jibbs is full of it," grunted Anton, turned to Maria. "I won't turn you in, but that doesn't mean you'll survive tomorrow's games."

"Oh, very true. Tomorrow is a boar hunt, or so the rumor goes," Mack beamed. "That is the first of three daily challenges. I would get some rest if I were you."

"Seems simple enough," muttered Maria.

Both men paused for a moment in shocked silence and then burst into laughter.

"You have no idea what's in store for you," said Mack, wiping a tear from his glasses.

Flags of all shapes and sizes, black, red, gray, and green, whipped back and forth in the chilling winds as they marked the staging area before a large open field. The sun couldn't break through gray clouds that spilled white fog on the ground, casting a dim haze over Glen Rio. Dozens of men and women stood around in groups, holding rifles, shotguns, and sharpened machetes at their sides. All of them were bounty hunters who had earned their tokens through blood and tears. All of them except for Maria. She felt so out of place in a crowd of killers.

"Did you know why crabs never need a lid when trapped in a barrel?" asked Mack, flinging his arm over her shoulder to whisper in her ear. "You see, the crabs are scared too. They know something is wrong, and very likely, their end is near. One gets to the edge and comes so close to freedom. It needs only to reach up and pull, but then something grabs its leg. It's the other crabs, its own brethren. You gotta understand the other crabs see this one dude nearly make it, and they decide if they can't get out, neither should anyone else. Thus, they keep themselves trapped. No need to watch them or put a lid over their bucket. Their nature rules over them. Now, you don't look like a crab to me, but I guess only time will tell. You should stick with us in the meantime," said Mack. Maria digested his story in silence.

There was something different about Anton and Mack. They seemed like brothers despite the fact they were very different both in appearance and character. Anton had grown gravely silent as he stood among his competitors, clutching his sawed-off shotgun with a small hatchet attached to the end. He held a Winchester lever action rifle with the barrel sewn off at his back. It had a scope on it and a beautifully carved bear on the wooden guard.

"He gets nervous so close to who he considers his enemies," whispered Mack. "You should, too. Some of these rats will shoot you just to get an advantage."

Maria eyed the hunters around them. The comradery of the previous day seemed to have washed away as they gave her soured looks. "Why don't they?"

"Because we could do the same," said Mack, drawing his revolver and holding it over his belt buckle. Maria matched the motion and regarded every hunter with suspicion as she passed by.

A woman with marble-white hair and an eye patch climbed up on an empty cart. Her arm was still in a sling.

"That's Dusty Rose," said Mack. "Arguably the scariest and craziest female this side of Mawbury Hills. You wouldn't want to cross her."

"She's the one who enforces the penalty of killing on the Rose Manor," said Maria.

"Well, yes, she and her aide, Maddie. The name suits her, by the way, both completely off their rockers," said Mack.

Dusty pulled her revolver and shot it in the air, a wide smile on her face.

A few of the bounty hunters cheered, but it was significantly less than at the town's main road the day before.

"Good morning, and welcome to the first day of the Bullet-Catcher Championship. This championship will set apart the elite among you from the chaff. Remember, there are no rules when off the manor property. Honor is left off the field. A boar roams the swamps. You are to kill the boar and bring me its tusks. Simple."

A loud howl like that of a rabid pig echoed in the distance as if to highlight Dusty Rose's words.

"Whoever wins takes with them $1000 dollars as a reward for today's challenge. Simple, now, let the hunt begin!"

No one cheered that time, yet the monetary amount made Maria pause. How good would it be to bring that money to Felix? It would pay for any of Lu's medical bills. Maria had to be the one to get the tusks and turn them in. She had to do it alone despite Anton and Mack's help. She had to think of her own first.

Are you a crab?

The thought surprised her as if it belonged to someone else, but she shook the feeling away. She had to focus.

The hunters gathered what belongings they had and began to mill into the swamp tree line. A thick strain lay on the air like an asphyxiating smoke, as sharp eyes and itchy trigger fingers melted into the underbrush. Maria didn't like the feeling one bit. She began to walk into the swamp, but a hand grabbed her shoulder.

"Wait," whispered Anton. She turned to him, and he held his rifle at his hip.

"But the boar. If someone else finds it first—" protested Maria.

"It won't be the boar that catches the first bullet," said Mack, matching Anton's tone. They stared at the hunters in the swamp. Before long, not even one could be seen.

"And—" whispered Mack.

The only sound was the deafening song from cicadas and other insects with a chorus of chirps and whistles.

"Now—"

Not even the boar could be heard howling in the distance anymore.

"It begins—"

No sooner had the words left Mack's mouth when gunfire rippled in the underbrush. Flashes of light were accompanied by muffled shots and horrific cries of the dying. It was an all-out shootout in the swamp. The undergrowth boiled with gunfire in all directions, almost as if the trees themselves had guns. Maria felt relief not being in the terse greenery. She almost lost her will and decided to simply leave, but she knew only death awaited her if she did. Maria could only stare until there was nothing more but silence. Not even the insects sang their song anymore.

"Why are you helping me?" asked Maria suddenly.

"It's a little late to be asking that question, don't you think?" responded Mack. He and Anton began walking to the tree line.

"You were in the wing with us," said Mack. "That makes you our partner, Twenty-two. Besides, you don't seem half-bad. Maybe a little misguided, but nothin' gunfire and a few brews can't fix. Unfortunately, in that order."

Maria felt the wooden coin in her pocket.

"Don't get comfortable," said Anton, pulling a sawed-off shotgun from behind his back and breaking the well open, loading a single shell into it. Maria shuddered at the small hatchet attached to the end. It had a nasty edge to it.

Maria glanced at her revolver. It was so boring and dull in comparison to those weapons. Despite this feeling, she felt a sense of safety with these two.

"Have you done this before?" asked Maria.

"Once. We got disqualified three years ago, but at least we made it out alive."

"How did you get disqualified?" asked Maria.

Mack leaned close to her ear. "Anton knocked the teeth out of Isaac 'The Wretch' McTurner before the hunt began. It wasn't technically the spilling of blood, just teeth, so he wasn't hunted down. It was conflict outside the actual championship day, so—"

"I see."

Then, they were in the swamp. The silence was the most frightening aspect of their entrance. They could not even hear footsteps, even though they knew other hunters were nearby.

"Could they all be dead?" whispered Maria.

Mack shook his head but remained silent. She spotted a body lying face down at the foot of a large tree. She could see his weapons glisten in the sparse sunlight poking through the sprawling canopy of green. Not more than a few feet away, she saw another body clumped in a mud-hole. The corpse was already sinking and would soon be lost in the mud, never to be found. She bit her lip and pulled the hammer of her revolver back.

Her gun was loaded with full-metal jacket bullets. They had the penetration power to go through thin walls and layers of wood, but would it be enough? She held the revolver at her hip and placed her fingers over the hammer in a fanning position, ready to fire. They walked slowly, Mack and Anton keeping an eye on the right and left as they moved forward. Maria scanned behind them, sweeping her revolver, careful not to—.

Suddenly, two shadows poked from a tree behind them, rustling through thick bushes. Maria shouted and fanned her revolver. Her shot hit the first shadow, exploding through his head in a sickly-red puff, and he fell to the ground dead, but the second one ducked behind a tree. Mack fired twice, matching her aim. Maria ducked into cover beside an old oak with thick branches, swung the drum of her revolver out, and slammed it against the palm of her hand. Thin bronze bullet casings slid out, and, using a speed-loader from her jacket, she jammed six rounds back into the drum. She flicked her wrist, closing the drum-well home.

Mack spat as he slid into a bush. He knelt beside her and quickly loaded two bullets into his revolver. "Twenty-two, how many did you see?"

Maria held up two fingers.

"Two! One down!" shouted Mack.

"What the hell are you yelling for?" whispered Maria, but then she realized Anton was not with them. In fact, he was nowhere to be seen. It was as if he had disappeared entirely, vanishing into the underbrush. She realized it was a callout for Anton. Then, they heard a muffled grunt and then a sound like a sack of potatoes falling into a pile of dried leaves.

"That's him," Mack smiled, standing up from the bushes. She followed suit and saw Anton looming above the second man's body with a bloodied shotgun blade. His hands were covered in gore, but his face reflected no emotion, save perhaps the muscles of his jaw over-straining.

"Think that's it," he said. "This was Doc Overton and 'Saint' John, looks like. I don't hear anyone else, not yet anyway."

"Was he really a saint?" asked Mack.

"He thought he was. I guess God must have disagreed," muttered Anton.

Maria turned at the sound of crushing leaves and saw two large green eyes staring right back at her. They were large, and beneath them were two large tusks poised to charge.

"Damn," was all she could utter before a monstrous boar screamed and broke through the bush, shaking the swamp. Anton didn't have time to move as he was directly in the path of the thundering creature. He looked up in shock. Suddenly, Mack charged in from his left, pushing them both out of the way.

The boar crashed into the tree, cleaving it in half, and stomping the dead bodies to a bloody pulp. Maria rushed away from the beast as fast as her legs could carry her. She could not stop herself and didn't even look back. That creature would kill them all, given the chance.

"*Lo siento*," she said repeatedly. Those two had watched her back, but she convinced herself they were giving their lives for her. It made no sense for all of them to die. When she had run for a few minutes, Maria rounded a gigantic tree and knelt down, weapon at the ready. She calmed her rapid breathing and waited there, listening intently. She didn't know how long, but she dared not move for fear of other hunters hearing her footsteps, or even worse, the boar catching her scent again and running her down.

She heard shooting in the distance and a loud yell. Despite something telling her to return, she was powerless to move. She brushed her black hair from her eyes and realized she was sweating profusely. Then, she heard a crunch of wet leaves just a few feet away. She held her revolver at the ready, but couldn't hear anything. Suddenly, the hum of the swamp reverberated in her ears and became like a chorus rising in a deafening crescendo. It almost hurt to listen, and she fought every urge to put her hands to her ears. Her chest ached, and she felt a sharp pain pierce into her shoulders and arms.

Then, she saw two yellow eyes glowing in a bush, but it wasn't the boar. It stood the height of a man, and then, just as she thought the volume of the swamp could get no higher, the sounds came to a halt, going completely silent. The thing emerged from the bushes, and Maria, in shock, lost control of her bladder.

It was a gator-like creature covered in dark green scales and a mouth full of sharpened teeth. Maria didn't have a clue what she was looking at, but the creature stood at nearly seven feet tall and wore brown pants and a white shirt that had been dirtied brown and had tears in them, revealing a muscle-bound chest like that of a man except covered in green scales. The creature screamed, but just before it could charge her, the swamp floor shook, sending ripples through puddles at her feet. The boar rushed through the undergrowth at the crocodilian and slammed into it, sending the angry but confused creature tumbling out of sight with a yelp.

The boar turned sideways to her, then turned to her with a snarl and stamped the ground. Maria didn't know what came into her, but she aimed her pistol and pulled the trigger. The boar turned sideways to glance at her just as the bullet pierced its right eye. The round exited the other eye instantly blinding the creature as it howled in pain. It shook its head, pawed the ground, and charged, but Maria leaped out of the way of the stampeding animal. Then, a thought crossed her mind so crazy it baffled her how quickly her arms responded to it.

She pulled a stick of dynamite from the bag at her hip and a match from her pouch, but before she could light it, the boar stopped in its tracks. It wheezed in pain but stood like a statue. Despite its grievous wound, it was listening for her.

Maria held her breath. She didn't dare move one step away for fear of giving away her position. Those few seconds stretched into eternity as a thick silence closed around her neck like a vice. She knew she could only hold her breath for so long. Then, she could hold it no longer. She finally whipped her hand down on her pants, and the phosphorus at the tip of the match instantly ignited.

She gasped for air, but the boar had heard it all. It grunted loudly and swung his massive tusks. Maria tried to leap out of the way, but she wasn't fast enough. The boar's tusks slammed into her side, knocking the wind out of her, and the point of the left tusk dug into her skin, slicing into her as she fell into the mud. She gasped for breath and felt hot liquid run down her spine. Maria realized she dropped the match and stick of dynamite into tar-like sludge. Despite the roaring beast, she heard the fizzle of the match going out. That's it. She was a goner. She stared up as the beast pawed the ground to run her over.

A shotgun blast left a harsh ringing in her ears. She looked up to see Anton's grim face. He moved away from the mud, stamping the wet ground as loudly as he could to draw the beast's attention away from her. This worked, and the boar snorted loudly, following his footsteps away.

"Don't move," whispered Mack. Maria turned to her right just behind a thick bush to see a worried look on his face. "Stay very still."

He held a monocle slightly above him, turning it this way and that above him. Then, Maria realized he was attempting to redirect the beam of the sun. She looked down at her side to see the stick of dynamite encased in mud. Luckily, the wick was still dry.

Suddenly, the tip exploded in a burst of sparks.

"You'd better hurry," said Mack. Maria nodded as the sparks began to eat up the chord. She stood up and saw Anton standing still just beside the boar. It was searching for him ravenously, swinging its head this way and that, stamping its hooves into the mud. This creature was pure evil.

She picked the dynamite up in her hand and fixed it to throw. Her eyes caught Anton's, and they locked for a moment. Time seemed to freeze for a split second, so much so that the pressure in Maria's forehead almost felt like her head was going to explode.

"Move," she mouthed, tilting her head at the stick of dynamite. Anton simply gritted his teeth and shook his head.

"Do it," he mouthed back.

A feeling of confusion overtook her. This man, a bounty hunter she barely knew, was willing to risk his life for this bounty. No, it was more than that. He was willing to risk his life for Mack. For her. She looked down at the lit dynamite in her hands. The spark was almost out of chord, quickly eating up to her hand.

"Hey!" she screamed at the boar. The beast turned wildly, foaming at the mouth and charged her.

Maria threw the dynamite as hard as she could, and the boar chomped on it the moment it touched its tongue.

She felt the heat first and then felt something like a train smash into her chest. The explosion blew her off her feet into the mud a few feet away. She heard the ringing in her ears again and struggled to stand up this time. She felt a sharp pain in her chest, like a knife poking into her ribs. It was as if she were caught in a painful dream and tried to wake herself from it. She saw Mack's face in the bright light, blinding her. She felt a strong grip and picked her up from the mud. It took her a moment to focus her eyes on Anton's grimy face.

"You did good. You did *very* good," Anton said with a few grunts.

Maria looked just past him at a pile of gore and fur. The head of the boar had been blown clean off, and bits of bone and meat had been scattered on the swamp floor.

"Good job with the repositioning," said Mack, climbing over the fallen tree branch. "At first, I thought you were abandoning us, but when the boar chased after you, I saw your plan. It was a good one. Very impressive for your first championship."

Anton walked to the pile of ground meat and knelt before it. He picked something up from the carnage and walked back to Mack and Maria.

He looked like he was about to say something when the crackle of gunfire erupted not too far away.

"This should stop the fighting," said Mack. He pulled out a flare gun from his belt, pointed it to the skies, and pulled the trigger. The red flare flashed up into the darkening clouds, marking the end of the challenge. Anton held something out to Maria. She stared at it in shock. It was a boar tusk with charred marks on the end.

"You're giving this to me?" asked Maria.

"You earned it," said Anton. "When you see Dusty Rose, you hold this out to her."

The gunfire ceased in the distance, and Maria, Anton, and Mack emerged from the swamps. They saw hunters to their far left and far right emerge, too. A few of them were wounded, being carried by their compatriots. One person screamed.

"You bastard! You killed him. You killed him in cold blood!" It was a young man, very likely his first championship as well. He was aiming his pistol at two hunters not too far from Maria. He pulled the trigger, and the hunters yelled out, ducking for cover.

Suddenly, a *zing* hit the young hunter in the head, blowing chunks of bone and brain matter onto the field. His body collapsed in a heap on the ground. His partner looked on and shook his head as he held his shoulder and left his buddy in the mud.

"Dumbass. He should have known better than to fire his gun after the challenge has ended," snapped Mack. "We're protected now."

Maria looked over to the shooter and saw Dusty Rose holding a smoking Sparks rifle with a long scope attached on it. She wore circular spectacles that rested low on her nose. She then loaded another round into the chamber and held the rifle at her hip. Maria shuddered. These hunters weren't messing around. The crowd from Glen Rio had gathered around to see the victors.

When they reached Dusty Rose, a few of the hunters embraced, and others shook their hands with respect.

"Good job," said one to another. Maria found this interaction strange as just a few moments ago, these men were shooting at each other with intent to kill. Dusty set the butt of her rifle to the ground and pulled out a cigarette from her coat pocket. She lit the end with a lighter and inhaled deeply. "Who shot the flare?"

"We did," said Anton. "Maria?"

She moved from behind Anton and held the broken tusk in her hand.

"Huh," grunted Dusty. "Less than two hours. Shame. I would have thought my pet would last longer. Looks like we have a winner!"

The growing crowd behind them cheered, and one person grabbed Maria's hand and shot it up in the air.

"Well done," said a hunter she didn't recognize.

"This belongs to you, kid," said Dusty, holding a wooden coin with the initials DR. "This is your second token, and with it, you can redeem the $1000 from the Rose Manor or keep the token for yourself, should you choose to. Those coins are more valuable than gold in these parts."

Maria took the coin but then saw a shadow behind Dusty. The man had silver eyes and red flowing hair affixed to a grim look on his face. His hand rested threateningly on his revolver. The face belonged to the unmistakably infamous man known as E. Gray.

"A*y mierda*," gasped Maria.

"Oh mierdha, indeed," said Dusty with a coy smile. "I believe you have something of Mr. Gray's."

Maria dug into her pocket and pulled out a small wooden coin very similar to the one she held in her other hand. The hunter snatched the coin away.

"That tusk would have been mine," growled E. Gray, turning to Dusty. "I demand retribution."

Dusty paused for a moment, thumbing the trigger guard of her rifle. "You lost your token. Your disrespect to our hallowed customs rests solely upon your head," she said.

"I would have beaten each and every one of you," he said with a nasty growl, eyeing each of the hunters in the eye. "You would all be dead meat."

"Doubt it," grunted Anton. He stepped before Maria.

"She is one of yours now?" growled E. Gray. "Huh, Bullet-tooth?"

"Looks that way," said Mack, tilting his head and throwing his arm over her shoulders. "Whatever the case may be, you can't harm her right now. Anyone carrying a coin such as this one during the championship is protected by the Rose Estate. You shoot her while no challenge is active, and you risk painting a target on yourself. Trust me, we don't miss easily."

"I know the rules, dammit," spat E. Gray, then glaring holes into Maria. "Just watch yourself, kid. You may be protected now, but I'll be gunning for you tomorrow. Just you wait."

He turned his back and melted away into the crowd of cheering faces.

"Holy hell," said Maria. "I thought I was *carne molida*."

"You still might be. *That's* a hunter you don't want to mess with," said Anton.

The crowd began to break apart, and Maria saw a man with a star-badge pinned on his chest walk before her with thumbs tucked into his bullet-belt. "You there! Don't move," barked the sheriff, keeping his thumbs in his belt. He spoke with such bravado that Maria felt his arrogance ooze in his stance of power. Yet, perhaps the sheriff knew that. The silver star at his breast gave him immunity, and he knew it. "I had a hunch you Quintana bastards would show up before long. It was only a matter of time."

Maria bit her lip and clutched the bounty token to her side. Dusty Rose moved in front of her and took a long drag of her cigarette, staring needles into the sheriff. He was young, and green, very green. She then let the smoke leave her nostrils with a sour smile.

"Who the hell are you?" she asked. "I don't remember calling for a sheriff's office. As a matter of fact, have we ever needed a sheriff in Glen Rio?"

A few of the bounty hunters laughed out loud, but others stared at the law with seemingly itchy trigger fingers. Maria herself turned sideways with one hand on the butt of her revolver.

"Don't you think about it. I am here on the authority of Commissioner Skinner. Where is Felix Quintana?" asked the man representing the law. He took his thumbs out of his belt, his confidence waning like night fog on a sunny Sunday morning. "My name is Sheriff Erik Matthews, and I'm placing you under arrest for the murder of Sheriff

Hardy and so much more. Now tell me, where are the others hiding? I know they're in Glen Rio somewhere."

"I don't think that's gonna happen, Sheriff," Dusty smiled, allowing smoke to rise from the edges of her mouth. She held her rifle on her hip and puffed her cigarette in her hand. "Half my hunters have warrants out for their arrest, and the other have court orders to hang. What kind of championship would it be if your kind simply waited for the season of the hunt to pick us up? I don't recognize your name or your face, so I will forgive your stupidity. I am permitted under Texican law to hold this championship, and as such, any carrier of a bounty token holds immunity from said law until the time the Bullet-Catcher Championship has found its victor and concluded."

The young sheriff glanced at his sides as the hunters closed in around him, his confidence now fully deflated. He knew there was no chance by himself.

"Looks like your luck hasn't run out," Erik said, glaring at Maria. "I'll be here when it does."

With that, he turned and left as hunters drew their guns and shot in the air, whooping wildly.

"And now, to declare our newest champion!" Dusty took a long drag, then flicked her cigarette into the dirt and stamped it out with the toe of her boot. "What's your name, girl?"

"It's Darien Ja—." It struck her that she didn't need to hide her identity anymore. The feds knew what she looked like and where to find her.

"What was that?"

"Maria Montenegro," she said.

"Give it up for Miss Montenegro!" said Dusty, grabbing her wrist and bringing it up into the sky. Hunters continued their shooting, and Anton put a hand on her shoulder. "You did good, Twenty-two."

"What happens now?" she asked.

Mack let out a whoop. "Now, we drink!"

Percy from Sweeney General generously gifted Dusty Rose and her bounty hunters three casks full of beer. Upon arrival, he even slammed the pegs in himself, much to the already vacuous cheer of the hunters. Maria's mug was constantly being filled by hunters, known and unknown, patting her back and congratulating her. On the other hand, a few in the saloon weren't so friendly. In fact, a handful of them sat at tables in the corners of the saloon, their unwavering eyes staring holes into her. A few of them had bandages around their heads or arms. Normally, she would never drink beer in a place where others she had exchanged lead with were drinking. It was such a quaint feeling.

She had heard that at least three had gone to Doc Jennings for emergency care. Nine were dead. She thought of Felix and Lu. She would have to see them tonight if given the opportunity. Now that she had immunity from the feds and E. Gray wasn't on her tail just yet, she could walk freely through the streets of Glen Rio.

"Hey, Twenty-two! Is it true you killed Sheriff Hardy?" asked Mack as he sat down at the table beside her with three mugs of beer. Anton sat across him and grabbed a mug, almost downing all of it in one drag.

"No," said Maria. She took a mug in one hand and quenched her thirst.

"When did you become a part of the Quintana gang?"

"Enough with the questions, Mack. If she wants to tell us, she will. Leave her alone," said Anton.

"When I was in the swamp, and that boar nearly killed me," began Maria, wiping foam off her upper lip. She paused for a moment, trying to find the words to put her fears in. She could have imagined the whole thing. After a while, she shook her head. She knew what she had seen. She had to tell them. "I saw a half-man, half-gator. It emerged from the swamp and screamed at me. I'm pretty sure it wanted to kill me."

She winced, expecting both Anton and Mack to burst into laughter. Their silence was unexpected, and when she looked into their faces, she saw they were solemn. Even Mack had turned a little pale.

"I've heard rumors of this crocodilian," said Anton. "I thought it was just that, a rumor."

"What the hell was that thing?" asked Maria.

"Dusty's new pet or bodyguard or something," said Mack. "Whatever it is, that thing listens to her and only her. It does her dirty work, as far as I know. I even heard Dusty goes out with that thing looking for bounties. Instead of shooting the targets, she lets the gator man eat them alive."

Maria shivered but was relieved at the same time.

"Dusty must have found out about you just after the championship began. If you hadn't won, the croc might have claimed you for dinner," said Anton.

That did not make her feel any better. She had been lucky; that much was true.

"I have to go," she said, tipping the last of her beer into her mouth.

"What? We just sat down!" protested Mack.

"I know, but I need rest. I'll see you boys on the east wing." She tipped her hat and left the Silver Bullet Saloon.

Maria stuck to the sides of the dirt road, careful to keep out of the rising moon's light. A few people walked the streets, but she didn't make eye contact. It was better to keep a low profile now that the feds knew who she was.

"Mar?"

The question came in the form of a whisper. Maria stood still and turned her head to see a shadow crouched in an alleyway. The shadow stood up, and she saw the shotgun barrel and squared shoulders.

"Felix."

"I wondered how long it would take for you to come find me. I hear your name come from the strangest places—well, that's not true. I hear your name everywhere. Maria Montenegro: champion of the first day of the Bullet-Catcher Championship," said Felix, emerging from the darkness into the pale moonlight. Maria could see the dark circles beneath his eyes. His cheeks were sunken in, and she could tell he hadn't really rested since their arrival. How could he?

Felix grabbed her shoulders and squeezed hard. "I could go for a warm meal right now. Maybe even a beer. Hmmm."

He sniffed her. "You smell like beer. How must it feel, Mar? Running from the law yet somehow galivanting through the street as if nothing at all is the matter, as if we aren't being hunted by the feds."

"I got immunity. As a participant—," began Maria.

"I don't give a damn. If anything, I feel you may have cut a deal with them. Are you the filthy rat, Maria?" growled Felix. He began to squeeze into her shoulders, causing her to wince. Maria began to whimper, and tears collected in her eyes.

"No, I would never do that. Listen to me, Felix, please. The Quintana is like a family to me. You took me in when I was starving and homeless. I would never turn my back on you. Listen, the grand prize of the Bullet-Catcher is $10,000 in addition to a mysterious prize! The first day gives $1000 dollars. I have the money in my pocket. I was just coming to give it to you."

When she mentioned the monetary amount, Felix instantly looked over her shoulder and relaxed his grip. "You have one-thousand, you say?"

"If I win, we could be set up for life. We would never have to fear anyone."

A sudden movement behind Felix startled Maria. A frail-looking woman in a brown cloak emerged and held a walking stick as she stumbled forward. "I knew our dear Mar would never betray us."

"Lu," gasped Maria. "*Dios mio,* I was afraid you wouldn't make it."

Lu struggled to stand up straight and drew the hood back from her head to reveal the right side of her face shredded to pieces. Her right eye socket was empty, and her nose and lips were pulled back. There were still bandages on her face that were soaked with blood, but at the very least, she was still standing. She was still alive.

"That concertina bomb really did a number on me, but I am still here," she said, gritting her teeth. The pain must have been immense, yet she stood tall, resisting the urge to buckle.

"Ren and Mateo?" asked Maria.

"Mateo got picked up, and he's being held in the town prison. He is keeping his mouth shut, that is for sure, or else we would have already been picked up. I cannot find Ren for the life of me. Either he is well hidden, or the feds already killed him," whispered Lu. It was clear she struggled to even draw breath, let alone speak.

"I'll find them," said Maria, wrestling herself from his grasp. She turned her backs to them and walked in the direction of the jail. After a few feet, she risked a glance behind her. Felix and Lu had disappeared as if they were ghosts. She shuddered and rubbed her shoulders. There would be marks on her arm for a while.

Maria took care to avoid the shadows of people milling about in the night and made her way to the prison.

The jail rested on the eastern end of Glen Rio, over-looking the Castor River that ran all the way around the town. It had originally earned itself that name due to the number of beaver dams that plagued the river during the town's founding. After a while, hunters came and exterminated all the beavers and broke their dams, yet the river retained its name. That particular area of the river that the jail rested near was dubbed the *Boca del Diablo*. This was because the jail was built on a steep hill, almost a cliff, and there was a thirty-foot drop onto the shallowest end of the river, where at the bottom were sharp rocks, almost like staves. A few escapees had tried their luck with a daring jump into the waters, only to smash their skulls or get impaled when they hit the dark waters. Felix had told Maria that story once, as he had been a prisoner for a few months in those very cells.

The prison was a white-washed brick building with six small rectangular cuts and two iron bars that served as windows near the roof. Every other window was a cell, and Maria knew that Mateo would be housed in one of them. She crept closer to the back of the prison and heard voices at the entrance. She wondered if it was one of the feds who was standing guard. Music from a gramophone played a soft tune, but she didn't recognize the song. Either way, it would be enough for her to see if Mateo was even alive at all.

Maria cupped her mouth to her lips and blew tenderly the sound of a dove. She then waited for a few moments, the rippling of the river echoing from far below.

"Renato, is that you?" came the hoarse whisper from within the cell.

"No, it's Maria."

"*Gracias a Dios*, You're alive. I thought for sure they got you."

"Not yet," said Maria. "Felix sent me. He wanted me to make sure you're still alive."

"I am. They beat me pretty bad, but I-wait, someone's coming," said Mateo. Maria heard the rustling of feet and hushed voices from within the cell. Then, nothing.

"I'll be all right. I have a plan to escape in the morning."

"Can I do something to help?" whispered Maria.

"No, I've got it all figured out. Find Ren. He needs your help."

"What happened?"

"We hid in a barn, but the farmer found us and flushed us out with a shotgun. Then, Sheriff Erik Matthews came around and picked me up. I lost Ren in the chaos. Please, you have to find him. I promised his mother to take care of him."

"I'm on it," said Maria. No more came from within the cell, so she just assumed there was no more to say. She didn't think it was a good idea Mateo turned her down. He would need all the help he could get from within that cell.

She left as quietly as she could without alerting the feds. The moon shone brightly high in the sky over the dirt street of Glen Rio. Maria kept to the right side of the street as she walked. Suddenly, a lone shadow crept through the middle, and she stopped in her tracks.

A man in a long coat and wide-brimmed hat stood in the middle of the road, holding guns crossed to his breast. Despite the darkness, the dark red tint of hair gave away his identity. Maria stared at him, and her hand wandered to the piece at her hip. Though Maria couldn't see his face, she knew it was E. Gray.

"Think very carefully about what you do next. I would hate to kill you here in the street like a dog all alone. No one is here to watch you die," said the man. She let her hand away from her revolver.

"Why are you in my way?" she said.

"You Mexican trash should never have come here. I have made it my personal duty to shoot every one of you," said E. Gray, putting one hand on his hip opposite his revolver and the other flicking the top of his hat back. Maria could see the sparkle of his black eyes. "Yet, there is one thing I hate more than a wetback, and that is a rat. I can't stand traitors and story corroborators. I've come to make a deal with you."

"What the hell are you talking about? I'm no rat," said Maria through clenched teeth. "Regardless, I would never make a deal with you. A racist, cruel man such as you deserves to lay six feet under."

"That may be true, but I also know you and your gang need me. You have guts, I'll give you that, but I know if you don't accept my help, you won't take one step outside of Glen Rio alive. You'll be buried on Cactus Hill along with the other nine new white crosses that have been placed there."

"Why do you give a rat's ass?"

"Because the rat is Dusty Rose. She isn't who you think she is. The legends are true: she made a deal with the Devil, and soon, we will all be sacrifices to her. Anyone holding a wooden token of hers has lost their soul."

"What?" asked Maria, sweat beading on her brow.

E. Gray nodded. "Unfortunately for you, you thought that coin might be your saving grace. It was your curse."

"How do you know that?"

"Because I have seen it. She is the shadow hiding behind it all. You would do well to distrust her."

"*Porque chingados* do you give a damn for? If she *is* behind it all, it changes nothing for me. The moment I finish the championship, we're gone."

"You are so far in over your head, it's disgusting," said E. Gray. With that, he turned, touching the tip of his hat, and he melted into the gathering darkness. "If you change your mind, once this is all over, I could use you to take her down. All I'm doing is just giving a sportsmanship tip; just sleep in tomorrow and don't show up. Don't get me wrong, I still want to kill you. Thing is, you are actually quite low on the list of people I want to feed hot slugs. It's just the way the butterscotch cookie crumbles."

E. Gray's words carried a menacing low growl, and even his shadow faded out of sight. The light of the moon faded behind a clump of clouds, and the threat of thunder rumbled not too far away.

Rain had begun to fall steadily by the time Maria reached the farmstead Mateo mentioned he and Ren had stayed the night before. It was a small farm with a granary and a mill placed beside a wooden half-home that had smoke coming from the chimney. A yellow light poured onto the dirt road from a scuffed window. She walked up to the window and set her hand on her revolver in her pants, ready to draw. Peeking through, she saw an old man with an eye patch eating soup with a shotgun resting on the table. She imagined it was probably the safer thing to do with so many bounty hunters roaming Glen Rio. Then, she realized the shotgun wasn't just any shotgun. It had the letters *RG* scratched into the metal of the barrel. Maria knew they stood for Renato Guerra, or since she'd known him the day they met in a seedy tavern on the Texican border, Ren. She didn't see him anywhere in the half-home, but then, as rain pattered softly on the brim of her hat, she heard a sound that made shivers run up and down her spine.

A chorus of raspy squeals broke through the sounds of rain like sharp thunder accompanied by a stench of something rotten, and Maria turned her head slowly to see a fenced-in pigsty. She saw the outline of four pigs milling about in the mud with horrendous snorts. Then, just as she was about to take a closer look, lightning flashed through the skies, and she saw a pair of boots sitting by a fence post. One of them still had half a leg sticking out, exposing the sharp end of bone wrapped in torn sinew. Maria gasped and put her hands to her mouth, unable to even speak as thunder rumbled like the beating of a thousand drums. She had found Ren after all.

Forcing her feet to move, she left the small farmstead and walked back to Rose Manor in shocked silence. She didn't even realize she was standing in the east wing staring at her door with a plaque and the black number 22 on it.

"Rough night?"

The voice startled Maria, and she turned to see Mack and Anton sitting in the lounge. She had walked past them without even noticing they were there. Anton cleaned a dismantled shotgun on the center table, wiping down the stock with a dirty rag. Mack studied her above thin wire spectacles low on his nose while holding a wrinkled newspaper on his lap. She realized tears were running down her cheeks, and she wiped them hurriedly. She pushed her door open and slammed it shut behind her without a word.

"It appears the answer is yes," said Mack, ruffling the newspaper and peering through his spectacles.

"She just lost her friend," came a voice that made Mack jump.

"Jesus Christ, Laura. Do you need to sneak up on us?" snapped Mack. Laura appeared from the hall and leaned on the doorframe, running her hand over her swollen belly.

"Us?" asked Anton.

"Oh, right. I forgot you got the brooding dark hunter nailed to a T," said Mack.

"I feel bad for her. She was dealt a rough hand," said Laura. "Wouldn't she be better off with us when this is all over? We could use a hunter like her."

"She did good today, but tomorrow may prove different," said Anton.

"What? Laura, do you know something we don't?" asked Mack.

"All I know is that the next challenge is in the Aqueducts. Be sure to keep your boots dry," she said, then disappeared back into the hall.

Anton grunted, and Mack shook his head. "How does she find these things out?"

"I dunno. Why not ask her? Everyone knows you have the hots for her," Anton grinned.

"I do *not!*" said Mack, but his cheeks flushed, clearly indicating his lie. "She would never want someone like me anyway. Ever since she escaped the fire in Mesa Frio, she's been different."

"You knew her as a . . .?" asked Anton.

"A whore? No, not like that. Though I did see her from time to time when I visited the town, I never had the balls to speak to her. Now that she's one of us, my tongue gets even more twisted."

"You miss every shot you don't take," shrugged Anton.

"Okay, Mr. Fortune Cookie. Why don't you talk to Twenty-two, then? I see you have the *hots* for her, too."

Now it was Anton's turn to flush, but he kept his tongue for a minute. He began to reassemble his shotgun and click it back into place. He let out a sigh when he had finished and looked at his partner. "She reminds me of my daughter, such spirit, such unwillingness to give in to fear. She was around Maria's age when she died."

"I didn't know. I'm sorry," said Mack.

"Nothing to be sorry for. The men who killed her have been rotting on the Zappalachian Mountain range for the better part of six years," said Anton. "C'mon, jackass, you need to get some rest too."

"Maria, wake up. Maria, you have to get up now."

She sprung up from her bed with a revolver in hand aimed squarely at Mack's chest. He looked down and then raised both hands to his sides. Maria gasped and lowered her gun, putting the hammer back with her thumb. She realized her shirt had come off during the night. She grabbed her coat and pulled it over her naked self. "*Que haces, hijo de puta?*"

"I don't know what that means. I didn't mean to startle you, but there is something you should see."

Maria dragged herself from the bed, shoved her arms into a white shirt, and buttoned it in the center. She grabbed her gun belt, but Mack shook his head.

"You shouldn't bring that now."

"What? Why?"

"Please, just follow me," said Mack. Maria grunted and then buckled her gun belt to her waist anyway. There was no way in hell she was leaving without her iron. She realized not much time must have passed since she tried to get some rest. The sun was nowhere close to rising. Maria realized she left her hat on the nightstand, but she thought better of going back. Whatever Mack wanted to show her, it must be urgent.

They left the Rose Manor estate, and Mack didn't say a word to her. He seemed on edge for some reason as he walked, his shoulders tense. Maria didn't have to know. If there was to be a shoot-out between her and the feds, she was ready. They entered Glen Rio proper, and Maria saw a crowd of people gathered in the town square under the watchful marble eye of the Native American female statue in the square. What Maria saw just a few feet in front of the statue made the warmth in her veins turn to ice.

A wooden gallows had been crudely built before the statue. What was so shocking wasn't the gallows themselves but the man hanging from it. Maria pushed her way through the crowd and saw Sheriff Erik Matthews standing beside the hanging man, holding a shotgun in his arms. He chewed on a burnt-out cigar, and as soon as his eyes locked with Maria's, he let out a cruel smile.

"Damn. I thought you'd get here sooner," he said. "You missed the best part."

She now stood at the foot of the gallows and looked up at the mangled body of Felix Quintana. He had been hanging for at least an hour at this point. His face had gone completely blue, and his eyes were red and bulging from his eye sockets. His shirt had been torn, and his boots were missing.

"No," whispered Maria. Her legs began to buckle, and her eyes flooded when an arm reached over and grabbed her shoulder. She looked up to see Anton on her right, holding her up. Mack stood on her other side with a deadly stare. Maria didn't know what it was, but standing beside the two legendary hunters filled her with a strange sense of strength. She wiped the tears away and stared up at the mangled body of her gang leader. Erik Matthews fell to one knee on the platform and, leaning on his shotgun, glared at her.

"In two days, you'll be hanging here beside Felix. Once the Bullet-Catcher ends, your ass is grass," said the young sheriff. Maria wanted to say something, but Anton moved her away from him.

"Let him speak his words. They mean nothing," he growled.

Maria allowed herself to be moved, and Mack and Anton made a path for her to leave. She caught a glance of a figure standing not too far away beneath the shadow of an awning and recognized the outline of the gunslinger E. Gray. He puffed a cigarette, and his eyes sparkled in the light of the falling embers, but he wasn't looking at her. He stared directly past her. Maria followed his gaze and saw a woman standing just a few feet behind the gallows. She had an eye patch and her left arm in a sling beneath a red shawl.

It was Dusty Rose.

Just a few hours later, a revolver sang in the distance, marking the beginning of the second day of the

Bullet-Catcher Championship. This time, the hunters weren't gathered for the start of the day, but instead, each group was assigned to an opening that led into a series of caves beneath Glen Rio, simply known as the Aqueducts.

"Today's challenge requires us to find an Incan necklace made of gold," said Mack. "Should be easy, right? The only question I have is where the hell did she get an Incan necklace?"

Maria didn't answer as she brought the edge of her hat up off her face. She was still very much shaken from seeing Felix hanging by the neck from a rope just a few hours earlier. In a lot of ways, he had been the closest thing to a father. She was still unable to believe he was gone.

She had tried to find Lu after that, but she was nowhere to be found. She worried her fate had concluded just like Ren's had. She learned that Mateo had indeed broken out, but his whereabouts were unknown as well. As far as she knew, she was the last one left of the Quintana Gang.

Anton regarded her in silence as he cracked the barrel of his shotgun open and slid a yellow slug, then snapping it back, pulling the hammer back with his thumb.

Maria pulled her revolver from her hip and slung the drum open to make sure it was loaded. She was running low on ammo and would need to see a bulletsmith before too long.

The moment they entered the aqueduct, all light, what little there was out in the darkened cloudy morning, melted into pitch-black. With the strike of a match, Mack lit a small lamp, closed the glass opening, and clipped it onto his belt. Maria knew they had to be very careful when it came to light. It could be a death sentence.

"Oh, I know that look," said Mack. "Bounty hunters should be the last of your worries down here."

As if on cue, Maria heard the furious flapping of tiny wings around her and had to bite her tongue not to scream.

Bats.

Suddenly, she felt a sharp bite on her shoulder, but when she swatted at it, the thing was gone. She felt a trickle of warm blood on her shoulder.

"Stay in front of Mack," grunted Anton. "They won't bother you in the light."

Maria made sure she stayed in the rays of his lamp as Anton threw on a heavy bear skin over his back. As it seemed, the bats wouldn't be able to chew through such thick hair and skin. They made their way deeper and deeper into the cavernous Aqueducts, and Maria heard trickling water all around her. After a while, she could no longer hear the flapping of bat wings, but now the darkness was so thick around them that the light from Mack's small lantern could barely cut through the shadows. A strange black mist enveloped them the farther they went.

"Where is this thing supposed to be?" asked Maria after a while. Exhaustion was starting to take hold of her bones, and she was ready for the end of the championship. Erik Matthews would be on her tail as soon as it ended. She would have another fight in store for her if she was unlucky. She supposed it would be even more unlucky if she lost.

Suddenly, Anton stopped in his tracks, and he held his hand out for Maria to stop.

"Someone has been here," he whispered.

"How do you know?" asked Mack, peering over his shoulder.

"See that water there?" asked Anton, pointing to a puddle.

"Yeah that's just mud, ole pal."

"Now, look over there," he said, pointing to a different puddle. "The water is clear, and the mud, undisturbed."

That must have been enough for Mack, for he cocked his rifle as quietly as he could. Suddenly, the ground beneath them began to move, shaking droplets of water from the stalactites above.

"Since when the hell does Glen Rio have earthquakes?" whispered Mack.

Anton stared at the puddles that were now all muddied. "Huh, I guess I was wrong."

The moment those words left his mouth, they heard that telltale hiss of an explosive being lit. Maria saw a flash and heard a loud bang that caused her ears to ring. Unable to see or hear, Maria felt something crash into her back and drive her to the cold, wet ground. She heard a *pop-pop-pop* in the distance, but as her vision and hearing began to return, the popping noise became much clearer and much closer.

"Stay down. Don't look up!"

Maria realized Mack was lying on top of her. He must have crashed into her the moment the flash grenade went off. Droplets from stalactites splashed water in her face, but then she saw they weren't drops of water from above but bullets skipping off the rock floor. Maria dared look up.

A man in a wheelchair fired his miniguns at them in a constant spray of lead, pinning them down. Bullets flicked overhead, and then, suddenly, they stopped. All that could be heard was the rotating barrels of the dry gun.

"Wait," said the man fiddling with a gun belt to reload, but he clearly was having problems. "Just stay right there for a moment. Don't move, ya?"

"Clifton? Is that you?" Anton called out.

"How many other paraplegics do you know that have damn miniguns attached to their wheelchairs? Of course, it's me!"

"He's got you there," whispered Mack as he got up and helped Maria to her feet behind a large boulder.

"Where's Horace and Ira?" Anton called out.

"Them bastards got shot up yesterday. Horace is at Doc Jennings, and Ira's dead. Anton, is that you?"

"Yeah."

"Well, come on out, you big dumb bastard. I got something for ya."

"You don't have any ammo left, you're out."

A round flicked overhead, making Anton flinch.

"You sure about that? I've still got a few tricks up my sleeve."

"He's always had a temper about him," said Mack to her.

"It doesn't have to be this way. I would hate to have to kill you," Anton called out.

"I need this. No way I'm going home empty-handed."

"We all need this, genius. That's why we're here," said Mack.

"Mack? You shut your mouth. Adults are speaking."

Mack grinned and shook his head.

Then, they heard a crisp *click*. "HA!"

A hail of bullets crashed over them in a second torrential downpour of gunfire. Chips of stone flicked over Maria and Mack, falling like molten stone flakes. Suddenly, the earth beneath them rocked, and the sound of crushing boulders echoed in the deep caverns of the aqueduct. Maria screamed as a stalactite smashed into the rocks directly beside her.

"Watch out," cried Mack a little too late. He tried to cover her, but she pushed him off. The shaking stopped, but the gunfire did not. Then, she dared peek her head around the boulder that was their shield.

Mack pulled her back.

"What the hell are you doing?" asked Mack.

"Shut up and don't touch me," she pushed him back.

"You'll get yourself shot!" he protested.

Maria drew her revolver and pulled the hammer back. She pointed the gun at him. "Don't make me shoot you, Mack. Stay put."

He held his hands up, a sullen look adorning his face. Gunfire flicked overhead. Maria took her hat off and peeked around the boulder again. She saw Clifton holding triggers of his machine guns, his grinning face, and burnt-red beard illuminated by muzzle flashes. His modified wheelchair was locked in place just beneath a loose stalactite, the sharp end rocking dangerously a few feet above Clifton.

Maria took aim at the rock and fired her revolver. The bullet smashed into the rock, and it fell, but much to Maria's dismay, the pointy end turned, and the heavy part slammed into Clifton's bald head. With a heavy grunt, he slumped back into his chair as the machine guns went silent and the smoking barrels ceased to rotate. All that could be heard was the droplets of moisture falling onto the smoking super-heated barrels with a hiss. Mack, Anton, and Maria emerged from their cover, weapons trained on the deadly paraplegic.

Maria raised her arm and leveled the revolver at Clifton's head, but Anton put his hand over the barrel and pushed it down slowly. He shook his head.

"Why not? He wanted to kill us," protested Maria.

"Maybe so," said Anton. He pulled a coil of string from his belt and began to tie the unconscious Clifton up. Then, when he was secured, he began to come to.

"Ah, hell," spat Clifton, trying to fight his restraints. Anton unhinged the machine guns from the sides of his wheelchair and let them down at his feet. "I guess this is it then."

"No, it ain't," said Anton, then stepping back and crossing his arms over his chest. "I know you've been deeper."

"How's that?" asked Clifton.

"The mud on your wheels," said Mack. "They have fluorescent algae only found at the basin."

"So, you've been to the Deep?"

"Once, a long time ago," grunted Anton. He stared holes into Clifton as he wiggled in his seat. "We were after E. Gray and *'El Cabrón'* for Scrapper bounty money they stole from us."

"Huh, shame what happened to Amador."

"That wasn't us."

"What happened?" asked Clifton.

"Well, they say he died in Salem to a ritual gone wrong, but that's a story for another time," said Anton. "Now, answer my question."

"So yeah, I've been down there today. Dusty sent me to check on the prize."

"There's something down there, ain't it? Dusty didn't just place you as the challenge, now did she?" asked Anton.

Clifton clenched his jaw and shook his head. Anton grunted and then grabbed him by the red beard and pulled him up against his restraints. He squealed, and his eyebrows flew up, looking into Anton's grim face. Maria realized she didn't ever want to have that stare in her face.

"I don't want to kill you, Clif. You and I have had our scrapes and been through our share of messes. Now, you're gonna tell me what's waiting for us down there."

"These things, I don't know what they are. I think they came from even deeper than anyone of us has ever been, from the earth's core. They are demons, they are. The Devil sent them."

Anton let go of Clifton, and he slumped back into his chair.

"The Devil didn't send them," said Anton. "You see, the Devil is our employer. Tell her next time Dusty sees me, she owes me for sparing you."

Clifton lifted his chin and gave a nasty grin. "They don't have a name, but they are countless. No one is going to win this thing. Dusty wants to start the Rose Hunters anew with everyone out—"

Suddenly, Maria heard a *zip* past her ear like the buzz of a bug or a mosquito. Anton's eyes widened, and it took him a few seconds to react. He clumsily grabbed his shotgun and swung back, but there was nothing but darkness behind them.

"Holy hell," said Mack. Anton and Maria turned to see Clifton smiling at them, but now a small red dot was placed in the middle of his forehead.

"Oh, Anton. Is that you? It's been a while. How've you been, old dog? Why are you looking at me like that?"

asked Clifton before his eyes rolled to the back of his head, and he slumped forward. A tiny trail of blood trickled from his forehead onto his lap.

Anton, Mack, and Maria ducked to their feet.

"*Hijo de—*. Where did that come from?" whispered Maria.

"I don't know. I didn't even hear the *pop*."

"Who the hell do we know who uses a silenced gun?" whispered Mack.

"*The Mosquito,*" grunted Anton.

"Joel Whitney," swore Mack, then turning to Anton. "Well, what do you wanna do about it?"

"Nothing. It's impossible to know where that shot came from."

"What if he shoots at us?" asked Maria.

"He won't. Clearly, whatever is down there, Dusty wants to remain a secret. She's willing to kill a Token Holder."

"You know, we can just leave. We aren't too deep into the Aqueducts," said Mack.

"That's what she wants, Mack. I don't know why this feels different, but something's off. Dusty is changing, like she knows something's gonna happen. I can feel it in my bones," said Anton.

"Is now the time to talk about this?" snapped Maria. "That mosquito is still out there."

"She's right," said Anton, suddenly standing up.

"What, you want to just walk out of cover?" asked Mack.

"Yeah. Let's find these demons," said Anton. "It's probably safe to do this." He flipped the lever on a small lantern clipped to his belt. The yellow light gave a soft, small glow to illuminate their footsteps. The three Rose Hunters walked away from Clifton's cold corpse. Maria took one last glance at his dead body and then followed Mack and Anton deeper into the aqueduct.

"Miners used to call this place El Pasillo Del Diablo, which, in Spanish means . . ." Mack paused as they walked and half-turned to Maria. "I guess I don't have to tell *you* what it stands for."

"No. You sure don't, *gringo.*"

"Anyway, they say the Devil emerged from hell in this place. For thousands of years, he roamed in these dark caverns, feeding off any creature or person unlucky enough to find its way into his grasp. For that time, he survived until one day, he met a child who had lost her way into the Aqueducts after a killer had murdered her father and grievously wounded her mother. The girl was afraid and cold, and the Devil saw the shadow of death following closely in his footsteps. Fortunate for the girl, Death and the Devil had been lovers at one time, and Death so did depart."

"Why do you speak differently when you tell a story?" asked Maria.

"You're *supposed* to speak differently when telling a story," snapped Mack. "Now, don't interrupt."

"The girl realized there was something very wrong with the thing she had encountered in the darkness of the abyss, but the Devil instead gave her a piece of raw rabbit. The girl recoiled in disgust as it had been a fresh kill but then pulled out a lighter from her dress. After a few minutes of scrounging up dried sticks from a nearby dead bush, the girl started a small fire by which she warmed herself and cooked the piece of meat. The Devil sat down beside her, and when the girl looked upon his countenance, she nearly lost her supper. The man wore a dirty black suit and tie, and his shirt was tattered and no longer white. His face was like a void where his mouth should be, and his eyes were alight like stars in the sky. The girl nearly turned tail and ran when the Devil held his hands up. 'I mean you no harm, girl. I only wish to escape this watery grave.'" Mack held his hands up to emphasize the character. Maria glanced at him and nodded to continue. "The girl said she didn't know how to get out. The Devil said he did."

"So why didn't he simply leave?" Maria asked.

"Because angels guard the entryway. Of course, the girl didn't understand this, but the Devil then pulled a small wooden coin from his pocket and held it up to the fire. The coin was of no note, and it was blank on both sides. 'This is worth more than gold,' said the devil. The girl took the coin. 'It's just wood,' she said. The Devil's face widened as he gave a cruel smile amid the void that was his face. The girl saw his serrated teeth and once again nearly turned tail to run. It was the soothing voice that halted her footsteps and calmed her beating heart. 'You want to live forever, kid?'"

Mack flashed a toothy grin. "The girl said 'Yes, of course.' The Devil replied. 'Then all you have to do is make a sacrifice of blood in my name every three years. Do this, and you will never die. You will be rich beyond your wildest dreams. You must spill blood in the swamps every year in my name. If you do not, you will lose everything you love. Help me escape these caves, and this token is yours.'"

"The girl took the token and held it in her hands like it was indeed gilded gold. 'Carve from this your initials and give this to anyone who might die for you.' Suddenly, the girl's eyes lit up as if it were the middle of the day despite being in the darkest part of the aqueduct, and she saw the path before her glow. She stood up and began to walk with the Devil close in tow. Little did the Devil know the Aqueducts were protected by a Circle of Midas placed there fifty years before by a group of Danish immigrants, and the moment he set foot in the sunlight, his soul was absorbed into a thousand tiny pieces that when they hit the ground, they turned into a thousand wooden tokens," said Mack as he fished the Rose token from his pocket and held it out in the scant light for Maria to see. She felt the token in her own pocket.

"Bull," grunted Anton.

"No, it's true," said Mack. "The girl took the tokens, and on her way into the then small town of Glen Rio, she stumbled upon a robbery gone wrong. Banditos had ransacked a carriage, taken all the valuables, and killed the owner, an old crone. However, they must have gone blind, for the old crone had died arched over a wooden box that they did not steal. Curiosity overcame the girl, and she pulled the body off. Then, opening the lid, she nearly lost the tokens in her hand. In the wooden box lay golden coins full up to the brim. The girl looked around, but there was no one to contest her find. She came upon a discarded sack within the destroyed carriage, and she set her tokens in and dragged the crate of gold away."

That must have been the end of the story, for Mack went silent suddenly. Maria only heard the trickling of condensation from the ceiling of the cavern.

"Those tokens the Devil turned into, are they the same . . .?" Maria twiddled her wooden token in her fingers.

"Yup. Or so the stories say. The girl's name was Dusty, and she took on the name Rose. They say her luck skyrocketed. She's the one who single-handedly took Loya Manor and transformed it into Rose Manor. So, now you know the story behind the tokens and we Hunters of the Rose."

"Holy hell," gasped Maria.

"She didn't do it single-handedly," said Anton.

"Oh, and how would you know that?" asked Mack.

"I was there that night. Now, pipe down," snapped Anton suddenly as he knelt on the ground and touched the wet rock at his feet. "Something doesn't feel right."

Maria realized they had walked into an opening in the claustrophobic rock walkways. She knew this as a breeze blew against her coat, and she could see glowing minerals in the dark. Four crisp gunshots snapped her from the view and made her draw her weapon.

"Another team?" whispered Mack.

Another three shots rang out. "This sounds different."

Suddenly, a flare went up and painted a red glare on the ceiling, casting shadows against tall, wet rocks. Maria saw a group of six hunters firing their revolvers, but they weren't shooting at each other. They were firing at the ground.

The ground itself was moving around them. Maria blinked hard. No, it was worse, so much worse.

"What is that?" gasped Mack. A dozen beetle-like creatures with fluorescent green carapaces flooded their feet. One bug sprang up at a hunter with pincers poised and snapped his arm in half. The hunter fell and twisted in agony but did not get back up. The bugs tore through the flesh of his back and chewed into him as the hunter screamed his agonizing last. Green acid poured from their mouths, eating up his flesh, and in a matter of quick moments, six hunters were downed, and their screams could no longer be heard echoing in the caverns. It was just the cursed clicking of pincers.

Anton turned with a look Maria would never have thought to see adorned on his face, pure terror. "Run."

Maria heard the ticks of crawling bugs behind them. Anton broke into a steady jog on a rock pathway on the right that led away from the ravenous bugs. Maria and Mack did the same. At that very moment, they heard a piercing series of chirps like that of a dying bird and then nothing at all.

"Run!" screamed Anton. He rushed ahead, the light of the lantern on his belt nearly out of sight.

"Hurry!" shouted Mack behind her. She ran until she heard a noise that spurred her feet even faster. It was the sound of a thousand creepy crawlies scurrying to feast on her flesh. She could hear the snapping of their razor-sharp pincers clicking over and over. She dared look back and saw dozens of green carapaces closing in behind them.

Then, Anton stopped in his tracks. Maria nearly crashed into him and had to turn and brace Mack to prevent him from colliding with them and sending them over a massive chasm. They stood on a thin lip of rock overlooking a black nothing far below. There was no way to know how deep the bottom went. All three hunters turned in unison and aimed their weapons at the mass of flesh-eating bugs closing in.

Anton fired his slug shotgun, creating an explosion of bug juice, torn translucent wings, and broken pincers. He then let the smoking shotgun fall to the ground and whipped his rifle out. He hip-fired his rifle, each shot bursting bugs into puffs of florescent green. Mack drew his revolver and fanned his shots from the hip, each bullet creating a puff of green guts and shattered shells. Maria took her shots at the bugs closest to her feet, but there were countless others behind them. A machine gun would really come in handy now, wheelchair or no. All this happened in a matter of seconds, and her weapon ran dry. Maria stuffed her hand into her pocket and fished out four bullets.

"Just one bullet, goddamn it. I need just one more," said Mack, tossing his spent revolver at the bugs. He pulled his knife out and shouted at the bugs.

Maria glanced behind her to see the edge of the chasm. There was nowhere to run. They stood at the tip of the rock lip. Anton swore and threw his spent rifle at the bugs, pulled a flare gun from his breast pocket, and fired. The flare shot into the crowding insects, and Maria saw there was no ground behind them. There was a sea of insects swarming as far as the eye could see within the cavern, with glowing green acid dripping from their small yet countless teeth just behind their clicking razor-sharp pincers. She screamed and fumbled with the bullets in her hand. Her heart beat out of her chest, and she felt her thoughts a heavy blur. It was over, but her mind refused to believe it. She would die a bloody death to a bunch of bugs.

Suddenly, the ground beneath her feet shook, and this tremor was not like the previous ones. Rocks began to crash onto the ground like bombs, then smash into bugs, spurting mists of green into the air. Maria dared to hope but then heard a terrifying crack just beneath the soles of their feet. Rock gave way, and Maria fell alongside Anton and Mack.

She must have hit her head because the next thing she knew, she was lying on something soft. She felt something warm drip on her face, and she coughed softly before succumbing to the dark.

A light, though small, shone its bright glow into Maria's eyes. She shook her head and sat up quite suddenly. Her head throbbed with pain, and she struggled to focus her eyes. It was a miracle she was still breathing. She looked at what she landed in and clutched a clump of moss. Her eyes must have adjusted to the darkness because the thin light gave enough glow to see the entire ground like a bed of purple and white.

"Mack? Anton?" she called out softly. No answer. She touched her forehead and realized the warmth on her face was her own blood. She heard the faint trickle of a nearby stream and dared herself to stand. Her leg pulsed with a vice-like pain, but as far as she could tell, she could still walk.

Maria winced and called out once more. "Mack? Anton?"

"Twenty-two?" came the soft answer. Maria stumbled to follow the sound of his voice. She found Mack lying against a rock, bleeding from his head, holding his side. She gasped as she touched a bloodied stalactite that pierced his side. It had gone clean through. "Mack?"

"Don't worry, it seems to have stemmed the bleeding. For now, this thing is keeping me alive."

"I'll go get help," said Maria, but then she looked around and realized she had no clue how to get out. The feeling of frustration was beginning to close around her throat like a rope.

"I'm going to be all right. Anton, he's right there," said Mack, pointing to a shadow lying down just a few feet away. Maria stumbled to him.

He lay on his stomach, and when Maria tried to push him over, he wouldn't budge.

"*Madre de Dios,* why are you so heavy?" said Maria as she pulled his arm and rolled him onto his back with all her strength. He was breathing despite being unable to open his eyes. Anton was bloodied as well and had a deep cut from his cheekbone to his forehead. His shirt was torn, exposing his chiseled chest that was scissored with small bleeding cuts. She heard faint clicking of pincers echoing in the distance, but it was fading. She pulled a handful of bullets from her pocket and slid them into the drum one by one. She flicked her wrist, driving the drum home, then shoved it into her pants. It may not be much, but if the bug swarm charged again, she would be able to take a few out before they consumed her flesh. She glanced at Mack. The boys were in no shape to run any farther. She shoved the thought of leaving them from her mind if she got attacked. She would deal with that dilemma if it happened and not before.

Maria decided it was best not to move him further. There would be no way she could carry him out of the Aqueducts, of that she was certain. She returned to Mack, who let out a strained, wheezing cough as she approached.

"He's alive for now. I have to go get help," said Maria.

"We won," whispered Mack.

"What?"

He held a bloodied finger up and gestured over her shoulder. Maria turned to see what he was pointing to when she saw a piece of gold on a necklace hanging from a stalactite. The initials DR were engraved on the face, and she realized that was where the light was coming from.

"Go and take it. Make this all worth something."

Maria stood up uneasily and walked closer to the stream. Something wasn't right. There was no other sound besides the trickling of the creak. It was much too quiet after the earthquake, and she felt like someone was watching her. Maria knew better than to ignore that feeling. She also knew better than to reveal what she was feeling. Instead of making a beeline to the necklace dangling from the rock, she slowed her footsteps, keeping her eyes nailed to the prize, and straining her ears.

The stream made listening tricky, but then Maria heard the telltale *click* of a revolver being cocked. She drew her revolver with lightning speed. She knew she had precious split seconds to find the target. She saw a pointy hat and fired three shots in quick succession. A shadow moved away, but it wasn't her target. She had shot a stalactite.

Maria darted behind the rock carrying the bounty and dug her hand into her pocket, desperately digging for more bullets. It was empty. She had only one bullet left.

"You're resilient, kid. I'll give you that."

Maria knew that voice. E. Gray's words echoed in the cavern, clouding her from pinpointing his precise location. She dared to look around the boulder with revolver raised, trying her hardest to keep her heart from beating in her ears. Her breaths came in small gasps, and her eyes darted from shadow to shadow to no avail.

"But you're blind to the truth. You're so far in over your head. Dusty Rose and her hunters, what do you think that is all about, eh? The Bullet Catcher Championship? Is it all just for a golden necklace? Or maybe a couple of tokens carved from wood? Don't you think there's something deeper?"

A bullet whizzed through the air and exploded just a few inches from Maria's face. Bits of rock blew into her face, forcing her from behind cover. Maria ducked behind another large boulder, spitting flecks of stone from her mouth.

"Fish in a barrel, every one of you. It doesn't have to end this way, you know. You could come with me. I wouldn't hurt you."

Maria knew if she spoke back, she was dead. That was his whole trick. This also meant he had a bead on her and was toying with her. She had precious moments to react, or else she would be toast.

Then, she saw something glint by her boot. It was Mack's lens. There were a few cracks in it, but that gave Maria an idea. She picked the glass up and held it in her left hand. She only had one shot, so she had to make it count. She turned to face the large boulder and pulled the hammer of her revolver back in her right hand.

Maria took a deep breath, and in one motion, brought her left arm, holding the glass out from behind the rock. She heard a gunshot, and the glass shattered in her left hand, a searing heat singing the flesh of her fingers. In that same instant, she poked on the right side of the rock and saw the gun smoke trail telegraph E. Gray's location. She aimed and squeezed the trigger.

She heard the soft pop of heated metal searing through flesh and breaking bones, followed by a tumble of a body onto wet rock. She let out a heavy sigh, but it was not over. She walked from behind the rock and brushed the glass from her hands. Maria felt a jolt of pain surge through her hand. Where her ring finger had been was nothing but a bloody stump. The bullet had cleaved clean through her digit, and bits of glass were still stuck into her flesh. She brushed her hand off. It would be nearly impossible to find her missing finger in the darkness.

Maria heard struggling gasps and walked over to E. Gray's body. He tried to sit up, but she put her boot on his shoulder and forced him down, pointing her revolver at his head.

"That was a good trick. Didn't expect that from you," he grunted with a bloody smile. The bullet had penetrated his neck, and he was bleeding profusely.

"What did you mean when asking me all that about Dusty Rose?" asked Maria. "Who is she really?"

E. Gray tried to laugh, but it only came off in a spurt of blood. "She's the Devil incarnate."

"I don't believe that."

"You don't? Then you're not as smart as you look."

"Any last words?" asked Maria. "Or should I let you bleed out?"

"Don't trust her or anything she says. If you were smart, you would shoot her in between the eyes the next time you see her."

"If you hate her so much, why do you play her games?"

"I was planning to kill her if I won. Never forget, it's all about her. It's not too late to save ourselves. Take your bounty reward and live for another hunt," said E. Gray, and then, blood pooled in his mouth.

"Guess that's just the way your butterscotch cookie crumbles," said Maria. He smiled wide at her words and coughed one last time as his eyes opened and remained still. His body struggled for a few moments and then went completely still. Maria reached into his coat pocket and pulled out a wooden token, the same one she had found on the streets what seemed like an eternity ago. She thumbed the token in her hand and heard raspy breathing. Maria ran back to Mack's side.

"Damn, he walked right by me," grunted Mack. "If only I had a bullet—"

"It's okay, Mack. Wait here, I'll go get help, I promise."

"I believe you. Better hurry, though. I can hear those bugs coming back. Oh, you're bleeding."

Maria nodded, tearing a piece of her shirt off and wrapping her hand in it tightly. She ran to the bounty rock, snatching the necklace, and followed the stream. Then, to her relief, she turned a corner and felt the cool breeze of morning air. The sun had risen in the sky, and she could see the path leading to Glen Rio. She felt exhaustion grip her like a vice, but she pushed the feeling off. Mack and Anton needed her.

Then, she paused. Who were those guys to her anyway? She had only just met them a couple days ago. With Felix dead, there was no reason for her to go back into the town. Maria could steal a horse and never return to Glen Rio. She stood there for a few moments, weighing her options. Then, she thought of Mack. He had been a friend to her, unlike anyone else before. He risked his life for her for sake. He didn't want her body nor use her for any other reason than a teammate.

But it was more than that. Mack and Anton belonged to a crew she wanted to be a part of. She felt something she had never felt before, even with the Quintana Gang, a sense of belonging.

She kicked herself for the thought down the dirt road and found herself pushing the doors open to the small hospital in town. There were dozens of hunters lying on cots with bloody bandages and slings for both arms and legs.

"Are you burned?" came the voice from within another room. The doc emerged from the room wiping blood off her hands, the shadow of a hulk of a man not too far away.

"Burned?" asked Maria.

"Yeah. Those bugs that Dusty sent you poor bastards into. Why the hell the Aqueducts would be a good place for sportsmanship, I'll never know."

"No, the bugs didn't get me. Anton and Mack are badly hurt. I need help, now!"

"Oh, boy. Anton's in trouble again. Who would have thought," snorted the doc.

The shadow entered from the room, barely able to fit through the doorway. His arms were the size of Maria's waist, muscle-strewn, and barely able to be contained in his sleeves. His brown hair was cropped short, and he had a mustache that connected to his thick sideburns. His brown eyes sparkled as he looked into Maria's face.

"Where?"

"Near the base of the Aqueducts following the southern path.

"I know this place. Lead on."

"Don't we need a horse or mule to carry them? Anton is very heavy."

"For you," snorted the man. He pushed past her, nearly knocking her to her feet. Maria let out a sigh and ran beside the man, who rolled up his sleeves. He pulled a mean-looking serrated knife from his belt and held its blade back. Maria decided to run ahead of him down the dirt path.

Once more in the Aqueducts, she breathed in the noxious air of the waterways beneath Glen Rio. The man pulled a small lamp from his hip.

"Thank you for helping me."

"Name's Paul Finley. I work for Doc Jennings and Doc Jennings alone. I'm probably one of the few people in this town who isn't in Dusty's pocket, so don't think that you and I are friends."

"Then why are you helping me?"

"I owe Anton my life. Now, where are they?"

Maria led Paul onto a sprawling moss bed and found Anton lying right where she had left him. He was still breathing under his bear coat, and then Maria looked just a little farther to the shadow of Mack lying by the rock.

"I told you I'd be back," she said, but she was met by silence. Suddenly, she heard the fluttering of bug wings.

"C'mon, Mack, we gotta get out of here. Those bugs are coming back," she said. Paul shone a light in his direction, and Maria's heart leaped up into her throat. Mack's face had been partially chewed off, exposing bone and sinew.

A bug lay on his chest, flapping its translucent wings. A rage built up in Maria, and she grabbed a rock and threw it at the bug, landing just beside Mack. The bug fluttered its wings and began to fly when Maria drew her revolver and fired at it. The bug exploded into a dozen pieces and fell to the ground.

Maria ran to his side.

"Mack. No," she said, falling to her knees beside what was left of him. Tears welled up in her eyes, and she touched his shoulder. "I brought help just like I promised. I held my end of the deal."

Suddenly, the light vanished, and she turned to see Paul carrying Anton on his shoulder, leaving Maria in the dark.

"Wait! What are you doing? Help me get Mack up."

The giant of a man stopped and turned his head slightly. "He's dead. Nothin' I can do for him now."

"No. He's not dead. He needs Doc Jennings," said Maria. She tucked her arm beneath Mack's shoulder and lifted him up, but the rock impaling him wouldn't let go. "I won't leave him."

"Then join his fate," grunted Paul.

"Get back here, you bastard!" shouted Maria.

Paul paused, holding Anton in his arms. He turned to her with a sad look in his eyes. "Do you know what it takes to be a Hunter of the Rose? It means you are already dead; you just don't know when or where. Every hunter has accepted this fate. Mack knew this. So does Anton.

You need to get it through your head. This is the only way to break your fear. And if you can't break it, you must move onward, scared. Take a piece of him with you. Weep for him. Mourn him well. Your memory is the only thing that will keep him alive at his peak, or else he shall fade into the dark, nothing, where the worst death truly awaits," said Paul as he walked away.

Maria turned to Mack's body, who now was lying on his back, and something fell out of his coat pocket. She picked it up and realized she held a necklace with a tooth affixed in the center. Char marks on the end revealed it to be the same boar she had killed with dynamite the day before. She clutched it in her hand and stared at fresh blood on the edge in the fading light as Paul left the Aqueducts.

The darkened skies threatened rain despite the sun still shining through it in the mid-morning. Sunlight wasn't so blinding, yet Maria still had to squint as she left the Aqueducts. She glanced at the bone necklace in her wounded hand but then looked up at the sound of a horse whinny.

She found herself surrounded by a row of horsemen with badges. Erik Matthews sat atop his steed with a burned-out cigar in his lips. His oiled mustache twitched as he chewed on the end.

"Maria Montenegro, you are under arrest as an accomplice to the murder of Sheriff Hardy. You will hang by the neck until dead in Temple for your involvement and membership in the Felix Quintana Gang," he said coolly with relaxed shoulders. He wasn't even going for his piece. Maria eyed the men with a cold stare. Then, Erik spat his cigar out and kicked the side of his horse once. The horse obeyed his command and stepped to the side.

Luisa sat on a horse just a few feet away with a brown shawl over her head. At first, Maria's heart sank, but then she realized Lu had no cuffs on her wrists. A wave of confusion crashed over, and Erik began to laugh.

"I can see your thoughts. I gotta admit, hunting you would have been much harder without our dear Lu."

Her wounds seemed to be healing as fresh bandages had very minimal blood on them. Lu evaded Maria's gaze, staring at the ground in shame.

"Good. I wouldn't be able to look anyone in the eye if I were a rat either," growled Maria.

"That's enough," said Erik, urging his horse to break their line of sight. "You're coming with us."

"Not so fast," said Maria, digging into her pocket and pulling out a golden necklace. She held it out before them. The golden inlays caught the scant rays of sunlight and glowed as if they had just been pulled from a furnace. A few of the sheriffs couldn't help themselves not to gasp. "I'm the winner of the day's challenge. Take me to the

Rose Manor per your agreement. It wouldn't do to cross someone like Dusty Rose."

Her words must have struck a chord with Erik, for his eyes darted from his men to her as if asking them to help him somehow. Lu moved her horse beside him.

"You can't let her get away. She has to die today," snapped Lu.

Erik turned to her. "If you ever breathe in my direction again, I will shoot you. Don't forget, the reason you're still alive is because of the deal we had. You're still a rat. Don't you ever forget that."

Lu melted away, keeping her eyes on the dirt, covering her face with her shawl. Maria's blood boiled as she watched the traitor lead her horse to the back of the posse. Whatever happened next, Maria would be sure to make her death painful. She began to walk at them.

Erik tossed iron cuffs into the dirt before her. "Put them on."

Maria clenched her fists but knew there was very little she could do. She slapped them onto her wrists and spat on the ground. Erik moved his horse just enough to give her room to walk past. The posse followed close; the constant *clop-clop* of horses behind her echoed along the dirt path ominously. They stared needles at her back, and she knew they had pistols trained on her. Maria glanced back and saw Lu staring at her. When their eyes met, she turned away and blushed. She knew she was a filthy rat. Every breath Maria took in was a testament that she hadn't completely gotten away with it. Not yet.

The posse marched Maria through the streets of Glen Rio until she found herself at the foot of Rose Manor. Erik and his posse dismounted and followed her close behind, hands on their irons. Two men stayed behind with Lu, remaining on horseback. Maria pushed the door open and walked onto polished marble floors. She spread mud on the tiles and caught a dirty look from a housemaid, but when she saw the sheriffs behind her, she kept her tongue. Maria marched past her and down a corridor with glass cases separated by an even space of ten feet. Sealed within were pieces of cloth, necklaces, and even guns. Maria reached the end of the hallway just past a single glass case that was empty and was met by a soft yellow light shining beneath a door.

Before Maria reached the office, the door creaked open, and a woman in a tight navy-blue suit stood by the large door. Her hair was tied into a tight bun, and the skin on her face was scarred and pulled back into a weird half-smile. She stared at Maria and the men behind her as she walked into the office.

Sitting behind a desk beside a fireplace with a crackling fire was Dusty Rose, with elbows on the desk and hands folded before her mouth. Her hair was down to her shoulders, and she had both eyes closed as if she were praying. Maria realized she had never seen Dusty without her eyepatch, and when she opened her eyes, nearly everyone froze in their steps. The door creaked to a close behind them.

Her left eye was closed, with a nasty-looking scar running across it. Dusty reached beneath her desk, and with a heavy sigh, tied the eye patch over her eye. She leaned back in her chair and saw the bloody necklace Maria clutched in her hands. Her hand throbbed, and her amputated finger began to bleed through the tight cloth once more.

Maria tossed the blood-crusted necklace onto the table and stared at Dusty.

"I did it. I won," she said.

"So it seems. You are not the one I expected to win. In fact, I am shocked you are still alive."

Maria glared at her, but Dusty seemed unfazed. A figure Maria hadn't seen before stirred in a dark corner, and a low growl emerged. Erik and the men took a step back as two yellow eyes glowed, staring needles at them.

"What the hell is that?" squawked one of the sheriffs.

The shadow moved in the darkness and then broke into the firelight to reveal anything but a man. Its skin was a dark shade of green with scales like armor along the muscle-ridden arms that looked like they could lift an ox with little effort. It had a tail that rested heavily on the wooden floorboards and had sharp dagger-like claws on the ends of its fingers. If Maria had to describe the creature, it would be as a half-man, half-gator. She slowly took a step back, realizing that the sheriffs were mimicking her movements, and she backed away from the monster. Despite the creature's imposing visage, it didn't take an aggressive stance. In fact, it merely stood there before Maria and the men. Perhaps that is what made it even more terrifying how relaxed it looked. It didn't even see them as a threat.

"Do you know why we have the Bullet-Catcher Championship every three years? It must have been a question that runs rampant among newcomers to my town. I see no reason not to be transparent. You see, the Devil provides power through blood. That much isn't a mystery. Anyone who knows anything about necromancy and the dark arts knows this. But, when it comes to me and my hunters, I become the conduit to their power. The more blood is spilled, the less runs through my veins," said Dusty Rose with a smile. "Every three years, I must prepare the championship, and my hunters must participate, or else we all run the danger of ruin. Anyone who carries a token and is not in Glen Rio gets hunted down by the undead and brought to hell to pay their debts."

Silence fell on the room with intoxicating expectation.

"There is still one more thing I must address. Is Sheriff Erik Matthews here?" asked Dusty. Erik pushed through the line of men, but it was clear his grit had been broken at the mere sight of the beast. He didn't even look at Dusty as his eyes were bolted to the creature.

"You have violated our treaty. That hunter is not yours. There is still one more day of the Bullet-Catcher," said Dusty.

Erik turned to his men and gestured at Maria for them to remove her cuffs. Sweat dripped down his cheeks, and he wiped some of it away with his forearm. Two sheriffs approached Maria and, with keys in hand, undid her cuffs.

She rubbed her wrists together.

"Hmm, you see, you were not to lay a hand on any of my hunters for the duration of the championship."

"Most of your participating hunters are dead or dying. Your infirmary is filled to the brim. The championship is over. I would wager Maria is the last hunter standing," said Erik. "I am ending the championship right here and now."

"You would fail that wager, Sheriff. You should have listened to Commissioner Skinner. He *did* warn you."

Erik's upper lip stiffened and curled into a frown. "How the hell do you know about that?"

"You would be surprised," said Dusty.

In a motion that can only be described as lightning-fast, Erik drew his revolver and held it at his hip. There was only a breadth of a second where he hesitated, pointing at the monster, but then turned the barrel of his revolver at Dusty. He pulled the trigger and fanned the hammer back, shooting each of his six bullets into her chest. Dusty flew back and fell to the floor, leaving a blood splatter on the wall. In a split-second, all that was left was a smoking barrel and Dusty's gurgling death breaths.

Maria's ears rang, but to her surprise, the gator man didn't move. It only regarded Erik with a mild annoyance. Even her aide calmly walked to her side and looked down. "Reducing ourselves to theatrics, are we, Ms. Rose?" she said.

Erik stood still like a statue; the smoke from his barrel was beginning to dissipate. No one moved a muscle, and a heavy silence fell on the room. Suddenly, a coughing fit emerged from behind the table, and the aide pulled a bloody Dusty Rose to her feet. She coughed, blood dripping from the edges of her mouth.

"Damn. I didn't expect a jellied spine like you to do that," Dusty said, wiping blood from her face. Then, she looked at the blood stain on her chest. She unbuttoned her shirt open to reveal four small bullet holes just between her breasts. Then, right before their eyes, six silver bullets popped out of the small holes and plopped onto the wooden desk.

"By God, it's true! The deal you made with the Devil, it's all true. You are a demon," gasped Erik, taking a step back into his men.

Dusty smiled and buttoned her bloody shirt back up. "Today is the third day of the Bullet-Catcher Championship, and today, Sheriff Erik Matthews, today you are a participant."

"Huh? What do you mean?" he asked, the terror in his voice no longer masked.

"The hunter who kills the most badges and brings them to me wins this final day of the championship. Earnest, dear, would you care to begin?"

For the first time, the creature bared its rows of jagged teeth at the sheriffs, its stature seeming to grow and spread a shadow of darkness over the badged posse. Then the thing opened its wide jaws and snatched Erik by the throat. It lifted the man off his feet and, in one motion of its arm, tore his throat out. Erik fell to the ground, gasping for air as blood dripped to the floor.

A searing panic overtook the room like a flash flood as the sheriffs turned to open the door, but it was locked from the other side. With shocking speed, the half-man half-croc leaped at the men. In two swings of its nasty claws, it cleaved two men in half. Blood spurted in the air, leaving behind a crimson mist. He grabbed another man by the arms and, with a deafening howl, pulled his right arm from the rest of his body. Then it chomped its head and crushed it like a melon.

One of the sheriffs managed to draw up his gun and fire, but the shot went wide, smashing into the wood ceiling just above the croc's head. The beast glared at the man and hissed. The man dropped his gun and began to scream wildly, falling to his knees, his eyes rolling to the back of his head. He scratched at his own face, drawing blood as if trying to peel his skin off. The croc reached down and grabbed his neck with his claws. Its five claws easily punctured the man's flesh as if it were a grape. It then let go, and the man fell to the floor in a gurgling mess of blood, attempting in vain to stem the flow. The gator man was a blur through the boiling blood spurting over the floorboards. After a few agonizing moments, none of the sheriffs in the room remained in one piece. Maria realized she had been holding her breath the entire time and then felt an involuntary rumbling in her stomach. She turned around and puked viscous, transparent liquid.

"Gather yourself, Ms. Montenegro. You draw breath yet. I would count that as a win," said Dusty as she fit her hat on her head. "Perhaps I am getting too far ahead of myself. Earnest, if you please."

The beast turned to Maria, its yellow eyes like embers of a dying fire piercing into her soul. She wiped vomit from the edges of her mouth and saw the fallen gun on the ground. She snatched it up in her hands but hesitated in threatening the beast. However, the croc didn't attack her. Instead, it moved over the pile of blood and gore and knocked on the door twice. She heard a *click* on the other side of the door, and it swung open with a slow creak.

"All done?" said a man as he entered the room. He wore a wide-brimmed straw hat with a tear at the front and beady black eyes like that of a rat glistened in its shadow. Maria instantly hated him.

"Yes, Mr. Whitney. Have someone clean this mess up," Dusty chuckled.

"You're the one they call the Mosquito, right? If it weren't for the stupid rules of this place, I would shoot you for what you did in the cavern. Coward," said Maria, glaring at the man. He melted back into the shadows, but she saw the glint of fear in his eyes. "Yeah, I would be scared. If our paths cross again, I'll make sure you end up with a bullet between your eyes."

"If it weren't for the rules of this place, Ms. Montenegro, you would be dead as well," said Dusty. "Now, get out. Never return to Glen Rio."

Maria didn't need convincing. She stepped over sliced limbs and cut pieces of meat, dripping blood on the floor. She cast a murderous glance at Joel as she past him by. Gunshots rippled outside, and they only got louder as she walked closer to the front door of the manor.

Maria emerged to the sight of gun smoke lingering in the air like a noxious mist. A rhythmic sound of guns popped in the distance, and she saw a man lying in the street face down beside a horse. Three others lay dead on the ground. She let out a sigh. It was over. She was free from the sheriffs, and she would escape the gallows for the meantime. The realization was almost too good to believe. Then, she saw a horse turn into the street, and the rider faced Maria.

Lu's face turned ghostly white.

Maria's lip curled, and she gripped the bloody revolver in her hand. Lu turned and kicked the sides of her horse, turning the steed fast away from her. Maria leaped to action and tucked the revolver in the back of her pants. She ran to the dead sheriff's horse. It snorted and bucked lightly, but Maria patted its neck.

"Hey, hey, it's okay, big boy. I just need to put a bullet in between that wench's eyes," she whispered into his ears. The horse seemed to understand as it stopped pro-testing against her presence. Maria leapt onto the saddle and spurred it on with the heel of her boot. The horse charged ahead with a loud whinny. A tiny voice popped into her head.

What about Mack?

Maria slapped the reigns in her hands against the horse's neck.

He needs to be buried, came the voice in her head again. It was her own voice, but the tone sounded foreign to her.

"*Callate*! Mack's dead. Nothin' I can do about it. But I can kill the one who sold me out."

Maria saw the brown rump of Lu's horse disappear into a brush leading to a dead forest. She kicked her horse after her. She passed a collection of thin birch trees, but then one of them exploded just above her. Maria ducked and pulled the reigns left, guiding her charging steed out of the straight line but still keeping sight of her prey. Lu's shawl flapped in the wind as she moved her horse away, but Maria saw her clearly as a mouse tried to scurry from a hungry hawk, and by God, her trigger finger ached.

Another birch tree exploded, but this one was ahead of her, and the bullet didn't come from Lu. Maria looked back to see four men on horseback with stars pinned on their chests charging after her with pistols in hand.

"*Pinche madre!*" spat Maria, yanking the reigns of her horse once again, but her eyes were still bolted to Lu. She looked back and then turned her horse away from Maria.

Bullets whizzed, exploding and branching overhead. If those gunmen closed the gap, their aim would lower, and she would be in trouble. She gritted her teeth but then heard the splashing of water ahead. Lu was attempting to ford the river. Maria smiled, realizing that she was attempting to ford the thickest part of the river. She may have been prettier, but she was always a little slow.

Lu struggled with the reigns, her wounds starting to bleed again through the wrappings in the rough, freezing waters. Her horse buckled, lost its footing, and fell into the waters, dragging Lu beneath the waves. She let go of the reigns and threw herself to the muddy riverbank. She had been carried through these very reeds just a few days prior.

Lu pulled herself from the grasp of the rivers and heard the desperate whinny of her horse being carried away by the strong currents. She then heard the stamping of horses on the other side of the bank. Four sheriffs rode past her, but they weren't looking in her direction. They were probably chasing Maria.

She thought better of signaling to them. Now, with Erik dead, their deal was null and void. They would likely shoot her on sight. She lay low in the reeds until she no longer heard their galloping horses. She waited there for what seemed like hours, though it could have only been minutes. The morning fog had finally dissipated, allowing strong rays of sunlight to shine down on her. After a while, she let out a sigh and picked herself up, only to find she was staring into the barrel of a revolver.

"Get up," said Maria through her teeth. Lu's face went pale white. She looked like she was going to say something when Maria leaned down and jammed the revolver into Lu's mouth, breaking her two front teeth. Lu whimpered, but Maria shoved the gun deeper, nearly making her choke. "No. You don't get to talk yet," said Maria. "You filthy rat. Felix was right about a traitor, but little did he know it would be you."

Lu whimpered again but offered no resistance.

"So weak. Puny," whispered Maria. The numbness in Maria's left hand began to fade, giving way to a piercing pain. "After I kill you, all that will be left of you will wash down the river. Only I will remember you, and even after a while, I won't even know what your face looks like. You will fade, and your death will mean nothing."

Lu began to sob, tears running down her cheeks. She seemed like she was trying to say *please*, but it was difficult to tell with the barrel of a gun in her mouth.

"Ren, Felix, and Mateo all died because of you. You are lucky they didn't figure it out," said Maria. She paused for a moment and then looked into Lu's eyes. "You were family to me. I thought of you as blood of my blood."

Maria pulled the revolver from her mouth. Lu let out a sigh of relief and brought her hands to her bleeding mouth. "I'm sorry. I was scared. I thought they would kill me."

"They probably would have," said Maria, wiping sweat from her forehead. "Did you know why crabs in a barrel never need a lid?"

Lu shook her head. She appeared still scared to move.

Maria sat down in the reeds beside her. The wind blew softly across the river at them. "You see, those crabs are scared too. They know something is wrong, and very likely, their end is near. One gets close to the edge and comes so close. It needs only to reach up and pull to be free, but then something grabs its leg. The other crabs see this and decide if they can't get out, neither should anyone else. Thus, they keep themselves trapped. No need to watch them; their nature rules over them. I see a crab in you."

"Why are you telling me this?" sobbed Lu.

Maria shook her head and looked to the south end of the river. "You always were pretty and stupid."

She raised her revolver and held it up without even looking. She pulled the trigger.

The bullet exploded skull and brain matter out the back of Lu's head, and she fell into the water with a soft splash like a sack of potatoes. The gunshot echoed across the river, disturbing a murder of crows nearby. Her body lay in the reeds, her upper torso bobbing in the waves, her legs an anchor in the soft mud. Lu wouldn't wash away until high tide.

"There she is!"

Maria dashed from the riverbank and leaped onto her horse. She probably should have drowned Lu instead of shooting her. She kicked herself for being careless.

The four horsemen closed in and cut off her escape. Maria pulled the reigns of her horse to a stop. They could shoot her easily at this distance. She raised her hands up slowly.

"We thought we had lost you," said the gunman, holding a rifle in his hands aimed directly at her head. Each one of them had rifles trained on her. "I should just shoot her like she shot her friend there."

They all chuckled but then stopped as a sound, the strangest Maria had ever heard, echoed up the river. It was like a song but with impossible sounds of varying pitches her mind couldn't comprehend. The sound came closer and closer, accompanied by light footsteps in the smooth mud. The gunmen turned their heads, looking for the source, equally as stunned.

Suddenly, a figure burst through birch trees carrying a long but thin sword on his back. The sound was coming from a black box at his hip. He was unlike anything Maria had ever seen before. His legs weren't normal but instead looked like glistening metal folded in on itself like the legs of a stork. He wore a wide straw hat on his head and a brown cloak over his shoulders. He tapped the box at his hip, and the strange sounds ceased.

"We have jurisdiction to take her with us. You are interfering with Texican State officials. What the hell are you?" asked a gunman, with rifles aimed at the strange newcomer instead.

"If you do not leave, we will drop you where you stand," said another.

"You carry the stench of death," said the third.

"I'd better not. Death usually smells of mess, and I just took a bath." The man threw his cloak over his shoulder and drew his blade with an echoing ring. Its sharp edge glistened in the rising sunlight, and he held it down pointed to the ground.

The way he stood by the riverbank struck Maria like a painting. Every movement was perfect, and he looked like he was about to dance more than fight the gunmen.

Maria's pursuers seemed to have gathered themselves as they trained weapons on him.

"Who the hell brings a knife to a gunfight?" One of the men laughed, but the tone of his voice betrayed fear. One of them, presumably the leader, brought his sights up and fired. The stranger elegantly brought his sword up in a glistening arc, and the bullet whizzed off the blade into a tree. The gunman aimed again and fired, but the stranger, in an elegant pirouette, blocked the bullet.

However, a piece of metal pierced the gunman's neck, and blood spurted from nasty gash. He grabbed his throat and fell into the sands of the riverbank, clawing at his face. Maria understood he had redirected the bullet with is sword. Her mouth fell agape.

The other two glanced at each other and opened fire. The stranger tapped the box at his hip, and pulsing sounds began to blare from it. Maria realized it *was* some sort of song, for she heard a person singing from the box, which baffled her even more. Then, the stranger put his sword pointed behind him, and he charged the gunmen. Their horses bucked as the stranger approached with his music. The gunmen opened sporadic fire, but the stranger was no longer on the bank. They looked up to see a figure fall from the sun. He dropped behind them into a rolling crouch with a sword out to his right. A single drop of blood fell from the tip of his weapon as the gunmen's heads rolled off into the sand.

He stood up and flourished his weapon into his sheath at his back. He bobbed his head up and down, moving his shoulders from side to side to the heavy beat of the sound. He was mouthing something when Maria realized he was singing and dancing to the song. Then, he hit the box, and the song stopped. He turned to Maria and flashed a smile. "I've been waiting for this moment. Pleasure to meet you. My name is Emmett."

The stranger had pale skin and long marble-white hair, just like Dusty's hair. Where his eyes should have been were some type of shiny goggles with thin yellow slits where the eyes should be. Maria stood up from the reeds, water dripping off her coat.

"What the hell are you?"

Emmett walked up to her and looked her up and down. "You seem unhurt. That's good. We have a long way to go."

Maria bit her lip. "Am I your prisoner?"

"Prisoner? No, I don't think you understand. You are the one I've been looking for," he said, then kneeling in the sand before her. "You are a Black Manor Ranger. Or you will be if I can find the damn place. You see, I lost it, clumsy me."

The words coming out of Emmett's mouth confused Maria even more. "I just barely escaped Glen Rio with my life. What the hell are you talking about?"

She knew better than to threaten the man with her revolver, but her patience was wearing thin.

"I want to shoot you so badly, but it's clear that would be a mistake. Just answer me simply. Are you a friend or foe?"

"Servant and seeker," said Emmett, rising from his knees. "I have come to take you to the Black Manor, or at least, to help me find it. You see, I've lost the damn thing, and Hortus, well, he's a little pissed that I haven't found you yet. Now, all my problems are gone, and you've been chosen. I'm to bring you to Hortus."

"For what?"

"Well, to save mankind, of course. All that's left of humanity is on this little rock, and soon this place will be destroyed as well. Only you can stop this. A Bad 'Un is near to this particular system."

"*Pinche madre.* I have no clue what you're talking about," said Maria. "I'm lucky to be alive."

"Just please, follow me to Black Rock Canyon. We will explain everything. We must hurry, though. There are other prospects in the ranger programs. You hunters make valuable killers, and there are many like Dusty Rose looking to exploit you."

"Including you?"

Emmett smiled and shook his head. "A year ago, I thought my world existed within the confines of this planet. Now, I can only say, with someone like you joining us, we have a fighting chance. I don't want you to work for me. I want to serve you. It is your choice."

"What if I say no?" asked Maria.

"I leave, and this becomes a bad fever dream. You will even doubt you met me at all. But I promise you will live to regret it."

Maria glanced over the river at Glen Rio. The gunshots had faded a while back, and nothing but smoke rose from the town. She had nothing to lose, and somehow, she felt Emmett knew it. He would have to answer more questions before she could trust him, but so far, the answers he had given seemed honest.

Maria nodded. "Where's your horse?"

"I don't need one."

Suddenly, Emmett's legs extended up with a strange mechanical sound, and he rose two feet above her. Maria approached the officer's horses and climbed up on one. Grabbing the reigns, she turned the horse to him.

"Lead the way."

"We had better hurry. Night is coming, and the manor will soon appear. We have to catch it."

Maria sighed in frustration, and then Emmett turned and sprinted down the sandy bank at an incredible speed. She slapped the reigns of her horse and spurred it on after him, kicking up sand in the air.

Two weeks later, Anton found himself on the hillside above *Boca del Diablo* before a gravestone with the name Mack Reynolds carved into the marble. It was hard to believe he was gone. Anton almost expected him to pat him on the back and ask what the hell he was here for. Why not go to the saloon for a cold drink? Anton smiled as the wind tingled at his ear, nearly reflecting that same sentiment. "You sure you should be out here in the wind like this? You only just woke up," said the voice of a woman. Anton didn't have to turn to see Laura walking up the path behind him. "First thing you did was pay a pretty penny for that stone. Mack would be grateful."

"Since I was born, there was only one thing I'm good at, and that's killing. This bounty hunter business has fed me and made death my sole companion for years. My uncle would call it what I deserved. I never wanted to be a hunter."

"What did you want to do? When you were a kid, I mean."

"I always thought I could make enough money off bounties to be a bulletsmith. I even wanted to come here to Glen Rio to meet the most legendary bulletsmiths in the region. I wonder if Mack's path and mine would have crossed then. I wonder if the outcome would be the same. I failed him. I pushed us farther into the Aqueducts. I should have had us leave to die another day. With Mack dead, I don't know what to do now."

"You can do nothing more for him, Anton. You loved him like a brother. To regret would mean to forget. Never forget him."

"I never will."

"Good. Because there is someone you and I know that we don't want to become a memory," said Laura as she pulled a folded piece of paper from her belt. She unfolded it and held it before Anton. His eyes widened, and he snatched it from her hands.

It was a wanted poster with a $300 bounty in large black letters at the bottom. It wasn't the small quantity that caught his eye but the depiction of Maria. The name Maria Montenegro was written above her picture.

"The hell is this? She earned herself a token. Dusty put a bounty on one of her own hunters?" asked Anton. "Impossible."

Laura nodded. "She gave an eloquent speech about it. Dusty really painted a pretty picture of how Maria usurped the winner of the Bullet-Catcher Championship, E. Gray, and murdered him after the winning. No holds barred. Take her token, and the bounty money is yours, she said."

"How many signed up for it?"

"Well, Amador rode into town this morning, and suffice to say, he's more than pissed his old partner is dead. He not only took the bounty but said that if anyone else killed her and claimed the token, he would skin them alive."

"That's good. Means less men to fight."

"He's taking four of the best hunters to find her. Clansy Portero, Micah McCullough, One-Arm Henry, and a new hunter by the name of August. The last one is barely more than a kid and has a bum leg, but Amador believes in him. They rode off west a few hours ago."

Anton shoved the paper into his pants pocket.

"I must find her. This is what Mack would have wanted," said Anton for the first time turning to a very pregnant Laura. She had a shotgun over her shoulder and held Anton's own shotgun in her arm. She tossed the weapon at him, and he caught it with a stunned look on his face.

"Sorry to say, your beautiful rifle was lost in the aqueduct. I don't think you'll ever see it again."

"Shame," he grunted.

"But! I saw two horses in the sheriff's barn. They won't need them anymore."

"Can you even ride?"

"Can you?" She smirked.

"Fair enough."

"From what I know, she was seen going west by the Castor River."

356

"Well, hell," said Anton as he threw the shotgun over his shoulder on a sling and cast one last glance at his friend's tombstone. He fished a single bullet and set it on the marble top tip-up. "I know what you're gonna say. If only I had a bullet for every time I went in half-cocked. Well, now you have that bullet."

"Ma'am?" came the voice from the other side of the door, interrupting the peaceful silence of the night.

Dusty lay in an ornate bed with soft lethargy-inducing pillows and blankets. She looked up from a book in her hands and glanced at the clock. It was nearly midnight.

"What is it, Maddie?" she asked, giving a heavy sigh.

"You have a visitor."

Dusty half-smiled and shook her head. "Let him in."

She saw her reflection in a mirror beside the door. Her marble-white hair was combed neatly over her shoulders, and her left eye didn't look entirely disgusting in the low light without her eye patch. It felt strange not to wear it as the door creaked open, and Commissioner Sam Skinner slid through, closing it behind him.

He wore a black leather coat that dripped moisture, and when he took off his black bowler hat, droplets of water fell from the brim. His brown eyes looked at her on the bed beneath the covers and blew air slowly from his mouth.

"Evenin', Ms. Rose. Didn't mean to arrive so late. This hellish mist nearly killed me and my horse."

"Would have been a shame, Commissioner Skinner," said Dusty, coolly. The look in her eye and the tone in her voice betrayed a luring hook that made something in between Sam's legs tingle. He shook the thought away. There was business to attend to.

"Right. Uhm, did you *have* to string my men up by their necks after they were shot dead? I saw them by the town square. Nice little wooden signs you made for them. Bounty traitors."

"You knew what would happen when they set foot in my town. It's what happens when someone gets too drunk on their power. Erik Matthews was a fool to try and hunt for the gang here and now. You sent him to die."

"I can't say that I'll miss that do-gooder. I always did hate the sound of his voice. Did you get a winner this year?"

At the thought of Maria, a frown decorated Dusty's face. "Some rat. It was supposed to be E. Gray, but he went and got himself capped. It was a random stray from Felix Quintana's crew who won."

"Unlucky."

"So it seems. Did you come to avenge your men? As you can see, I'm harmless."

"Dusty Rose doesn't need a gun to cause harm," said Sam with a knowing shake of his head. "And it's for that reason, I am here." He unclipped a pair of steel handcuffs from his belt.

"I thought you weren't going to avenge him."

Sam flashed a half-smile. "I don't give a damn about Erik. I came because of the twenty deputies you had shot and killed like dogs in the street. *That* I cannot ignore. I came because I have been tasked with bringing you in. Don't think you can wriggle your way out of this one."

"Is all that steel just for little old me?" said Dusty, sitting up and letting her blanket fall from her shoulders and holding up one arm to cover her breasts. Sam dropped the cuffs on the floor, his eyes widening as he swallowed hard.

"Oh, I hope you aren't done with those," said Dusty, throwing the covers from her legs to reveal her complete nudity. She covered between her legs with one hand and moved her arm over her breasts. She caught her reflection in the mirror. Not a single wrinkle or loose fold of fat blemished her perfect skin. Her hair reached down to her buttocks, and she had well-chiseled leg muscles. As a matter of fact, her entire body was laced with well-carved musculature, including her arms, abdomen, and back. She had earned a body like this through the rigorous taxing work it took to be the head of Rose Manor.

"Dear God," gasped Sam. "You should be nearing seventy by now, yet you look like my granddaughter. Did you really make a deal with the Devil?"

Dusty turned sideways to show off the curvature of her round ass and shook it as if she had a tail. "Such a nasty thing to say to a woman ready to be bedded. Truth is genetics. Of course, I don't think you want a history

359

lesson about me right now. I think you have something else on your mind, don't you?"

"Damn, Dusty. If I weren't a suspicious man, I would think you knew I was coming."

"Not yet, you're not." She let her hands down and approached him with a seductive stride. "I believe you've earned this."

She moved her hand in between his legs to conjure a heavy sigh from the commissioner. She saw a bulge in his pants rise even further.

"I said, I am here because I have been tasked with bringing you in. You have to answer for your crimes."

"Is that so, big boy?" she squeezed his bulge, and his legs nearly buckled. "Maybe you should take your jacket off."

Dusty let go of him and fell onto the bed. Without need for further convincing, Sam stripped his jacket off as if it were on fire and threw it on the floor. He shrugged his suspenders off and began to unbutton his shirt. He turned to approach the bed.

"Uh-uh. Pick those up. You're gonna need them," said Dusty, pointing to the cuffs beside the pile of clothes. Sam grunted, and she saw a bead of sweat fall from his forehead. She couldn't help herself but smile.

It was almost too easy. Sam leaned down and picked the cuffs up.

Click.

He froze at the sound of a revolver's hammer being pulled back. He turned to see Dusty holding a gun aimed at his head. Sam grunted and held his hands up. "I knew it was too good to be true."

"Oh, *that* deal ain't off the table just yet. You see, I fancy you, Sam. I just wish you had a little more backbone."

"Meaning?"

"Look at what's on the end table. Pick it up."

Sam turned to see what she was gesturing at. He saw a small circular coin in the center. He walked over to it and picked it up. Carved into the center were the letters D and R. He turned it over.

"It's made of wood," said Sam.

"Careful now. In these parts, that right there is worth more than gold," Dusty grinned.

"This is a bounty token?"

This made Dusty's smile disappear. "You are quite the sleuth, aren't ya? I want you to keep that."

"I can't work for you, Dusty. Hunting men is behind me. Besides, I'm the commissioner."

"Good. I want you to remember that. That's not why I want you to have my token, though. You see, I want you to pay the Salem Twins a visit. They have something they owe me, and they refuse to pay up. I need them to come to Glen Rio. You are my messenger. You give them that. When you do, tell them it's time to awaken Mad-Dog Tannen. They'll know what that means."

Sam turned pale. "The Salem Twins are mad. They shoot people for looking at them wrong. You know what they say. They make Glen Rio—" He cut his words short.

"They make Glen Rio look like paradise," said Dusty, finishing his sentence. "Well, they say beauty is in the eye of the beholder. Now tell, me, Sam, doesn't this look like paradise to you?" She opened her legs and moved her free hand seductively from her belly down to touch in between her thighs. Dusty gave a soft, beckoning moan. That was all Sam could withstand before melting like a pail of warm water on a pile of sugar. He shoved the token into his pocket before undoing his belt and shoving his pants to his ankles. He was already fully erect.

With her thumb, Dusty set the hammer home and tossed the gun onto the bed harmlessly just before Sam launched himself onto her. She could feel his hot breath on her neck and allowed herself to be swallowed up by the pleasure of his touch. He wasn't hard to look at either. In a way, she had been wanting this for a while. She would never reveal this minuscule detail, but sometimes, The Plan and desire go hand in hand.

He kissed her neck and began rubbing into her navel. She pinched his nipple.

"Are you going to keep me in suspense?" whispered Dusty into his ear before biting it. Sam penetrated her, and a wave of pleasure washed over Dusty in shivers. She moaned as Sam began to fall into a passionate rhythm. He clutched the bedsheets and grunted over and over again.

Dusty allowed herself to be pulled by the undertow of lovemaking, succumbing to her primal desires.

Sam stopped suddenly and sat up, grabbing Dusty by the waist and flipping her over on her stomach. He grabbed her ass and squeezed hard as he mounted her from behind. He began pounding into her, making her toes curl, feeling her legs spasm with greedy lust.

She opened her eye and caught something in the window. Two reptilian eyes glowed yellow in the darkness just outside her bedroom in the bushes. As Sam pushed repeatedly into her, Dusty smiled, and then her left eye opened to reveal a metal eyeball with a red iris beneath. Two mechanical tendrils, thin as shoelaces, darted from her eye and slithered to the lamp at her bed. They coiled around the lever and snuffed the wick out, plunging the two into darkness. Only Dusty's eye glowed red in the heat of passionate lovemaking.

"I'm gonna smoke this dude like a brisket."
—*Oscar Sweeney during his hunt for the deserter Lieutenant Jim Cadney at the Battle of Graw Hill. He was found dead with a bullet between the eyes.*

Mother Love

A year after the Bullet-Catcher in Glen Rio.

The pungent smell of moonshine burned Jonesy's nostrils despite the corks jammed firmly into the bottles jangling against each other. He carried twelve bottles of hooch in a crate from Mrs. Ann Blankenship's carriage into the Silver Bullet Saloon. The toe of his boot caught on a loose plank on the floor and launched him into a table where a drunk had been sleeping face down on the surface. The crate fell to the floor with a loud thud, and the bottles of glass fell out and rolled beneath the tables. The drunken man fell backward onto his chair, his eyes wide in surprise. This racket stirred everyone from their drunken stupor, drawing ire from their looks as the rays of sun began to poke through the windows. Blood rushed to Jonesy's face, and he could feel the intense heat on the back of his neck and ears. He picked himself up and grabbed the bottles up one by one. He reached down beneath a table to snatch one that had rolled deep.

"You dumb bastard!" growled a drunk man from that very table as he smacked Jonesy across the face. He had coppery white hair and a diseased-looking mustache with bits of dried slobber and beer. His deep green eyes flashed, and he took a step back and clumsily pulled a revolver from his belt. "Can you imagine the headache you just gave me? You're going to give me all your money. I need a drink right now."

Jonesy found himself staring up the barrel of a revolver.

"I'm sorry," said Jonesy, bringing his hands up slowly. He could feel a warmth dripping down the legs of his pants.

"Damn right you are—what?—are you pissing yourself, boy?" The anger in the man turned to boisterous laughter. "How old are you?"

"Fourteen," coughed Jonesy, tears streaming down his eyes.

"Hah! Too old for that, don't you think?" heaved the drunk, tears streaming down his eyes with laughter.

The sharp click of a gun stopped his hyena howling as Jonesy saw the barrel of a gun pointed right up to the drunk man's temple. His smile quickly turned to a look of terror. Jonesy turned to see Mr. Darrens holding his hand cannon leveled at the drunk's head.

"Drop the gun. I can't have you threatening the help," he said, his nicely trimmed black mustache firm on the top of his lip accentuating the frown on his face. He meant business.

The drunk gave a nervous laugh and jammed the revolver back in his pants. "I was just teasin'. You have a clumsy nincompoop on your hands, Darrens. You ought to get rid of him."

Mr. Darrens brought his revolver down as the drunk man went to a different seat and sat down, nearly instantly snoring as he let his head down on the wooden table. He shoved his piece into his pants.

"Go on," said Mr. Darrens.

"What?" asked Jonesy, standing up and wiping tears from his cheeks.

"Get. You have outworn your welcome, and I will harbor you no longer, your father be damned. He would be sorely disappointed in you if he were still alive. Look at you. What a joke," growled Mr. Darrens. "Go tell your hag of a mother never to send you here. Next time, I'll let you eat the bullet. Go on, git!"

With that, Mr. Darrens grabbed Jonesy by the collar and threw him out the double doors. He landed on the ground hard as a rumble of laughter erupted within the saloon. Jonesy picked himself up, his pride fully poached, rubbing his shoulder. He swore under his breath, glaring through the double doors. He stumbled down the dirt road to a small shack beside the abandoned church, the wet spot on his pants instantly going cold as a cool breeze blew against him.

His cheeks flushed as he stopped just outside the shack. He knew who was waiting for him inside and what she would say. Overgrown thorn bushes crowded around the wooden panel walls of his house. As Jonesy approached, the stench of Chamberlin's Colic Remedy wafted through the door. Though it was dark, he could see the glint of his mother's eyes piercing him through the darkness.

"Well, what happened now?" came the voice from within. Jonesy sniffed, fighting tears from his eyes as a tightness gripped around his chest.

"Mr. Darrens kicked me out."

"What did you do?"

"I-I—"

"Never mind. I don't want to hear it. It's probably going to be some silly excuse. Next time, do me a favor and walk down the path to Castor River, and don't come back," said Momma, her eyes glinting with hatred as she spoke. Jonesy curled his lip and pushed the door open, his chest tightening as he closed the door behind him. He walked up to the water basin and splattered water onto his face.

"You're a disgrace, Jonesy. I should have thrown you into the mud the first minutes of your miserable, pathetic life. Damn. Your father might still be alive to get us out of this mess."

Her words cut like a knife, but Jonesy tried to shrug it off.

"I'm sorry, Momma."

"I'd say so," she grunted. "Put some more oil in that lamp, boy. See if you don't muck that up too."

Jonesy did as his Momma instructed and picked up a pail of oil by the foot of the bed. He fitted a steel spigot at the top and tilted it into the lamp on a table. Then, he set the pail down and turned the wick switch, shedding light in the room. He almost wished he hadn't.

Momma had wet the sheets again. Eight long years since his stepfather Roy Biggs had been killed, and Jonesy struggled to even recall his face. From what he was told, a murderer named Oscar Sweeney had gone demented and killed him in cold blood. He and Momma were lucky to have survived. Yet, he was never found by the law or after when Momma placed a bounty on Oscar Sweeney's head. The bounty collected dust for eight long years at Rose Manor. Afterward, they had to sell the farm for pennies on the dollar and move into a small wooden shack close to the jail cells in Glen Rio. He couldn't hold down a job no matter to save his life.

"You've always been a disappointment, Jonesy. Your father knew it, and so do I," growled Momma.

"Roy wasn't my father. You told me my father was a Hunter of the Rose."

A look of anger flashed over Momma's face, but it quickly faded.

"I . . . I didn't think you knew. Who told you?"

"They call me a bastard. They call you far worse."

She slapped Jonesy across the face. He recoiled and took a step back. It didn't hurt too badly anymore, but her blow still carried a sting. Momma's look changed to a look Jonesy wasn't too familiar with. Her brown eyes widened, and she pursed her lips.

"Oh, my poor boy." She grabbed his arm and pulled him close, wrapping her arms around him awkwardly. "The cards have always been stacked against us, but I have the solution. I need your help."

"What can I do, Momma?" The momentary flash of embrace suddenly made Jonesy's eyes flood with tears. He grabbed hold of his Momma, wishing to never let go.

"The Rose Manor was always meant to be mine. The Loyas stole it from us. My sister, your aunt Dusty, took it back, but then, in her greed, she banished me. She was always selfish and cruel. The only reason she allowed us to return to Glen Rio was because she wanted to take *care* of me. Tell me, how many times has that bitch visited me? How many times has she asked how I am doing? Why the hell are we living in this run-down shack and not at Rose Manor?"

"Not once," whispered Jonesy.

"Not once, indeed. Well, you love your Momma very much, don't you, Jonesy?"

Jonesy nodded sheepishly.

"Yeah, you are dim, but even a retard like you can see the injustice of our situation. You know I deserve so much more."

"What do you want me to do, Momma?"

"I'm tired of living in this squalor. You are ready now; I can see it. Go to Rose Manor. Ask for a job. Earn Dusty's trust. That's all I want for now. Pretty soon, I will unveil my plan to you, but for now, just go and be my eyes and ears. Learn everything you can from them. Don't muck this up."

He nodded and stood up.

"If you do this, Jonesy, you'll have changed my mind about you. Before you go, change my bedsheets."

Jonesy wiped sweat from his forehead as he entered the pristine stables of the Rose Manor. The stalls were polished pearl white full of horses of colors brown, black, and gray. Jonesy had no clue if they were male or female or even what kind of horse they were. One thing he could definitively tell was they were magnificent to look at. Each one had been brushed clean, and not one speck of dust or mud dotted their skin. Their fur glistened in the rays of the sun. Men wearing leather boots and fitted in fine shirts and pants strapped saddles onto the horses' backs. They mounted them and then rode off into a nearby field in a single elegant line, kicking up dust in their wake. Even the horses' trot looked calculated and precise.

Jonesy didn't have the talents of a bounty hunter. He didn't even own a gun. That alone discounted him from that kind of work. The stables were his best bet for finding a job in Rose Manor, and even then, it was a long shot. He had no experience with horses. He clenched his fists, remembering his promise. He would make Momma proud. Maybe then, her gaze would soften, and her tongue would cease to be so sharp.

Jonesy watched the horses, completely enthralled by their parade as the men rode away. Dust began to settle to reveal a lone figure in the courtyard with their back turned to him. It was a woman in black leather pants and a tight black suit coat. She had short, raven black hair cropped against her pale cheeks. Her back was more than straight, as she had her arms behind her back, holding a riding crop in her right hand. Despite the mid-summer heat, she wore black gloves. Jonesy imagined it couldn't be too comfortable, especially in the sunlight.

She half-turned her head at Jonesy, and he gasped. The skin of her cheek was peeled back on her mouth like it had been caught in a hook, giving her a permanent half-smile. Several hooks, for that matter. He could still see the snow-white scars like comets streaking across her skin. Her eyes were piercing blue that seemed to slice into his skull and sift through his thoughts. He instinctively took a step back as she brought her riding crop and slammed it onto the palm of her gloved hand.

"What are *you* doing here?" she asked, still not fully facing him. "Strangers are not wanted here, and I've never seen you before."

"I've come for work."

She snorted and turned, looking him up and down. "We only hire professionals. Your kind has no place here."

"Please, I just need work. It doesn't matter what. I can clean the stables or brush the horses."

"Filthy beggar. We give no handouts," snapped the woman. "Now beat it before I beat you."

A cough echoed in the stables behind Jonesy, and the woman turned to another figure leaning against the wooden stall. It was another shrouded individual, but Jonesy knew who this one was. Dusty Rose's bifocals glinted sunlight off the dark lens as she lit a cigarette and took a drag. She blew smoke from her nostrils and then nodded to the woman in front of him. She took off her hat, revealing a crown of shoulder-length white hair. "That's my kin."

"You've got to be kidding me," grunted the woman, shaking her head. "This is Jonesy?"

"Yes," he said. The woman smacked him across the face, sending him to one knee. His face grew hot, and a thin streak of blood marked just above his chin.

"That's yes, *ma'am*. You will speak to me with respect. Did your mother teach you no manners? What am I saying? Of course, she didn't."

"I'm sorry," whispered Jonesy as he stood up. This only brought another sharp blow across his face, sending him back to the ground.

"I hate false apologies. Only say sorry if you mean it. Never say it to attain sympathy. You will only be known as weak."

Jonesy stood up, but this time no tears, fell down his face. He clenched his hands and glared right back at her. He expected another blow at this gesture of defiance, but this time, she let the riding crop down to her side.

"There he is. It seems you're not as pathetic as you look," she said. "My name is Maddie, but you will call me ma'am or Ms. Maddie."

Jonesy didn't quite know what to say. He just stood there. She looked at Dusty, and for a split second, Jonesy thought they were communicating without words. She finally nodded and glared at Jonesy.

"When the horses return, I want them all bathed and brushed. You will dress them for the night. I will harbor no complaints, or I will have you run out of this place so fast your head will be spinning for weeks. I'll make your mother look like a saint, understood?"

"Yes, ma'am."

"Now, get ready. The riders will return soon," said Maddie as a dust cloud led by a team of horses and their riders approached rapidly. Jonesy kicked off into the stables. Dusty blew smoke between her lips to form a large 'O' in the air.

"You sure about this?" asked Maddie.

"It's about time. I've been waiting for him to have the balls to come to me," said Dusty. "When his mother's claws release him, he may be worth a damn. Give him the opportunity, but don't go easy on him. In fact, the tougher you are on him, the better."

"He's a Glen Rio rat."

"You were a Glen Rio rat long ago when I took you in," said Dusty, taking another drag from her cigarette and letting it out her nostrils. "Truth is, Maddie, when everyone else discovers this forgotten planet, and they will, the massive potential my hunters possess will cause a Glen Rio rush. There is no better killer in the galaxies than a gunslinger with a reason or a bounty. I want the Hunters of the Rose to stand at the pinnacle."

"You want me to give him a token?"

Dusty shook her head and tossed the cigarette butt on the ground, then crushed it beneath the toe of her boot. "Not yet. He must earn it. Keep him in the stables for now. I want you to measure the worth of his grit. Perhaps my instinct may be vindicated."

For the next three months, Jonesy woke up with the stable hands before the sun rose and would go to bed long after it had gone down. At first, he would lay down sore on his bed, if you could call a rough straw cot a bed, unable to move his legs or arms. They ached with so much pain he could hardly bring them up to wash himself, yet he knew if he did not, he would receive a beating from Maddie. Rarely a day went by that he didn't feel the snap of her whip on his arms, legs, or back. It was better than serving whiskey at the saloon, he told himself. He was so exhausted he would fall asleep the moment his head touched his rough leather-skin pillow, not even minding he didn't have a blanket. The three other stable hands, boys not much older than him, kept to themselves, not speaking to him, even going so far as to avoid any kind of interaction. Jonesy wondered if they were directed to ignore him seemingly at all costs. They even went out of their way to never catch his gaze. Perhaps it was better this way anyway.

At first, this bothered Jonesy, but seeing he really had no choice, he much preferred it after a while. He was never really good at making friends. He simply focused his mind on work. It felt strange not to be completely out of place in the stables of Rose Manor. After a while, the work began to make sense as callouses began to collect on his fingertips and palms. His arms and legs, though sore the first few weeks, began to take on strength, and he could see the muscles of his arms and legs begin to take form. The job finally clicked, and he didn't have to be reminded how to clean a stable, bathe and brush a horse, or fix a saddle and bit. After a while, even the stable hands began to acknowledge his existence and prefer him for his precise work. Unease turned to pride as he familiarized himself with horses, saddles, and bits to precision. When the riders left one of Jonesy's stalls, they needn't worry about a damn thing save for the ride ahead and sale at the market. For the first time in Jonesy's life, he felt like he had found a place where he belonged.

A place to call home.

Yet, something tugged the back of his mind. The words of his mother.

"*. . . Don't muck this up.*"

He had made a promise and would be true to his word. For now, he just had to earn their trust like Momma instructed. But what did she have planned for Dusty? It couldn't be anything good, could it?

He would visit that shack nearly every day once the sun had gone down. Momma lay in bed in the same place for many years since they moved there, but she made no comment to the strength he was building. She made no comment about the patchy beard filling in, no longer just peach fuzz. Even so, Jonesy began to treat taking care of her as taking care of one of Dusty's horses. He ignored the abuse and set his mind to task. He had to make sure to shift her body from time to time to avoid sores collecting on her buttocks and back, which had a very high potential for infection. She often wet herself, so Jonesy was always prepared to change and wash the bed sheets. Today was one such day. He was soaking the soiled linens in the kitchen sink when Momma handed him a small black box.

"It's time, Jonesy," she said out of the blue. Once he had her bedsheets soaking in soapy water, he knelt to her bedside. She handed him a rectangular black box no larger than his hand.

"What is this?" Jonesy asked, taking it from her.

"Be very careful with that. One whiff will knock you out for hours. If it's dissolved in tea or beer, it will knock you out forever."

"It's poison."

Momma nodded. "It's time for revenge. When the time is right, slip it into Dusty Rose's drink and step away."

Three men shrouded in black entered the small hut and set what seemed like a sack of potatoes on a table. Two had face coverings and wide-brimmed hats with pistols tucked into their gun belts. The third wore a scowl and a face only a mother could love. They all smelled of sweat and hard riding,

"Rick and his crew have been dealt with," said the third, revealing a short two-barrel shotgun around his arm. "Where's the pay?"

Momma smiled to reveal rows of yellow cracked teeth. "Not much cash but enough blow." She tossed them a small bag, and the third man picked it from the air. He put a finger into the bag, then in his mouth. He smiled.

"Will do."

"Stick around. I may have further use for you," said Momma.

"Oh? Are we talking small fry?"

"Not at all," said Momma. "Once this shrimp does his job, I'll alert you boys to your task. Don't blow through all that just yet, you hear? I'll need your trigger fingers sober. After I get what's mine, you lose yourselves however you please."

The third man smiled back.

"Momma?" I asked.

"What?" she snapped.

"There is someone I would like to request you leave alone when you take over Rose Manor," said Jonesy, mustering as much courage to look her in the eye. He pictured Maddie standing tall behind him with her arm behind her back. This image filled Jonesy with courage, and his hesitation left him.

"Spare Maddie. When the time comes, please leave her alone."

"Boy's found a soft spot," said the third man with a cruel grin. "She's not much of a looker, though. Guess any lay is good lay, even as ugly as she is."

This made Jonesy blush, and he clenched his fists. Even so, Momma's expression seemed to soften for the first time in his life. She nodded. "I know the wench. When it goes down, I won't put in orders to kill her. Even so, she'd better not get in my way."

Jonesy nodded with relief. He had to find a way to keep her away from the manor when the time came.

"Have you gotten inside the manor yet?" asked Momma, as if she could read his mind.

He shook his head.

"Well, what the hell have you been up to, boy? Don't tell me you've simply been working in the stables. Get the hell back there and do what the hell I sent you to do."

It was the end of the day, and the horses had been bathed, brushed, and put in their stalls for the night. Jonesy dared wander close to the manor grounds, scouting the outer perimeter. He carried the small black box in his pocket when he heard a sound that piqued his curiosity. It seemed like someone was chopping wood for a fire, only it was one hundred degrees outside. Who the hell would need a fire?

Jonesy turned a corner and saw Maddie standing before a wooden target with a rusted bucket over its head. She held three sharp knives in between the fingers of her hands. Suddenly, he heard a *thump,* and all three knives were no longer in her fingers. Jonesy looked at the target to see the knives embedded in the wooden face of the target. She hadn't even shifted her posture as she threw, he noticed in astonishment. With lightning speed, she drew three more knives from her belt, and this time, he saw her throw them. Throw isn't the correct term when describing the action she took. It was more like she flicked her hand, and the knives were launched with extreme speed and force from it. He couldn't even see the knives sail through the air until they hit their target with three loud *thuds,* this time just slightly beneath the first three.

She cursed at herself and stamped the ground.

"I'm getting old, goddamnit," she said to herself, rubbing her forearm.

"Ma'am?" asked Jonesy, straightening his back.

"Jonesy?" asked Maddie, not even turning to look at him.

"Horses tucked in early for the night, just as you requested."

Maddie nodded and drew three more knives from her belt. She knuckle-rolled the knives in her hands, making them *flick* in between her fingers as if they were claws.

"Is something the matter, ma'am?" he asked.

"How long have you been here? Three, four months?" she asked, raising a finger and peering at the target over the tip.

"A year next Tuesday," said Jonesy with a curt nod.

"You've learned a lot and grown too. Not a man, not yet, but very soon will be," said Maddie, turning to him and flashing her broken grin. Jonesy had become altogether used to seeing her grotesque visage. He often wondered how she had attained such gruesome scars but knew better than to ask. To do so might earn a lash from her whip. She turned sideways and threw the knives, but this time, she missed the target entirely. The knives spun into the brush behind it.

"Dammit" she snapped.

"How do you do that? I can't even see you throw the knives until they hit the target."

"But I didn't hit the target."

Jonesy guffawed at her words and shook his head in unbelief. She was a perfectionist through and through.

"It's a skill I learned from someone long ago. He believed the strength of the arm could far outdo the destruction of gunpowder. It's a skill you must practice daily or else lose it. Unfortunately, he failed to mention that even if you *do* practice daily, time will still claim your arm. I guess that's the price of growing old."

"Could you teach me?" asked Jonesy

Maddie snorted and turned to face him. "Only Blind Gideon from the Aqueducts could ever teach you what you needed to know, that is, if you could persuade him to do it. That is if he would choose to. *You* could never find him, even if you wanted to. He was always very . . . *unique.*"

She stared at him for a split second, then tilted her head. "You've earned a lesson at the very least, Jonesy. Stand right here and take this. Careful. It's viciously sharp."

Maddie held out a single throwing knife in her hand out to him. Jonesy grabbed the cold steel of the blade and watched the glint of sunlight roll across the razor edge. She moved the blade in his fingers so that the point was away from them.

"The first and most important thing you must learn is to hold your blade tight. If you drop the blade, you will slice your toes off, and then you're forever useless," said Maddie. She put one foot forward and straightened her posture into a slender, practiced position with one hand behind her back.

"You must be relaxed when you throw the knives. Your stance must be impeccable."

Jonesy straightened his back to imitate her, but he felt anything but relaxed.

"The second most important thing you should know is when you use a knife, you must commit to discretion. Nine out of ten times, a bullet will be faster than your throw. Well, ten for you. Thus, you must use the element of surprise on your side to win a fight. Once you have revealed your hand, things can go wrong. You must strike first because you won't get a second chance. Once you lose control of a situation, you will never get it back."

Jonesy eyed the target and threw the blade. It flew clumsily in a slow arc at the target and pinged on the barrel, then flailed harmlessly to the ground. Maddie snorted. "At least you hit the target, kid."

A bell rang from the direction of the barns, suddenly interrupting their conversation. Maddie slipped the remaining knives beneath her blazer. Jonesy's eyebrows flew up as he saw rows of steel knives over her chest on a crossed belt. Discretion, indeed. He couldn't even have imagined she had those weapons on her, let alone an entire arsenal of blades.

Two of the stable hands ran to them. One of them had a rifle in hand.

"What happened?" asked Maddie.

"Horse thieves," said one.

"Any details?"

"It looks like strays from Conley's farm. They took three. One of them is Dusty's favorite chestnut."

"We better get them back before Dusty finds out, or it will be our necks hanging by a noose," said Maddie. She took the lead as they walked to the stables. "That farm mysteriously burns to the ground, and those horses had no proprietor. They belong to us now. Hunt them down."

"Hunt them?" asked Jonesy.

"Bring out the hounds," said Maddie. "No mercy for thieves."

Jonesy followed them to the barns to find a row of five riders on horseback. One of them held the reins to an American Quarter Horse with golden hair and a white mane. It was Jonesy's favorite horse, and seeing her ready to ride always set his heart right. They waited patiently for Maddie as she grabbed the reigns of her horse and heaved herself up.

"Get me the thoroughbred, the black one," said Maddie as she heaved herself up on her horse.

A stable hand, a young one having recently joined, stepped to, and before long brought the horse saddled and ready up to them.

"You ready, boy?" asked Maddie. "Today, you ride with us."

Jonesy touched the horse's side. It had been brushed and sported a beautiful sheen on its black hide and hair. He put his foot in the stirrup and pushed himself up. The horse grumbled with a snort and shook its mane. He leaned down and patted the beast on its side.

"Here," said a stable hand. He tossed a repeater rifle at Jonesy. He caught it in his hands, and then the man handed him a handful of bullets. "Put that in your pocket."

Jonesy did as he was instructed.

Without a word, Maddie slapped the reigns of her steed, and they shoved off into the waning sunlight.

"Roarke has them down by the Pup Canyon. Maybe they think they can hide," said a rider on Maddie's right.

Her gaze remained unwavering as she led the posse across the plains, chased by a cloud of dust that loomed over their shadows. They went down into a collection of canyons and slowed their horses down. The thieves knew their horses would not simply be able to race through. Maddie came to a complete stop. The seven horses stood in a line with the riders itching at their triggers. They sat there for a moment while the wind blew softly against their backs.

A squat man with tangled hair and a patchy gray beard emerged from the darkness. Despite his grotesque stature and appearance, Jonesy recognized him as a bounty hunter of Dusty Rose. This was no ordinary man, not one to underestimate.

"Roarke?" grunted Maddie, fishing a bronze coin from her picket and flicking it at the man. He caught it with one hand and shoved it in his pants pocket. "Right time and place once more."

"They know you're coming. There's at least eight of them," he said shoving the coin into his pocket.

"That rules them out as Conley strays," said Maddie.

"If not the Conleys, then who?" asked Jonesy. "Who else would dare steal from Dusty Rose?"

Roarke nodded. "I heard them speaking Spanish. It could be the what's left of the Felix Quintana Gang. Mateo was never found."

"No way. The sheriffs killed them all," said a rider.

Maddie unbuttoned her blazer and held her right hand close to her belt.

"Dismount," she whispered.

The posse did as she ordered, and Maddie walked into the canyon. Jonesy realized his heart was beating like a drum, and his hands were shaking. He followed Maddie close behind as the others fell in behind him.

"Take a deep breath, Jonesy. Swallow the lump in your throat. Force the pain in your chest away. Furthermore, dismount the thoughts that ride on your physical pain. They will rule your grit. The shakes will go, but so will you if you don't breathe," said Maddie. Jonesy did as she said and held the rifle at his hip and finger on the trigger, sweeping his weapon across the way ahead. Dried bushes adorned the narrow path, but then Jonesy saw the ground open up into a series of caves.

Going in there would be suicide. Maddie walked down into the canyon without hesitation. Jonesy stuck close to her, keeping his gun pointed where Maddie's was not looking. She held her hands crossed inside her jacket.

If Jonesy, didn't know better, she would seem to be a crazy person walking into a canyon defenseless.

That's exactly what the first masked thief thought when he saw her. His last mistake was to emerge from cover with a revolver in hand and finger on the trigger. Maddie raised her arms, but the knives were already embedded into the thief's chest. He fell over, barely able to gasp as his last breath escaped his lungs. Another peeked around a boulder and squeezed a round off that sailed over Maddie's head, but she turned, and Jonesy only heard the quick whistle of her blades as they sliced through the air and jabbed into the man's neck, instantly slicing deep into both sides. Geysers of blood spewed from his neck, and he fell into a flailing mess. Then, the fight began in earnest.

Three gunfighters emerged like prairie dogs from the entrance of a cavern. Maddie threw one blade, but it landed on the ceiling of the cave. She instantly ducked behind a boulder as hot slugs flicked against the top, showering her in flecks of stone. Jonesy brought his rifle up to his eye and pulled the trigger just as two stable hands fired their weapons. Bullets instantly filled one man with lead as he fell forward from the caves. His body dropped like a rag doll into the dirt. The other two thieves disappeared back into the cave.

"Gregory!" shouted Maddie, clutching her shoulder. She was right. Even the strongest hand was no match for a bullet. Fortunately, the round seemed to have only grazed her arm. A stable hand with a pristine beard and a smoking cigar approached from behind Jonesy. The man named Gregory looked at him and winked. "Watch this."

He pulled a stick of dynamite from his belt and brought the wick up to his face. He puffed the cigar, the embers glowing yellow within, and the wick burst into sparks. He reared back and threw the dynamite into the cave. Jonesy heard a desperate yelp just before the cave exploded, spewing fire, rock, and chunks of flesh and clothing.

More rounds zipped overhead, and Jonesy saw a man in a cave farther away leap atop a horse.

"Jonesy! Stop him from running, but *don't* kill him. He's not yours to take," shouted Maddie as she winced at the pain in her shoulder. He felt a spur in his heels and salivated with anticipation. He ran back to his thoroughbred and mounted it with one leap. He kicked its side, and the horse charged out of the caves with a curt whinny.

Jonesy emerged from the canyon onto a plateau and was met by a fierce wind that beat at his chest. He squinted his eyes and saw a shadow on horseback racing fast away. Then, he saw the glint of silver in the sunlight.

Jonesy ducked just as a round whizzed over his head. He kicked his horse forward and stood straight, raising his repeater rifle sights up to his eyes. He paced his breath and pulled the trigger. The sights bounced up as the horse galloped forward, sending his bullet way too far above his target's head. He readjusted, cocked the lever back, and fired again, his round going too far once again. He ducked as the shadow fired back.

Then, he took a deep breath and let it out slowly. He squinted his eye and waited. Just as his horse's hooves left the ground, he fired. His aim was true, and his bullet sailed through the air at his target. He saw a puff of red mist, and the shadow fell from his horse and hit the ground hard. Jonesy pulled the horse's neck to the left hard and leaped off onto the ground, landing on his feet. His boots dug into the earth, but he wasted little time bringing his rifle back up to his sights. He cocked the lever, grabbed three loose rounds, and fed them into the slim carrier tube without looking. He then patted the lever back expertly and brought the sights up to his head.

The shadow had tried to stand up but was struggling. Jonesy took a few steps to him with his jaw tightened.

"Don't move!"

"I wasn't trying to," said the shadow. "It's kind of difficult to be still with a bullet in your gut."

No sooner had those words left his mouth that he flipped over like a fish. Jonesy dodged to the left and ducked as three rounds buzzed, just missing his side. Then, he stood still and pulled the trigger back on his smoking revolver.

"You're out," said Jonesy as he let his rifle fall to his hip.

"Damn," said the shadow as he let a smoking silver revolver fall from his hands. It plopped on the dirt beside him. "Look, dude, I just needed to make some extra money. I haven't had a bounty in months. You don't know what it's like. Please, it's just you and me. Just tell Dusty I ran away."

"If she puts a bounty on your head, you're as good as dead anyway," said Jonesy.

"If you kill me, y*ou're* as good as dead. No one touches a Hunter of the Rose without facing—," then, his eyes widened. "Wait, I know you."

Suddenly, it struck Jonesy that he *did* know who this shadow was. His deep green eyes begged at him, and he held his hands up. He still had spittle crusted in his coppery white mustache.

"You're the kid from the saloon, the one who spilled the hooch," he said, his face turning from worry to a cruel smile. "I know all about you, kid. You're the sad sap who has that naggy wench as a mother. I would have never imagined a runt like you to end up working for Dusty. I felt bad for getting you fired, so I paid her a visit."

He let his hands down and pushed himself off. "She couldn't move, but damn, she could use that mouth. I paid her pretty well, too, after you left that day. I'll go visit every now and again. She never has anything good to say about you, though," he snorted. "Give it up, boy. You'll never belong to Dusty's crew. You don't have the grit. Now, stand back, and let me go."

The man stood up, and there was a red spot on his lower torso. He looked behind him. "Went clean through, lucky me."

He then grabbed his revolver and shoved it into his pants. "Later kid. Next time I see ya, I'll shoot ya."

Jonesy aimed at his back and pulled the trigger. The man yelped as Jonesy pumped every round he had into his back, slamming the lever action back and forth. He fell into a smoking heap. A pool of blood spread beneath the man, and he did not move again. The wind smacked against him, stealing his dying breath.

Jonesy walked to the man and realized tears had fallen from his eyes. He wiped the moisture from his cheeks and stood over the man. He heard the galloping of a horse behind him and saw Maddie dismount her horse in one leap.

"Does he have a token?"

Jonesy kicked the coat of the dead man open, and a wooden token fell out.

"Don't touch it!" she shouted. "Step away from the token, Jonesy."

"I couldn't let him live," said Jonesy, turning to her.

Maddie drew a knife from her belt.

"Oh, is that meant for me?" asked Jonesy.

"Only another hunter can kill a member of the Rose. If Dusty learns you killed a Token Holder, she will put a bounty on you. They will tear you apart. If I kill you now, I will make it quick. I will make it painless."

Jonesy held his rifle at his hip, but he didn't aim at her. Not yet. "You said to use the element of surprise against someone with a gun. You said you weren't faster. If you haven't killed me yet, then you're not going to."

Maddie brushed a strand of black hair behind her ear. She smiled, showing her broken yellowed teeth. "You were paying attention. Unfortunately, for you, I don't need the element of surprise. *You'll* never be fast enough."

Then, Jonesy leaned down and snatched the wooden token from the ground.

Her eyes widened in horror. "No!"

"It's too late. This makes me one of the Hunters of the Rose," said Jonesy. He grimaced as pain shot up and down his arm, and an upside-down triangle with a screaming skull appeared like a brand on his wrist. Then, it disappeared as if it had never been there to begin with.

"I can take his place," said Jonesy, licking his teeth.

"That token wasn't yours to take. Dusty doesn't think you're worth it."

"What about you? Do you think I'm worth it?" asked Jonesy. Silence descended onto the plateau save for a whistling wind that blew across the brown grass. Jonesy fingered the trigger of his repeater, but Maddie was telling the truth. He would never be fast enough. Maddie hesitated, and for the first time since Jonesy had seen her, he saw a look of doubt in her eyes. She gritted her jaw and glanced down at the ground. The wind whistled a chorus of unease between the two. The silence was deafening. After a while, she looked up. The look of doubt was gone.

Maddie shoved her knife into her belt beneath her blazer.

"She will know what happened even if I don't tell her. She has an uncanny way of finding out even the darkest secrets. She will know that you killed him, even if he was a piece of filth," said Maddie.

"He stole these horses from her. She has to see that as some sort of vindication."

Maddie nodded as a gust of wind blew against her blazer, revealing the rows of knives on her waist and chest. "Fair point. I hope your gamble pays off. You're going to see Dusty. It's better if she hears everything from you. You gotta get cleaned up first."

Jonesy let his rifle to his side and felt his elbow touch the black box Momma had given him in his pocket. He would never have a better chance.

Burnt orange rays lined the horizon in a blood arc as Jonesy pushed the door to the washrooms. He climbed into the water trough, peeled his dusty clothes off into a pile, and grabbed the water pail with both hands. He could feel the sticky stench of sweat wash off as he poured the tepid waters over his shoulders. Brackish red water collected at the base of the water trough, and he scrubbed himself with a white towel. It quickly went brown. After he had finished, he wrapped himself in a towel and stepped from the trough.

Jonesy heard the sound of water in the backroom and was astonished he hadn't heard anyone else enter.

He made his way into the washroom hall, felt the heat of warm water, and saw a shadow standing in a large bathtub. He drew the divider back and saw Maddie bare naked, standing in a trough of steaming water. Jonesy gasped as he saw her entire body laced with nasty white scars. She had what looked like bite marks on her torso, arms, and legs. Where her breasts would have been instead was a clump of scar tissue where it almost looked like her chest had been opened at the sternum and closed up in a clumsy manner.

He realized what he was doing and averted his gaze.

"I'm sorry, ma'am. I didn't think anyone else would wash here."

Maddie smiled as she grabbed a towel on a rack and wrapped herself in it. The wound on her shoulder had been cleaned and wrapped well. It was simply a matter of taking rest, which was something Jonesy wasn't entirely sure she could do. He dared look at her again. The scars were simply beyond grotesque; he could hardly look away.

Maddie sat on the edge of the tub, and she slumped her shoulders. "I bathe here from time to time, to remind myself where I came from."

It was strange to see her in such a vulnerable state. Normally, the stoic wall of a woman would give the idea that she could harbor no weaknesses. Yet, here and now, she seemed like a knight without her armor, like a bastion without a shield. She put her hands over her shoulders and then, just in front of Jonesy, she began to sob.

Shock took hold of Jonesy as he stood there watching her break down. He didn't know how long she had cried, and he stood there simply staring. Finally, Maddie wiped her tears away and let out a sigh.

"Fifteen years ago, I had a son, a weakling of a boy, sick most of his life, and his bones would crack just by touching them. Even then, I loved him. Every smile he gave was a breath of air into my lungs, a beat of spirit into my heart. All his life, he only knew pain, yet those few moments of peace were everything to both of us. Doc Jennings arrived shortly after in Glen Rio with promises to cure his ailing bones. She remained true to her promise. Soon, my boy could stand on his own without his bones breaking, and strength was returning to his body. He would laugh and play, and soon, he could run. One day, I returned from a rough ride with Dusty, only to find him gone. The door was open, and my heart fell to my feet when I heard screams for help in the swamp down the road. I ran and called for him, but all that answered were the growls of a hundred gators.

"With a revolver in one hand and dagger in the other, I went into the swamp. The first gator I found had seen me enter and stalked me. It nearly tore my leg off had I been careless. I stabbed the beast through the skull, quickly dispatching it, but another was upon me. I heard a roar, and a third charged and leaped, grabbing my arm and tearing deep into it. I shot it through the head, and it fell, but with my arm clamped, dragging me into the mud. The one at my leg did a death roll, but it, fortunately, didn't have a good enough grip that it slipped off, tearing only a few pieces from my leg. Then, it disappeared back into the darkness.

"I lay there in the sinking mud, knowing I could only rest for a few minutes before I would be forced to make a move or succumb to the tar of the swamp. I looked up and saw beady yellow eyes all along the swamp grounds. They were waiting for me.

"Then, I heard a voice. It was calling out to me. It was my son. I jammed my dagger into the jaws of the beast and cut my hand from its grasp. With renewed vigor, I ran deeper into the swamp, bleeding and surely losing my mind. I heard his voice like an echo, and I stopped because I heard him all around me. They were screaming.

"The yellow eyes charged in like demons. I shot the first two in the head, downing their gaping jaws instantly, but two more darted behind me. They grabbed my legs and forced me to the ground. I found myself face-to-face with the largest gator to ever live. It was almost as big as a house, and it snapped over my head. The thing's breath was like a suffocating gust of hot ash, and I heard a crack. I could taste blood, knowing well it was my own, but I was not dead yet.

"I jammed the dagger into the bottom of the thing's jaws. I heard it grunt in pain every time I jabbed the blade into its scaly flesh. It let go, and for a split second, I thought I was free.

How wrong I was. The instant it let go, it slammed onto me, pushing me onto my back and laying on top of my body. I still remember the weight of him crushing my legs. The other gators watched all around as if waiting for the kill to tear apart whatever was left of me. The beast tore my chest open, and I was sure I was dead. At that moment, I saw myself in the swamp as if I was standing over my own body. I could see the gator tear my flesh away, exposing bone and sinew. I didn't feel pain, strangely enough. I only felt an intense heat squeeze my chest like a vice, forcing the air from my lungs.

"Suddenly, the pain lifted, and I was sure I was dead. When I forced my eyes open, I saw a man standing over me. Man isn't the correct term, however. It was a half-man, half-gator. He picked up the beast with one hand and tore it in half as if the gator was made of paper. The other gators fled, or at least I think they did. I saw no more yellow eyes in the undergrowth of the swamp. The only glowing yellow eyes I saw were on that *thing*. It carried me back, but I lost consciousness. The next thing I remember I was in this very room, bandaged with Dusty standing over me. The gatorman was long gone. She was always obsessed with that thing skulking in the swamps."

Silence descended upon them both. Jonesy dared speak. "Your son? Did you ever find him?"

"No. After a few months, before Doc Jennings had fully patched me up, I recruited a few Rose Hunters, and we purged the swamp of gators. I knew the chances were less than slim. Regardless, I never found him. They didn't even leave a piece of him for me to mourn or bury."

"What was his name?"

Maddie shook her head. "Not today, Jonesy. We have a meeting to attend. I hope you know the words to say. Your future will be decided tonight."

Jonesy turned to leave, but just before he did.

"Jonesy."

"Yes, ma'am?"

"Who you are reminds me of how my son was before he was taken. You share his smile. Regardless of what happens tonight, I'm proud of you."

Jonesy felt strange being so clean. His hair was combed and tied into a brown ponytail. He hadn't realized how long it was getting. He hoped there would be time later to cut it. Maddie had given him a fancy pair of brown pants and a starched shirt. He felt the shape of the black box in his pocket. He wasn't entirely sure how to do what he had been working on for the better part of a year, but he would try. One thing was for certain; he would not return to Momma empty-handed.

If you do this, you will have changed my mind about you. Don't muck this up.

Then, he glanced at Maddie, who walked beside him, her boots clicking against the hard tile of the manor floor. He wondered what it would mean to her. If Dusty were to die, would Momma really be able to take the manor for herself? Would her *vaqueros* be capable enough to take Dusty's legendary hunters on?

It had to start with him. He had to get her out during the meeting with Dusty. He and Dusty must be alone.

He found himself standing in front of her study door when Maddie walked up to it and pushed it open. Dusty Rose sat on her desk with long riding boots, black pants, a blue shirt, and suspenders. Her marble-white hair rested on her shoulders, and she had a black eye patch on her face. She held a collection of papers in her hand, and she looked up. When her eye locked with Jonesy, she smiled and set the papers down.

"Dear nephew," she said, "I hear nothing but good things about you. You may yet fulfill your potential. But first, I hear you've killed a Token Holder. Care to sit down?"

She gestured to a couple of chairs in a corner. Though much time had passed since the first time Jonesy had set foot in the study room, there was still a metallic hint of blood. Perhaps she liked it this way.

As he sat in a lavish leather chair, Jonesy saw a pot of coffee on a small corner table. The small box in his pocket seemed to get warm, as if it was burning a hole in his pants. He felt sweat drip down his neck.

"Do you know what happens to anyone who lays a finger on my hunters without authorization?" asked Dusty. She walked to the coffee pot and poured herself a cup, only to take a sniff and set it back on the table. "Maddie, dear. Seems my coffee has gone bland. Care to get us a refill while I speak with Jonesy here?"

"Of course, ma'am," said Maddie with a curt nod. She left the room without a word. Dusty sat across from Jonesy. Now was the perfect time.

"I asked you a question," her firm voice shook Jonesy from his thoughts.

"You place a bounty on their heads."

"Indeed," she said, her eyes piercing into him. "Maddie informed me that you picked up a token. You killed Bill Basterson, not much of a hunter but a Hunter of the Rose, nonetheless. I've had men killed for far less."

Jonesy craned his neck. "I couldn't let him live."

"Did his words inflame you that much you had to take his life?"

"What?" Jonesy gasped. They were alone when the murder happened. Not even Maddie was close enough to hear the words exchanged. He grabbed the arms of the chair and clutched them.

"A better question is, did your mother's words motivate you that much to attempt the life of your aunt?"

Jonesy's heart jumped into his throat, and shivers ran up and down his spine.

"She's been so cruel to you, and yet, you do her bidding. You could have just walked away; did you know that? I wish my hunters had as much devotion to me as you do to her, misplaced though it is," said Dusty, rounding the chair and resting her small hands on his shoulders. She kneaded them in a faux massage, but Jonesy felt anything but relaxed.

"I don't know what you mean," hesitated Jonesy, but he knew he had been outed. The black box in his pants felt like hot coals against his leg. Dusty laughed, her voice dancing in the stillness of the night. "Take it out, that box in your pocket."

Jonesy involuntarily pulled the box out. He stared at the silver inlays decorating the ornate receptacle.

"Open it," said Dusty. Maddie entered the room with a hot coffee pot in hand, and a confused look adorned her scarred face.

Jonesy opened the box, and Dusty held her coffee cup out. Maddie obediently poured the coffee into her cup until it was full.

"Well, do your thing. Show me what it would have been like should I be an idiot," she said, holding the coffee cup out to Jonesy. He turned the box upside down and dumped what looked like ash into the steaming cup.

"This was Emily's plan all along? Seems archaic, doesn't it? To use poison?"

She put the coffee cup up to her lips.

"Dusty, what are you doing?" asked Maddie.

"It takes a Devil to look evil in the eye and not blink," she said, coolly. Without hesitating, she then tipped the cup and took a long gulp. She brought it down onto her lap and burped. "A tad too sweet."

Jonesy's jaw dropped as she inspected the dark, steaming drink and then stared at him. Dusty, with the cup in her right hand, then pulled a revolver from in between the newspapers in her lap with her left hand. It was a sleek silver Caldwell Conversion revolver with strange cuts along the length of the drum. She flicked the revolver, the drum popped open, and she put her finger over one bullet. Then, she tilted the revolver up, and five bullets clattered onto the floor, except for the one where her finger was placed. She then slammed the drum home, spun it with the palm of her hand, and cocked the hammer back. She did this all expertly with only one hand in a matter of split seconds, and then she set the revolver on her lap pointed at Jonesy.

"You ever heard of the game Russian Roulette?"

Jonesy tried to swallow, but he was unsuccessful. Sweat began to collect at his brow as he shook his head.

"It's simple. You take all the rounds of a revolver just like I did, leaving only one in the drum." She clutched the revolver in her hand and raised it at Jonesy. She pulled the trigger, and the hammer slammed home with a crisp *click*. Jonesy jumped in his seat, and he felt his heart pulsating in his ears.

Then, she smiled, pulled the hammer back, and spun the drum again. This time, she put the gun to her own head and pulled the trigger. It clicked home, but nothing else happened. Jonesy realized he was holding his breath and let it out, gasping to fill his lungs with oxygen. Dusty smiled as if satisfied by his reaction.

"Simple," she said, tilting the cup in her right hand back up to her mouth and taking a swig. She set the cup beside her on the end table and allowed the pause in the room to inflate with strained silence. "It becomes complicated when its poison, right? Or maybe, not so much. Do you think the game can be played like this?"

She then held the cup out to Jonesy. "Take it."

Jonesy's eyes widened, and his hands began to shake. "No-I—"

"Oh," said Dusty, giving him a look and raising an eyebrow. "Are you not asking yourself why nothing has happened after I drank those leaves?"

"It's not—It's not poison?"

"That's got to be it, right? Maybe your wench of a mother didn't realize this was chamomile tea and not poison? Only one way to find out. Maddie?" Dusty asked, holding the cup out to her. Maddie hesitated but reached out, taking the steaming cup in her hand.

"No," gasped Jonesy, sitting straight, but Dusty raised the revolver in her hand and pointed it at him.

"This game's not over," she said. "Perhaps a new name for this is deserved. 'Rio Roulette.' I like that."

"I'm sorry. I-I don't know what I was thinking," said Jonesy.

"I do. My sister has a way of manipulation that is uncanny. I thought time would soften her up, but it has done the contrary. I can't trust her, and you've shown me I can't trust you either."

"I-I don't want to die."

Dusty raised an eyebrow and craned her neck. "I don't want you to die either. You had so much potential."

She held the cup once more out to Maddie, and she took it in her hand.

"You've been a faithful servant. This is your final act of service to me," said Dusty looking her dead in the eye.

Maddie straightened her back and gritted her teeth. "I know why I'm doing this." She took the cup and downed the remainder of the drink. Then, she dropped the cup on the floor with a *clank*. Maddie stood there, staring at Jonesy for a moment.

He gasped as a drop of blood dripped from Maddie's nose. She grunted, clearing her throat, which turned into a cough. She fell to her knees, clutching at her stomach as nasty black bile spewed from her throat onto the floorboards.

"No," gasped Jonesy. He was unable to move from his chair, and Dusty only smiled, revealing a perfect row of teeth. Maddie heaved and brought her eyes up to meet Jonesy's gaze. Blood dripped from her eyes, and then she fell to the floor with a thud and ceased to move as black liquid dripped from her lips.

"Not done yet," said Dusty as she raised her revolver. "You have one last play. You ready?"

Jonesy's shoulders fell forward, and tears began to fall from his eyes. "No, I-I didn't mean for any of this."

"You just meant for me to die so my sister could take the manor over with her raggedy-ass hunters, and everything would be okay. You could then become the son she always wanted. The forgiven son, right? I'm afraid that was never in the cards for you." She squeezed the trigger of her revolver, and the hammer slammed down. Jonesy squeezed his eyes shut, but nothing happened.

"You're lucky today," said Dusty, standing up. Finally, as if a great weight had lifted from his shoulders, Jonesy left his chair and knelt by Maddie's side. He brought his arm under her head and picked her up, but her eyes were glossed over, red and bleeding, staring at the ceiling. Jonesy cradled her neck as foam collected at the edges of her mouth. "I didn't mean for any of this."

He could feel warmth leave her body, her broken lips creating a look of agony on her deadened face. Tears dripped from his chin onto her pale skin.

Then, the door opened, and Jonesy turned to see a hideous figure standing in the doorway. At first, he thought the man wore a gator-skin trench coat, but after he took a closer look, he realized that it *was* his skin. It had yellow eyes that glowed like coals of the sun. Its jagged teeth were lined crookedly in its mouth.

"Earnest, take Maddie outside. Her usefulness has come to an end."

To Jonesy's shock, the gator man did as he was told, as if he, too, was under Dusty's spell. He picked Maddie up with one arm, and her limp body dangled as if she were nothing but a wet towel to him.

"Take this one to the stockades. Rogen will be here on the morrow. He'll take care of this garbage," said Dusty, her back turned to Jonesy. She craned her neck to look at him out of the corner of her eye, and he saw a tear drip from her cheek. That was all he caught before the gator man grabbed him by the jacket and pulled him into the hall.

The gator man growled low. Jonesy felt his legs move, but they did so without him commanding them. When he finally came to, he realized he sat in a cold and cramped room closed shut by an iron grate.

The iron grate to the small jail swung open, and Dusty walked in. Her spurs clinked faintly on her gator-skin boots as she stopped in front of him. She wore simple brown pants and a white shirt beneath a slim leather jacket. Her pale-white hair was down, and she eyed Jonesy hard with her right eye. A man walked in behind her.

"Well, this is him," she said.

The man walked into the light and knelt before him. He smelled of old leather and hard riding. His thick wiry white moustache fell over his mouth and dripped over his chin.

"He's just a boy," he said in a thick accent Jonesy couldn't place. "It's hard to believe Maddie's gone."

Dusty fished a wooden coin from her pocket and knelt on the other side of Jonesy. She grabbed his wrist and placed the coin in the center of Jonesy's palm. He frowned as a small black mark appeared on his arm. It looked like a small diamond with a skull in the center. It flashed bright red, and then it disappeared. It was almost as if he had imagined the brand appearing at all.

"You're giving him a token? It's a death sentence," asked Rogen, the worry accumulating in his voice.

"Maddie was the closest one I ever had to a friend. She was irreplaceable. I want my nephew to learn what it means to take away one of my most prized possessions. Take him north. I never want to see his face again."

"Dusty. What you're asking me . . ."

"Rogen. Listen to me carefully. Take him to what's left of the Conley farms. There are a few left over who still slumber beneath the earth. Understood?"

"He's just a boy."

"He killed the only one who cared about him. Now, no one in this world gives a damn what his fate turns out to be," said Dusty, then grabbing Jonesy up by the collar and lifting him up. "You'll die alone on barren earth with no one to celebrate your death save for the maggots that will feast on your rotting corpse. Remember these words when you breathe your last."

The man named Rogen grabbed Jonesy by the shoulder and pulled him to his feet.

"You know where to find me if you need me," said Rogen.

"I'll send Nilah if I need you. Get him the hell out of my sight."

Rogen slapped the reigns to the old donkey, and the cart lurched forward onto the dirt path. Jonesy sat in the cart bed beside three thick bundles of pelts and two bundles of kindling. The air had mysteriously gone cold and nipped at his nose and cheeks, and the sky hung overcast above him. Flecks of snow began to fall around them.

As they went from road to thicket, tears streamed from his eyes, and he sobbed and sobbed until he could no longer cry. He curled up in a ball beside the pelts. Rogen glanced back at him. At first, he kept a wary eye on him, but it became clear the boy wasn't going to make a move. Dusty was right. He was broken.

"And I killed her," he whispered. Rogen sharpened his ear to the whisper, but Jonesy said nothing more.

Rogen made camp along the trail, and then the snows began to fall. He quickly set upon making a fire, and before long, he was beginning to warm himself up. Jonesy made no effort to shield himself from the cold. Rogen watched him slink away from the fire, and he frowned.

"Boy, you will catch something if you don't get yourself warmed up," he said, but Jonesy didn't answer. He stood up, walked to the cart, and grabbed a pelt from the bundle. It would be dark soon, and the night could bring any number of curious predators, human or otherwise. Rogen also grabbed a sawed-off shotgun and loaded two shells. The boy could become problematic. It never hurt to be prepared.

He walked back to the small fire, and Jonesy was sitting up with knees up to his face. As Rogen pulled the pelt open, he studied Jonesy. It wasn't usual that he took a marked boy away. He wasn't even old enough for his first shave. He threw the pelt onto Jonesy's shoulders, but just as he did, the boy bolted up from the fire and reached into Rogen's side, pulling a revolver from his hip.

Jonesy stood up with the revolver leveled at him. Rogen bared his teeth and held his hands up.

"What do you think you're doing, boy?"

Tears welled in Jonesy's eyes, but he pulled the hammer of the revolver back and put the barrel to his own head. He screamed and pulled the trigger. The hammer hit home with a rough *click*.

Nothing happened.

Defeated, Jonesy fell to his knees, dropping the weapon into the snow at his feet, melting into tears.

"Holy smokes, boy!" said Rogen with a heavy slap to Jonesy's head, shoving him to the snow. He reached down and picked up his revolver. "I would never leave it loaded around a marked man. What the hell happened back there?"

"The way she looked at me when she was dying. She didn't hate me, not even then. Please, just leave me to die," sobbed Jonesy, curled in a ball in the snow. "That's what this coin and the mark means, doesn't it? I've heard the stories. If I don't return to the Bullet-Catcher in four years, the dead will rise up from the ground and chase me until I'm dead. They say that coin is worth more than gold, but it's a curse. Good. I deserve to be cursed. I didn't want to kill her. I didn't mean to kill her. I should have just drank the cup myself!"

"Get up, boy," said Rogen as he grabbed Jonesy and picked him up from the ground. Then, in a move that shocked Rogen to the core, he wrapped his arms around Rogen's waist and squeezed tight. The boy trembled in his arms and wept. Rogen held his hands to the side as Jonesy trembled, sobbing on his chest.

"What a heckin' mess," grunted Rogen. He pushed the boy off himself to the ground. "Stop crying."

Jonesy fell over into the snow.

"I said, *stop crying.*"

Rogen knew threatening to shoot the boy wouldn't work. Death was what the boy wanted. *No,* he said, smiling to himself. *That's what he* thinks *he wants. He hasn't lived long enough. Unfortunately for him, he won't.*

Rogen reared back and kicked Jonesy in the stomach as hard as he could. Jonesy grunted and flew into a fit of coughs. When Rogen heard him sob again, he kicked him for a second time. "I said, stop crying."

Silence descended on the camp, only being broken up by Jonesy's strained gasps. He no longer had the strength to even cry. Rogen stared over the boy. He felt sorry for him in that moment. He heard about his mother, that Devil wench, and her mistreatment of him. Poor sod didn't even have a father to bring him up right. He might be too mucked up by now. Perhaps the best thing to do was end his life before he caused more harm to others and himself.

Rogen sat down by the small fire and threw the pelt over a broken tree. He then lay his head down on it and let out a heavy sigh. He adjusted the hat over his face but kept just enough room to keep an eye on him. This would prove to be a long trip.

The next morning, Jonesy startled awake, tormented by nightmares without reprieve. The waking daylight did very little to alleviate his dreams and instead turned them into daymares. Despite Rogen having offered him a cut of salted meat to break his fast, he simply held it in his hand, sitting in the mule cart. Snow fell in little specks that stuck to his skin, but he did little to warm himself.

Rogen puffed at a cigar as he slapped at the reins of a mule he called Grunt. He pulled a small book from his belt and held it up to his eyes as he directed the mule across the narrow path. Jonesy shivered as he stared at the man with thick shoulders and bear pelt strapped over his chest.

Silence was his only company as the thick forest gave way to rocky mountains. The cold seemed to augment, accompanied by the gust of frigid wind that beat at his back. He huddled beside the bundle of pelts in the cart but refused to warm himself by them.

"You will lose a toe, boy," said Rogen in a fatherly tone of warning. He had turned his head over his shoulder and was staring at Jonesy with a cigar in his mouth. A cloud of smoke and fog escaped his mouth as he spoke. He held a finger stuck in a book that read *the Holy Bible* in gold lettering along a black leather spine. "It will only get colder."

"You brought me here to die," said Jonesy. "Hell won't care if I fall without a toe."

"That much is true," said Rogen with a shrug. "It will be dark soon. The night will not treat you kindly."

He turned back to reading the small black book.

"How can you read that?" asked Jonesy.

For a long while, Rogen didn't answer. In fact, it seemed like he wouldn't. Jonesy huddled against the wooden rail of the cart, and then his gruff voice broke the monotony of the squeaking cartwheel.

"You're right. How can a Devil read the Holy Book? I used to scoff at God and his word when I was your age. Love of your own children and grandchildren will make you do silly things. Therefore, God wouldn't listen if I prayed for my own soul. If I show up at the pearly gates, they would be locked, for the dark evil that follows me wherever I go is unbroken. So, I pray for the souls of my daughter-by-law and my two grandsons. If I have a chance to trade my soul and, in turn, save theirs, I would take it in a heartbeat. Now, my sole purpose is to eradicate evil so they never have to look it in the eye. You see, I have to be a Devil so they never have to shudder in fear of the darkness. I fight for a world I'll never see but one that is worth dying for, for them. You're a Devil, too. Hell is the only place for us. Only question is, are you too corrupted to be left alive this side of death?" asked Rogen. He looked up at the stars. "A world without men like me is a fantasy. Someone needs to take out the trash, and it won't be the pious or men of pure heart. I'll go to hell for them to get to heaven."

"You're telling me you and Dusty are the ones to take out the trash?"

Rogen snorted. "When you learn what's out there, you will be grateful for women like Dusty. You will be grateful for her devils like me."

Then, Jonesy realized the cart had come to a complete stop. They sat along a path looking over a ravine. Below were nothing but sharp rocks. Rogen stepped off his seat and grabbed Jonesy by the collar, heaving him over the edge of the cart. He held him over the steep cliff. Jonesy clutched his arm with a whimper.

"You didn't care so much for your life when you put that gun to your head. You care about it now?"

"If I fall, I may not die," said Jonesy. He tried to gain traction by pawing the tip of his boots on the ground to no avail. Rogen was simply too strong.

"I keep on having a dream. I am flying far above the ground, but I am surrounded by darkness. I can see nothing above me or below, and I have no concept of time or place. Then, a wilderness appears at my feet. I see my grandsons and my daughter-by-law, unaware that I am watching over them. I get a feeling watching over them that everything will be all right, so long as I breathe. In that dream, I feel like a guardian angel. I hope they see me the same way. So long as I keep on having that dream, I know I am alive," said Rogen. "I can walk into hell, and the flames of the fire will not harm me."

"I don't want to die," blurted Jonesy. This caused Rogen to tilt his head with his eyebrow raised. "Why would you want to live? You killed the one person who ever cared about you."

"I must make it up to her. I can never be forgiven, but maybe I can trade my soul for that of an innocent. If I follow you into hell, maybe the path will be opened for someone who deserves it."

Jonesy felt Rogen's grip on his collar soften. He pulled him closer from the edge.

"Now, you're getting it. Don't let Maddie die for no reason. This world is much bigger and darker than you can possibly imagine. Everything you know in Glen Rio is nothing compared to what lies beyond the stars. We live in a petri dish, and there is a sick, twisted evil up there. If you want to know what something like that is, you must have the capacity of evil yourself."

"I don't know how to do that."

"I'll give you the option. Either you come with me, and I take you to the one who will teach you what it means to be a devil on a leash, or you die there on those rocks below. I will warn you. If you come with me, you will wish I had thrown you down."

Jonesy nodded. "I'll do it. Whatever you tell me to make up for what I've done."

"Oh, it won't be me you'll be making it up to. I'm taking you to see an old friend, and I have a feeling he will want to get his claws on you. He won't make it easy, especially after what you've done."

The least Jonesy could do is suffer for the right to live. Living would be his penance for Maddie.

Rogen pulled Grunt's reigns at the mouth of a cave. The cave had stalactites jutting down from a rock lip that made it seem like the jaws of a beast. Jonesy stared into the darkness of the cave, but he could see nothing past a few feet into the hole. Rogen cleared his throat and stepped off the driver's seat.

"This is it."

"This is what?" asked Jonesy, hesitating for the first time.

Rogen stood at the cave entrance, and Jonesy could tell there was the same hesitation in the look on his face.

"Many years I spent here. I'm glad it's you who's staying here and not me," said Rogen, gritting his teeth and clenching his fists. "Little tip for ya. Stay in the light. Never let the fire go down."

"What is this place?" asked Jonesy.

"This is where the Aqueducts begin."

Jonesy's eyebrows flew up. "The Aqueducts? The same ones beneath Glen Rio?"

"It begins here beneath this mountain," said Rogen. He pulled a small whistle from his pocket. It was a wooden piece made of white wood. Strange designs were carved into the body, traced with red ink. Rogen put the whistle to his lips and blew softly. A low-pitched sound emanated from the whistle that bounced off the sides of the cave into a twirling echo, going farther and deeper into the mouth of the Aqueducts. Jonesy realized Rogen only blew into the whistle for less than a second, but the sounds not only crescendoed as they went into the cave system but also seemed to go louder. Then, the sound collapsed on itself. Everything went silent.

"Now, we wait," said Rogen as he leaned against the cart and pulled a pipe from his jacket. He lit the contents with a match and puffed away. Jonesy looked into the darkness of the cave.

"How long are we going to wait here?"

"As long as it takes. We ain't going nowhere until he answers my call."

"Who is *he*?"

Rogen smiled and let out a smoke cloud from his nostrils. Hours passed, and he stood there against the cart, simply staring into the cave. The bowl of Rogen's pipe went cold, but still, he chewed the lip. Jonesy found that he couldn't stand so still, especially with the cold taking hold of his body. He could feel the tingling of black foot in his feet. If he stayed still for too long, he knew he would surely lose a digit.

Jonesy climbed onto the cart, sat on the end of the bed, and began to massage his feet. Finally, he heard the shuffling of boots deep within the cave. He stood up from the cart and approached the cave entrance.

"It's about damn time," said Rogen. Then, the sounds stopped. Jonesy squinted but could see nothing in the darkness.

"Who's the boy?" came a gruff voice shrouded in shadow.

"Dusty sent him to die. I want to think he isn't totally lost."

"Dusty usually is a good judge of character. If she thinks he deserves death, he usually does."

Rogen glanced at Jonesy. "He's had it rough."

"So, it is true. Maddie is dead?" There was a hint of sadness in the tone as he spoke despite the monotone nature of his voice.

"He's worth more than filth, barely, but more," said Rogen. Jonesy heard the shuffling again, and an outline appeared from the dark of the cave. Jonesy could see his eyes, but still not clearly. They were wide, bigger than any eye he had ever seen. They were blue.

"Do you think yourself so adept at gathering the measure of a man with only a bare naked eye? Dusty knew better. What would she think if she learned you disobeyed her and brought him to me instead of throwing him off a cliff?" asked the stranger. His voice was ridiculously raspy and seemed to be distorted, as if coming from somewhere else and not his open mouth. It was cold and devoid of emotion. He didn't even seem to care that through Jonesy's actions, Maddie had paid his price.

"What stands before us is a cursed man with no token to hold. He's a dead man. You're his only hope. If he completes your task, I will give him one to bear. He will be a Hunter of the Rose when he returns to Glen Rio for his reckoning but not before," said Rogen.

"He won't make it back to Glen Rio. Once he sets foot into these Aqueducts, he will never leave. The Crone will make sure of it."

The man finally emerged from the shadows, and Jonesy gasped. He was tall, nearly eight feet high, and thin beyond belief, nearly skeletal. His neck was lanky and seemed like it could snap at any moment, carrying a thin-skinned skull. Blue veins popped around his shaven head like his vessels were straining to refill with blood. Then, Jonesy looked into the man's eyes. They weren't blue. They weren't even eyes. Where his eyes should have been were blue-like spectacle lenses embedded into his very eye sockets. Where his mouth should have been was a circular grid and dozens of tiny cables running the shape of his jaw intertwined with his long brown beard. Jonesy took a step back, his hand wandering to the pistol at his hip.

"What the hell are you?" asked Jonesy.

The stranger looked down at him, a faint whizzing sound emanating from his mouthpiece. He seemed completely alien.

"I forget my visage is uncommon on this planet. The strain of gravity has been lost on my body from thousands of years of travel. I—" his voice cut off, and he turned his head to Rogen.

"This little one got the better of Maddie?"

"It's complicated."

"Must be."

"Yeah, and who are you?" asked Jonesy, looking up into the stranger's face.

"I'm Blind Gideon, boy. Maddie was always my favorite. I have half a mind to throw you off the cliff myself."

Jonesy lowered his gaze. "I never meant for anything like that to happen."

"You seek redemption?"

"In any way I can."

"Huh, well then." Jonesy looked into Blind Gideon's emotionless face. His visage was so unsettling as the man breathed in what seemed mechanically. His throat was raspy, but his lenses never shifted from Jonesy. It was like looking into the face of a statue. Then, he turned his back to him and disappeared into the cave.

Jonesy gave an uneasy look to Rogen, and he gestured after the strange man. Jonesy looked into the cave.

"What's down there?"

"Just Mad-Dog Tannen."

Epilogue

The cool of a late fall breeze blew on Rogen's bear coat as he heaved an axe over his head and brought it down on a block of wood, cleaving it into two. The blocks fell carelessly into the knee-tall grass at his boots. Rogen wiped the sweat from his forehead and grabbed another cut of lumber. He set it on a cutting block and stood back. The callouses in his hands rubbed against the master-crafted wooden grip. The head of the axe was a beaten iron that Rogen had forged at Glen Rio. The wooden body had been replaced twice, but the last one he had carved himself from a hickory tree. He sported the names of Nilah and his two grandsons on the body. Then, he had Nilah etch blessings onto the wooden body with her carving knife. It wasn't the first time Rogen stopped to admire her craftsmanship.

Rogen inhaled suddenly and brought the axe down on the block. He paused to catch his breath and heard the laughter of children strewn through the peaceful wind in his ears like a susurrus of sparrows. He looked to the cottage and saw his two grandsons, Jonah and Eli, playing in the field. Nilah appeared in the doorway, looking out to her sons. She called for them, her voice like an angel's call. They stopped their play and obediently went into the cottage. The door closed after them.

Rogen couldn't help but smile. His heart warmed in his chest as his nose caught the smell of freshly baked pecan pie. His mouth watered, and he thought it better to finish his task quickly so he could have himself a slice before his two grandsons ate every last bit. He placed another cut of lumber on the block and raised his axe above his head.

Suddenly, the axe flew out of his hands. Rogen gasped as he realized the axe didn't fly out of his hands so much as it was *pulled* away. He looked behind him to see where the axe went, but he didn't hear it fall in the tall weeds. Small stones and loose flecks of grass floated up to his eyeline. He felt his coat rise, and then his feet lifted up off the ground.

A red glow burned on his chest, and he tore his shirt open to see three triangles encircled by a misshapen square there in between his pectoral muscles. It burned like hot coals, but the pain was overshadowed by his alien circumstance.

A bright light shone above him like the sharp gaze of the sun, only it wasn't the sun. When Rogen looked up, he saw his axe twirling up above him into the light and saw a saucer-like object floating above him like a giant mechanical eye. The edges of the object shone polished silver like the largest clock face he had ever seen. Strange lights blinked green and red off and on. Rogen's body lifted above the tree line, and he felt his heart fall into his boots as he looked down. He must have been twenty feet into the air and steadily going higher.

He tried to shout, but when he did, he heard himself at the bottom of a barrel full of water, merely the whisper of an echo. He saw the cabin far below his feet shrinking in size as he ascended. Rogen flailed his arms and legs to steady himself but failed, tumbling head over heels over and over again. Higher and higher, he went into the sky and finally disappeared into the light of this giant eye.

As the capture ship closed its tractor cannon and blasted off to the mothership dead in orbit, no one on the surface could even guess where Rogen disappeared. His shouts were not heard, and his body was never found. When Nilah called out to him hours later, she was answered only by the stark silence of the night and the sweet whistle of wind in the trees. Rogen was never seen in Glen Rio ever again.

TO BE CONTINUED

Printed in the USA
CPSIA information can be obtained
at www.ICGtesting.com
LVHW010948190824
788333LV00008B/5